SOUL HUNTER

'I SAW YOUR Emperor. A handful of times, back in the age before he betrayed us all.'

The sword slid into the admiral's chest with sickening gentleness, inch by slow inch, charring the dusty white Battlefleet Crythe uniform as the powered blade burned the material where it touched. The blade's tip sank into the bone of the command throne behind the mortal's back, forming yet another bond between the admiral and his station.

The effects were immediate. The bridge lighting flickered, and the ship itself groaned and rolled, tormented, like an injured whale in the black seas of Nostramo. The admiral's death flooded the ship's machine-spirit, and Talos withdrew the blade in a harsh pull. Blood hissed on the golden blade, dissolving against the heat.

'And,' the Night Lord said to the dying man, 'he was no god. Perhaps not a man,' the Astartes smiled, 'but never a god.'

By the same author

CADIAN BLOOD

More Chaos Space Marines from the Black Library

STORM OF IRON
Graham McNeill

DARK APOSTLE
DARK DISCIPLE
DARK CREED
Anthony Reynolds

A WARHAMMER 40,000 NOVEL

AARON DEMBSKI-BOWDEN

SOUL HUNTER

A NIGHT LORDS NOVEL

Katie, will you marry me?

A BLACK LIBRARY PUBLICATION

First published in Great Britain in 2010 by
BL Publishing,
Games Workshop Ltd.,
Willow Road, Nottingham,
NG7 2WS, UK.

10 9 8 7 6 5 4 3 2 1

Cover illustration by Jon Sullivan.

A CIP record for this book is available from the British Library.

UK ISBN: 978 1 84416 810 1
US ISBN: 978 1 84416 811 8

Printed and bound in the UK.

IT IS THE 41st millennium. For more than a hundred centuries the Emperor has sat immobile on the Golden Throne of Earth. He is the master of mankind by the will of the gods, and master of a million worlds by the might of his inexhaustible armies. He is a rotting carcass writhing invisibly with power from the Dark Age of Technology. He is the Carrion Lord of the Imperium for whom a thousand souls are sacrificed every day, so that he may never truly die.

YET EVEN IN his deathless state, the Emperor continues his eternal vigilance. Mighty battlefleets cross the daemon-infested miasma of the warp, the only route between distant stars, their way lit by the Astronomican, the psychic manifestation of the Emperor's will. Vast armies give battle in His name on uncounted worlds. Greatest amongst his soldiers are the Adeptus Astartes, the Space Marines, bio-engineered super-warriors. Their comrades in arms are legion: the Imperial Guard and countless planetary defence forces, the ever-vigilant Inquisition and the tech-priests of the Adeptus Mechanicus to name only a few. But for all their multitudes, they are barely enough to hold off the ever-present threat from aliens, heretics, mutants – and worse.

TO BE A man in such times is to be one amongst untold billions. It is to live in the cruellest and most bloody regime imaginable. These are the tales of those times. Forget the power of technology and science, for so much has been forgotten, never to be re-learned. Forget the promise of progress and understanding, for in the grim dark future there is only war. There is no peace amongst the stars, only an eternity of carnage and slaughter, and the laughter of thirsting gods.

PART ONE

TRAITORS' UNITY

'My sons, the galaxy is burning.
We all bear witness to a final truth – our way is not the way of the Imperium.
You have never stood in the Emperor's light.
Never worn the Imperial eagle.

And you never will.

You shall stand in midnight clad,
Your claws forever red with the lifeblood of my father's failed empire,
Warring through the centuries as the talons of a murdered god.

Rise, my sons, and take your wrath across the stars,
In my name. In my memory.
Rise, my Night Lords.'

– The Primarch Konrad Curze,
at the final gathering of the VIII Legion

PROLOGUE
A GOD'S SON

It was a curse, to be a god's son.

To see as a god saw, to know what a god knew. This sight, this knowledge, tore him apart time and again.

His chamber was a cell, devoid of comfort, serving as nothing more than a haven against interference. Within this hateful sanctuary, the god's son screamed out secrets of a future yet to come, his voice a strangled chorus of cries rendered toneless and metallic by the speaker grille of his ancient battle helm.

Sometimes his muscles would lock, slabs of meat and sinew tensing around his iron-hard bones, leaving him shivering and breathing in harsh rasps, unable to control his own body. These seizures could last for hours, each beat of his two hearts firing his nerves with agony as the blood hammered through his cramping muscles. In the times he was free from the accursed paralysis, when his reserve heart would slow and grow still once again, he would ease the pain by pounding his skull against the walls of his cell. This fresh torment was a distraction from the images that burned behind his eyes.

It sometimes worked, but never for long. The returning visions would peel back any lesser torment, bathing his mind once more in fire.

The god's son, still in his battle armour, rammed his helmed head against the wall, driving his skull against the steel again and again. Between the ceramite helmet he wore and the enhanced bone of his skeleton, his efforts did more damage to the wall than to himself.

Lost in the same curse that led to his gene-father's death, the god's son did not see his cell walls around him, nor did he detect the data streaming across his retinas as his helm's combat display tracked and targeted the contours of the wall, the hinges of the barred door, and every other insignificant detail in the unfurnished chamber. At the top left of his visor display, his vital signs were charted in a scrolling readout that flashed with intermittent warnings when his twin hearts pounded too hard for even his inhuman physiology, or his breathing ceased for minutes at a time with his body locked in a seizure.

And this was the price he paid for being like his father. This was existence as the living legacy of a god.

THE SLAVE LISTENED at his master's door, counting the minutes.

Behind the reinforced dark metal portal, the master's cries had finally subsided – at least for now. The slave was human, with the limited senses such a state entailed, but with his ear pressed to the door, he could make out the master's breathing. It was a sawing sound, ragged and harsh, filtered into a metallic growl by the vox-speakers of the master's skull-faced helm.

And still, even as his mind wandered to other thoughts, the slave kept counting the seconds as they became minutes. It was easy; he'd trained to make it instinctive, for no chronometers would work reliably within the warp.

The slave's name was Septimus, because he was the seventh. Six slaves had come before him in service to the master, and those six were no longer among the crew of the glorious vessel, the *Covenant of Blood*.

The corridors of the Astartes strike cruiser stood almost empty, a silent web of black steel and dark iron. These were the veins of the great ship, once thriving with activity: servitors trundling about their simple duties, Astartes moving from chamber to chamber, mortal crew performing the myriad functions that were necessary for the ship's continued running. In the days before the great betrayal, thousands of souls had called the *Covenant* home, including almost three hundred of the immortal Astartes.

Time had changed that. Time, and the wars it brought.

The corridors were unlit, but not powerless. An intentional blackness settled within the strike cruiser, a darkness so deep it was bred into the ship's steel bones. It was utterly natural to the Night Lords, each one born of the same sunless world. To the few crew that dwelled in the *Covenant*'s innards, the darkness was – at first – an uncomfortable presence. Acclimatisation would inevitably come to most. They would still carry their torches and optical enhancers, for they were human and had no ability to pierce the artificial night as their masters did. But over time, they grew to take comfort in the darkness.

In time, acclimatisation became familiarity. Those whose minds never found comfort in the blackness were lost to madness, and discarded after they were slain for their failure. The others abided, and grew familiar with their unseen surroundings.

Septimus's thoughts went deeper than most. All machines had souls. This he knew, even from his days of loyalty to the Golden Throne. He would speak with the nothingness sometimes, knowing the blackness was an entity unto itself, an expression of the ship's sentience. To walk through the pitch-blackness that saturated the ship was to live within the vessel's soul, to breathe in the palpable aura of the *Covenant*'s traitorous malevolence.

The darkness never answered, but he took comfort in the vessel's presence around him. As a child, he'd always feared the dark. That fear had never really left him, and knowing the silent, black corridors were not hostile was all that kept his mind together in the infinite night of his existence.

He was also lonely. That was a difficult truth to admit, even to himself. Far easier to sit in the darkness, speaking to the ship, even knowing it would never answer. He had sometimes felt distant from the other slaves and servants aboard the vessel. Most had been in service to the Night Lords much longer than he had. They unnerved him. Many walked around with their eyes closed, navigating the cold hallways of the ship by memory, by touch, and by other senses Septimus had no desire to understand.

Once, in the silent weeks before another battle on another world, Septimus had asked what became of the six slaves before him. The master was in seclusion, away from his brothers, praying to the souls of his weapons and armour. He had looked at Septimus then, staring with eyes as black as the space between the stars.

And he'd smiled. The master rarely did that. The blue veins visible under the master's pale cheeks twisted like faint cracks in pristine marble.

'Primus,' he spoke softly – as he always did without his battle helm – but with a rich, deep resonance nevertheless, 'was killed a long, long time ago. In battle.'

'Did you try to save him, lord?'

'No. I was not aware of his death. I was not on board the *Covenant* when it happened.'

The slave wanted to ask if the master would have even tried to save his predecessor had the chance arisen, but in truth he feared he knew the answer already. 'I see,' Septimus said, licking his dry lips. 'And the others?'

'Tertius... changed. The warp changed him. I destroyed him when he was no longer himself.'

This surprised Septimus. The master had told him before of the importance of servants that could resist the madness of the warp, remaining pure from the corruption of the Ruinous Powers.

'He fell by your hand?' Septimus asked.

'He did. It was a mercy.'

'I see. And the others?'

'They aged. They died. All except for Secondus and Quintus.'

'What of them?'

'Quintus was slain by the Exalted.'

Septimus's blood ran cold at those words. He loathed the Exalted.

'Why? What transgression was he guilty of?'

'He broke no law. The Exalted killed him in a moment of fury. He vented his rage on the closest living being. Unfortunately for Quintus, it was him.'

'And... what of Secondus?'

'I will tell you of the second another time. Why do you ask about my former servants?'

Septimus drew breath to tell the truth, to confess his fears, to admit he was speaking into the ship's darkness to stave off loneliness. But the fate of Tertius stayed trapped within his forethoughts. Death because of madness. Death because of corruption.

'Curiosity,' the slave said to his master, speaking the first and only lie he would ever say in his service.

The sound of booted footfalls drew Septimus back to the present. He moved away from the master's door, taking a breath as he glanced unseeing down the hallway in the direction of the approaching footsteps.

He knew who was coming. They would see him. They would see him even if he stayed hidden nearby, so there was no sense running. They would smell his scent and see the aura of his body heat. So he stood ready, willing his heartbeat to slow from its thunderous refrain. They would hear that, too. They would smile at his fears.

Septimus clicked the deactivation button on his weak lamp pack, killing the dim yellow illumination and bathing the corridor in utter blackness once more. He did this out of respect to the approaching Astartes, and because he had no wish to see their faces. At times, the darkness made dealing with the demigods much easier.

Steeled and prepared, Septimus closed his now-useless eyes, shifting his perceptions to focus entirely on his hearing and sense of smell. The footfalls were heavy but unarmoured – too widely spaced to be human. A swish of a tunic or robe. Most pervasive of all, the scent of blood: tangy, rich and metallic, strong enough to tickle the tongue. It was the smell of the ship itself, but distilled, purified, magnified.

Another demigod.

One of the master's kin was coming to see his brother.

'SEPTIMUS,' SAID THE voice from the blackness.

The slave swallowed hard, not trusting his voice but knowing he must speak. 'Yes, lord. It is I.'

A rustle of clothing, the sound of something soft on metal. Was the demigod stroking the master's door?

'Septimus,' the other demigod repeated. His voice was inhumanly low, a rumble of syllables. 'How has my brother been?'

'He has not emerged yet, lord.'

'I know. I hear him breathing. He is calmer than before.' The demigod sounded contemplative. 'I did not ask if he had emerged, Septimus. I asked how he had been.'

'This affliction has lasted longer than most, lord, but my master has been silent for almost an hour now. I have counted the minutes. This is the longest he has been at peace since the affliction first took hold.'

The demigod chuckled. It sounded like thunderheads colliding. Septimus had a momentary trickle of nostalgia; he'd not seen a storm – not even stood under a real sky – in years now.

'Careful with your language, vassal,' the demigod said. 'To name it an affliction implies a curse. My brother, your master, is blessed. He sees as a god sees.'

'Forgive me, great one.' Septimus was already on his knees, head bowed, knowing that the demigod could see his supplication clearly in the pitch darkness. 'I use only the words my master uses.'

There was a long pause.

'Septimus. Stand. You are fearful, and it is affecting your judgement. I will do you no harm. Do you not know me?'

'No, great lord.' This was true. The slave could never tell the difference in the demigods' voices. Each one spoke like a predator cat's low snarls. Only his master sounded different, an edge of softness rounding out the lion-like growls. He knew this recognition was due to familiarity, rather than any true difference in the master's tone, but it never helped in telling the others apart. 'I might guess if told to do so.'

There was the sound of the demigod shifting his stance, and the accompanying whisper of his clothing.

'Indulge me.'

'I believe you are Lord Cyrion.'

Another pause. 'How did you know, vassal?'

'Because you laughed, lord.'

In the silence that followed those words, even in the darkness, Septimus was certain the demigod was smiling.

'Tell me,' the Astartes finally spoke, 'have the others come today?'

The slave swallowed. 'Lord Uzas was here three hours ago, Lord Cyrion.'

'I imagine that was unpleasant.'

'Yes, lord.'

'What did my beloved brother Uzas do when he came?' The edge of sarcasm in Cyrion's voice was unmistakable.

'He listened to the master's words, but said none of his own.' Septimus recalled the chill in the blackness as he stood in the hallway with Uzas, hearing the demigod breathe in harsh grunts, listening to the thrum of his primed battle armour. 'He wore his warplate, lord. I do not know why.'

'That's no mystery,' Cyrion replied. 'Your master is still in his own war armour. The latest "affliction" took hold while we were embattled, and to remove the armour would risk waking him from the vision.'

'I do not understand, lord.'

'Don't you? Think, Septimus. You can hear my brother's cries now, but they are muffled, filtered through his helm's speakers and further constrained by the metal of his cell. But if one wished to hear him with a degree of clarity... He is screaming his prophecies into the vox-network. Everyone wearing their armour can hear him crying out across the communication frequencies.'

The thought made Septimus's blood run cold. The ship's demigod crew, hearing his master cry out in agony for hours on end. His skin prickled as if stroked by the darkness. This discomfort – was it jealousy? Helplessness? Septimus wasn't sure.

'What is he saying, lord? What does my master dream?'

Cyrion rested his palm against the door again, and his voice was devoid of the humour he'd hinted at before.

'He dreams what our primarch dreamed,' the Astartes said in a low tone. 'Of sacrifice and battle. Of war without end.'

CYRION WAS NOT entirely correct.

He spoke with the assurance of knowledge, for he was all too experienced with his brother's visions. Yet this time, a new facet was threaded through the stricken warrior's prophecies. This came to light some nine hours later when, at last, the door opened.

The demigod staggered into the hallway, fully armoured, leaning against the opposite wall of the corridor. His muscles were like cables of fire around molten bones, but the pain wasn't the worst part. He could manage pain, and had done so countless times before. It was the weakness. The vulnerability. These things unnerved him, made him bare his teeth in a feral snarl at the sheer unfamiliarity of the sensation.

Movement. The god's son sensed movement to his left. Still pain-blind from the wracking headache brought on by his seizures, he turned his head towards the source of the motion. His ability to smell prey, as enhanced as every sense he possessed, registered familiar scents: the smoky touch of cloying incense, the musk of sweat, and the metallic tang of concealed weaponry.

'Septimus,' the god's son spoke. The sound of his own voice was alien; scratchy and whispered even through the helmet's vox speakers.

'I am here, master.' The slave's relief was shattered when he saw how weak his lord was. This was new to them both. 'You were lost to us for exactly ninety-one hours and seventeen minutes,' the slave said, apprising his master in the way he always did after the seizures struck.

'A long time,' the demigod said, drawing himself up to his full height. Septimus watched his master stand tall, and was careful to angle away the dim beam from his lamp pack, casting its weak illumination onto the floor. It still provided enough light to see by, bringing a reassuring gloom to the hallway.

'Yes, lord. A long time. The afflictions are getting longer.'

'They are. Who was the last to come to me?'

'Lord Cyrion, seven hours ago. I thought you were going to die.'

'For a while, so did I.' There was the serpentine hiss of venting air pressure as the demigod removed his helm. In the low light, Septimus could just make out his master's smooth features, and the eyes as black as pools of tar.

'What did you dream?' the slave asked.

'Dark omens and a dead world. Make your way to my arming chambers and make preparations. I must speak with the Exalted.'

'Preparations?' Septimus hesitated. 'Another war?'

'There is always another war. But first, we must meet someone. Someone who will prove vital to our survival. We must go on a journey.'

'To where, lord?'

The demigod gave a rare smile. 'Home.'

I
NOSTRAMO

A LONE ASTEROID spun in the stillness of space. Tens of millions of kilometres from the closest planetary body, it was clearly no natural satellite belonging to any of the planets in the sector.

This was good. This was very, very good.

To the keen eyes and knowing smile of Kartan Syne, the hunk of rock twisting endlessly through the dead space of Ultima Segmentum was a thing of beauty. Or rather, what it represented was a thing of beauty, because what it represented was money. A great deal of money.

His vessel, a well-armed bulk trader by the delightfully ostentatious name *Maiden of the Stars,* sat in a loose orbit around the vast asteroid below. The *Maiden* was a big girl, and she threw her weight around when it came to tight manoeuvres, but while Syne hated a little meat on his women, he loved a little bulk to his ship's hull. The sacrifice of speed for greater profit was worth it.

Pirates were no issue. The *Maiden* bristled with weapons batteries, all bought with the profits of his mining runs. Often he'd settle for a finder's fee, but in cases like this – and cases like this were few and far between – he felt the need to fall into orbit and set his servitor teams on the surface to start digging. They were down there now, lobotomised lords of their own little mining colony. It had only been a handful of hours since planetfall, but already his automated crews were hard at work.

Lounging in his command throne, Syne watched the occulus screen as it displayed the asteroid spinning below, grey-skinned and silver-veined, a massive shard of untapped profit. He glanced at the data-slate in his hand for the hundredth time that hour, reading the figures from the planetary scan. He smiled again as his dark eyes graced the numbers next to the word 'Adamantium'.

Holy Throne, he was rich. The Adeptus Mechanicus would pay well for a hull full of precious, precious adamantium ore, but better yet, they'd pay a High Lord's ransom for the coordinates of this rock. The trick would be to leave enough ore here for the Mechanicus's exploratory vessels to confirm the intense value, but still have a cargo hold full of collateral when he approached them. Given the amount of the rare metal woven through the vast asteroid below, that wouldn't be a problem, not at all.

He glanced at the figures again, feeling a smile break out across his handsome face. The glance became a gaze, and the smile became a grin. This smirking leer was broken less than three seconds later, when proximity alarms began to ring across the *Maiden*'s untidy bridge.

Servitors and human crew moved about the circular chamber, attending to their stations.

'A report right about now would be just wonderful,' Kartan Syne said to no one in particular. In answer, one of the servitors slaved to the navigation console chattered out a babble of binary from its slack jaws.

Syne sighed. He'd meant to get that servitor replaced.

'Well, I'm none the wiser, but thanks for speaking up,' Syne said. 'How about an answer from someone who isn't broken?'

Blood of the Emperor, this was bad. If another rogue trader had chanced upon this site, then Syne was entering the murky waters of profit-sharing, and that would end in tears for all concerned. Worse yet, it could be the Mechanicus itself. No finder's fee, no hull full of rare ore, and no room to negotiate, either.

Navigation Officer Torc finally looked up from his monochrome screen and the bright runic writing trailing across it. His uniform was about as official as Syne's own, which meant both men would have looked at home in an underhive slum.

'It's an Astartes vessel,' Torc said.

Syne laughed. 'No, it's not.'

Torc's face was pale, and his slow nod halted Syne's laughter. 'It is. Came out of nowhere, Kar. It's an Astartes strike cruiser.'

'How rare,' the trader captain smiled. 'At least they're not here for the mining, then. Bring us about and let's have a look at this. We might never see one again.'

Slowly, the view in the occulus changed from a gentle blur of stars to settle on the warship. Vast, dark and deadly. Jagged, long and lethal. Midnight blue, wreathed in bronze trimmings, blackened in places from centuries of battle damage. It was a barbed spear of violent intent: the fury of the Astartes in spaceborne form.

'She's a beauty,' Syne said with feeling. 'I'm glad they're on our side.'

'Uh... She's on an approach course.'

Kartan Syne turned from the majestic view to frown at Torc. 'She's doing what now?'

'She's on an approach vector. It's bearing down on us.'

'No,' he said again, without laughing this time, 'it's not.'

Torc was still staring at his data display screen. 'Yes, it is.'

'Someone give me its transponder code. And open a channel.'

'I've got the identification code,' Torc said, his fingertips hitting keys as he looked into his screen. 'It reads as the *Covenant of Blood,* no record of allegiance.'

'No allegiance code. Is that normal?'

'How am I supposed to know?' Torc shrugged. 'I've never seen one before.'

'Maybe all Astartes vessels do this,' Syne mused. It made sense. The Astartes were famously independent of traditional Imperial hierarchy and operation.

'Maybe.' Torc didn't sound too sure.

'How's that channel coming along?' Syne asked.

'Channel open,' murmured a servitor, its head attached to the communications console via several black cables.

'Let's get this sorted out, hm?' Syne lounged in his throne again, clicking the vox-caster live. 'This is Captain Kartan Syne of the trading vessel *Maiden of the Stars.* I have claimed this asteroid and the profit potential therein. To my knowledge, I am in no violation of any boundary laws of the local region. I bid you greetings, Astartes vessel.'

Silence answered this. A pregnant silence, that gave Syne the extremely uncomfortable feeling the channel was still live and the Astartes on board the other vessel were listening to his words and choosing not to reply.

He tried again. 'If I have erred and claimed a source of profit already marked by your noble forces, I am open to negotiation.'

'Negotiation?'

'Shut up, Torc.'

Torc didn't shut up. 'Are you insane? If it's theirs, let's just go.'

'Shut *up*, Torc. Do the Astartes even mine for their own materials?'

Again, Torc shrugged.

'We have precedent to stake the claim,' Syne pressed, feeling his confidence ebbing. 'I'm just trying to keep our options open. Need I remind you that there's also the matter of over a hundred servitors and several thousand crowns worth of heavy-duty mining equipment on the surface of the asteroid? Need I remind you that Eurydice is down there with the digging teams? We won't get far without her, will we?'

Torc paled and said nothing for a moment. Needless to say, he'd been adamant in his advice to keep Eurydice on board and curtail yet another of her 'I'm bored, so I'm going' jaunts off the ship.

'The cruiser's still bearing down on us,' Torc said.

'Attack vector?' Syne leaned forward in his throne.

'Maybe. I don't know how these vessels attack. They have one hell of a forward weapons array, though.'

Syne liked to think he was a genial soul. He enjoyed a laugh as much as the next man, but this was getting quite beyond the realm of light entertainment.

'Throne of the God-Emperor,' Torc swore in a soft voice. 'Its lances are primed. Its... *everything* is primed.'

'This,' Syne said, 'has crossed the border into ridiculous.' He clicked the vox live again, failing to keep a note of desperation out of his voice. 'Astartes vessel *Covenant of Blood*. In the name of the God-Emperor, what are your intentions?'

The reply was a whisper, edged with a smile. It hissed across the *Maiden's* bridge, and Syne felt it on his skin

– the chill of the first cold wind that always precedes a storm.

'Weep as you suffer the same fate as your corpse god,' it whispered. 'We have come for you.'

THE BATTLE DID not last long.

Combat in the depths of deep space is a slow-moving ballet of technology, illuminated by the bright flickers of weapons fire and impact explosions. The *Maiden of the Stars* was a fine enough vessel for what it did; long-distance cargo hauling, deep-range scouting and prospecting, and fighting off the grasping attentions of minor pirate princes. Its captain, Kartan Syne, had invested years of solid profit into the ship. Its void shields were well-maintained and crackling with multi-layered thickness. Its weapons batteries were formidable, comparable to an Imperial Navy cruiser of similar size.

It lasted exactly fifty-one seconds, and several of those were gifts; the *Covenant of Blood* toyed with its prey before the killing strike.

The Astartes strike cruiser drew closer, opening up with a barrage of lance fire. These cutting beams of precision energy slashed across space between the two vessels, and for several heartbeats, the void shields around the *Maiden* lit up in flaring brilliance. Where the lances stabbed against the shields, a riot of colours rippled around the trader ship, like oil spreading across the surface of water.

The *Maiden's* shields endured this beautiful punishment for a handful of seconds, before buckling under the warship's assault. Resembling a popping bubble in almost all respects, the void shields collapsed with a crackle of energy, leaving the *Maiden* defenceless except for its reinforced hull armour.

Kartan Syne had the wherewithal to get his bridge crew together by this point, and the *Maiden* returned fire. The barrage from the trader's conventional weapons batteries was monumentally weaker than the lance strikes of the Astartes ship. The *Covenant of Blood* drifted ever closer, its own shields now displaying the rippling colours of attack pressure, except – much to the unsurprised dismay of Syne – the warship's shields showed no strain at all. The approaching vessel ignored the minor assault. It was already firing its lances a second time.

This time, with the shield bubble popped, the lances ate directly into the *Maiden's* hull. Predatory incisions were made in the steel flesh of the prey vessel, and the lances tracked and turned, beams of cutting laser fire neatly slicing through the lesser vessel's armour. The *Maiden* had barely responded, yet it was already listing, losing stability, and shaking apart from half a dozen detonations across its length. The *Covenant* had picked the paths of its lances with due care, targeting explosive sections of the ship: the engine core, the plasma batteries, the fuel chambers.

The strike cruiser broke off, its engines roaring into the silence of space to put distance between itself and its crippled prey.

On the *Maiden's* bridge, as his ship rattled and shook with myriad explosions, Kartan Syne glared into the occulus screen as the graceful warship speared away. For a sickening moment, he recalled when he'd hunted grey lynxes on Falodar, and the time he had seen one of the great cats kill one of the equine beasts that served as its preferred prey. The lynx had struck in a blur of movement, ripping great wounds in the horse's throat and belly, then retreated to watch the creature bleed out and die. He'd never forgotten that. At the time, he'd suspected the planet was tainted somehow, to breed such behaviour in the fauna.

'You remember Falodar?' he asked Torc.

There was no response. The bridge was a maelstrom of shouts and alarms, as the crew and servitors fought hopelessly to hold the ship together. The noise annoyed Syne. It wasn't like their struggles could actually achieve anything now.

Syne was still watching the occulus when the final lance strike came. He saw it reaching out towards him, a beam of migraine-bright white that hurt his eyes, seeming to stretch an impossible distance across the stars.

It arrived in a flash of burning light that blessedly silenced the panic around him once and for all.

EURYDICE MERVALLION SAW the *Maiden* destroyed in orbit. She stood staring in horrified awe as it exploded under the lance strikes of another vessel, but even peering into space through her magnoculars, the enemy ship was too distant to identify with any clarity. Whatever it was, it outgunned the *Maiden* by a vast degree. That meant she was probably dead, too.

As deaths were concerned, this was hardly how she'd imagined she would go out. Perhaps it was her mutational gift that led her to such assumptions, but she'd always assumed her end would come when Kartan Syne ordered her to find a way through some horrendously difficult warp storm, and the *Maiden* was another 'lost with all hands within the Sea of Souls' footnote in some minor chronicle. She certainly never assumed she'd live to be interred in the undervaults of House Mervallion, but that suited her fine, anyway. House Mervallion, as Navigator Houses went, wasn't worth much in her eyes.

And truthfully, not in anyone's eyes.

Mervallion was one of the lesser-known families within the myriad cluster of minor Houses: small, lacking influence, providing relatively mediocre Navigators, and largely devoid of wealth – all of which added up to why the Navis Nobilite had seen her assigned to a semi-respectable (at best) junker like the *Maiden of the Stars*, under the command of a weasel like Kartan Syne.

Still, despite the weakness of her bloodline and pedigree, she figured she deserved a better death than *this*.

The camp, such as it was, was unfinished. A bulk lander sat in the heart of the base, surrounded by teams of servitors still unloading the mining vehicles and drill columns. In an ungainly, cheap and uncomfortable atmosphere suit topped by a glass sphere for a helmet, Eurydice watched the black sky, ignoring the servitors around her. They shambled around in their modified protective suits, machine parts spinning, tensing, locking and unlocking as they wheeled equipment into position and constructed what should have been a fully-functional mining operation.

She couldn't help feeling annoyed. What a stupid, pointless way to die. Even if the unknown enemy up there didn't land, she was still marooned. Her lander wasn't capable of warp flight, so her ability to find the Astronomican didn't matter a damn, and she had no supplies for any serious travelling even if she did somehow have the capacity to leave this barren rock behind.

What she did have was an indefinite air supply within the lander, about three weeks' worth of food, and about one hundred servitors that were still getting ready to mine adamantium from a mineral-rich asteroid. The mindwiped slaves lacked the intelligence to realise their mother ship was now nothing more than debris in space.

Not for the first time, she regretted taking the job with Syne. Not that she'd had any choice, of course.

Three years earlier, she'd been dressed in the black toga traditionally worn by her family while on Terra, kneeling before the Celestarch of House Mervallion in his throne room.

'Father,' she had said, head cast down.

'Eurydice,' he replied, his voice flat and toneless as it bleated in a metallic drone through the bulky voxsponder unit replacing the lower half of his face. 'The House calls upon you.'

Those words sang through her body like a chill in her blood. Nothing would be the same again. At twenty-five standard years of age, duty had finally called her into service. Still, she couldn't meet his face. Eurydice knew her father was lucky to have survived the destruction of his speeder six months before. The juvenat surgeries to repair his body had been both extensive and costly, but he was far from the man she remembered from her youth. House Mervallion, even as part of the Navis Nobilite, could hardly afford to flush a fortune into the regeneration treatments the Celestarch would need to restore himself to wholeness. She hated to see him so ruined.

But it was his burden to bear. He had chosen to ignite the rivalry with House Jezzarae. He had signed the contract that brought about the death of Jezzarae's heir. As far as she was concerned, Eurydice figured her father deserved his speeder being sabotaged. She had no time for the petty feuds and revenge debts that linked the Navigator Houses more completely than any bonds of blood.

'Who has purchased the talents of our House, father?'

It would be wrong to say she'd dreamed of this day. At least, not with any real excitement. Between House

Mervallion's station and the fact she was the eighth of her father's daughters, laughably distant from even scenting an inheritance, she'd known as long as she could remember that she was destined for life on some mass-conveyance scow. No glory, no honour, no excitement. Just a pittance bleeding back to the family coffers.

But she couldn't help it. Now the moment had come, she dared to imagine what lay ahead. The thrill of hope prickled her skin, and she felt herself smiling. Perhaps she would be chosen to guide one of the Imperial war vessels through the Sea of Souls, part of the Imperium's unending crusades. Perhaps even the Astartes...

'The rogue trader,' her father said, 'Kartan Syne.'

The words meant nothing to her. Nothing, except to kill her hope like a candle guttered by sudden wind. No rogue trader dynasty of any worth would stoop to purchasing a daughter of House Mervallion.

It had been a satisfactory three years, though. Of course, fending off Syne's smirking advances had been no treat, but she'd seen a wealth of the segmentum in her tenure as the *Maiden's* Navigator. She came to know the ship as well as she knew the crew. Awake or asleep, she would hear the old girl's voice in the creaks of the hull and the grumbling engines. She was a placid thing, the *Maiden*, and her complaints were gentle. Eurydice had liked her.

But it had been unfulfilling. Of course it had. Especially when one considered the money hadn't even been all that great. True, she'd raked in more than she would have expected, permitted a small allowance to her personal finances as well as the tithe to House Mervallion, but she was hardly living comfortably. Syne was always spending massive sums of Imperial crowns on upgrading his precious fat matron of a ship, and wasn't that just *so very hilarious* in light of recent events. Good job, Captain Syne. All those guns certainly helped when it really counted.

Very calmly, with another glance around the camp and its busy servitors, she spoke a stream of curses that would have made any within her family utter a prayer for her apparent degeneracy. Several of the words in this barrage of invective were made up, but remained obscenely biological.

All of her worries quickly became moot, however. Unarmed, stranded on an asteroid, not as rich as she'd like to be (and doomed to die within the month anyway) Eurydice watched a fireball streaking down from the starry sky.

'Tomasz?' she spoke into her vox-mic, hailing the mining operations chief. She wasn't entirely alone down here, but a dozen technicians and the pack of armsmen with her hardly mattered if the enemy was capable of ending the *Maiden's* journeys in the blink of an eye.

'Yes, my lady?' came the response from the other side of the camp.

'Uh. Problems.'

'I know, my lady. I know, we see them coming, too. You must get to safety.'

'Really? Where's safe?'

He didn't respond. She looked over her shoulder at the four armsmen; they never left her side when she was out of her trance chambers. They were staring as well, over to the horizon, at something inbound.

'Lady Mervallion,' the leader, Renwar, voxed. 'We need to leave the site. Come with us.'

'Sounds fun, but I'll die here, thank you.'

'Lady...'

'You can run if you like. I think with Syne dead, you're excused from needing to guard me with your lives.'

'Lady, the secondary landing site–'

'Is over two weeks' march from here,' she laughed. 'You think we can outrun their landing vessel?'

'Lady, please. We have to go.'

'I don't have to do anything. We don't have time to fire up the lander, and we'd likely be shot down if we tried. And while the four of you look awfully proud with your shotguns, I doubt they will do much against whatever is coming our way.'

The soldiers shared worried glances. 'Lady,' Renwar said, not meeting her eyes, 'can't you... use your powers?'

'My what?'

'Your eye, my lady. With all due respect. Can't you kill them?'

Her forehead itched. Covered with a black bandana, her third eye, the gift of her Navigator heritage, pulsed softly beneath the material. She wanted to scratch, which was impossible in her glass helmet.

What could she say? Her powers were weak? Her eye didn't work that way? She'd never even tried to employ it in such a manner?

'Just go,' she sighed. 'Syne is dead. We have no way off this rock, and I'm not coming with you to the second camp.'

The men moved away in silence, and she felt their relief all too clearly. Guarding her had been a pleasure for none of them. Fear came with the duty. She was too different. She saw into the warp, and no sane soul wanted anything to do with those who stared into the empyrean.

The thought never depressed her. From birth, it had always been this way. The unease of other humans was so ingrained within her perceptions that she barely noticed it happening.

'Tomasz?'

'Yes, my lady?'

'Are you taking the servitors?'

'We planned to leave them as a distraction, my lady.' She chuckled at that. Bloody cowards. Eurydice waited as the technicians and armsmen started their low-gravity loping run to the south.

Soon she was alone but for the continued unpacking and unloading of the hundred servitors all around. The fire in the sky grew, drawing closer. Whoever or whatever had killed Syne and the rest of the crew – she wouldn't exactly call them her friends, but Torc hadn't been so bad – was evidently on its way to kill her.

'Well,' she said, using a word that had featured heavily in her last tirade, 'shit.'

THE LANDING PARTY consisted of four demigods and one mortal. Septimus, in an old atmosphere suit, trailed behind the lords Cyrion, Uzas, Xarl and his own master. Their boots made the gunship's gang ramp shake as they stalked down to the asteroid's silver-grey surface.

The human slave allowed himself a moment of smiling reflection as he glanced skyward. It wasn't much of a sky – just stars, like always, no clouds or sunlight – but it was enough of a change to keep him smiling as he followed the demigods.

Septimus's master led the small group, clad in his battle armour, breathing the chemical-tasting recycled air within his helm. His visor display, tinted crimson through ruby eye lenses, flickered from servitor to servitor as the squad moved through the small camp. In his dark fists was an ancient bolter, loaded and primed, though he doubted he'd have cause to fire it.

'Servitors,' he said, for the benefit of those back aboard the *Covenant*. 'Technical servitors, outfitted for mining. I count a hundred and seven.'

'Perfection,' drawled a voice over the vox. It was a wet, burbling growl, like a wolf with a throat full of tumours. Septimus's own vox-link allowed him to listen to the demigods speaking. He shivered at the voice of the Exalted.

The squad moved in patient precision around the camp, utterly ignored by the labouring servitors. The bionic slaves paid them no heed at all, mono-tasked as they were to perform their current operations.

'Final count is one hundred and seven,' Septimus's master repeated. 'Most of these could be easily refitted for our use.'

'Who cares?' another voice snarled. Septimus watched as Xarl stopped in his patrol ahead. Skulls, some alien and some human, were mounted on Xarl's war-plate. Several dangled on chains from his belt, forming layered faulds that covered his thighs. 'We did not come here for mindless slaves.'

'Yes,' one of the others growled, most likely Uzas. 'We must not delay here. The Warmaster calls us to Crythe.'

'Septimus,' the master said, turning back to his servant. 'Confirm the asteroid is what we seek.'

Septimus nodded, already scanning a gloved handful of dust and small rocks. His handheld auspex display showed a series of green bars in perfect alignment with a previously imprinted pattern.

'Confirmed, master.'

The bulk lander from the *Maiden* towered above them all. Its armament was pathetic, but with the most irritating timing imaginable, the single laser turret mounted upon its hull opened fire on the demigods below. Inside the grounded ship, Eurydice Mervallion sat at the helm console, directing the turret's aim through a distorted pict-link, scowling at the blurry screen and not hitting a damn thing.

Outside, the squad remained unharmed, taking cover behind six-wheeled ore loader trucks and drilling tractors. They watched the lone turret unleashing its minor rage, the red beams pulsing into the dusty ground, nowhere near any of them.

'Under fire,' Cyrion voxed to the *Covenant*. He sounded amused.

'Barely,' Septimus's master amended.

'I've got this one,' Xarl said, rising out of cover, his bolter in his fist. It shuddered once, the echo of its fire transmitting over the vox but not in the airless atmosphere. On the side of the lander, the single weapon detonated under the kiss of the explosive bolt shell.

'Another glorious victory,' Cyrion chuckled in the silence that fell afterwards. Septimus couldn't help but smile as well.

'Do we truly have time for this idiocy?' Xarl grunted.

'Someone is alive in there,' Septimus's master said quietly. The squad looked up at the cargo lander, its blocky sides and the gaping maw of its landing bay, lit from within by dim yellow light. 'We must face them.'

'This is insignificant prey,' Xarl argued.

Uzas grunted an agreement. 'The Warmaster calls. Battle awaits us in Crythe.'

'Yes,' Xarl voxed back, 'let this weakling prey rot.'

Cyrion spoke up, cutting them off. 'This prey is someone capable of managing a hundred servitors. They almost certainly possess technical skill. Such skill will be of use to us.'

'No,' Septimus's master breathed. 'The prey is much more than that.'

Xarl, draped in skulls, and Uzas, his dark armour sporting a cloak of light brownish leather that had once been the skin of a hive-world's royal family, both nodded their reluctant assent.

'A prisoner, then,' Xarl said.

'Night Lords,' came the wet growl of the Exalted, 'move in.'

THEY DIVIDED UP once they were inside. The lander was large enough that even separated it would take them up to fifteen minutes to sweep the entire hulk. Uzas took the storage decks and the cargo hold. Xarl made for the bridge and the crew deck. Cyrion remained outside, watching over the servitors. Septimus and his master moved towards the engineering deck.

Septimus drew his own weapons as he followed the reassuring bulk of his master. Two laspistols, Imperial Guard standard issue, were gripped in his fists.

'Put those away,' his master said without turning around. 'If you shoot her, I will kill you.'

Septimus holstered the pistols. The two figures moved down a row of silent generators, each one twice as tall as a man. Their boots clanked on the metal gantry of the floor. Beyond the threat, which was hardly out of character for any of the demigods, something in his master's answer caught his interest.

'Her?' he asked over a direct vox-link to his master.

'Yes.' His master advanced, his weapons undrawn but his gauntleted hands tensed into claws. 'Even had I not seen her in my vision, I can smell her skin, her hair, her blood. Our prey is female.'

Septimus nodded, shielding his eyes again from the glaring illumination of the strip lighting above. It ran the length of the chamber, just as it had in the previous three chambers.

'It's bright in here,' he said.

'No, it's not. The ship is on low power. You are just used to the *Covenant.* Be ready, Septimus. Do not, under any circumstances, look at her face. The sight will kill you.'

'Master–'

The demigod held up a hand. 'Silence. She is moving.'

Septimus couldn't hear anything, except his master's vox-clicks as he changed channels to address the rest of the squad.

'I have her,' he said, and calmly turned to catch a blur of shrieking movement that launched at him.

EURYDICE HAD BEEN watching from her darkened hiding place between two rumbling generators. She had no weapon except for a crowbar that she'd scrounged from her tools, and although she'd been scowling alone and telling herself she would go down fighting, kicking and screaming, that pledge faded a little when she saw the two figures coming down the gantry. One was a human, armed with two pistols. The other was a giant, well over two metres tall, and wearing archaic battle armour.

Astartes.

She'd never seen one before. It was not a pleasant sight. Awe met fear, mixing to form a feeling of dread in the pit of her stomach and a sour taste that doggedly coated her tongue no matter how much she tried to swallow it. Why were the Astartes attacking? Why had they killed Syne and destroyed the *Maiden*?

She retreated into the shadows, willing her heart to calm, and gripped her crowbar in sweating fists. Maybe if she aimed for the joint where his helmet met his neck? Throne, this was insane. She was dead, and there was nothing she could do about it. With a mirthless grin, she suddenly regretted all the mean things she'd said to... well, to everyone. Except to Syne. He was always an arse.

For all her faults, her spiteful tongue among them, Eurydice Mervallion was no coward. She was the daughter of a Navigator House, even if their name wasn't worth spit, and had looked into the madness of the warp and guided her ship safely each and every time. The sight of a demigod stalking closer to her made her head ache and her guts tighten, but she kept the promise she'd made to herself. She'd go down fighting.

They drew near, walking down the aisled gantry. Eurydice's forehead itched with fierce sensitivity, and with her free hand, she pulled off the bandana of black silk. The recycled air of the lander's internal atmosphere tingled unpleasantly on her third eye, even closed as it was. As naturally as drawing a breath, she opened the eye slowly, feeling the uncomfortable tingle intensify, on the edge of irritation now. The tickling connection of the eye's milky surface meeting the air forced a shiver through her body. It was a sickening sense of vulnerability. The eye saw nothing, yet it felt the warm, scrubbed air brush over its soft surface with every movement she made.

She was ready. Eurydice clutched the crowbar in both hands again.

The giant passed slowly, and as he did, she leapt at him with a cry.

The crowbar banged against his helm with the dull clang of iron on ceramite. It was a strange sound, half a metallic chime, half a muted and echoless clank. She swung with all her strength coupled with a rage born of desperation. The impact would have staved in the head of a human, and had she chosen her target better, Septimus's skull would have collapsed under the blow, killing him instantly. But she chose the Astartes.

That was an error.

The bar had already struck three times before she realised two things. Firstly, her furious strikes against the giant's helm were barely even causing him to move his head. His skull-faced helmet glared at her with ruby eye lenses, juddering only slightly under each of her flailing strikes.

Secondly, she hadn't landed yet. That was what sent her into a writhing panic. He'd caught her as she jumped, and was holding her off the ground with his hand around her throat.

The realisation hit her when he started to squeeze. The pressure on her throat choked her so suddenly, so completely, that she didn't even have time to squawk a cry of pain. The crowbar landed one last time, deflected from his forearm by the dark armour he wore, before it clattered to the ground with a reverberating clang. She couldn't hear it; all she heard was her own heart thundering in her ears. Eurydice kicked out at him as she dangled, but her boots clacking against his chestplate and thigh armour met with even less success than her crowbar had.

He wasn't dying. Her eye... it wasn't killing him. All her life she'd heard tales that allowing any living being to stare into a Navigator's third eye would result in some arcane, mystic, agonising death. Her tutors had insisted this was so – a by-product of the Navigator gene that granted her this obscene and priceless mutation. No one understood the reason behind it. At least, no one in the ranks of House Mervallion, but then

Eurydice knew she'd only ever had access to tutors of relatively poor quality.

She stared at the giant with her third eye wide and open, as her human eyes narrowed in breath-starved pain. Yet the Astartes stood unfazed.

She was right. Had the demigod looked into her sightless eye the colour of infected milk, he would have died instantly. But behind the crimson lenses, his own eyes were closed. He knew what she was. He had foreseen this moment, and a true hunter didn't need every sense to bring down prey.

Her vision started to swim. She couldn't tell if she was really being pulled closer to him, but his skull helm filled her sight, bone-white and blood-eyed. The giant's voice was low, inhumanly low, grinding like distant thunder. As her vision misted and finally blackened, the demigod's words followed her down into unconsciousness.

'My name is Talos,' he growled. 'And you are coming with me.'

SEPTIMUS'S MASTER WAS the last to leave the asteroid. He stood on the surface, his boots leaving eternal prints in the silver-grey dust, and he looked up at the stars. Stars he didn't recognise from the last time he'd stood upon this rock and stared up into the heavens. This asteroid had been a world once – a planet far from here.

'Talos,' Cyrion's voice crackled over the vox. 'The servitors are loaded. The prisoner is ready to be taken to the mortals' decks aboard the *Covenant*. Come, my brother. Your vision was true, there was much to discover here. But the Warmaster calls us to Crythe.'

'What of those who fled?'

'Uzas and Xarl have ended them. Come. Time eludes us.'

Talos knelt, seeing how the dust clung to his black-blue armour in an ashen covering. Like sand sifting through his fingers, he watched a fistful of the dust cascade from his open hand.

'Time changes all things,' Talos whispered.

'Not everything, prophet.' That was Xarl, his voice pitched in respect as he waited in the gunship. 'We fight the same war we've always fought.'

Talos rose to stand once more, making his way to the waiting Thunderhawk. Its engines cycled live, blasting dust away in all directions as it readied for the return flight, where the *Covenant of Blood* waited in orbit.

'This rock came a long way,' Cyrion voxed. 'Ten thousand years of drift.'

Uzas chuckled. It wasn't that the emotional significance was lost on him. It was simply that the situation held no emotional weight in his mind at all. He couldn't have cared less.

'It was good to come home again, hmm?' he said, still smirking inside his helm.

Home. The word left a burning afterimage in Talos's mind – a world of eternal night, where spires of dark metal clawed at the black sky. Home. Nostramo. The VIII Legion's home world.

Talos had been there at the end, of course. They all had. Thousands of the Legion standing on the decks of their strike cruisers and battle-barges, watching the shrouded world below as the end rained down upon it, piercing the caul of cloud cover, tearing holes in the dense blanket of darkness in the atmosphere and revealing a venomous illumination: the orange glow of flame and tectonic ruination blazing across the surface. The skin of the world split, as if the gods themselves were breaking it apart out of spite.

And in a sense, they were.

Ten thousand years before, Talos had watched his world burn, shatter, and crumble. He'd watched Nostramo die. It was sacrifice. It was vindication. It was, he told himself, justice.

Ten thousand years. To Talos, his life measured from battle to battle, crusade to crusade, it had been no more than a handful of decades since his home world burned. Time was enslaved to unnatural laws in the regions of hell-space where the Traitor Legions hid from Imperial retribution. It was maddening, sometimes, to keep track. Most of his brethren no longer tried.

Talos's boots thudded on the ramp as he boarded the gunship. Once inside the hangar, he cast a single glance at the herd of lobotomised servitors standing impassive in the deployment bay, and thumped his fist against the door lock pressure pad. The ramp withdrew and the blast doors slammed shut in a grinding chorus of hydraulics.

'Do you think we'll ever see another shard that size?' Cyrion asked as the Thunderhawk shuddered into the air. 'That must have been at least half a continent, all the way down to the outer core.'

Talos said nothing, lost for a moment in the memory of raging fire flickering through breaks in dense cloud cover, before an entire world came to pieces before his eyes.

'Back to the *Covenant*,' he finally said. 'And then to Crythe.'

II
VISION

'Surprise is an insubstantial blade, a sword worthless in war.
It breaks when troops rally. It snaps when commanders hold the line.
But fear never fades.
Fear is a blade that sharpens with use.
So let the enemy know we come. Let their fears defeat them as everything falls dark.
As the world's sun sets…
As the city is wreathed in its final night…
Let ten thousand howls promise ten thousand claws.
The Night Lords are coming.
And no soul that stands against us shall see another dawn.'

– The war-sage Malcharion
Excerpted from his work, *The Tenebrous Path*

TALOS WALKED THE corridors of the *Covenant*, wearing his battle armour without the confining presence of his helm. While he lacked the vision-enhancing modes the helmet's sensors offered, there was a comforting clarity in piercing the ship's darkness with his natural sight.

The mortal crew struggled to see in the blackness, their eyes too weak to perceive the trace illumination emitted by the ship's powered-down lighting. They were permitted lamp packs, allowing them to see in the dark when they must move from one part of the ship to another. To the Nostramo-born Astartes, the gloom simply didn't exist. Talos moved through the wide passageways, nearing the war room, which had long since become the meditation chambers of the Exalted. A natural attuning, coupled with the genetic manipulations performed on his brain during his ascension into the ranks of the VIII Legion, meant he saw the *Covenant's* interior as clearly as dawn on a far brighter world.

Cyrion, clad in his own war-plate, drew alongside. Talos glanced at his brother, noting the creases of strain around Cyrion's black eyes. It was strange to see one of his fellow Legionnaires show signs of age, but Talos was under no delusions. Cyrion was struggling under the pressure of his own curse – one that weighed upon his brother far more heavily than Talos's own visions wracked him.

'You're not coming in with me,' Talos said, 'so why are you following?'

'I might come in,' Cyrion replied. Both of them knew how unlikely that was. Cyrion avoided the Exalted at all costs.

'Even if you wanted to, the Atramentar will bar your way.' They walked through the labyrinthine halls of the great ship, accustomed to the silence that framed their presence.

'They might,' conceded Cyrion. 'They might not.'

'I'll let you keep that mistaken belief for another few minutes, Cy. Don't ever say I am not a generous soul.' Talos scratched the back of his shaven head as he spoke. One of his implant ports, a socket of chrome in his spine just above his shoulder blades, had started aching these past few days. It was an irritating, dull pulse at the edge of his attention, and he felt the vibrating hum of the symbiotic coupling there that merged him to his armour. The machine-spirit of his war-plate must be appeased soon, and Septimus would need to be set to work preparing the unguents and oils that Talos used to tend to his inflamed junction sockets. The invasive neural connections from his armour into his body were growing aggravated from the amount of time he spent in battle. Even his inhuman healing and physical regeneration could only cope with so much.

In better days, several Legion serfs and tech-adepts would have tended to his bionic augmentations and monitored his gene-enhancements between battles. Now he was reduced to a single slave, and as talented as Septimus was as an artificer, Talos trusted no one to come near his unarmoured form – not even his own vassal, and especially not his brothers.

'Xarl is looking for you.'

'I know.'

'Uzas, as well. They want to know what you saw while afflicted.'

'I told them. I told you all. I saw Nostramo, a shard of our home world, spinning in the void. I saw the female Navigator. I saw the vessel we destroyed.'

'And yet the Exalted summons you now.' Cyrion shook his head. 'We are not fools, brother. Well… most of us are not. I make no claims for Uzas's state of mind. But we know you are going to meet the Exalted, and we can guess why.'

Talos cast him a sidelong glance. 'If you are planning to spy, you know you are doomed to failure. They won't let you in.'

'Then I will wait for you outside,' Cyrion conceded. 'The Atramentar are always such wonderful conversationalists.' He wouldn't be distracted. 'This summons is about your vision. We're right, aren't we?'

'It's always about them,' Talos said simply. They walked the rest of the way in silence.

The war room was at the heart of the ship – a vast circular chamber with four towering sets of doors leading in from the cardinal directions. The Astartes approached the southern door, taking note of the two immense figures flanking the sealed portal.

Two of the Atramentar, chosen warriors of the Exalted, stood in wordless vigil. Each of the elite Astartes wore one of the Legion's precious remaining suits of Terminator armour, their hulking shoulder guards formed of polished silver and black iron forged into the snarling skulls of sabre-toothed Nostraman lions. Talos recognised the two warriors by their armour's insignia, and nodded as he approached.

One of the Terminators, his war-plate etched with screeds of tiny golden Nostraman runes detailing his many victories, growled down at Talos and Cyrion.

'Brothers,' he said, the words a slow intonation.

'Champion Malek.' Talos nodded up at the warrior. He was head and shoulders above most mortal men himself, well over two metres tall. Malek, in the suit of ancient Terminator plate, was closer to three.

'Prophet,' the voice drawled deep and mechanical from the tusked helm. 'The Exalted summoned *you*.' He punctuated his words with the crackling threat of his gauntlet's claws wreathing themselves in coruscating energy.

'You,' the Atramentar repeated, 'and you alone.'

Cyrion leaned against the wall, magnanimously gesturing for his brother to go ahead without him. His theatrical bow brought a smile to Talos's pale features.

'Enter, prophet,' said the other Atramentar warrior. Talos knew the figure from the heavy bronze hammer it carried over its shoulder. Its Terminator helm, instead of sporting the half-metre tusks Malek favoured, was marred by a vicious bone horn spiking from its forehead.

'My thanks, Brother Garadon.' Talos had long since given up demanding that others stop referring to him as a prophet. Once the Atramentar had followed the Exalted's tendency to use the term, it had spread across the *Covenant* and stuck fast.

With a last look back at Cyrion, he entered the war room. The doors closed behind him, sealing with a click and a hiss.

'So,' Cyrion said to the silent, towering Terminators. 'How are you?'

Only two souls were present in the room: Talos and the Exalted. Two souls facing each other across an oval table that had once seated two hundred warriors. Around the edges of the room, banks of cogitators and vox-stations sat idle and silent. Centuries before, they had been manned by live crew: Legion serfs and a small army of servitors. Now the *Covenant's* remaining crew strength was focused on the bridge and the other vital sections of the ship.

'Talos,' came the draconic growl from the other side of the table. The darkness was ultimate: so deep it took Talos's vision several moments to tune through the blackness and make out the other figure in the chamber. 'My prophet,' the Exalted continued. Its voice was as low as the purr of the warp engines. 'My eyes into the unseen.'

Talos regarded the vaguely humanoid shape as his sight resolved into an approximation of clarity. The

Exalted wore the same relic armour so revered by the Atramentar, but… changed.

Warped. Literally. Occasional flickers of warp lighting rippled across the surface of the armour. The witchlight gave off no illumination of its own.

'Captain Vandred,' Talos said. 'I have come as ordered.'

The Exalted breathed out, long and soft, the amused exhalation ghosting through the air like a distant wind. It was the closest the creature could come to laughing.

'My prophet. When will you cease this use of my ancient name? It is no longer entertaining. No longer quaint. Our forgotten titles mean nothing. You know this as well as I.'

'I find meaning in them.' Talos watched as the Exalted dragged itself closer to the table. A mild tremor shook through the chamber as the creature took a single step.

'Share your gift with me, Talos. Not your misguided reprimand. I control this. I am no pawn of the Ruinous Ones, no avatar of their purpose.'

The chamber shuddered again as the Exalted took another step. 'I. Control. This.'

Talos felt his eyes narrowing at the old refrain. 'As you say, brother-captain.' His words caused another breathy exhalation, at once as gentle and threatening as a blade stroked across bared flesh.

'Speak, Talos. Before I lose what little patience remains to me. I indulged your desire to seek a rock in the void. I allowed you to once again walk the surface of our broken home world.'

'My desire? My *desire*?' Talos pounded a fist onto the surface of the war room's central table, hard enough to spread a cobweb of cracks from where his fist landed. 'In a vision, I saw a fragment of our home world in the lightless black, and I led us there. Even if you don't believe that's an omen, it still brought over a hundred new servitors into the ship's crew, and a *Navigator*. My "*desire*" greatly benefited the Legion, Vandred. And you know it.'

The Exalted drew a breath. As the air was sucked into the commander's altered throat, it sounded like a banshee's wail.

'You will address me with respect, brother.' The words were meaningless; it was the softness of the warning that made Talos's blood run cold.

'I stopped respecting you when you changed into... this.'

'Standards of decorum must be maintained. We are the VIII Legion. We are not lost to the madness that grips the others who failed alongside us on the surface of Terra.'

There were a hundred answers to that, each more likely to get him killed than the last. With a swallow, Talos finally said simply 'Yes, sir.' This was no time to argue. In truth, it never was. Words changed nothing. The corruption within the Exalted ran too deep.

'Good,' the creature smiled. 'Now speak of the other truths you saw. Speak of the things that matter. Tell me of the wars,' the Exalted finished, 'and the names of those doomed to die.'

So Talos told him, immersing himself in the flames of those memories once more, and...

...at first, there is nothing. Darkness, blackness. It is almost like home.

The darkness dies in a genesis of fire. White-hot and sun-bright, it sweeps across his senses. He stumbles and falls, kneeling on the red rock of another world. He's lost his holy weapons... his bolter and blade... When his vision clears, they are not in his hands.

A sudden strength invades his system. His armour's senses track the waxing and waning of power and life within his body, flooding him with stimulants to keep him in the battle even when his inhuman physiology would require succour. They rush through his blood now, electrifying muscles and deadening nerves.

As they reach his brain, his vision clears. Coincidence or providence, the warrior doesn't care. Rubble everywhere. And there, shattered and cast aside like a puppet with cut strings, another warrior in the colours of the VIII Legion. Talos moves to him, knowing he must reach the fallen brother before anyone else.

He makes it. Targeting sensors flicker and beep as they lock onto other figures moving through the insane dust-smoke all around, yet he's the first to reach the broken corpse. But no sword... no bolter...

His targeting crosshairs zero in on the fallen warrior's blade, outlining it in a threat display reticule and streaming data about the sword's construction. He blink-clicks the details of metal composites and power capacity away, and grips the blade with both hands. A press of his thumb on the activation rune starts the chainsword roaring.

The others are closing in now. He has to be fast.

The chainblade kisses the dark ceramite armour of the dead Astartes, grinding against the war-plate for several fevered seconds before biting through. Talos carves in a quick sweep, hurling the sword aside once it has performed its function.

One of the others is Uzas. He bounds forward like a beast, ignoring Talos, his hands tearing at the dead warrior's helm. By the time he has pulled it free, Talos has retreated from the scavenging, carrying the severed forearm he earned. Once the meat is removed from the armoured arm, the gauntlet could be reworked and...

* * *

...THE EXALTED BREATHED out once more, its laugh-breath exhalation.

'Who was it?' he asked. 'Who will fall, to be plundered in death?'

'It was... They wore...'

...armour of midnight blue, like everyone in the Legion. But the helm's faceplate is painted red, a leering scarlet skull. Talos...

'...DIDN'T SEE CLEARLY,' he said to the Exalted. 'I think it was Faroven.'

Talos closed his right hand into a fist, listening to the quiet growl of the servos in every knuckle joint. The gauntlet was stiff, and Septimus had said several times it would soon need to be replaced. It was old, that was all. The years had worn it down, and although much of his armour had been replaced over time, his gauntlets were both pieces of his original mark IV war-plate.

It did not trouble him to think of looting his fallen brethren the way it might trouble a mortal to plunder the dead. The Night Lords Legion had lost much since their failure to take the Throne of Terra, and their capacity to forge new Astartes armour was severely limited.

Looting the dead was a forgivable necessity in the endless war.

Talos opened his hand, slowly articulating his fingers. 'Yes,' he said as he watched the hand move, thinking of the night to come when this gauntlet would be replaced by another. 'It was Faroven.'

The Exalted made a sound Talos had heard many times – a grunt of dismissal, callous and curt.

'When he dies, you are welcome to whatever you take. His demise will be no loss to the Legion. Now continue. An explosion. Rubble and smoke. The plundering of Faroven's wargear. And then?'

Talos closed his eyes. 'And then…'

…he sees his sword. There, lying across a spill of rubble, the gleam of the blade already dulled by a thin layer of dust. He scrambles for it, his boots crunching on the gravel underfoot – rock chunks that were the towering wall of a manufactorum until moments ago.

The blade is in his hands, a masterwork of form and function. The hilt and cross-guard is crafted from bronze and polished ivory, forming the outstretched wings of an angel. Between the wings, set into the base of the blade on both sides, rubies the size of a mortal man's eyes have been cut and shaped into crimson teardrops. The blade itself is forged of adamantite stained gold, with High Gothic runes hand-scribed along the weapon's length detailing a long and illustrious lineage of fallen foes.

Talos had killed none of them, for this blade was never forged to be his. He grips it now, feeling the reassuring weight of the stolen weapon, as comfortable in his hands at this moment as it was a decade before when he'd taken it from the dying grasp of an Imperial champion.

Aurum. The blade was called Aurum – the power sword of noble Captain Dumah of the Blood Angels. Its kiss was death; like all power weapons, a ravaging energy field tore apart solid matter with every strike. But Aurum was forged when the Imperium was young, when the tech-priests of Mars were as much artisans as keepers of secrets.

Three times, Legion brothers have tried to kill him for this sword. Three times, Talos has slain his kin to defend this prize.

He rises, activating the power cell within the hilt, burning the dust from the golden blade in a hissing rush.

Lightning, tight and controlled, dances across the sword's length, bright enough to hurt his Nostraman eyes.

Talos moves across the rubble. The sounds of battle are returning now. The rubble-dust is clearing. He has to find his bolter before the enemy comes to sweep through the sector they've just annihilated with unbelievable firepower.

He... he can't find it. What is that accursed noise? That thunder? The world is falling apart...

Blood of the Ruinous Ones, where is that weapon...

He...

...STAGGERED UNDER THE wave of memory, as real to him in the war room as it was when the vision first struck. The Exalted grunted its displeasure.

'What is wrong? What happened next?'

'The sun,' Talos said. 'The...

...sun has died.

He raises his head to the sky, all thoughts of seeking his bolter forgotten. A moment before it was high noon, now the sky is dark as dusk. An eclipse. It must be an eclipse.

And it is.

In a way, it is.

Targeting reticules lock on the behemoth that swallowed the sun. Information Talos doesn't see slides in jerky lines across his retinas, beamed into his eyes from his helmet's sensor interface.

Alarms chime in time to the warning runes' flickering, and as he looks up, he recalls why the explosion had levelled this part of the city. He looks up at the explosion's cause.

Warlord-class. His sensors flicker the words over and over, the alarm chimes becoming screams in his ears, as if he doesn't know what he is seeing. As if he needs to be warned that it's death itself. Over forty metres of

Mechanicus vengeance has come to destroy them all. It's taller than any buildings that remain standing.

Its gargantuan weapons pan and aim, tracking the ant-like forms of the Astartes below. Its arms – cannons the length of trains – split the sky with the sound of a thousand gears grinding – just aiming, not even firing yet. Lower, they aim. Lower.

The city shakes again, even before the Titan fires, purely because the iron god is moving. The vox fires into life, voices bellowing in anger as the Imperial war machine strides closer.

'Heavy weapons!' he roars into the vox general channel. 'Land Raiders and Predators, all guns on the Titan!' He doesn't even know if there are any of the Legion's vehicles left in one piece, but if they don't form a response of some kind, the Titan will end them all.

With the sound of habitation towers falling, the Titan takes another step.

And with the sound of a world dying, it fires again.

Talos...

...OPENED HIS EYES, only then realising they'd been closed.

The Exalted had come closer while Talos was in the grip of the vision. 'Titans are no surprise,' the creature said. 'A forge world is the Warmaster's priority target within the Crythe Cluster.'

Talos shook his head, his lip curling slightly as he made out the edges of the Exalted's horned visage in the dark.

'We are going to be slaughtered. We will stand in the path of the Mechanicus's god-machines, and our eyes will burn in the light of their fire.'

'And what of the Warmaster's own forces?' the Exalted pressed, his eagerness lending an edge of impatience to his burbling tone. Talos was reminded of a deep cauldron brought to the boil.

'What of them, sir?'

'My prophet,' the Exalted drawled, with an unfamiliar hint of kindness. Talos tilted his head to regard his leader, suppressing a growl. The Exalted was trying to mask his irritation, most likely, to keep his pet seer from losing his own temper at the questioning. 'Talos, my brother, you see so much, yet so little.'

The Exalted smiled – a portrait of too many fangs and acidic drool. Talos glared into his lord's black eyes, and the twisted face of a man he'd once admired.

'That is my question,' the Exalted leered. 'Where *are* they? Do you see them? Do you see the Black Legion?'

'I can't...

...see them. Anywhere.

Above, the metallic gods make war. Titan against Titan in the ruins of a shattered city. The air is a solid storm of cannonfire bursts and thunderous grinding as war machines loose their wrath upon one another. The Titans have forgotten that battle playing out around their feet now, and the Night Lords – those that remain – regroup in their towering shadows.

Talos reaches his transport, the Land Raider's sloped, dark hull like a beacon in the maelstrom around. And that's when he sees Cyrion, still half-buried in rubble, almost a thousand metres away.

It's not a clean sight, nor an instant identification. The distance is significant, and at first Talos just sees a struggling figure emerging from stone wreckage, the minute movement catching his eye purely by chance.

He blink-clicks the visor's zoom symbol. A name rune flashes up on his retinal display – Cyrion – as his targeting systems lock onto his brother as an invalid target.

He breaks into a run.

Another target – Uzas, Invalid Target – flashes up in runic code. Uzas reaches Cyrion first, climbing down the rubble behind the staggering, wounded Astartes. Talos runs harder, faster, somehow knowing what's coming.

Uzas raises his axe and...

'...AND WHAT?'

'And nothing,' Talos replied. 'It's as I've said. The Warmaster will send us against the Titan Legion of Crythe, and we will suffer severe casualties.'

The Exalted let the silence extend for several moments, letting his voiceless displeasure speak for him.

'Am I dismissed, lord?' Talos asked.

'I am far from satisfied with this meagre recollection, my brother.'

Talos's smile was crooked and genuine. 'I will endeavour to please my commander next time. As I understand it, prophecy is not an exact science.'

'Talos,' the Exalted drawled. 'You are not as amusing as you think you are.'

'Cyrion says the same, sir.'

'You are dismissed. We draw near to Crythe, so make final preparations. Ensure your squad is in midnight clad within the hour. We strike at the Crythe Cluster's penal world first, then move on to the forge world.'

'It will be done, sir.' Talos was already leaving when the Exalted cleared his throat. It sounded like he was gargling something that was still alive.

'My dear prophet,' the Exalted grinned. 'How is the prisoner?'

III
THE WARMASTER CALLS

'Nostramo has died, and with it, our past.
The Imperium burns, promising a future of ash.
Horus failed, because his plans grew from seeds of corruption – not wisdom.
And we failed because we followed him.
We do not do well when leashed to the wills of others,
And when bound by the words of leaders that do not share our blood.
We must choose our wars with more care in the centuries to come.'

– The war-sage Malcharion
Excerpted from his work, *The Tenebrous Path*

EURYDICE AWOKE TO a darkness so deep she feared she'd been blinded. She sat up, her shaking hands feeling the relative softness of a cot bed beneath her. The smell around her was a strong mix of copper and machine oil, and the only sound apart from her breathing was a distant but ever-present background hum.

She knew that sound. It was a ship's drive. Somewhere, on a distant deck, this vessel's great engines were propelling it through the warp.

The image of a skullish helm leering at her with crimson eyes drifted through her returning memory. The Astartes had taken her.

Talos.

Eurydice moved her hands to her throat, feeling the tenderness there, aching to the touch, hurting to breathe. A moment later, she reached for her forehead. Cold metal met her questing fingers. A small, thin band of iron or steel... fastened to her forehead. It covered her third eye. She felt the tiny rivets where the plate was drilled and fixed to her skull, just the right size to imprison her genetic gift.

There was the sudden clank of a bulkhead door opening, whining open on old hinges. A blade of light, muted and yellow, stabbed into the room. Eurydice drew back from the painful brightness, squinting to make out the source.

A lamp pack. A lamp pack in someone's hand.

'Rise and shine,' the figure said. He entered the room, still nothing more than a silhouette, and seemed to be adjusting the lamp pack in his hands. For a moment, everything went black again.

'May the Powers take this bastard thing,' the man grumbled. Eurydice wasn't sure what to think. She was tempted to fly at him blindly, lashing out to knock him down and flee. She would have, she was sure of it, if her head would just stop spinning. With the return of vision, even for a moment, came the realisation that she was sickly dizzy, right to her stomach. She doubted she could even stand up.

Light was restored when the man switched the lamp pack to a general glare instead of a focused beam. Still very dim, the cone of light projecting from the pack spread across the ceiling and illuminated the cell-like room with a glow almost reminiscent of candlelight.

Her dizziness peaked as her returning vision swam again. Eurydice threw up the remains of her last meal aboard the *Maiden of the Stars*. Torc had cooked. Catching her breath, she spoke in ragged gasps.

'Throne… that tasted bad enough going in.' The sound of her own voice shocked her. It was as muted and weak as the light from the lamp pack. That Astartes, Talos… he'd half-strangled her. Even the memory made her blood run cold. His eyes, drilling into her own, red and soulless and devoid of humanity.

'Don't say that word,' the man's voice was soft.

She looked up at him now, wiping her mouth on her sleeve and blinking exertion tears from her eyes. He looked about thirty, thirty-five. Scruffy hair hung in ash-blond locks to his shoulders, and silvery yellow stubble showed he'd not shaved for several days. Even in the darkness, with his pupils enlarged to see in the gloom, she saw his irises were the green of royal jade. He'd be attractive if he wasn't a kidnapping son of a bitch.

'What word?' she asked, touching her sore neck.

'*That* word. Do not use Imperial curses or oaths on this ship. It will offend the demigods.'

She didn't recognise his accent, but it sounded strange. He also pronounced every word carefully, taking care to form his sentences.

'And why should I care about that?'

She was proud of the defiance she forced into her voice. *Don't let them know you're scared. Show your teeth, girl.*

The man spoke again, his soft voice a contrast to her scathing demands.

'Because they have little patience at the best of times,' he said. 'If you anger them, they will kill you.'

'My head hurts,' she said, gripping the edge of her cot. Her throat tensed and saliva thickened on her mouth. Throne, she was going to be sick again.

She was. He stepped back a little, avoiding the ground zero site of her messy purging.

'My head is on fire,' she said afterwards, and spat to clear her mouth of the last traces.

'Yes, from the surgery. My masters did not want you killing me when you awoke.'

Again she felt the metal plating covering her forehead, blinding her third eye. The panic she thought she was hiding so well pushed that worry aside in favour of another. Through the murk of her thoughts, she voiced the first of a thousand questions she desperately needed answered.

'Why am I here?'

He smiled at that, a warm and honest smile that Eurydice could have gladly punched off his handsome face. 'What the hell is so funny?' she snapped.

'Nothing.' His smile faded, but remained in his eyes. 'Forgive me. I was told that was the first thing everyone asks when they are brought aboard. It was the first thing I asked, as well.'

'So why is that funny?'

'It isn't. I just realised that with you among us, I am no longer the newest in our masters' service.'

'How long was I out?'

'Eight standard hours.' Septimus had counted the exact minutes, but doubted she'd care about that level of detail.

'And you are?'

'Septimus. I am the servant of Lord Talos. His artificer and vassal.'

He was annoying her now. 'You speak strangely. Slow, like an idiot.'

He nodded, his face set in calm agreement. 'Yes. Forgive me, I am used to speaking Nostraman. I have not spoken much Low Gothic in…' he paused to recall, '…eleven years. And it was never my first language, anyway.'

'What's Nostraman?'

'A dead language. The demigods speak it.'

'The… the Astartes?'

'Yes.'

'They brought me here.'

'I helped bring you aboard, but yes, they did.'

'Why?'

Septimus cleared his throat and sat down, his back to the wall. He looked like he was settling to get comfortable. 'Understand something. There is only one way off this vessel, and that is to die. You are here to be offered a choice. It will be simple: life or death.'

'How is that a choice?'

'Live to serve, or die to escape.'

The truth surfaces, she thought with a bitter smile. She could feel the fragility of her grin, like all her fear was trapped behind clenched teeth. It turned her tongue cold.

'I'm not a fool, and I know my mythology. These Astartes are traitors. They betrayed the God-Emperor. You think I'll serve them? Throne, no. Never.'

Septimus winced. 'Be careful with that word.'

'To hell with you. And to hell with serving your masters.'

'Life in their service,' Septimus said in a musing tone, 'is not what you might expect.'

'Just tell me what they want from me,' she demanded, a shake in her voice now. She gritted her teeth again to stop it.

'You are gifted.' Septimus tapped his forehead. 'You see into the immaterium.'

'This can't be happening,' she said, and at last her voice was as soft as his. 'This cannot be happening.'

'My master foresaw your presence on that world,' the slave pressed. 'He knew you would be there, and knew you would be of use to the Legion.'

'What world? It was just an asteroid.'

'Not always. Once, it was part of a world. Their home world. But that's not important now. You can navigate the Sea of Souls, and that is why you are here. The Legion is not what it once was. Their flight from the Emperor's light happened many centuries ago. Their... what is the word? Inf... Infra... Damn it. Their resources are running out. Their relics and machines of war are eroding without maintenance. Their mortal attendants are succumbing to age.'

Eurydice didn't resist the urge to smirk. 'Good. They're traitors to the God-Emperor.' She felt a little of her spirit returning, and risked another smirk. 'Like I care if their guns don't fire.'

'It is not that simple. Their inf... infra–'

'Infrastructure.' Throne, what a simpleton.

'Yes. That's the word. The Legion's infrastructure is shattered. Much knowledge has been lost, and many loyal souls; first in the Great Heresy, and then in the wars since.'

She almost, almost said, *'My heart bleeds'*, but settled for a silent smile, hoping her discomfort didn't show through it.

Septimus watched her, sharing the silence for several moments.

'Was your life before coming here really so wondrous,' he said, 'that this opportunity has no value to you?'

Eurydice snorted. That question wasn't even worth answering. Being kidnapped and enslaved by mutants and heretics wasn't a step up from anywhere. She was just surprised they weren't torturing her yet.

'You are not thinking clearly,' Septimus smiled, rising to his feet. She realised with an uncomfortable swallow that he was carrying two holstered pistols at his sides, and a hacking machete the length of her forearm strapped to his lower leg.

'You will witness sights no other mortals ever have the chance to see.'

Does he think that's supposed to be tempting?

'I'd rather not damn my eternal soul just to learn a few secrets.' She hesitated, watching him carefully, the smile in his eyes and the way he lounged comfortably against the wall. His easy grace unnerved her. He was hardly a lunacy-driven heretic, like she'd expected to find in a vessel of the Archenemy.

'Why are you here?' she snapped. 'Why did they send you?'

'You are afraid, and it's making you angry. I can understand that, but it would be better for you if you kept your temper. I must report every word of this to my master.'

She hesitated at that, but wouldn't be cowed. 'Why did they send you?'

'Acclimatisation,' he smiled again. 'Easier on you to speak with another human, than one of the Astartes.'

'How did you come to be here?' she asked. 'Were you kidnapped?'

He shrugged a shoulder, and his jacket whispered with a rustle of smooth material. 'It's a long story.'

'I've got time.'

Without warning, the ship shuddered violently, shaking to the sounds of the hull straining. Septimus braced himself by gripping the wheel-lock of the bulkhead door. Eurydice swore as the back of her head smacked against the wall with bruising force. For a few seconds she saw nothing but dancing colours.

'No,' Septimus said, raising his voice over the shaking of the ship. 'Time is the one thing we don't have.'

Eurydice blinked annoying tears of pain from her eyes, listening to the protesting hull as metal squealed and screamed. She knew this sound, too. The vessel was falling out of warp, breaking into realspace.

In a hurry.

'Where are we?' she yelled.

Her answer was a shipwide vox message, crackling with distortion, echoing from thousands of speakers across the myriad decks of the *Covenant*.

'Viris colratha dath sethicara tesh dasovallian. Solruthis veh za jass.'

'And that means *what* exactly?' she shouted at Septimus.

'It... doesn't translate well,' he called back, already working the wheel-lock.

'Throne of God,' she muttered, the words swallowed by the shaking all around her. 'At least try!'

Sons of our father, stand in midnight clad. We bring the night.

'It means,' he looked back over his shoulder, '"Brothers, wear your armour. We are going to war". But as I said, it doesn't translate smoothly.'

'War? Where are we?'

Septimus dragged the door open and moved through the oval portal. 'Crythe. The Warmaster, blessings upon his name, has summoned us to Crythe.'

Septimus stood in the doorway. Waiting.

'Crythe was days away...' she said. 'Weeks, even.'

'My masters know many secrets. They know the warp and the pathways through, in the shadows away from the False Emperor's light. These will be the paths you will also learn to walk.' He paused, as if considering her. 'Are you coming?'

Eurydice watched him for several moments. Was that a joke?

He didn't look like he was joking.

She rose on unsteady legs, hesitantly taking his offered hand. The ship juddered again and she knew that, at least, was not the warp drive catching its breath.

Septimus led her from the room, his lamp pack beaming the way. He noticed the look on her face as the ship rattled and shook.

'It is weapons fire,' he said, reassuringly. 'We are under attack.'

She nodded, but had absolutely no idea why he seemed so calm about it.

'Where are we going?' she asked.

'My master told me of the Legion's attack plan.'

'So?'

'So we are going to be ready in case that plan goes wrong. Do you know what a Thunderhawk is?'

RINGING A WORLD called Solace, the vessels of Battlefleet Crythe were stalwart in their defence, punishing the invaders for daring to assault an Imperial planet. It would be recorded as the largest void engagement ever to occur in the sector, with casualties in the millions.

The *Covenant of Blood* had torn back into realspace in the middle of an orbital war.

THE CRYTHE CLUSTER.

Five worlds, spread across five solar systems, allied in profit and a shared defence. Brought into the Imperium of Man during the Great Crusade ten thousand years before, it was an empire within the Imperium – a lesser reflection of fair Ultramar in the galactic east.

Hercas and Nashramar: two hive-worlds with productive, stable, sprawling populations forming the core of the star cluster. These were supplied in turn by Palas, an agri-world with a climate so ideal and harvest potential so rich it exported enough resources to feed the entire cluster.

The fourth world was Crythe Prime itself, named for the Imperial commander responsible for bringing the region into compliance with the Emperor's will after the decadent years of Old Night. Once, it had been a populous hive-world – the third of the trinity: Crythe Prime, Hercas and Nashramar. Several thousand years ago, its mineral deposits were exhausted by the ceaseless efforts of the Mechanicus and the planetary economy collapsed. Refugee transports left the world in increasing numbers over a number of decades, and rather than leave the barren world alone, a recolonisation was undertaken by the Adeptus Mechanicus itself.

The Crythe Prime of late M41 was an industrious forge world, equipping the sizeable and well-trained Crythe Highborn regiments of the Imperial Guard, and serving as the manufactorum home world of the Titan Legion, the Legio Maledictis.

The fifth and final world was Solace. Here, based around an orbital shipyard fortress, was the heart of Imperial strength.

The planet below the starfort was a third populated world, though unlike Crythe Prime, Solace had always been devoid of mineral worth and natural resources. The world was a barren rock, empty but for the hive-like prison complexes rising from its surface, home to hundreds of thousands of criminals drawn from across neighbouring sectors and the hives of the Crythe Cluster. A penal world, guarded by the might of the Imperium, used as a base for Imperial Navy and

Astartes counter-piracy efforts in the star cluster. Only Crythe Prime, in the augmetic grip of the Mechanicus, was a stronger target.

Lord Admiral Valiance Arventaur commanded the unbreakable might of Battlefleet Crythe. Countless escorts, dozens of cruisers, all led by the jewel in the battlefleet's crown: the colossal Avenger-class grand cruiser, *Sword of the God-Emperor,* a city of cathedrals running down the ship's spine, home to thousands of souls.

Had this been the entirety of the Throne's might in the sector, still it would have stood as a defiant and implacable foe, but the lord admiral could also count on the support of a garrison of the noble Astartes Chapter, the Marines Errant, who were permanently on deployment to crush the piracy rife within the sector. Their vessel, the Gladius-class frigate *Severance,* was a lethal blade used against the heretics that dared prey upon the trade routes of the Emperor's loyal subjects.

It was to Solace that the Warmaster first brought his wrath. Break the defences of this fiercely guarded world, tear the strength from the Holy Fleet, annihilate the Astartes presence here... and the Crythe Cluster would surely fall. So went the great Despoiler's plan.

The Exalted's plan fit neatly within this framework. To succeed before the Warmaster's eyes, he would call upon his calculating, tactical genius.

TALOS VIEWED THE interior of the pod through the ruby hue of his helm's eye lenses. His squad didn't even take up half of the twelve thrones within the confines of the pod. They needed to recruit soon. The losses incurred the past few decades had hurt the remnants of the VIII Legion's 10th Company to the point where – at best – the Exalted could raise no more than fifty Astartes.

The process to engineer new warriors was painstaking and slow, and the Legion's forces aboard the *Covenant of Blood* were severely lacking in fleshsmiths and technicians capable of gene-forging children into Astartes over the course of a decade.

Xarl always commented on the empty thrones. Every time the squad came together in a drop-pod, a Thunderhawk, a boarding pod, their Land Raider... anywhere they stood ready in the moments before an engagement, he would bring it up.

'Four of us,' he grunted, right on schedule. 'This is bad comedy.'

'I'm just aggravated it was Uzas that survived on Venrygar,' Cyrion said back over the vox. 'I miss Sar Zell. You hear me, Uzas? It's a shame you made it instead of him.'

'Cyrion, my beloved brother,' Uzas growled in reply, 'watch your mouth.'

For a moment, Talos was back in his vision, seeing Uzas's axe rise as he approached from the rubble behind Cyrion...

'Sixty seconds,' a mechanical voice blared over the pod's speakers. It jolted Talos back to the present with a sickening lurch of perception.

'I'd like to state,' Cyrion said, 'that this is the most foolish use of our forces I can recall.'

'Noted,' Talos said softly. It wasn't his idea to use a pod deployment, but complaining about it now wasn't going to change a thing. 'Stay focused.'

'Furthermore,' Cyrion ignored his brother's reprimanding tone, 'this will see us all dead. I guarantee it.'

'Be silent.' Talos turned in his throne, making his restraint harnesses pull tight over his bulky war-plate as he faced his squadmate. 'Enough, Cyrion. The Exalted gave us our orders. Now sound off.'

'Uzas, aye.'

'Xarl, ready.'

'Cyrion, aye.'

'Acknowledged,' Talos finished. 'In midnight clad, on my mark. Three, two, one. Mark.'

All four back-mounted power generators clicked live, feeding artificial strength through their suits of armour, boosting their physical levels far beyond even the inhuman power already within their gene-engineered bodies. Talos's visor display powered up, filtering his crimson vision with scrolling white status text, ammunition counters and dozens of stylised icon runes scattered at the edges of his sight. He blink-clicked three specifically, frowning as one of them kept flickering in and out of focus.

'Uzas,' he said, 'your identification rune is still unstable. You said you'd get that fixed.'

'My artificer... suddenly died.'

Talos clenched his jaw. Uzas had always been murderous with his slaves, be they Legion serfs or augmented servitors. He treated them like worthless playthings, toying with them to sate his own private amusements, and the only reason his armour was even sustainable was because he plundered his fallen brothers with a diligence few other Night Lords adhered to.

'We do not have the resources for you to entertain your bloodlust with the murder of slaves, brother.'

'Maybe I can borrow Septimus to repair my armour.'

'Yes, maybe,' Talos said. Not a chance, he thought.

'Forty-five seconds,' the launch servitor's voice crackled.

'Stow weapons for transit,' Talos ordered.

He checked his bolter one last time, turning it over in his fists. A beautiful weapon, and one that had served him well since before the Great Betrayal. He'd fired the weapon on Isstvan V, and scythed down countless numbers of the Salamanders Legion as part of that fateful battle. Just holding the boltgun in his gauntlets was enough to give him a thrill of pleasure, as real and tactile as a flooding rush of combat stimulants from his armour's drug infusion ports in his spine and wrists.

It was called *Anathema*. The name, in flowing Nostraman script, was embossed along the side in black iron. Talos held the weapon lengthways against his right thigh, as if holstering a pistol. He blinked at a small icon on the edge of his display, and the thick electromagnetic strip along the firearm's edge went live. With a clank of metal on metal, the bolter clamped to his leg, waiting to be drawn in battle once the release icon was confirmed with another blink.

With his bolter secured, he checked the sheathed blade – too long to be tied to his hip while he was seated – secured to the pod's sloping wall by strips of magnetic coupling. The angel wings of the crosspiece hilt were the white of fine marble. The ruby teardrop between the wings glittered in the red gloom, darker than its surroundings, a drop of blood on blood.

Aurum and *Anathema*, the tools of his trade, his relics of war. His lip curled as his heart started to beat faster.

'Death to the False Emperor,' he breathed the words like a whispered curse.

'What was that?' voxed Xarl.

'Nothing,' Talos replied. 'Confirm weapon check.'

'Weapons stowed.'

'It is done.'

'Weapons, aye.'

'Thirty seconds,' the voice issued forth again. The Dreadclaw-class pod began to shake as its thrusters cycled up to full power. Although it would be fired from its socket, the pod's attitude thrusters still needed to be burning hot to guide them on target.

'10th Company, First Claw,' Talos spoke into the general vox-channel. 'Primed for deployment.'

'Acknowledged, First Claw.' The voice that replied was low, too low for even an Astartes. The Exalted was on the bridge, speaking to the squads preparing for battle. Talos listened to the other squads sounding off as the pod started to shake with increasing violence.

'Second Claw, ready.'

'Fifth Claw, ready.'

'Sixth Claw, aye.'

'Seventh Claw, primed.'

'Ninth Claw, prepared.'

'Tenth Claw, ready.'

None of those squads were complete, Talos knew. The centuries had been unkind. All of Third Claw had been slaughtered at the Battle of Demetrian, by the accursed Blood Angels. Fourth and Eighth Claws had both died piece by piece, battle by battle, until the last surviving members were absorbed into other understrength Claws. Uzas had been Fourth Claw once. Talos hadn't been thrilled by that particular inheritance.

'This is Talos of First Claw. Give me a soul count.'

'Second Claw, seven souls.'

'Fifth Claw, five souls.'

'Sixth Claw, five souls.'

'Seventh Claw, eight souls.'

'Ninth Claw, four souls.

'Tenth Claw, six souls.'

Talos shook his head again. Including his own squad, it racked up to thirty-nine Astartes. A skeleton crew would remain with the Exalted aboard the *Covenant*, but it was still a grim figure. Thirty-nine of the Legion were ready for deployment. Thirty-nine out of over one hundred.

'Soul count confirmed,' he said, knowing every Astartes on the vessel was patched into this vox-channel. He doubted the significance of the figure was lost on any of them.

'Ten seconds,' the servitor intoned. The pod was shuddering in its cradle now alongside the six others, like a row of jagged teeth pushing from a giant's gums.

'Five seconds.'

The vox was filled with a frenzy – dozens of roaring Astartes, calling out for vengeance, for blood, for fear, and the memory of their primarch. Inside First Claw's pod, Xarl howled long and loud, a sound of unrestrained glee. Cyrion whispered something Talos couldn't quite make out, most likely a benediction to the machine-spirits of his weapons. Uzas cried out a string of oaths, promising bloodshed in the name of the Ruinous Powers. He invoked them by name, crying out like a fanatic in ecstatic worship. Talos bit back the urge to rise from his restraint throne and shoot his brother dead.

'Three.'

'Two.'

'One.'

'Launch.'

IV
VOID WAR

'It has been said by tacticians throughout the ages of mankind that no plan survives contact with the enemy. I do not waste my time countering the plans of my foes, brother. I never care what the enemy intends to do, for they will never be allowed to do it. Stir within their hearts the gift of truest terror, and all their plans are ruined in the desperate struggle merely to survive.'

– The Primarch Konrad Curze,
Allegedly speaking to his brother,
Sanguinius of the Blood Angels

THE EXALTED SAW void warfare as infinitely more graceful than any surface attack.

He excelled in personal combat and had reaped a bountiful harvest of life with his own claws, but it wasn't the same. Such savagery lacked the clarity and purity of a void hunt.

Even in the years before he became the Exalted, when he had simply been Captain Vandred of the Night Lords 10th Company, he had taken his greatest battle-pleasures from those moments of orbital and deep space warfare where everything played out to perfection.

And he was no simple observer in those moments. He prided himself on making the perfect battles come to pass, and it was a pleasure he'd taken with him through all his changes. It was a matter of attuning one's perceptions to the realities of scale and dimension involved within a void war. Most minds, mortal and Astartes alike, could not truly fathom the distances between ships, the sheer size of warring vessels, the scars left by each and every type of weapon against hulls of different metals...

This was his gift. The Exalted *knew* void war, seeing its grandeur within his swollen mind the way other men saw the weapons in their hands. His vessel was his body, even without the primitive tech-links engineered by the Mechanicum to merge man and machine. The Exalted bonded with the *Covenant* by familiarity and his modified perceptions. Merely by standing on the bridge, he felt the ship's heartbeat in his bones. Simply gripping a handrail allowed him to hear its screaming voice as it fired its weapons. Others would feel nothing more than vibrations, but others were blind to such nuances.

The *Covenant of Blood* had a fine history of pulling through engagements against long odds and taking part in some of the most savage conflicts to involve the VIII Legion. Its reputation – and, by extension, the reputation of the warband that had once been the 10th Company – was assured through a record of space battles won, largely thanks to the void warfare skills of the Exalted.

As his precious, prided vessel broke into realspace, the creature that had once been Captain Vandred stared at the eye-shaped occulus screen that dominated the forward wall of the strategium deck. His own eyes were unchanged by the mutations that had twisted his physical form, remaining the pure black of the Nostramo-born, and these obsidian orbs glittered with reflected light from the dozens of crew consoles and the detonations lighting up the occulus before him.

By necessity, the strategium endured a greater level of illumination than the rest of the ship, so the mortal crew could perform their duties with ease. The Exalted spared a sweeping glance around the multi-layered chamber now, ensuring all was in readiness.

It seemed so.

Servitors slaved to their stations jabbered and droned and worked consoles with a mix of bionic and human hands. Mortal crew, including several former Imperial Navy officers in service to the Legion, worked at stations of their own or supervised teams of servitors. Few consoles or strategium positions stood empty. Operations here were far too critical to suffer under a lack of manpower. It was almost the way it should be, the way it had been before the Great Betrayal, before the slow decline of the Legion's strength had begun, and the Exalted revelled in this echo of a greater age.

He took all of this in within the space of a single thump of his heart, before returning his attention to the occulus once more.

And there it was. War in its grandest form. A theatre of destruction where hundreds, even thousands of lives were lost with the passing of each second. He allowed himself several moments to drink in the sight, to relish the sight of the life-ending explosions, no matter which side sustained the casualties.

The feeling threatened to edge into euphoria, and the Exalted clawed his focus back. He had not earned his title by weakness and self-indulgence. Duty came first.

The Exalted likened void war to the feeding frenzy of sharks. Few memories of his pre-Astartes life ever bubbled to the surface of his warped memory, but one in particular returned to him each time he brought his passions to bear in spaceborne battle. As a child, on several coastal journeys with his father, he had witnessed the eyeless barrasal sharks that would group together to hunt the great whales of the open ocean. They would form a pack, yet without any real bonds, for they rarely aligned their movements or worked together – they simply did not kill each other as they hunted the same prey. When each shark would strike at an exposed killing point on the great whale, it was instinct, not cooperation, that drove them. Instinct for the quickest kill.

Void warfare seemed much the same to the Exalted now. Each ship was a shark swimming in the three-dimensional battlefield of space, and only the most talented fleet commanders could harness their instincts and bring their forces together into an efficient hunting pack. The Astartes creature smiled, baring black gums and fanged teeth as he watched the occulus. He was no fleet commander. His own talents had never been in bringing about such a pack unity.

In fact, quite the opposite. He had no desire to inspire tactical union within the fleets he sailed with. All he cared about was the dissolution of order within the enemy's armada.

The easiest way to win a void battle was to ensure no enemy commander achieved tactical unity for his own forces. If their overall cohesion was compromised, each vessel could be isolated from any potential support and torn apart, alone, piece by piece.

It was an approach the Night Haunter had honoured the Exalted for on no small number of occasions. As the primarch himself had said, it was worthless to know an enemy's plans. The foe should be defeated before his plans even come into play.

THE WARMASTER'S CRYTHE invasion fleet had translated into the system several days before – that much was obvious to the Exalted as soon as the Night Lords strike cruiser tore from the warp. Dozens of broken hulks of vessels, their shattered metal skins declaring allegiances to either side in the conflict, hung powerless in the void, destroyed in the opening phases of the war.

The Exalted ordered its helmsmen to guide the ship through this silent graveyard, engines burning to reach the main battle, where the Warmaster's fleet had at last forced the Throne's forces into an orbital defence.

The creature's eyes drank in the sight of ancient names on the flickering hololithic display. Great vessels that had waged war for thousands of years, their names and titles etched into the flooding tides of the Exalted's memory despite the turning of time.

There, the *Ironmonger*, which served the Legion of Primarch Perturabo. There, the *Heart of Terra*, still with the scars it earned when it laid siege to the world it was named for. And ringed by dozens of smaller vessels, in the heart of the storm, the *Vengeful Spirit*.

The Exalted gestured with its claw.

'Make for the Warmaster's flagship as you transmit our identity codes, then break formation and engage ahead of the fleet.'

The *Covenant of Blood* streaked into the maelstrom of the orbital battle, and the Exalted pictured the command decks of Imperial vessels as another mighty ship joined the Archenemy host. Console alarms would sound, orders would be shouted... It was delightful to envisage, even if just for a moment.

But the *Covenant* was vulnerable. It burned its engines white-hot as it powered past the *Vengeful Spirit,* past the Chaos vanguard.

This had to be done fast.

Even a cursory glance at the occulus revealed to the Exalted that the battle result was inevitable. The Imperial fleet was doomed. He watched the icons on the wide holographic display table before his oversized command throne, seeing their slow dance through three dimensions. In a matter of moments, he saw the outcomes of each icon's motion, calculating the many ways every vessel might move in relation to the others. A game of many – but ultimately finite – possibilities, unfolding before his eyes.

Again, he looked to the occulus. The forces of the False Emperor were still numerous enough to inflict severe harm upon the Warmaster's attacking fleet, and that was what counted. Victory at too high a price was no victory at all.

As he grinned, his eyes leaked tears of oily blood. The dark tears ran cold down a face as pale as porcelain, showing every vein beneath in thick, black cables. Muscles in his face strained and his tear ducts tingled. The Exalted was not used to smiling. It had been too long since entertainment of this calibre had been forthcoming, and better yet, the Warmaster was watching.

It was time to make the most of it.

Two Imperial ships stood out from the pack. Two targets that had to be destroyed in order to dissolve the hopes of tactical unity. The Exalted had marked both of them, and relayed his desires to the strategium crew. They worked now to make his intentions a reality.

The *Covenant of Blood* raged through the battle, taking incidental damage on its void shields from the few fighters and light cruisers that had reacted fast enough to its sudden arrival. A speeding shrike of blue-black and bronze, it speared between two ships of similar size to itself, ignoring the barrage from their broadsides.

By the time they had come about to give chase to the diving blade of a ship that had evaded them, they were already engaged by other vessels. These new attackers bore the black and gold of the Black Legion, the Warmaster's own Astartes.

The *Covenant of Blood* didn't even slow down. The Night Lords hunted larger prey.

An Astartes strike cruiser was a powerful ship, excelling in actions of surface bombardment and blockade-running. In void warfare it was a dread enemy, for while it lacked the offensive capability of a battle-barge or heavy cruiser of the Imperial Navy, because of its armaments and dense shielding, it would make short work of most vessels of a similar size. Had the Exalted joined the orbital battle above Solace by lending the fury of the *Covenant's* lances and weapons batteries, the Night Lords would have made a significant and useful contribution, worthy of praise.

That, however, was not enough.

The greatest threat from an Astartes strike cruiser was its cargo. While the *Covenant* had weapons capable of levelling cities and shields that could take punishment for hours on end without flickering, its deadliest and most feared weapons were already leashed into their deployment pods and awaiting the moment of launch.

The Night Lords cruiser was a huge and weighty ship, yet graceful despite its bulk. It rolled, shark-like, slow and smooth, as it dived towards the much larger Gothic-class ship, the *Resolute.* The Imperial cruiser was a monument as much as a warship: a small city of cathedral-like structures jutted from its central spine, and its aggressive beauty was an inspiration to the small fleet of support ships that streamed around it, orbiting like satellites in its presence.

The occulus aboard the *Covenant* was blinded by the release from the *Resolute's* lances. The larger ship was still target-locked on the Warmaster's attacking vessels – it had had no time to bring its furious weapons array to bear on the new arrival yet – although the support ships in its shadow began to power up to destroy the racing Night Lords cruiser plunging into their midst.

The Exalted watched as one of the icons situated behind the *Covenant's* symbol winked out of existence. The *Unblinking Eye* was no more, coming to pieces under the final assault of the *Resolute*. A Black Legion ship: one of the Warmaster's own.

Strange, thought the Exalted, to have endured for millennia, just to die here. The *Unblinking Eye* had been at the Siege of Terra ten thousand years before. Now it was debris and an ignoble memory of failure.

Then it was the *Covenant*'s turn. The strategium shuddered again, and not gently.

But the shields were holding, the Exalted knew. He felt the ship's skin as keenly as he felt his own. Three ships firing abeam, and… something more.

'Shields holding,' a mortal officer called to the command throne. 'Weapons fire from three light cruisers and incidental fire from a fighter wing.'

Fighters, it chuckled. How quaint.

The Exalted instantly assimilated this information into his overall vision of the icon formation ballet unfolding before his eyes. The *Resolute* had been his first target because its shields were already down. He'd known from the moment the battle hololithic display had flickered into life that, from its place in the formation, the Gothic-class cruiser had fallen back from the fighting to restore its void shields. The minor fleet spinning around it like parasites only confirmed his deduction. It was one of the larger ships in the Imperial fleet, swarmed by protectors as it sought to restore its defences. It was clearly key to the defence.

The Exalted snarled harsh manoeuvre orders, and the *Covenant* strained to obey. It began below the *Resolute,* and with engines howling, it climbed hard. Shields still holding, rippling as they reflected incoming fire, the strike cruiser sliced almost vertically up past the *Resolute's* starboard side. The Night Lords ship presented almost no target to the masses of broadsides, though they fired anyway. It was a curious move by the standards of traditional void warfare. Running abeam of the ship would have allowed for a more standard exchange of heavy broadside batteries as the ships coasted alongside each other, but lancing vertically seemed to achieve nothing at all. Although the *Resolute's* broadside volley went tearing off into space, completely wasted, the *Covenant's* weapons batteries would have also done almost nothing – if they had actually fired. The guns of the Night Lords vessel remained silent.

Aboard the *Covenant of Blood,* all of the human strategium crew were still crying out or throwing up in the aftermath of the insane gravitational forces from the manoeuvre. Several had passed out. The Exalted wiped bloody tears of joy from his cheeks.

That had been divine.

'Confirm,' it said simply to the servitor at the pod launch console.

'Seventh, Ninth and Tenth Claws deployed,' the half-machine slave murmured in response.

'Contact?' it demanded.

'Confirmed,' came the toneless reply. 'Boarding pods confirm successful contact.'

A moment later, a familiar voice crackled over the strategium vox-speakers.

'Exalted,' it said in the deep resonance of the Astartes. 'This is Adhemar of Seventh Claw. We are in.'

All this smiling made the creature weep more aching tears. They had just run a gauntlet of Imperial vessels through the heart of the enemy fleet, and by the time the officers of the *Resolute* realised what had happened, three squads of Astartes would be butchering their way to the command decks.

Truly, that had been divine. The *Resolute* and the fleet leadership on board were as good as dead. Once the other Imperial crews heard of the slaughter aboard their key vessels, fear would spread like a merciless cancer.

One down, one to go.

'Helm,' it said as the strategium shivered under another barrage. 'Make for the *Sword*. All power to the engines.'

'Lord,' an officer close to the throne cleared his throat. 'The enemy flagship's shields are still raised.'

Not for long. 'Approach vector: insidious predation.'

'Aye, lord.'

The Exalted licked its lips with a black tongue. 'Fire all forward lances and torpedoes at hull section 63 as we move across her bow. Time the firing of the bombardment cannon to coincide with the exact moment our lances and torpedoes strike.'

That was no easy feat. A dozen servitors and mortal officers hunched over their consoles, working their controls and calculations.

'It will be done, lord,' assured the nearby officer.

The Exalted couldn't recall his name. Either that, or it had never learned the human's name, it wasn't sure. The creature knew the man as its bridge attendant, and that was all it needed to know. 'But–' the man hesitated.

'Speak, human.'

'My lord, Exalted of the Dark Gods... This attack vector will bring us within the *Sword*'s firing solution for fifteen seconds.'

'Thirteen,' the Exalted corrected with a death's head grin. 'And that is why as soon as we fire our prow weapons, the ship will execute a Coronus Dive, full burn on the engines with port thrusters overloaded by seventy per cent. We will roll while holding maximum sustainable negative yaw and pitch for ten seconds.'

The officer went paler, if such was even possible for a man who hadn't felt sunlight on his skin in decades.

'Lord... we're too large a vessel for–'

'Silence. You will coordinate this attack run with main armament weapons fire from the vessels *Ironmonger, Vengeful Spirit,* and the *Blade of Flame*. Align with their strategiums and inform them of our intent.'

'As you say, lord.' The officer swallowed. His eyes, the Exalted noted, were a particularly rich brown. They did not flicker here and there in his nervousness, as did most mortals' in the presence of the Exalted, but he was still reluctant to speak his mind in the presence of his liege. The reasons for this were fairly obvious, of course. Arguing with the Astartes always, always ended in blood and pain.

The ship moaned a long, agonised heave as it passed through the forward fire arc of another sizeable cruiser. Again, the Night Lords ship declined to defend itself, letting its shields take the impacts while it stormed to its chosen target.

'Speak, human,' the Exalted repeated. 'Entertain me with your thoughts in these moments before our victory.'

'A Coronus Dive, lord. The g-forces alone are likely to kill us, and the attitude thrusters will be offline for weeks with the burnout. The risks–'

'Are acceptable.' The Exalted nodded to the officer. 'The Warmaster is watching, mortal. And so am I. Bring my wishes into being, or you will be replaced by one more capable of doing so.'

The officer should have known better. When he turned back to his station and whispered under his breath 'This will destroy the damn ship...' he should have known the Exalted would hear.

'Bridge attendant,' the Astartes smirked.

The man didn't turn around. He was too busy working his console, sending binary orders to the minds of the strategium servitors to prepare for the madness to come. 'Yes, lord?'

'If this is not flawlessly done, I will feed you your own eyes, and you will die tonight, skinless and howling for mercy that will never come.'

The bridge fell quiet, and the Exalted grinned wetly.

'I do not care about overhauling the attitude thrusters, nor the slaves that will die in the repairs. A Coronus Dive, as close as this vessel can come to such a manoeuvre, timed with weapons fire from the three named ships.

'Do it now.'

IT WAS BEYOND audacious.

The *Ironmonger*, *Vengeful Spirit* and the *Blade of Flame* pulled into position, supporting the Night Lords' manoeuvre by firing their weapons in a coordinated burst, though from a significant distance. The Exalted suspected their own captains aligned with his plan out of amused curiosity rather than the belief it would actually work, but then, their lack of courage was their cross to bear.

Almost every fleet captain on both sides stared – at least for a moment – at the *Covenant of Blood*, the only vessel of the Warmaster's fleet to run the gauntlet of enemy lines, as it sliced past the massive Avenger-class grand cruiser *Sword of the God-Emperor*. Many captains also recognised, to their disbelief, that the ship was in the initial movements of a wrenching, spinning, maddened Coronus Dive.

It began its attack run in the face of incredible firepower. Ghosting through the great ship's fire arc, the *Covenant* suffered the rage of the *Sword's* forward lances and weapons batteries which were already spitting torrents of fury against the enemy ahead. The Night Lords vessel endured the assault of supreme weapons fire that had been destined to hit other Chaos ships, and its shields first cracked, then shattered, within a matter of moments.

To all observers, it seemed the *Covenant of Blood* was sacrificing itself in a ramming run. And it would succeed, too. That much weight, inertia and explosive capability would burn out the *Sword's* shields and gut the ship to its core.

But the *Covenant* didn't ram its prey.

It returned fire just as its shields died, unleashing a blistering barrage of lances, solid shells and plasma fire from its prow weapons batteries, as well as a precisely timed single magma bomb warhead, principally designed for surface attack, from its bombardment cannon.

This payload struck the *Sword* just as massed fire from the three other Traitor Astartes vessels coordinated their prow weapons on the same target. It was as close to the shark-like unity of the black sea sharks as the Exalted could have imagined, but that was hardly foremost in the Night Lord commander's mind.

All of this unleashed punishment was enough, barely, to achieve the Exalted's desires. The colossal *Sword of the God-Emperor*, pride of Battlefleet Crythe, flagship of Lord Admiral Valiance Arventaur, no longer shimmered behind an invincible screen of rippling energy.

Its shields were down, overloaded by the sudden savage assault of the Astartes strike cruiser.

The Exalted was not a fool. He knew void war, and he knew the capabilities of his foes, the strength of their weapons, and the power of their vessels. He knew the *Sword of the God-Emperor* was bristling with failsafes and auxiliary generatoriums, and his attack had inflicted no real damage to the enemy flagship beyond temporarily overloading its shields by giving them too much to absorb at once. They would be back online within moments – a minute at the very most – multi-layered and strong once more.

The *Covenant of Blood* veered sharper than a cruiser of its size had any right to do, throwing itself into a potentially terminal rolling dive alongside and past the grand cruiser it had almost rammed. Alarms hammered the senses of all her crew across the ship. The bladed spear of a vessel roared down into its dive, taking secondary fire from the *Sword's* broadsides as it plunged past. It didn't return fire. A single volley from the mighty Imperial flagship pounded the *Covenant's* port weapons batteries into nothingness.

Still twisting as it slid past, the *Covenant* trailed a path of shed debris. Halfway through its plunge, the Exalted felt that one perfect moment of connection with the battle.

Here.

Now.

Even as his ship was being torn apart by Imperial guns, he felt the moment with unbroken clarity, and growled a single word.

'Launch.'

'THREE,' THE SERVITOR'S voice had said.

'Two.'

'One.'

'Launch.'

Talos felt his world lurch from under him, every muscle locking tense. It wasn't a feeling of falling, exactly, nor one of dizziness. His altered senses were resistant to matters of unbalance and unreliable perception. Where a human would have been painting the pod's interior with vomit and passing out from the pressure of launch, the Astartes on board merely suffered mild sensations of discomfort in the pits of their stomachs. Such was the blessing of biologically reconfigured perceptions.

'Impact in five seconds,' the pod's automated voice chimed from everywhere and nowhere at once. Talos heard Uzas wheezing into the vox, gleefully counting down the seconds.

Talos counted silently, bracing when a single second remained. The pod's guidance thrusters kicked into life with a jolt almost as bad as the impact that came a moment later. The pod smashed into its target with hull-breaching force, echoing within the pod itself like a dragon's roar.

A rune flickered on his retinal display in twisting Nostraman script, and in the shuddering aftermath of impact, Talos hammered a fist onto his throne's release pad. The restraints unlocked and disengaged, and the four Astartes of First Claw moved from their seats without hesitation, weapons clutched in dark fists.

The pod's hatch opened with a grind of tortured metal and a hiss of escaping air pressure. Talos spoke into the vox, his voice smooth and assured as he looked out into a steel-decked arching corridor: his first view of the interior of the *Sword of the God-Emperor.*

'*Covenant,* this is First Claw. We are in.'

SWORD OF THE GOD-EMPEROR

'Poison will breach any armour.
When faced with an invincible foe, simply bless his bloodstream with venom.
His own racing heart will carry the poison faster throughout his body.
Fear is a venom just as potent.
Remember that. Fear is a poison to break any foe.'

– The war-sage Malcharion
Excerpted from his work, *The Tenebrous Path*

LIEUTENANT CERLIN VITH listened in on the vox-net, from his position on the bridge.

Orders had come from the highest authority: repel the boarding party currently rampaging through the operations decks below the bridge. Cerlin knew there were other boarding parties moving elsewhere across the ship, but they would be handled by other squads of armsmen. Vith had his orders, and he intended to see them through. His men guarded the bridge, and he had a host of reinforcements on the way.

He wasn't worried. The *Sword of the God-Emperor*, his home for the past twenty years, was as grand a ship as any in His Majesty's Holy Fleet. Over 25,000 crew called the warship home, even though a sizeable chunk of those were slave labourers and servitor wretches working their lives away in the sweathouse enginarium decks. You didn't board a vessel this big.

At least, Vith amended, not if you intended to survive.

It was true enough that the *Sword* wasn't in front-line service, anymore. Equally true, the glorious ship had been sidelined from the major battlefleets, but she still stood as the invincible jewel in the crown of Battlefleet Crythe. It was a sign of the times, that was all. The Avenger-class was a brawler, a close-range battler, designed to rage into a maelstrom of enemy ships and give out a beating twice as bad as any it took. It had the firepower to do it, but fell out of favour with admirals over time, when such blunt tactics were frowned upon by an increasingly defensive Imperium.

This is what Cerlin told himself. This is what he believed, because the officers said it so many times.

Cerlin's beloved *Sword* wasn't out of the running forever. She was just out of fashion. He'd told himself this time and time again, because although he was just a soldier in service to the Golden Throne, he took great pride to be serving where he was. Above all, Lieutenant Cerlin Vith ached for front-line service once more. He burned to gaze out of a porthole and see the blackish bruise of distorted warp space that made up the Great Eye – the nexus of the Archenemy's influence.

So he wasn't worried now. The *Sword of the God-Emperor* was unbreakable, undefeatable. The shaking of the ship was the endless vibration of its own guns unleashing hell upon the accursed Archenemy. When the shields had fallen a short while ago, they'd been raised again within a single minute. And even if they fell again, the hull wreathing them all in protective, loyal armour was as strong as a righteous man's faith.

Nothing, but nothing, would ever kill the *Sword*.

He repeated these words within his mind, not a trace of desperation in his silent voice. The fact they'd been boarded was... Well, it was madness. What sane enemy would ever attempt such a thing? He literally couldn't conceive of the tactics at play. What fool of a commander wasted the lives of his men by hurling a handful of them into a ship that boasted over twenty thousand souls ready to defend it?

It was time to teach the first boarding party the error of their ways.

Apparently their vessel had pulled some nice stunts to get them here, if the vox-talk from the strategium was anything to go by.

Well, whatever the truth, they'd managed to come aboard a ship that hadn't seen invaders in over a dozen years, so maybe the admiral – blessings upon his name – was right. Maybe this *was* serious.

But Cerlin had a reputation for dealing with serious business. That was why more often than not, he was the one that saw duty defending the command decks.

Vith led the decorated platoon known as Helios Nine, with a record of distinction and superior marksmanship that wouldn't have shamed an Imperial Guard sniper. He handpicked the men and women of Helios Nine, turning down promotion twice in the last ten years because he didn't want to be raised above the station he felt best suited him. Commanding a dozen armsman squads would mean he had a lot of mediocrity in with his finest soldiers. Commanding Helios Nine meant he commanded nothing but the best of the best.

Helios Nine even dressed like they meant business. On the occasions they were tasked to descend into the depths of the *Sword's* belly and bring some order to the criminals and scum labouring beneath the civilised decks, their sleek, dark carapace armour with its flaring sun symbol on the chestplate was a sign for every slave and serf to look busy and keep to the rules. Helios Nine – the 'Sunbursts' and the 'Niners' to the conscripted slave colonies in the ship's bowels – were well-known for their ruthless demeanour. A famous predilection for a merciless eagerness formed the core of their reputation, brought about from many instances of executing slaves that dared hint at disobedience or dereliction of duty.

Helios Nine numbered fifty men and women, spread across the command decks, squad by squad. Forty-nine of Vith's favourite killers standing ready for the enemy, and Vith himself with the lead squad, backing the admiral's throne.

Every member of Helios Nine packed a shotcannon for maximum short-range damage without risking the ship's hull. He didn't need to look around to know his men were ready. They were born ready and had trained to be readier every day since. Nothing would take them down.

Lieutenant Cerlin Vith believed this without a doubt until the first reports came in over the vox.

'...bolters...' one of the crackled cries had said.

He'd swallowed, then. *Bolters.*

That wasn't good.

More reports crackled in his ears, flooding in now from armsmen squads elsewhere on the ship. The transmissions were broken and patchy, distorted by the running battles as well as the war raging outside the ship. But he was hearing more words he didn't like, more words he didn't want to hear.

'...require heavier weapons to...'

'...falling back...'

'…Throne of the Emperor! We're…'

As he stood in the centre of the low-ceilinged chamber of the main bridge, Cerlin tapped the micro-bead vox pearl in his ear, adjusting the needle mic to the edge of his lips.

'This is Vith. Enginarium teams?'

'Affirmative, lieutenant,' the response from the squads defending the ship's plasma drives crackled in his ear. The teams guarding the enginarium chambers were, if memory served, the Lesser Gods, the Death Jesters, the Lucky Fifty and the Deadeyes. Vith had no idea which officer he was talking to – the vox wasn't clear enough – but they were all solid, dependable squads. Not Helios Nine standards, by any means, but good enough in a scrap. The reception was punctuated by violent shrieks of distortion that prodded at Cerlin's hangover with cruel fingers.

'I'm getting vox chatter about bolters and all kinds of death breaking loose,' he said.

'Affirmative, lieut…' the voice repeated. 'Be advised that boarders are…'

'Are what? That the boarders are what?'

'…st…'

'Command team? Enginarium defence command team, this is Vith, repeat.'

'…th… es…'

Wonderful. Just wonderful.

It was easy to immerse himself in his own world, removed from the larger battle. The bridge was a chaotic hive of activity: naval officers shouting and moving from console to console as they devoted their attention to the war raging outside the ship. Servitors chattered and droned as they obeyed the orders called at them. Almost a hundred crew, human and lobotomised slave alike, working to keep the *Sword* unleashing its full lethal potential against the enemies of the Golden Throne.

With a moment's effort, Vith blanked it all out. His world was restricted to snippets of incoming vox chatter, and the immediate area around Lord Admiral Arventaur's throne. Raised on a platform to look down upon the bridge below, the throne accommodated the admiral's slender, jacketed form with apparent comfort despite the arching backrest made from the curving ribs of some strange xenos creature. Admiral Valiance Arventaur reclined in his bone throne, his temples thick with cables and wiring that bound him to the chair, and in turn, to the ship's systems.

Vith knew the admiral – eyes closed and seemingly lost in meditation – was allowing his consciousness to swim within the ship's machine-spirit. He knew the admiral felt the hull like his own skin, and the racing efforts of the crew within the steel halls like the blood that beat through his own body.

And again, Vith cared little for it. Keeping the old man alive was all that mattered. The admiral had a war to fight, and it looked like Vith did, too.

The thunder of the ship taking hits was still audible, but the hull itself was stable for the moment. Several of the armsmen shared glances.

'Sir,' one of the ones closest to the front of the column said to Cerlin. 'I know that sound. I served on the *Decimus,* and we did several boarding actions with the Astartes. The Marines Errant Chapter, sir.'

Cerlin didn't turn. His gaze remained fixed on the sealed and locked double doors in the starboard side of the chamber. The thunder was coming from there, and he knew the sound, too. It had taken a moment to recognise, because he'd never expected to hear it on board his own ship.

There was no mistaking the distinctive boom of bolt weapons.

They'd been boarded by Astartes. Traitor Astartes.

Finally, confirmation of the enemy was coming from all angles. Naval ratings relayed to each other that the enemy ship diving past them was a confirmed Astartes vessel, excommunicated for heresy, registering as the *Covenant of Blood*.

This was really information that would have been more use to Vith before he'd been comfortable on the command deck with only fifty men.

'Helios Nine,' he voxed to the soldiers scattered across the outer ring of the chamber. 'Enemy nearing the starboard doors. Show no mercy.'

He spared a glance at the lord admiral, seeing the old man sweating, teeth clenched, eyes closed as if in the grip of some strenuous nightmare.

The starboard doors exploding inwards stole his attention right back to where it should have been.

WHEN THEY HAD first come aboard, Talos had disembarked from the twisted wreckage of the hull where the pod had impacted, *Aurum* in one hand, *Anathema* gripped in the other. Despite ten minutes of infrequent fighting since then, he'd barely fired his bolter once. The same with Cyrion or Xarl. The squad was conserving its ammunition for when it really counted – once they reached the bridge.

Their pod had struck the enemy ship in the densely-populated upper gunnery decks, and the resulting slaughter was a time-consuming annoyance that had grated on all their nerves.

Except Uzas. Uzas had loved every moment of ploughing through the terrified crew as they put up what defences they could with tools and personal sidearms. The bark of his bolter was like a hammering in Talos's head, unwelcome and aggravating.

At one point Talos had slammed his brother against the arching wall of one passageway. Under fire from a retreating rabble of gunners ahead, he had thudded Uzas's helm against the metal wall and snarled through his speaker grille.

'You are wasting ammunition. Control yourself.'

Uzas writhed out of his brother's grip. 'Prey.'

'They are *unworthy* prey. Use your blades. Focus.'

'Prey. They are all prey.'

Talos's fist cannoned into the other Night Lord's face, denting his helm's faceplate. It slammed his head back into the wall a second time, louder than gunfire. From the cluster of mortal crew at the end of the passageway, a solid round clanged from Talos's shoulder guard. He ignored it, blinking to clear his visor display of the flashing warning runes.

'Control yourself, or I will end you here and now.'

'Yes,' Uzas had finally said. 'Yes. Control.' He reached for his fallen bolter. Talos could see the reluctance in his brother's movements as Uzas clamped the weapon to his thigh plate and drew a chainsword.

His restraint had not lasted long. As the squad came to another chamber that housed one of the grand cruiser's weapon turrets, he'd opened fire on the servitors that hadn't received orders to flee when the human crew had run moments before.

Talos led on, no longer caring if Uzas fell behind. Let him gorge on his need to instil terror. Let him waste his efforts on mindless servitors, just for the hope of seeing a flicker of fear in their eyes before the end.

They moved with speed, slaughtering the ill-equipped crew that were foolish enough to stand before them. Most lacked the courage to remain, or had the good sense to flee, but not all of the mortals ran.

Sergeant Undine of the armsmen squad Final Warning stood his ground, as did a total of seven of his men, their shotcannons firing a barrage down a narrow corridor at the advancing Astartes.

Talos's slanted eye lenses flickered with dull threat warnings, and his helmet's sensor muted the sound of their ammunition striking his war-plate to the sound of hailstones clattering to the ground. Undine's courageous last stand, and that of the valiant members of Final Warning, ended several seconds later when Talos waded through them, swinging *Aurum* with several annoyed curses. These delays were getting on his nerves, and while shotcannons offered little threat to his armour's integrity, this kind of massed fire might strike a vulnerable joint or socket, and slow him further.

And not all those who failed to flee offered any real resistance. Dozens of mortals stood in paralysed awe, locked in terror, as giants from mankind's nightmares strode past them. They stood open-mouthed, muttering nonsensical benedictions and pointless prayers at the sight of Traitor Astartes in the flesh.

Talos, Cyrion and Xarl ignored these. As they moved on, the sound of a chainblade told them that Uzas was apparently not content to let the fear-struck wretches live.

Finally, Talos thought as he rounded yet another corner.

'The bridge is beyond these doors,' Xarl said, nodding at the sealed portal ahead. At the end of the wide thoroughfare corridor, the double doors stood closed and grim. Uzas pounded a fist against them, just once, resulting in nothing more than a small dent and the clang of ceramite against adamantium – a rock meeting an anvil.

'Prey,' Uzas said. The others heard his voice thick with saliva. He was drooling into his helm. 'Prey.'

'Be silent, freak,' said Xarl. The others ignored Uzas as he started to claw at the locked bulkhead like a caged animal needing release.

'These won't blow,' Cyrion said. 'Much too thick.'

'Chainblades, then.' Xarl was already revving his up.

'Too slow.' Talos shook his head and hefted *Aurum*. 'This has already taken too long,' he said as he advanced with his stolen power sword.

HELIOS NINE WAS ready when the Night Lords hit them.

Under Vith's orders, they'd taken up positions around the bridge chamber. The sheer number of adjacent passages offered a wealth of cover and corners to shoot around. The bridge crew were too rapt in the orbital war. They had their duties to attend to, and although nervous glances were cast at the starboard door, every officer present needed his attention on the void battle, which kept them hunched over consoles and staring up at the wide vista offered by the occulus screen.

No one, least of all Helios Nine, had expected the reinforced doors to give way so easily. Over a metre thick, metal layered upon metal, the doors had stood unbroken since the ship's construction almost two thousand years ago.

Vith cursed as the explosion sounded. The Traitor Astartes had cut their way deep into the doors in order to lay explosives at the point where conventional detonators could actually sunder the command deck bulkheads.

Throne of the Emperor, where were his reinforcements?

'Helios Nine!' he shouted over the vox, without any idea if they could even hear him over the echoing thunder. 'Repel boarders!'

Unseen by Vith and any of the armsmen, the old admiral's eyes opened. Bloodshot, intensely blue, and narrowed in rage.

THE EXPLOSION, AND the clutch of blind grenades that followed, was the signifying event that pulled the mighty *Sword of the God-Emperor* out of the close-pitched void war.

In many of the records that would come to be written on the Crythe War, the Avenger-class grand cruiser remained a powerful force in the Imperium's defence until its eventual destruction. Admittedly, the storming of its bridge was the blow that crippled the ship, leaving it robbed of some of its former effectiveness, but it continued to fight with all honour.

History can be a humorous thing indeed, when written by the losers.

Curiously absent from Imperial records documenting the battle was that the *Sword* spent its final half hour of life in relative indignity, robbed of its glorious fury and its expected honourable last stand. Instead it unleashed its reduced rage, directionless and limping, while it was systematically torn apart by the Warmaster's cruisers – among them, the *Covenant of Blood*, which was not shy about opening fire on a vessel even while its own Astartes were on board. A swift and decisive victory demanded no less, and Astartes engaged in boarding actions were trained to withdraw immediately upon completing their objectives.

The blind grenades thrown by First Claw rattled as they skidded across the mosaic-inlaid floor of the bridge chamber, detonating within a half-second of each other. A thick burst of black smoke spread from each grenade, and while the smoke screens belched out by each device were nowhere near enough to blacken even half of the vast bridge, that was never the intention with which they'd been deployed. The four grenades clanged across the deck towards the forward gunnery station and exploded there, blinding the dozen officers and servitors at the prow weapons consoles.

As the naval ratings staggered back from the blinding cloud of smoke, the servitors remained where they were – slaved to their stations and emitting monotone warning complaints at the low level electromagnetic radiation in the cloud that stole their sight.

At that moment, the forward guns of the great *Sword* fell silent.

On another vessel, the Exalted grinned, knowing First Claw had reached the enemy bridge.

Several of the *Sword's* bridge crew cried out blessings to the immortal Master of Mankind. Among them, only the most pious and the most desperate actually believed the God-Emperor would save them.

Helios Nine, blessed with a paradise of cover in the form of angled work stations and railings, raised their weapons as one, drawing beads on the savaged starboard door.

A figure emerged, blacker than the shadows from which it stalked. Vith took in the sight – a towering killer, too large in all ways to be considered human, clad in bulky ceramite plate forged in a forgotten era. He drank in the details within the space of a single heartbeat: in one hand was a blade of gold, as long as Vith was tall, sparking with lethal power and still dripping molten metal from the door it had sliced through. In the other fist, an oversized bolter with a wide muzzle, open like the maw of some great beast.

Its helmed visage was painted with a skull's staring face, bone-white over midnight blue, with glaring red eye lenses lit up from within. A scroll, tattered and burn-marked by small-arms fire, was draped across its left shoulder, the surface of the creamy paper covered in runes alien to Vith's eyes. On the other shoulder a clutch of short chains hung from the ceramite, bronzed skulls hanging from the dark iron links like morbid fruit, rattling as the figure moved.

Vith's tearing eyes took in one detail above all others. The ruined Imperial eagle across the figure's chestpiece, carved from ivory and since marred by blade strikes to scar the symbol in a simple but effective act of desecration.

The armsman leader had no comprehension that the Night Lord had taken the chestpiece from a fallen Astartes of the Ultramarines Chapter a few years before. He had no idea that ten thousand years ago when this warrior had first worn his own war-plate, only the favoured III Legion, the Emperor's Children, had been granted the honour of wearing the aquila upon their armour. He had no idea Talos wore it now, even defiled, with a comfortable sense of irony.

What Vith did know, and all that mattered, was that a Traitor Astartes had come into their midst, and that unless he ran – maybe even if he did run – he was a dead man.

Vith was many things. An average officer, perhaps. A little too fond of his drink, certainly. But he was no coward. He would die with the words so many Imperial soldiers had died with on their lips across the millennia.

'For the Emperor!'

As noble as the sentiment was, his cry was utterly swallowed by what the Night Lord did next.

Talos's retinas were bombarded with chiming runes flickering across his visor. Target upon target upon target, detailing white flashes where weapons were visible. A single step into the chamber, he didn't raise his weapons, nor did he seek cover. As soon as he emerged from the broken doorway, he threw his head back, blanking his visor of all the threat runes, and he *screamed*.

It was a roar no unaugmented human could ever make: as resonant and primal as a feral world reptilian carnosaur. The roar, already inhumanly loud, was amplified by the vox speakers in Talos's helm to deafening levels. Powered as it was by his three lungs, the cry stretched out for almost fifteen seconds at full strength, echoing through the corridors of the *Sword* in a flood of sound. The crewmen plugged into their consoles felt it physically, sending tremors through the vessel's steel bones. Across the ship, tech-priests and servitors linked to the ship's systems felt the machine-spirit soul of the *Sword* shiver in response to the unearthly roar.

On the bridge, Lord Admiral Valiance Arventaur, at one with the *Sword's* machine-spirit in a way infinitely more intimate than any other, began to cry blood.

All of this went unnoticed by the armsmen surrounding their commander. They, like every other human in the sweeping circular chamber, were on their knees, hands clutching at their bleeding ears. Several would have killed themselves to escape the sense-shattering sound, had they been able to reach for their guns, which lay discarded where they fell.

Talos lowered his head, seeing the threat runes blink back into existence. The smoke cloud was thinner now, but drifting to cover much of the command deck. Everyone, every single mortal on the bridge, was prone. The *Sword* idled in space, most of its guns fallen silent. Talos imagined the Warmaster's fleet converging on the ship now, the eyes of every captain glinting with murderous intent.

Time was short. The Claws deployed on the *Sword of the God-Emperor* had a handful of minutes to achieve their mission objectives and get back to their pods before they were killed in the coming destruction.

In that moment, something happened that Talos would never forget to his dying day. From fifty metres away, through a break in the smoke and past the staggering forms of deafened crew, he met the admiral's eyes. They bled thick red tears, the same trickles that ran from his nose and ears, but his expression was unmistakable. Never, in the countless years Talos had made war against the servants of the False Emperor, had one of the Imperial wretches glared at him with such hatred.

He treasured the moment for the single, blood-warming instant it lasted, then whispered a single word.

'Preysight.'

At the soft command, his suit's machine-spirit complied, masking the red-tinged view of his eye lenses in a deep, contoured series of blues. Through the smoke, even through the cover of consoles and work stations, the bridge crew were revealed to him in a maelstrom of blurry orange, red and yellow smears of heat sources against the cold blueness around.

Cyrion, Xarl and Uzas stepped up behind him, and he heard their whispered commands as they activated their own hunting vision.

With thermal sight active, they stalked forward, blades and bolters coming up to spill the blood of the *Sword's* best and brightest as the mortals scrambled to recover their weapons.

THE ADMIRAL WAS the last to die.

By that point, the bridge was a charnel house. Through the dissipating smoke that finally succumbed to the emergency air scrubbers, all one could see were the ruined bodies of a hundred crew and their slain defenders, Helios Nine. The four Night Lords moved here and there, taking chainswords to consoles and ripping the nerve centre of the failing *Sword of the God-Emperor* to pieces.

The names of the slain were meaningless to Talos, and he had no idea that the last to fall by the admiral's throne, shotcannon pounding out its ignorable bark, had been Cerlin Vith.

Vith wheezed out the last of his life through his ruptured lungs, unable to lift his chin from his chest. He had been irrelevant to Talos, an irritating thermal blur, and the Night Lord had dispatched him with a simple thrust of his golden blade. As Vith fell, Talos kicked him from the throne's podium, his attention already elsewhere as Vith's head cracked on a railing and the mortal descended slowly into death.

Lord Admiral Valiance Arventaur stared up at the creature who would be his murderer. The blood-coloured eyes of Talos's helm stared down at the old man merged to his chair. Now, it made sense why the admiral had not raised himself up in the bridge's defence. The mortal did not exist – in the flesh – below the waist. His uniformed torso was directly bound to his command throne by snaking cables sutured against his pelvis, linking him bodily to the ship as surely as the tendril-wires in the back of his head tied his consciousness to the *Sword's* machine-spirit.

Talos wasted perhaps a second wondering when the admiral had submitted to this invasive, restrictive surgery, and how long he had been confined here – a living piece of the vessel he commanded – bound to his throne as a half-human mess of flesh, wire, cables and fluid exchange tubing.

He wasted that second and then, gripped by curiosity, he wasted another by asking 'Why would you do this to yourself, mortal?'

He never got an answer. The admiral's unshaven chin trembled as he tried to speak. 'God-Emperor,' the old man whispered. Talos ignited his power blade again, shaking his head.

'I saw your Emperor. A handful of times, back in the age before he betrayed us all.'

The sword slid into the admiral's chest with sickening gentleness, inch by slow inch, charring the dusty white Battlefleet Crythe uniform as the powered blade burned the material where it touched. The blade's tip sank into the bone of the command throne behind the mortal's back, forming yet another bond between the admiral and his station.

The effects were immediate. The bridge lighting flickered, and the ship itself groaned and rolled, tormented, like an injured whale in the black seas of Nostramo. The admiral's death flooded the ship's machine-spirit, and Talos withdrew the blade in a harsh pull. Blood hissed on the golden blade, dissolving against the heat.

'And,' the Night Lord said to the dying man, 'he was no god. Perhaps not a man,' the Astartes smiled, 'but never a god.'

The admiral tried to speak once more, his hands trembling as they reached out to Talos. The Night Lord gripped the dying shipmaster's frail hands and left them folded over the blade wound in his chest.

'Never a god,' Talos repeated gently. 'Know that truth, as you die.'

With the admiral's last breath, the lights on the bridge failed forever.

THE CREW OF the *Sword of the God-Emperor* might have regained control of their ship, except for two factors in the Night Lords' attack.

First and foremost, the teams of crew and armsmen that reached the bridge found the helm and every control console in the room ruined beyond use, displaying the jagged wounds left by the chainblades of First Claw. Using low-light visors to see in the darkness, these would-be saviours also found the admiral dead in his throne of bone, his face set in a twisted expression that lay somewhere in the ugliness between pain, hatred and fear.

The command decks might have been savaged beyond fast repair, but the under-officers aboard the *Sword* had only to ensure the grand cruiser could move from the battle, and its armour could easily sustain it until it could thrust clear of the orbital war. Efforts were redoubled in tech crews and officers racing to the enginarium decks, which was where the second factor came into play.

Talos and First Claw had not been alone.

The second impediment to regaining any semblance of control over the ship was that the secondary enginarium sector was in the hands of the enemy. While this section of the ship was nowhere near as vital to overall function as the main engine decks, it was a significant disruption to power flow and drive efficiency. The Night Lords hadn't hit the primary sections and allowed themselves to be drawn into protracted firefights. They'd hit all they needed to hit; enough to take the *Sword* out of the fight with a minimum of delay and effort.

Teams of armsmen stormed the massive engine chambers seeking to oust the invaders, but Second and Sixth Claws had left their pods with their bolters barking, and held their ground until the order to leave. When that order finally came, the defiant Imperials retook the subsidiary enginarium chambers, only to find a farewell gift left by the Night Lords, who had fastened explosives to the same hull section that their pods had breached in the first place. When the detonators counted down to zero, the explosives took out a vast section of the already compromised hull wall, leaving a sizeable portion of the secondary enginarium decks open to the void.

This killed any hope of crew transit to and from the primary enginarium decks alongside the starboard edge of the grand cruiser, and left the secondary engines silent and dead. Directionless, with neither a brain nor a beating heart now that the bridge and enginarium were disabled, the *Sword of the God-Emperor* rolled in space, naked without its shields, taking a million scars from the weapons of the Warmaster's fleet.

In the space of half an hour, a handful of Astartes had killed several hundred Imperial souls, kept the two key areas of the vessel disrupted and only loosely in loyal control, and made their escape after ensuring no significant repairs could be made in time.

Aboard the *Covenant of Blood*, the Exalted – already anticipating the praise he would receive from the Warmaster – ordered the helm to run close to the suffering *Sword* and be ready to receive boarding pods back into the starboard landing bays.

His personal screens mounted in the arms of his command throne spilled digital data in a ceaseless stream of green runes on a black setting.

Second Claw had disengaged and awaited retrieval.

Sixth Claw, the same.

Fifth Claw... no contact. No contact since launch. The Exalted suspected the pod had been destroyed almost as soon as it left the *Covenant*, hammered into nothingness by the pulverising fire from the grand cruiser's broadsides. A shame, certainly. Five souls lost.

But First Claw... Their pod was still attached. The last to be fired from the *Covenant*, their pod hadn't impacted as close to their target objectives as the others.

'Talos,' the Exalted drawled.

'THIS ISN'T HAPPENING.' Cyrion had to smash his chainsword against the wall to free it of the spasming, screaming armsman he'd impaled. 'We're not going to make it in time.'

First Claw was embattled in the myriad corridors between the bridge and the gunnery deck where their boarding pod had struck the hull. Around them, the great ship shuddered violently, already breaking into pieces. The Night Lords had no idea how much of the *Sword* was still intact, but from the screams trailing across the hacked enemy vox, there wasn't going to be anything left worth speaking of within the next few minutes.

They'd met a flood of Imperial crew coming their way, which at first had been a surprise and had quickly become an annoyance. As they'd butchered the mortals running at them in the low-ceilinged corridor, Xarl had joked that it was amusing to see humans running towards them for a change.

'Makes the hunt all the easier,' he smiled.

'You say that,' Cyrion replied, 'but you have to wonder what they're running from if *we're* a more pleasant option.'

Xarl reached for a running female officer, grabbing her by the throat to drag her into a headbutt that caved in the front of her skull and snapped her spine. He hurled the body into the oncoming horde, knocking several people from their feet to be trampled by the advancing Astartes. Her blood was smeared across Xarl's helm, starkly dark against the skull-white of his painted faceplate.

'I see your point, brother,' he said to Cyrion.

As Talos listened to the scraps of enemy vox that reached his ears, *Aurum* rose and fell with mechanical precision, almost without any attention at all. A picture built up in his mind – a picture of the ship ahead and the horrendous damage it was taking as the Warmaster's fleet picked it apart like a flock of vultures worrying a fresh corpse.

'It seems,' he spoke calmly, 'the gunnery decks between here and our pod are taking the brunt of fire from our fleet.' His bolter roared once, but the range was too short. The high-calibre shell pounded right through a running Imperial's chest and out his back, to explode against the wall beyond.

Cyrion chuckled as he saw.

'What do we do?' Uzas, more coherent now, asked as he laid about left and right with his combat blades. 'Can we cross the suffering sections?'

'Gravity is out, and they are ablaze,' Talos replied. 'No, we need to get back to the bridge. Close to it, at least. Even getting to the pod will take too long. The ship is in pieces already, and the crew are swarming like ants in a kicked hive.'

'Then we kill our way there!'

'Be silent, brother,' Talos told Uzas. 'The sheer number of lives we need to end is the main reason this will take too long. The gunnery deck must be in pieces by now. These mortals are coming from there.'

'How do you know?'

'Uniforms, Xarl,' Talos replied.

Xarl, always one to need the proof of his own eyes, grabbed another human attempting to flee past. The man's uniform looked like every other – white and generic. What was Talos talking about? He lifted the struggling man off the ground by his greasy hair, holding the officer's yelling face close to his bloodstained faceplate. Through the vox speakers in his helm's snarling mouth grille, Xarl's voice came out at insane volume.

'Tell me where you are stationed. Is it the gunnery de–'

The officer – quite deaf now – hurriedly drew a pistol in shaking hands and fired it point-blank into Xarl's face. The small slug pinged against the ceramite, knocking Xarl's head back a little before ricocheting with a wet crack back into the man's own forehead. Xarl took one look at the deep red groove in the man's skull and dropped the corpse, swearing in Nostraman. He could hear that bastard Cyrion laughing over the vox.

'Fine,' he said, ignoring Cyrion's laughter. 'Why the bridge?'

'Because it has several decks beneath it that won't explode if a lance strike hits them,' Talos said. 'And because I'm going to do something we may regret.'

With those words spoken, he blink-clicked the spiralling rune on his retinal display that represented the *Covenant*.

* * *

THE EXALTED LISTENED to its prophet's voice more than the actual words he spoke. Talos sounded calm, but there was a hard edge of irritation in the Astartes's tone. They were cut off from their pod, and it would evidently take too long to fight through the panicked crew.

It nodded its horned head as it relayed the orders to a servitor manning one of the lance gunnery stations.

'You. Servitor.'

'Yes, lord.'

'Lock a single lance on the three decks beneath the main bridge of the enemy flagship. Cut at the angles I am transmitting now.' It tapped a blackened claw on a number pad mounted on the arm rest of its throne. 'Break off fire after exactly one-point-five seconds.'

Yes, that should be enough. Penetrate the hull. Cut deep, excise the metal meat, without doing too much damage. Tear a chunk of hull away, and expose the command decks to the void. It might just work, too.

It would be a shame to lose the prophet if this failed.

'Lord,' spoke one of the mortal officers. The Exalted noted with only faint interest that the man still wore his old Imperial Navy uniform, from over a decade ago.

'Speak.'

'Servitors in Bay Five report a Thunderhawk is readying to launch. It requests clearance.'

The Exalted nodded again. It had been expecting that. 'Let it go.'

'Servitors also report, Exalted one, that the crew is not Astartes.'

'I said to give them clearance,' the Exalted burbled, low and wet, saliva stringing between its fangs.

'A-as you say, lord.'

The Exalted turned to the gunnery servitor it had addressed before.

'Ready, lord,' the servitor murmured.

'Fire.'

THE SHIP SHUDDERED again, more violently than ever before.

'That was close,' said Xarl. His suit's stabilisers kicked in, but he'd almost had to grip the arching wall of the passageway for support. First Claw had withdrawn to the command decks, no longer seeking to carve their way through fleeing human crew elsewhere. Here, in the darkness of the halls webbing beneath the bridge chambers, the Night Lords sheathed their blades and locked their bolters to thigh guards with magnetic seals. The ship's lighting here was dead, a legacy of the lord admiral's murder and the wounding of the *Sword's* machine-spirit, and four pairs of crimson eye lenses glared out into the blackness, seeing everything in crystal clarity.

Distantly, as the ship's tremor subsided to a background shudder again, Talos's helm auditory sensors picked up a faint sound wave: a series of metallic clangs, faded with distance.

'You hear that?' Xarl asked.

'Bulkheads closing,' Cyrion acknowledged.

'Move faster,' Talos ordered, and the squad broke into a run, their heavy boots thundering on the steel decking. 'Move much faster.'

Dimly, in his right ear, he heard a familiar voice.

'Master?'

The Night Lords sprinted through the blackness, rounding several corners and smashing aside the few crew that lingered, hiding and panicking, in the darkened hallways.

'The squad,' Talos breathed into his vox mic, 'is using frequency Cobalt six-three.'

'Cobalt six-three, acknowledged, master.'

'Confirm our location runes.'

'Locator runes sighted on my augury screens. Lord Uzas's rune is flickering and weak. And... Lord, the ship is breaking apart, with eighty per cent damage to the–'

'Not *now*. Has the *Covenant* fired?'

'Yes, master.'

'I thought so. We seek the closest deck to the voided sections of the command levels.'

The silence stretched for five seconds. Six. Seven. Ten. Talos could imagine his servant scanning the hololithic display of the degrading grand cruiser, watching the locator runes of First Claw as they navigated the tunnels.

Twenty seconds.

Thirty.

Finally... 'Master.'

The shuddering was so violent that both Cyrion and Uzas were thrown from their feet. Talos staggered and left a dent in the hull where his helm crashed into the metal. The ship was coming apart now. No question.

'Master, stop. The left wall. Breach it.'

Talos didn't hesitate. The wall – which looked no different from any other in their headlong flight through the dark passageways of the command decks – exploded under the anger of four bolters.

Beyond the wall, just for a moment, was fire.

Beyond the fire was nothing but the infinite night of space, sucking the four warriors into the void with a greedy breath.

PAIN FLOODED HIM.

Talos looked down... up... at the planet below... above. A dreary rust-red rock decorated by thin wisps of cloud cover. He wondered what the air would taste like.

Stars spun past his field of vision, and he stared without truly seeing.

Then, a slowly-turning cathedral, a palace of stained glass and a hundred spires, on the back of the burning *Sword*. He saw none of this, either.

Blackness took him for a moment, which blessedly dulled the pain. When it passed, he tasted blood in his mouth, and was blinded by the bright warning runes flashing across his vision. He tried to vox Cyrion, Xarl, Septimus... but couldn't recall how to do it.

Pain, like light from a rising sun, bloomed in his skull again. Voices spoke in his ears.

'Armour: void sealed,' one of the runes said. Talos tried to move, but wasn't sure he could. There was no resistance to his movements, no traction to anything he did, to the point he wasn't sure he was moving at all.

His vision turned once more, revealing pinprick stars and shards of metal spinning slowly nearby. It was difficult to see clearly, and that worried him more than anything else. One of his eye lenses was darker than it should be, blurry and black-red with dim, watery runes. Blood, he realised. There was blood in his helm, coating one of his eye lenses.

One of the voices resolved into something approaching clarity. It was Xarl, and Xarl was swearing. Xarl was evidently swearing about blood.

Talos's vision turned, and then he saw Xarl suspended by nothing, drifting in the blackness, his brother's skulls on chains floating around his armour like a dozen moons orbiting him. He felt thunder, a powerful tremor, as Xarl's reaching hand slammed into his chest.

'Got him,' Xarl grunted. 'Hurry up, slave. My leg's smashed to hell and I'm bleeding into my armour.'

Septimus's voice came from the garbled darkness. 'I'm drifting in now.'

'Do you have the others?'

'Yes, lord.'

'Confirm you have Uzas.'

'Yes, lord.'

'Huh,' Xarl's voice lowered. 'Shame.'

Talos, now blinded by the blood smearing both his lenses, gripped Xarl's wrist as his brother held him. He felt his senses refocusing, and although he was sightless, the unearthly silence and weightlessness told him all he needed to know. He was in space, without any propulsion, turning in the darkness without any control at all.

'This,' he said through gritted teeth, 'was the stupidest idea I've ever had.'

'Glad you're still alive,' Xarl laughed, his voice hard and edged. 'You should have seen the way you hit your head on the way out.'

'I can feel it now.'

'Wonderful. You deserve it. Now shut up and pray that accursed little runt you trust doesn't crash our damn Thunderhawk.'

VI
AFTERMATH

'If there is nobility remaining within Konrad's Legion, then it is hidden deeply beneath too many layers of twisted lusts, deviance, and disobedience. Their ways are foolish, ill-considered and a hindrance to the orderly flow of controlled war. The time is coming when the Night Lords must answer for their behaviour and be brought back into the doctrine of Imperial warfare, lest we lose them to their own deviant hungers.'

– The Primarch Rogal Dorn,
Recorded commentary at the
Battle of Galvion, M31.

TEN MINUTES AFTER First Claw had destroyed the wall separating them from the vacuum of space, the four of them stood in the strategium of the *Covenant of Blood*, arranged in a half-crescent at the base of the Exalted's raised throne. Two of the Atramentar – Malek and Garadon again, Talos noticed – flanked the former captain, their weapons deactivated but held at the ready.

The Exalted paid little attention to the mundane aspects of the orbital war now. The beauty of its void dancing was done, and it merely awaited the accolades due for its boldness. For now, the Exalted was content to let its under-officers move the ship into the formations of the larger battle and add the strike cruiser's formidable guns to the onslaught.

Battlefleet Crythe was finished. The *Resolute* and the *Sword of the God-Emperor* were well on their way to becoming burned-out wrecks in orbit around Solace, and the lesser ships were being savaged by the overwhelming firepower of the Warmaster's fleet.

The deck shook as the Exalted nodded its acknowledgement down at the four warriors of First Claw.

'Nicely done,' the creature said.

Talos was bareheaded. His helm had been mauled in the final escape from the burning *Sword*, when the pull of the void had crashed his head against the breached wall as he was sucked out into space. Xarl was limping and favoured his right leg – he'd almost lost it in the same instant that Talos had narrowly escaped decapitation – and even his enhanced Astartes physiology was struggling to re-knit bones that had almost been reduced to gravel. Cyrion and Uzas were physically unharmed, but Cyrion's internal organs were still tense and working in frantic heat from the brief time in the void. His war-plate had been compromised by an unlucky shotcannon spread that had damaged his chestplate, and he'd needed to hold his breath for several minutes once his armour had vented all air pressure in space. Uzas, with a lucky streak the other three had long begun to curse, was grinning, utterly unscathed.

'You are insane, Vandred.' Talos spoke up to the command throne on its raised dais. His shaven head was a mess of scabbing and dried blood-trails as his gene-enhanced Larraman cells clotted his blood at the wound on his crown.

Immediately, the atmosphere soured. Both of the Atramentar brought their weapons to bear: Malek hunched the shoulders of his brutish Terminator warplate, and thick claws slid, crackling with force, from the armour's oversized gloved fists. Garadon's hammer hummed with building energy as it sparked into life.

Talos might have been handsome had he been left as a man. With his enlarged Astartes features, he'd ascended from the ranks of classical humanity, but there was still something recognisably imposing and inspiring in the way he looked. His black eyes, stony with rage, glared up at the Exalted, and Talos had no idea just how much he resembled a sculpted marble statue from the heathen ages of Old Earth.

'What did you say, my prophet?' the Exalted asked, purring the way a contented lion might.

'You,' Talos pointed up at the altered figure with *Aurum*, 'are insane.'

The ship shivered under the attentions of Imperial guns. No one paid attention, except for the mortal crew at their stations that ringed the unfolding scene between their masters.

The Exalted licked its fangs. 'And by what leap of the imagination do you arrive at such a conclusion, Talos?'

'There was no need for such risks. I heard about Fifth Claw.'

'Yes, a shame.'

'A *shame?*' Talos almost went for his bolter. His hesitation was evident in his body language, for Malek of the Atramentar stepped forward. Both Cyrion and Xarl raised their bolters and aimed at the elite guards either side of the throne. Uzas did nothing, though they all heard the chuckling from his helm speakers.

'Yes,' the Exalted said, utterly unfazed by the standoff. 'A shame.'

'We lost five Astartes in a single operation. For the first time in *millennia,* 10th Company is below half-strength. We have never been so weak.'

'10th Company,' the Exalted smirked, preening and condescending. '10th Company has not existed for millennia. We are the warband of the Exalted. And this night, we have earned much honour in the eyes of the Warmaster.'

The confrontation would change nothing. Talos lowered his blade, letting his anger bleed from him like corruption from a lanced boil. He buried the urge to blood his sword with the life fluids of the Exalted. Sensing the change in him, Cyrion and Xarl lowered their bolters. Champion Malek of the Atramentar stepped back into position, his tusked helm watching impassively.

'Fifth Claw is no more,' Talos said more quietly. 'We are in dire need of recruitment. We cannot function for long with barely forty Astartes.'

He let the unwelcome words hang. Every one of them knew the decades of attention and effort recruitment would require. To sustain a company's fighting strength, it needed a great deal of materiel and expertise to gene-forge new Astartes from prepubescent male infants. The *Covenant of Blood* lacked almost all of what would be required, which was why no recruitment had been done since the Great Betrayal. The remains of 10th Company had been fighting with the same warriors since the Horus Heresy.

'Change is inevitable,' the Exalted growled. 'The Shaper of Fate is with us, and it knows the truth of this.' At those words, the Atramentar both nodded their heavy helms in respect. Uzas grunted a monosyllabic sound that could have been respect or pleasure. Talos felt his skin crawl, and his dark eyes narrowed.

'Who are we to answer the demands of the Ruinous Ones? We are the Night Lords, the sons of the eighth primarch. We are our own masters.'

'The Shaper of Fate demands nothing,' the Exalted said. 'You do not understand.'

'I have no wish to understand the entities you are enslaved to.'

The Exalted smiled, patently false, and waved a clawed gauntlet. 'I am tired of reminding you, Talos. I control this. Now leave before First Claw joins Fifth in no longer existing.'

Talos shook his head at the threat, disgusted it had even been made, and smiled back before stalking from the strategium.

Once they were outside the bridge, Cyrion voxed to Talos. 'He is worse than before.'

'As if that was possible.'

'No, brother. His fear. I can feel it boiling beneath his skin. He is losing the fight with the daemon that shares his body.'

Septimus and Eurydice were still in the port hangar bay.

The Thunderhawk *Blackened* sat on its landing pad, occasional jets of pressurised steam venting from its ports as the raptor-like gunship cooled. The boosters at the rear of the troop-carrying attack ship matched the gunship's name, the engine exhausts charred from decades of orbital and sub-orbital flight. Septimus was diligent in ensuring *Blackened* remained in as good a condition as could be expected, but he was an artificer first and foremost, not a tech-priest. His skills lay in repairing and maintaining the master's weapons, not keeping an ancient gunship flying.

Eurydice watched the slave as he sat on the deck of the landing bay in the shadow of the Thunderhawk, turning his master's skull-faced helm over in his hands.

'This,' he said to himself, 'is not going to be easy.'

It was a miracle the helm hadn't come to pieces: it was severely dented on the left side where Talos's head had smashed into the edge of the breached wall once the vacuum had pulled First Claw into space. Eurydice said nothing. She was still unnerved by the shaking of the ship, and replayed the last hour over and over within her mind. Powering up the Thunderhawk... Taking it out into the middle of an orbital battle... Throne, this place was insane.

Septimus looked up at her, his jade eyes narrowed. She wondered if his thoughts matched her own. As it happened, they did.

'It's not always that bad,' he said without a smile.

She grunted what might have been an agreement. 'Is it ever worse?'

'Often,' Septimus nodded. 'If you think the Astartes are bad, wait until we go to the crew decks.'

She didn't answer. She didn't want to know.

Septimus held up the oversized helm once more. 'I should get started on this.' But he didn't move. He was lingering, she knew.

Finally, she bit. 'You're not allowed to leave me alone.'

'The only way you may leave my presence is if one of us is dead.'

Her forehead, and her permanently sealed third eye, ached with sudden ferocity. It felt as though her warp-gaze sought to stare through the steel and slay the foolish, cocky slave before her.

'I hate it here,' she said, before she even realised she was going to speak.

'We all hate it here,' he nodded again, speaking slowly, and not just because of his awkward Gothic. He spoke as if stating the obvious to a slow child. 'We all hate it here, more or less. We are worthless to them. They are demigods.'

'There are no gods but the Emperor,' Eurydice sneered.

Septimus laughed at that, and his casual blasphemy grated against her. 'You are a heretic.' She said the words softly, but unpleasantly.

'As are you, now. Do you think the forces of the Throne would welcome you after even a short time on board a Traitor Astartes vessel?' His humour faded. 'Open your eyes, Navigator. You are as ruined as the rest of us, and this ship,' he gestured at the dimness of the launch bay around them, 'is your home now.'

She drew breath to argue, and he held up a hand, cutting her off.

'Enough arguing. Listen to me.'

He let the skullish helm rest on his lap as he scratched the back of his neck. 'This is the 10th Company of the VIII Legion. Thousands of years ago, they would have had serfs and servitors and Astartes enough that me taking a relic Thunderhawk out into the black would have been punishable by death. They lack resources, including the souls to serve them.'

'A fitting fate,' Eurydice smiled coldly. 'They're traitors.'

'You think that smirk you wear hides your fear.' He met her eyes and stared for several moments. 'It doesn't. Not from me – and definitely not from them.'

The smile left her face as quickly as it had arrived.

'I don't deny that they are heretics,' Septimus continued, 'but let me put it another way. Have you ever heard of Lok III?'

She reluctantly moved to join him, seated on the Thunderhawk's gang ramp in the gloom of the spacious hangar bay. Across the cavernous area, other Thunderhawks sat idle and silent, untouched in years. Decades, perhaps. Cargo trucks and munitions loaders sat equally lifeless. Fifty metres away, a lone servitor lay slack and unmoving on its back, its grey skin rendered greyer by the touch of dust. It looked like it had lost power and collapsed, left there to decay in the presence of these venerable war machines. Eurydice couldn't take her eyes from the corpse. Its skin was withered and drawn tight against its bones, almost mummified, though actual decomposition was probably delayed because of the machine parts fighting off decay in the organic sections that remained.

She shivered. It was all too easy to see how this ship was a hollow image of itself.

'No,' she said at length, taking grim comfort in his body heat as she sat next to him. The *Covenant* was so cold. 'I've never heard of Lok III.'

'Not much to hear of,' he admitted, then lapsed into silence, thinking.

'I've not seen much of the galaxy,' she said. 'Syne kept most of our prospecting runs within a handful of sectors to save on journey costs. Also, I...'

'You what?'

'My family, House Mervallion, is on the lowest tier of the Navis Nobilite. I think Syne was worried about pushing me too hard. Worried his Navigator was of... poor quality.'

Septimus nodded, with a knowing look in his eyes Eurydice didn't like. When she expected him to comment on her confession, he merely cut back to his previous line of conversation.

'Lok III is far distant, close to the region of space known to Imperial records as Scarus Sector.'

'Half the galaxy away.'

'Yes. I was born there. It wasn't a forge world, but it was close. Manufactories covered the planet, and I worked as a hauler pilot, ferrying cargo to and from the orbital docks down to the manufactorum that employed me.'

'That's... nice.'

'No, it was boring beyond words. My point should be obvious. Yes, I'm considered a heretic because of my allegiance. Yes, I am indentured to traitors who make war upon the Throne of Terra. And yes, there's darkness within this ship that hungers for our blood. But I see things in a realistic light. What I have now is better than death. And once you learn how to walk in the dark places here... it's almost safe. It's almost a real life.

'I lived a life of repetition – another tiny cog in a vast, dull existence. But this? This is different. Every week will bring something new, something incredible, something that takes my breath away. Rarely in a good way, I confess.'

She looked at him. He was *serious*.

'You're serious,' she said, for lack of anything else to say.

'I am. As an artificer and a pilot, I'm given a great deal of freedom on the ship. I am valued.'

'A valuable slave.'

He narrowed his eyes as he looked at her. 'I am trying to keep you alive. If you don't adapt to this existence, your life ends. It's that simple.'

After a long pause, she asked, 'Are you happy?'

'I suspect you think that's a very insightful and cutting remark.' Septimus gestured around the hangar bay again. 'Of course I am not *happy*. I am a slave to heretical demigods, and I live on a vessel touched by indescribable darkness. The mortal crew lives in fear of the things that stalk the ship's lightless decks, and those things are not always the Astartes.'

Septimus chuckled after he said the words, the sound low and devoid of mirth. In his hands, the skull helm grinned up at them both.

'So how did they take you?' Eurydice asked.

Septimus didn't look up from the helm. 'They attacked Lok III. I was originally taken to serve as a pilot, and the hyp... hypno–'

'Hypnotic?'

'Hypnotic. Yes.' Septimus spoke the word a few more times as if tasting it. 'I'm not sure if I forgot that word, or just never knew it. As I said, Gothic was never my first language. But the process was agony. They teach through mental conditioning and hypnotic implantation programs that burn information directly into the mind. That is why I can fly a Thunderhawk – though even after a decade, not with the skill of a true Astartes pilot.'

She scanned the hangar bay again, imagining how it would look as it should have been: a hive of industry and activity, crew running here and there, servitors and munitions loaders rattling and clanking across the rune-marked floor, the howling of turbines as gunships roared in the moments before launch.

It must have been so impressive. It was, she hated to admit it, close to what she'd hoped for herself: guiding the vessels of the Astartes across the stars.

'He has you fixing his armour now,' she said, looking back to Septimus. 'Is that a demotion?'

'Technically, a promotion. Artificers are the most respected serfs in a Legion's armoury.'

She laughed, the sound alien and echoing in the hollow hangar bay.

'What's so funny?' he asked.

'You're not exactly up to your neck in respect.'

'You only say that,' he smiled, 'because you have not seen everything, Octavia.'

'Why do you call me that?'

'Because I am the seventh of my master's servants. And you are the eighth.'

'Not likely.'

'Already your defiance is fading. I hear it in your voice.'

'You're imagining it.'

'That's a shame.' He rose to his feet, the broken helm in his hands. 'Because if I am, you'll be dying very soon.'

As Talos confronted the Exalted, and as Septimus spoke with Eurydice, the last vestiges of the orbital battle played out to their inevitable conclusion. Battlefleet Crythe was annihilated, and the few surviving vessels that managed to flee into the warp are of no further relevance to this record, though most distinguished themselves in their own ways when they merged with other sector battlefleets.

Consolidation came next.

The Warmaster's forces had destroyed the Imperial Navy presence in the area, and his fleet hung in the atmospheric reaches above the penal world, Solace. The insignia displayed by the vessels of his gathered fleet were myriad. The slitted Eye of Horus marked a full seven Black Legion vessels – a massive portion of their mighty fleet – while the fanged skull of the Night Lords was evident on both the *Covenant of Blood* and its much larger sister ship already among the fleet, the battle-barge *Hunter's Premonition*. The majority of the fleet was made up of bulk transports carrying legions of the lost and the damned: Imperial Guard and planetary defence forces that had turned traitor and sworn allegiance to the Warmaster's cause across recent campaigns. All in all, the Warmaster came to Crythe with the capacity to unleash over two thousand Traitor Astartes and more than a million human soldiers. Pride of place within the fleet was given to the vast hulks belonging to Legio Frostreaver, once of the Mechanicum of Mars. A full Titan Legion at the Warmaster's beck and call, numbering almost a dozen god-machines of varying classes.

Such a Chaos fleet was rarely seen outside of the Warmaster's holy wars against the Emperor's worlds, and word of this gathering of the Archenemy spread throughout the nearby Imperial planets, with fearful talk of a new Black Crusade in the Despoiler's name.

With Solace fallen and the Navy crushed, the war for the Crythe Cluster was only just beginning. Long-range scanners told a grim tale, unnerving even for the captains of this lethal battlefleet. The forge world, Crythe Prime, remained ringed by a vast fleet answering to the Adeptus Mechanicus, which had steadfastly refused to answer Battlefleet Crythe's hails for help. Curiously, the Marines Errant vessel *Severance* had withdrawn to Crythe Prime to side with the Mechanicum instead of fighting and dying with the Imperial Navy.

Time was of the essence, and every officer in the Warmaster's fleet knew it. The Imperium of Man would answer this aggression with fury of its own, and alongside Naval reinforcements, Imperial Guard and Astartes armies would be en route from the moment the first astropathic cries for aid had been sent by the beleaguered Battlefleet Crythe.

The *Covenant of Blood* pulled close to its kin-ship, the powerful battle-barge *Hunter's Premonition*. The larger ship had been one of the Legion's flagships before the scattering of the Night Lords over the centuries, and it was an awe-inspiring sight to those who hadn't gazed upon an example of their Legion's strength in many years. Even the Exalted, though he was loath to admit it, felt moved by the sight of the princely vessel, a lance of midnight blue edged in gold and bronze.

He wanted it. He wanted command of that vessel, and all upon the deck saw that need burning in his obsidian eyes.

The destruction of Battlefleet Crythe was not the only reason the Warmaster had ordered Solace taken first. Just as important as the death of the orbital defenders was the preservation of the population below. Had Lord Admiral Valiance Arventaur been more familiar with the Archenemy – instead of spending most of his career fighting eldar raiders – he might have turned the guns of his beloved *Sword of the God-Emperor* on Solace itself, destroying the population centres of the penal world and denying the Warmaster his prize. Ultimately, this would have done much more to save the Crythe Cluster.

But, of course, he had not. He had died with a sword in his heart, whispering incoherent curses at his murderer.

The Chaos fleet hung in space around a world with almost a million prisoners: rapists, murderers, heretics, thieves, mutants and criminals of a thousand other stripes – all held in appalling conditions and discarded by an Imperium that loathed them for their deviance.

Within the hour, while the hulks of Battlefleet Crythe were still flaming wrecks in space, the Warmaster's troopships began their landing. On the surface, hundreds of thousands of potential new warriors watched the skies burn, staring up through the windows of their cells as deliverance – and freedom – came for them.

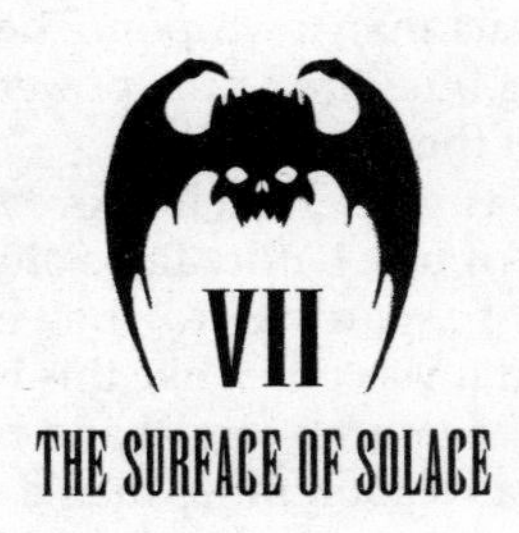

VII
THE SURFACE OF SOLACE

'Talos. The prophet of the Night Lords. Bring him to me.'

– Abaddon the Despoiler
Commander of the Black Legion,
Warmaster of Chaos

TALOS AND XARL locked blades.

The sparring chamber was, like most of the *Covenant*, a shadow of its former activity. In the centre of the chamber, which was tiered and inclined much like a gladiatorial arena, the two Astartes duelled alone, Talos's deactivated power sword clashing against Xarl's stilled chainblade. With respect to the weapons' machine-spirits, the brothers practised with their own swords instead of practice blades, but kept them unpowered.

Xarl's chainsword was a standard-issue Astartes weapon, incredibly tough and resistant to damage, with vicious serrated teeth honed to monomolecular points. But *Aurum*, the blade taken from a slain captain of the Blood Angels, was a relic of incredible potency. A standard power sword would sunder even an honourable blade like Xarl's *Executioner*, and *Aurum* was closer to an artifact than a weapon. They duelled without the crackling blue fire of the power sword and the roaring whine of the chainblade.

In a way, it was worse. Their movements reeked of training instead of true battle. Talos always felt the relative silence of sparring to be unnerving and unsatisfying, and it was times like this he dwelled most on how he had been gene-forged and bred for the battlefield. He was a weapon more than a man; never was it more obvious than in the moments of his disquiet.

By mortal standards, it would have been considered a duel of the gods. The blades sliced the air faster than the human eye could follow, clash upon clash in a storm of relentless speed and force. Had any Astartes been witnessing the fight, they might have seen with a deeper clarity. Both warriors were plainly distracted, their thoughts elsewhere, obvious in every minute hesitation and flicker of the eyes.

Around them, banks of human-sized passages formed into the arena walls had once housed a small army of combat servitors, engineered for practice and destined for destruction under the blades of the Astartes that came to hone their skills here. Such days were long past. The halls where the servitors had trundled from storage-engineering chambers beneath the arena were silent and lightless, another reminder of a time now gone forever.

Talos felt his anger swell up as he leaned back and deflected a throat cut. Melancholy was not something that sat well with him. It was alien to his thoughts, yet of late it would cling there like it belonged.

That made him angry. It felt like a vulnerability in his defences, a wound that wouldn't heal.

Xarl sensed the frustration in his brother's blows, and as their deactivated swords locked again, Xarl leaned in close. Their faces – already similar due to the genetic enhancements that moulded their bodies – glared into one another with mirrored anger. The bitter gaze from their black eyes met as surely as the blades in their hands.

'You're losing your temper,' he snarled at Talos.

'I'm annoyed that I need to go easy on you because of the leg,' Talos growled, nodding almost imperceptibly down at Xarl's healing limb.

In response, Xarl hurled his brother back with a laugh, disengaging with surprising grace for one who relied so often on fury to win his fights.

'Do your worst,' he said, smiling in the darkness. Like all areas of the *Covenant of Blood* restricted to the Astartes alone, the sparring chambers were utterly lightless. No hindrance at all to the dark eyes of the Nostramo-born, but in former days combat servitors had required night vision visors and aural enhancer sensors to aid with detecting movement.

Talos came on again, his guard high as he executed a flawless series of two-handed cuts from the left designed to force Xarl onto his right leg more and more. He heard his brother's pained grunts as he defended himself.

'Keep it up,' Xarl said, still not even breathing heavily despite the fact they'd been duelling at an inhuman pace for almost an hour. 'Still need to get used to taking weight on this leg again.'

Instead of pressing the attack, Talos stopped.

'Hold,' he said, raising a hand.

'What? Why?' Xarl asked, lowering *Executioner*. He looked around the silent, dark arena, seeing nothing but the empty rows of witness seats, hearing nothing but the dim growl of the ship's orbital drives, smelling nothing but the sweat from their robed bodies and the faint tang of centuries of weapon oil. 'I sense no one nearby.'

'I saw Uzas kill Cyrion,' Talos said, apropos of nothing.

Xarl laughed. 'Right. That's good. Are we going to fight or not?' In a moment of uncharacteristic concern, Xarl tilted his head to regard his brother. 'Has your head not healed? I thought it was fine.'

'I am not joking.'

In the darkness, pierced with ease by the vision of one born on a sunless world, Xarl saw his brother's black eyes regarding him without a trace of humour.

'Are you speaking of your vision?'

'You know I am.'

'You saw wrong, Talos,' Xarl said, spitting onto the decking. 'Cyrion is easy to hate. He is corrupted in the worst of ways. But even a rabid fool like Uzas would never kill him.'

'Cyrion is true to the Night Haunter,' Talos said.

Xarl snorted. 'We've had this argument before. He is an Astartes that knows fear. That is as corrupt as can be imagined.'

'He understands fear.'

'Does he still hear the daemon warring within the Exalted?'

Talos let the silence answer for him.

'Exactly,' Xarl nodded. 'He can sense fear. That is unnatural. He is corrupted.'

'He senses it. He does not feel it himself.'

Xarl looked down at his chainsword, silent in deactivation. 'Semantics. He has been corrupted by the Ruinous Ones, as surely as Uzas has. But they are still brothers, and I trust them – for now.'

'You trust *Uzas?*' Talos tilted his head, curious now.

'We are First Claw,' Xarl answered, if that justified everything. 'At least the corruption within Uzas is visible. Cyrion is the dangerous one, brother.'

'I have spoken to Cyrion about this many times,' Talos warned, 'and I tell you, you're wrong.'

'We'll see. Tell me of this vision.'

Talos pictured again the sight of Uzas, an axe in hand, moving over the rubble of a shattered building, leaping at Cyrion as he lay prone. He explained it to Xarl now, as faithfully as he could, omitting nothing. He spoke of the blaring war horns of the Titans above and the dusty grey stone of the fallen buildings, still magma red in places where the rock had been cooked by the towering god-machines' guns. He described the fall of the axe, the way it hooked into Cyrion's neck joint, and the blood that flowed in the moments after.

'That does sound like Uzas,' Xarl said at length. 'A vicious kill, and perfectly made against helpless prey. I am no longer so sure this was a foolish joke of yours.'

'He despises Cyrion,' Talos pointed out. He moved to the side of the arena, where *Aurum's* sheath rested against the metal wall. 'But I have been wrong before,' he said over his shoulder.

Xarl shook his head again. He looked more thoughtful than Talos had ever seen him, which was disquieting purely for its unfamiliarity. It occurred to him for the first time that perhaps Xarl was one of those that invested great faith in his prophetic curse. He seemed almost... unnerved.

'When?' Xarl said, 'A handful of times in how many years? No, brother. This has the stench of unwelcome truth to it.'

Talos said nothing. Xarl surprised him by speaking more.

'We all trust you. I don't like you, brother – you know that. It is not easy to like you. You are self-righteous and you take risks as foolish as the Exalted sometimes. You assume you lead First Claw, yet were never promoted above any of us. All you were was an Apothecary, yet you act like our sergeant now. By the False Throne, you act like the Captain of 10th Company. I have a hundred reasons to dislike you, and they are all valid. But I trust you, Talos.'

'Good to know,' Talos said as he sheathed the blade and stood once more.

'When were you last wrong?' Xarl pressed. 'Humour me. When was the last time one of your auguries went awry?'

'A long time ago,' Talos said. 'Seventy years, perhaps. On Gashik, the world where it never stopped raining. I dreamed we would see battle against the Imperial Fists, but the planet remained defenceless.'

Xarl scratched at his cheek, musing.

'Seventy years. You've not been wrong in almost a century. But if Cyrion does die, and you were right that he isn't corrupt, we could use his progenoid glands to gene-forge another Astartes in his place. No loss.'

Talos considered drawing the blade again. 'The same could be said for the death of any one of us.'

Xarl raised an eyebrow. 'You'd harvest Uzas's gene-seed?'

'Point taken.' And it was. Talos would sooner burn that biological matter into ash before he saw it implanted within another Night Lord.

Xarl nodded, clearly distracted as Talos carried on. 'If this comes to pass, I will kill Uzas.'

Talos wasn't even sure he heard him.

'I will think on this,' Xarl replied, and without another word, he walked from the arena, descending into the deeper darkness of the ship. After the awkwardness of the brotherly candour a moment before, this was much more like the Xarl Talos had grown to tolerate – stalking off in silence, keeping his counsel to himself.

Caught between the desire to follow Xarl and seek out Cyrion, Talos was denied the choice a moment later.

Thudding footsteps drew his attention as another figure emerged at the first tier of witness seats. Lightning-marked armour, too bulky even for Astartes war-plate.

'Prophet,' said Champion Malek of the Atramentar.

'Yes, brother.'

'Your presence is required.'

'I see.' Talos didn't move. 'Inform the Exalted I am currently engaged in my meditations, and will attend him in three hours.'

The sound of a rockslide avalanche rumbled from the hound-like helm of Malek's Terminator armour. Talos assumed it was a chuckle.

'No, prophet, it is not the Exalted that demands your presence.'

'Then whom?' Talos asked, his fingertips stroking the sheathed hilt of *Aurum* at his hip. 'No one demands my attention, Malek. I am no slave.'

'No? No one? And what if the presence of the Night Lord prophet was demanded by Abaddon of the Black Legion?'

Talos swallowed, neither scared nor worried, but instantly on edge. This changed things.

'The Warmaster wishes to speak with me,' he said slowly, as if unsure he heard correctly.

'He does. You are to be ready within the hour, along with First Claw. Two of the Atramentar will accompany you.'

'I need no honour guard. I will go alone.'

'Talos,' Malek growled. Talos still looked up at him. None of the Atramentar had ever used his name before, and he felt a terrible gravity within the use of it now.

'I am listening, Malek.'

'This is not the time to stand alone, brother. Take First Claw. And do not argue when Garadon and I also stand with you. This is a show of strength as surely as the Exalted's tactics in the void war.'

It took several seconds, but Talos finally nodded. 'Where is this meeting taking place?'

Malek held up a massive power fist, his Terminator armour clanking and the servo-driven joints snarling as he moved. Four blades slashed from his knuckles, each one as long as a mortal man's arm. At a command word Talos didn't hear, the lightning claws lived up to their name, becoming wreathed in a crackling power field that brought stark, viciously flickering light to the blackness of the arena.

'Solace,' Malek replied. 'The Warmaster walks the surface of his most recently conquered world, and we are to meet him there.'

'The Black Legion,' Talos said after a few moments, a dark little smirk crossing his features. 'The Sons of Horus, with a heritage of treachery as great as their fallen father.'

'Aye, the Black Legion.' Malek's claws slid back into their housing on the back of his massive armoured fists, locked until reactivation. 'Which is why we are going in midnight clad.'

THE SURFACE OF Solace was the mixed, dusty red-brown of old scabs and burned flesh. It was an ugly world in all respects, even down to the taste of the air. Because of intense volcanic activity raging across the southern hemisphere for centuries, the myriad mountain ranges breathing fire into the atmosphere left the thin air tasting of ash across the planet.

The spires of the penal colonies were no easier on the eyes than anything else on the surface: towers of red stone, clawed and brutish, jutting like broken blades from natural mountain formations. The Gothic architecture so beloved of many Imperial worlds was in evidence here, but in its crudest and most unskilled execution. Whoever designed the prison spires of Solace – if indeed any real design had taken place at all – knew all too well how the world would be home to souls that barely counted as part of the Imperium. His prejudice against the prisoners that were destined to come to this world and rot under its dull skies was all too obvious in the architecture.

The Night Lord Thunderhawk *Blackened* streaked across the weatherless sky, its pilot adjusting thrust output as the gunship broke from orbital to atmospheric flight.

'On approach,' Septimus said, easing back on one of the several levers that handled the gunship's thrust. In the creaking control chair, which was obviously made for a larger pilot, he clicked a cluster of switches and watched the vivid green hololithic terrain display – updated every few seconds from auspex returns. Altitude dropping gently, speed falling, he spoke without taking his eyes from the console's displays.

'Internment Spire Delta Two, this is the VIII Legion Thunderhawk *Blackened*. We are on southern approach. Respond.'

Silence greeted his attempts at communication.

'What now?' he asked, over his shoulder.

Talos, armoured and armed, standing behind the pilot's throne, shook his head. 'Don't bother repeating the hail. The Black Legion is hardly noted for excellence in re-establishing infrastructures upon the worlds it conquers.'

Cyrion was making final reverent checks over his bolter. 'And we are?'

Talos didn't turn to his brother. In the spacious cockpit, where all of First Claw stood behind Septimus and Eurydice in the pilot and co-pilot thrones, Talos watched the thin, dusty red mist breaking apart over the front windows as they closed in on their destination.

'We do not conquer worlds,' Talos replied. 'Our mandate is not the same as theirs, nor is our ultimate aim.'

Keeping himself out of their debate, Septimus waited until he was sure they would say no more. 'Five minutes, master. I'll bring us down on the spire-top landing platform.'

'Your flying is improving, slave.' It was Xarl who stepped forward, resting a gauntleted hand on the back of Septimus's chair. There was nothing comforting in the gesture. Septimus could see their reflections in the viewscreen. All without their helms – Talos, handsome and stern; Cyrion, weary with a half-smile; Xarl sneering and bitter; and Uzas, dead-eyed and licking his teeth as he stared at nothing in particular.

And Eurydice. He noticed her reflection last, still unused to her presence. She met his eyes in the reflection on the cockpit window, and offered him an expressionless glance that could have meant anything. Her hair, scruffy and chestnut brown, framed her face in choppy locks. The iron strip still concealed her third eye, and Septimus often found himself wondering just what it would look like.

She wore the ragged, dark blue jacket and trousers of the Legion's serfs, though getting her into the loose uniform had been no easy feat. She'd only relented to Septimus's insistence when he pointed out how bad she smelled still wearing the same clothes they'd captured her in weeks before.

They hadn't branded her, yet. The tattoo beneath his clothes that covered his shoulder blades itched as if in sympathy with his thoughts. A winged skull, in black ink mixed with Astartes blood.

If she gave her allegiance – if she survived – she'd be branded soon enough.

Ahead of them, the thin mist parted to reveal a clawed cluster of peaks, topped by a spire that could only be their destination. Talos and the others reached for their helms, sealing them in place. Septimus was familiar with the differences between them, as familiar to him as their natural faces. Cyrion's helm was older than the other death masks, a mark II design with narrowed eyes and an almost knightly aesthetic. He wore few trophies, but his armour was decorated in great detail with jagged bolts of blue-white lightning. Twin storm bolts streaked from his ruby eye lenses like forked tears.

In contrast, Xarl's helm was the newest – a mark VII piece, taken from a recent engagement with the Dark Angels. He'd ordered one of the few remaining artificers to modify it, with a hand-painted daemonic skull covering the faceplate. He displayed trophies with relish and pride: alien and human skulls hanging from chains across his armour, scrolls of past deeds draped across his shoulder pads.

Uzas wore a grim-faced mark III helm, the paintwork crudely done with little care. Stark against the dark blue was a red palm print with splayed fingers, done with his own hand dipped in blood and pressed against the helm's face.

Talos's helm, a studded mark V design freshly repaired by his servant's craftsmanship, featured a skulled face of creamy bone, with a Nostraman rune branded black into the forehead. When Septimus had been reshaping the helm on the artificer deck of the *Covenant*, Eurydice had asked what the sigil meant.

'It's like "in midnight clad",' he said, repainting the bone face with both reverence and the ease of familiarity. 'It doesn't translate well into Low Gothic.'

'I'm getting tired of hearing that.'

'Well, it's true. Nostramo was a world of high politics and a complicated underworld that infested all layers of society. The tongue has its roots in High Gothic, but much had changed through generations of unique phrasing by faithless, trustless, peaceless people.'

'Trustless and peaceless aren't words.' Despite herself, she smiled, watching him work. She was growing used to his stumbling attempts to speak the universal tongue.

'My point stands,' Septimus said, painting bone white around the left eye lens. 'Nostraman is, by Gothic standards, very grand and overly poetic.'

'Gangsters like to think of themselves as cultured,' she said with a curl to her lip. To her surprise, he nodded.

'From what I gather of Nostraman history, yes, that's the conclusion I draw as well. The language became very... I don't know the word.'

'Flowery.'

He shrugged. 'Close enough.'

'So what does that symbol mean?'

'It's a combination of three letters, which in turn stand for three words. The more complex a symbol, the more likely it is that a number of concepts and letters make up the final sigil.'

'Sorry I asked.'

'Fine,' he said, still not looking up from his duties. 'It means, directly translated: "Ender of lives and collector of essences".'

'What is it in Nostraman?'

Septimus spoke three words, which sounded beautiful to her ears. Smooth, delicate, and curiously chilling. Nostraman, she decided, sounded like a murderer by her bedside, whispering in her ear.

'Shorten it for me,' she said, feeling her skin prickle at the sound of his voice speaking the dead language. 'What does it mean, direct translation or not.'

'Equivalently, it would mean "Soul Hunter",' he said, holding the helm up now and examining his work.

'Is that what the other Night Lords call your master?' Eurydice asked.

'No. It is the name bestowed upon him by their martyred primarch father. His favoured sons within the VIII Legion held... titles, or names, like that. To the Legion, he was Apothecary Talos of First Claw, or 10th Company's "prophet". To the Night Haunter, lord of the VIII Legion, he was Soul Hunter.'

'Why?' she asked.

And Septimus told her.

THE THUNDERHAWK SETTLED on the landing platform with a gush of vented steam and the clank of its landing claws locking, taking the gunship's weight. Under the cockpit, the gang ramp lowered on groaning, grinding hydraulics. Once it had slammed down onto the deck, the Night Lords disembarked, weapons armed.

Talos led the way, *Aurum* active and *Anathema* drawn. First Claw came behind him, bolters up. Behind them, with servo-joints growling and heavy boots thudding onto the decking, came the Terminator-clad Atramentar warriors Malek and Garadon.

In the moments before *Blackened* had touched down, Septimus had been ordered to stay with the gunship. Although she wasn't included in the order – in fact, the Night Lords were still essentially ignoring her – Eurydice remained with Septimus.

'Septimus,' Talos had said, 'if anyone approaches the Thunderhawk, warn them once, then open fire.'

The serf had nodded. *Blackened* possessed a vicious armament: several heavy bolters mounted on the wings and flanks of the vessel, crewed by limbless servitors slaved directly to the gunnery consoles. The weapons were also fireable from the main cockpit console, which was fortunate considering the depleted state of 10th Company's servitor complement: only half of the Thunderhawk's heavy bolter turrets were actively crewed. Several of the other gunships aboard the *Covenant of Blood* completely lacked a servitor crew.

The Astartes moved with cautious speed. The decking was clear, open to a starlit sky only thinly veiled by colourless clouds. At the north side of the thruster-burned platform, a small shelter with a double door led into the spire beneath.

'Looks like a lift,' Xarl nodded to the small building.

'Looks like a trap,' Uzas murmured. As if on cue, the double doors opened with a whirr of mechanics, revealing four figures lit by the internal lights of an elevator.

'I was right,' said Xarl.

'I probably was, too,' Uzas persisted.

'Silence,' Talos growled into the vox, and the order was echoed by Malek of the Atramentar. Talos considered objecting to the champion issuing orders to his squad, but then technically, First Claw was no more his to command than it was Malek's. And Malek held overall rank.

The dark figures left the wide elevator, stalking onto the platform with a graceless, lumbering stride that matched the Terminator-gait of the Atramentar.

First Claw raised their bolters in perfect unity, each one drawing a bead on a different figure. Malek and Garadon brought their close combat weapons to bear, flanking the Astartes.

'Justaerin,' warned Malek. They knew the term. The elite Terminator-armoured squad of the Sons of Horus 1st Company.

'Not any more.' Talos didn't lower his bolter. 'We don't know if they have kept that title. Times change.'

The four black-armoured, red-eyed Terminators approached, their own weapons raised. Brass-mouthed double-barrelled bolters, and an ornate arm-mounted autocannon with twin barrels the length of spears – all aimed at the new arrivals. Where the Night Lord Terminators wore dark cloaks around their bulky forms, spiked trophy racks arced from the Black Legion's hunched backs, displaying a varied selection of Astartes helms from various Imperial Chapters. Talos recognised the colours of the Crimson Fists, the Raven Guard, and a number of Chapters he'd never encountered. Inconstant Imperial dogs. They divided and bred like vermin.

'Which one of you is Talos?' The lead Terminator's voice came through his helm speakers like a detuned vox – all crackles and rasps.

Talos nodded at the Black Legionnaire. 'The one aiming his blade at your heart, and his bolter at your head.'

'Nice sword, Night Lord,' the Terminator rasped, gesturing its storm bolter at *Aurum* pointed at his chestplate. Talos sighted down the golden blade, reading the lettering across the warrior's armour: FALKUS, in faded indentations.

'Please,' Cyrion voxed over the intra-squad channel, 'tell me that rhyme wasn't his attempt at wit.'

'Falkus,' Talos said slowly, 'I am Talos of the VIII Legion. With me is First Claw, 10th Company, as well as Champion Malek and Garadon, Hammer of the Exalted, both of the Atramentar.'

'You give yourselves a lot of titles,' said another of the Black Legion Terminators, the one with the long-barrelled autocannon. His voice was lower than the first's, and he sported a horned helm similar to Garadon's.

'We kill a lot of people,' Xarl replied. To punctuate his words, he trailed his bolter across the four Black Legionnaires. It was posturing of the most brazen, unsubtle, even childish kind. It galled Talos that such theatrics were necessary.

'We are all allies here, under the Warmaster's banner,' the cannon-bearer said. 'There is no need for such a display of hostility.'

'Then lower your weapons first,' Xarl offered.

'Like the nice, polite hosts you are,' Cyrion added.

One of the squad, Talos wasn't sure who, had privately voxed back to Septimus on board *Blackened*. He knew this because the heavy bolters mounted on the starboard cheek and wing tips rotated to lock onto the four Black Legion Terminators.

Nice touch, he thought. Probably Xarl's idea.

The Warmaster's warriors lowered their weapons a moment later, evidently neither gracious about the fact, nor with any real unity of movement.

'They move carelessly,' Garadon voxed, his disgust obvious in his tone.

'Come, brothers,' said the first Black Legion Terminator, inclining his brutish helm. 'The Warmaster, blessed scion of the Dark Ones, requests your presence.'

Only when the Black Legionnaires stalked away first did the Night Lords lower their weapons.

'You remember when we used to trust each other?' Cyrion voxed.

'No,' Xarl said.

'Let's get this over quickly,' Talos cut in. No one argued.

THE PRISON LOOKED to be in a riot.

As they descended, the lift's windows revealed floor after floor of expansive red chambers flooded with howling, screaming, fighting, running prisoners. On one floor, the windows showed a yelling man's face, his fists beating on the glass and leaving bloody stains. He fled as soon as he saw what occupied the interior, which was lucky for him, as Uzas had been about to fire his bolter and end the fool's life.

'These will all be rounded up by our slaver ships, ready for the war against the forge world,' the cannon-bearing Legionnaire growled in his guttural cant. 'For now, we are letting them enjoy their first taste of blood-lust since they were incarcerated.'

'We freed them,' the leader, Falkus, said. 'We deactivated their restraining cells and granted them their liberty. They are using their first acts of freedom to butcher the internment guards that still live.' He sounded both proud and amused.

Muted through the lift shaft walls, gunshots could sometimes be made out amongst the howls. Evidently, not all the guards were going down easily.

The lift trembled once as it came to a halt on a floor that looked no different than any other. A horde of prisoners, many bare-chested and armed with cutlery or chunks of furniture as weapons, seemed to be beating each other to death with great enthusiasm.

Until the doors opened.

Of all the founding Legions to turn from the light of the False Emperor, Talos most despised the Black Legion, the Sons of Horus, for how far they had fallen in the years since their primarch father's death. In his eyes, they were an amalgamation of every sin and deviation across the sphere of mortal experience, armed and armoured as Astartes without a shred of the nobility that they once possessed. They consorted with daemons en masse, fighting beside them and listening to their warp-whispers for shards of wisdom. Just as the Exalted, daemon-corrupt and a shadow of the man he once was, revolted Talos – so too did the Black Legion in their wanton embrace of the Ruinous Powers.

But as the lift doors opened, he felt, just for a moment, a glimmer of why they lived as they did.

The floor before them was a long chamber with a central corridor and walls consisting of cells on both sides, looking across at one another. All the cell doors stood open. Smeared here and there were the remains of guards slaughtered by the newly-freed prisoners. And the prisoners themselves – perhaps three hundred gangers, murderers and violent criminals – were all suddenly silent.

Silent and kneeling, their heads bowed towards the lift.

The Black Legion Terminators heaved their spiked bulks from the lift, tromping down the central corridor without paying any attention to their worshipful supplicants. Their power was obvious. They did not live in restraint, suffering through a lack of slaves, taking pains not to reveal themselves to an enraged Imperium. And that, just for a moment, spoke to Talos. He understood them, even though he hated them.

The Night Lords followed, and Talos suspected the others were as eager to reach for their sheathed weapons as he was. Humans brought to obedience through fear; that he was used to. But this... this reeked of something else. The sense of something sulphurous was in the air, not entirely drowned out by his breathing filters. Something sorcerous or daemonic, perhaps, to inspire such terrible reverence in such a short time.

At the end of the corridor, another set of doors led into a square chamber, the lights dimmed almost to nothingness. As soon as the doors closed behind them, Talos heard the melee in the prison block begin once more. Somehow, that sound was more reassuring than the silence.

The chamber they had arrived at had been a mess hall. In the initial riots following their freedom, the prisoners had devastated it utterly, and what remained was a junkyard of broken tables, stools and the corpses of twenty-two guards and inmates in varying states of dismemberment. Several other doors led deeper into the internment complex, but Talos would never see any more of the prison than this.

'What a creature Man is...' said a figure in the centre of the wrecked room, '...to spend its first moments of freedom destroying its own lair.'

The Black Legion warriors knelt, their joints emitting low snarls at the unfamiliar movements. Terminator armour was not designed to pay reverence to others. It was designed to kill without end, without mercy, without respite. Talos's jaw clenched at the sight of the Warmaster's elite bowing down. Even the Atramentar, 10th Company's finest, never knelt before the Exalted.

The figure in the centre of the room turned, and Talos met the eyes of the most powerful, most feared being in the galaxy. The figure smiled warmly.

'Talos,' said Abaddon the Despoiler, Warmaster of Chaos. 'We must speak, you and I.'

VIII
WARMASTER

'When in the heart of the foe, show only your strength.
Never bare your throat, never sheathe your sword.
We are Astartes. Not diplomats. Not ambassadors.
We are warriors all.
If you are within the enemy's fortress, you have already breached his best defences.
You hold all the advantages.
Use them.'

– The war-sage Malcharion
Excerpted from his work, *The Tenebrous Path*

ABADDON SMILED AS he spoke.

A smile was the last thing Talos had been expecting.

In his own suit of Terminator war-plate, the Warmaster dwarfed his men and the Atramentar alike, and the consummately crafted black ceramite he wore was bedecked in ornate finery, emblazoned with brass and bronze edges, and bearing the glaring, slitted, fire-orange Eye of Horus on the centre of his chestplate. A cloak of grey-white fur, the hide of some huge wolf-beast, was draped across his massive shoulders. As with his elite warriors, his back sported spear-like trophy racks, each of them impaling a clutch of Astartes helms. Several of them were at the right angle to stare lifelessly at Talos, their dead gaze an unsubtle reminder of the millions of lives lost to the Warmaster's machinations in ten thousand years of rebellion and heresy.

His right hand ended in a vicious power claw of archaic, unique design. The bladed talons, as long as an Astartes's arm, curved and glinted in the half-light of the flickering wall lamps. Horus, favoured son of the Emperor, had worn that gauntlet in the Great Crusade and the Heresy that followed. He'd used it to slay the angel Sanguinius, and wound the Emperor unto the edge of death. Now the dread weapon graced the fist of his gene-son, the leader of his fallen Legion.

That weapon alone almost brought about the urge to kneel, to show respect to the one who carried the blades of ultimate heresy.

But it was the Warmaster's face that drew Talos's attention above all else. Abaddon would never be considered handsome, and the regal lethality emanating from him was nothing a human could project. His face was lined and scarred from centuries of battle, the marks across his pale skin speaking of a thousand battles on a thousand worlds. His head was shaven but for a topknot of his blue-black hair.

In his eyes, Talos saw the death of the galaxy. They burned with inner light, made bright by the dreams of conquest that infested his every waking moment, yet tinged with desperate fury, a longing to inflict vengeance upon the heart of the Imperium.

Like Chaos itself, Abaddon was a clash of contradictions.

And Talos hated his warm, welcoming smile. He could almost smell the corruption beneath the man's skin, a rank scent of charred metal and polluted flesh that teased the edges of Talos's senses.

'You smell that?' he voxed to First Claw.

'Yes,' from Xarl. 'I smell spoiled meat and... something more. They are ripe with corruption, all of them. The Terminators are likely mutated under their armour.'

From there, their replies deteriorated in usefulness.

'The Warmaster smells like he's been boiling human flesh in engine oil,' Cyrion ventured, slightly less helpfully.

All Talos got back from Uzas was an acknowledgement blip – a single burst of quiet static indicating an affirmation.

'I thank you for coming to meet me, brother,' the Warmaster said, his words graceful where his voice was not. It rumbled from his throat, guttural and feral, another contradiction to add to the growing list. Talos wondered how much of this was intentional, designed to throw supplicants off-guard when they came before the great Despoiler.

'I have come, Warmaster,' Talos said, and his targeting reticule locked onto the Black Legion commander, flashing white as it registered the weapons on his person. The Talon of Horus. The storm bolter attached to the great lightning claw. The blade at the Warmaster's hip.

Threat, a Nostraman warning rune flickered across his retinal display. Talos didn't dismiss it from view.

'And you do not kneel,' Abaddon said, his growl not quite letting the words become a question.

'I kneel only before my primarch, Warmaster. Since his death, I kneel before no one. I mean no disrespect.'

'I see.' Talos's attention was drawn to the Talon of Horus for a moment as the Warmaster gestured with the scythe-like claws to the door. 'My brothers, and honoured Night Lord guests... Leave us. The prophet and I have much to discuss.'

Talos's vox-link clicked live. 'We'll be nearby,' Cyrion said.

'We will remain with the Justaerin,' Malek grunted. Talos could hear his eagerness with troubling clarity.

Cyrion had picked up on it, too. 'You sound like you want them to start something.' Neither of the Atramentar replied, though the others could make out muted vox clicks as the two Terminators shared private communication.

Once they were alone in the ruined mess hall, Talos scanned the room, his eyes panning over the wreckage.

'This is not the kind of place I had expected to find you, sir.'

'No?' Abaddon stalked closer, his movements lumbering in the heavy plate, yet somehow more threatening than other Terminators. It was the economy of his movement, Talos realised. The Warmaster's every movement was precise, measured and exact. He wore the armour like a second skin.

'A destroyed mess hall in an internment spire. Hardly the place to find the one who once led us all.'

'I still lead you all, Talos.'

'From a certain point of view,' the Night Lord allowed.

'I wanted to walk the halls of this prison spire myself, and I have neither the time nor the desire to stand upon worthless ceremony. I was here, and I demanded your presence. So it is here that we meet.'

Talos felt his skin crawl at the superiority in the commander's tone. Who was he to speak to one of the sons of Konrad Curze in this way? A captain in a broken Legion, now twisted by the favour of daemons. He deserved respect for his might, but not obeisance. Not fealty or subservience.

'I am here, Warmaster. Now tell me why.'

'So I might meet you, face to face. The Black Legion has its share of sorcerers and prophets, Talos.'

'So I have heard.'

'They are precious to me, and vital to my plans. I take great heed of their words.'

'So I have also heard.'

'Indeed.' The hateful smile came again. 'I wonder to myself, where do you fit in? Are you content with the existence your Legion offers you? Do they respect your gift for what it is?'

And then it was clear: he knew what this was about. How alarmingly unsubtle...

The Night Lord suppressed a growl of anger, eyes narrowed on the flickering *threat* rune that still played across his visor display. His armour's systems tracked his rising heartbeat and, suspecting battle, flooded his veins with potent chemical stimulants. It took several moments for Talos to exhale a shivering breath and speak, ignoring the burn of his energised muscles.

'I am a breed apart from the creatures you call sorcerers, sir.'

Abaddon ceased his vague pacing, looking at his reflection in the silver sheen of his claws. 'You think I do not detect the disapproval in your tone?'

'Evidently not, my lord. It is disgust, not merely disapproval.'

Now Abaddon looked to him, the claws of his relic Talon slicing the air in silent, slow strokes by his side. It almost seemed a habit of his, the way a bored man might crack his knuckles. The Despoiler's claws were always in motion, always cutting, even if it was just air.

'You insult me, Night Lord,' Abaddon mused, still smiling.

'I cannot change the heart of my Legion, Warmaster. I am as you name me: a Night Lord. I am no warp-touched sorcerer, or fallen weaver of spells. I share the gene-seed of the Night Haunter. From my father – not the Ruinous Powers – did I inherit this... gift.'

'Your honesty is refreshing.'

'I am surprised you think so, Warmaster.'

'Talos,' Abaddon said, facing the Night Lord once more. 'Another Black Crusade is in the making.' Here he paused, holding up his claw, and Talos was forcibly reminded of a painting he had once seen of Horus, clutching a burning world in that same gauntlet. He'd assumed, at the time, the world was supposed to be Terra. Ironic then that the painting depicted Horus's ultimate failure – in his grip burned the one world he couldn't conquer.

'This time...' the Warmaster closed his unnatural eyes, and the silver talons trembled, '...this time, the fortress worlds around the Cadian Gate will burn until their surface is nothing but an ashen memory. This time, *Cadia itself* will die.'

Talos watched the Warmaster, saying nothing, until his self-absorbed ecstasy faded and he opened his eyes once more. The Night Lord broke the silence that stretched between them by walking to the corpse of an inmate and kneeling by the body. The man had bled a great deal across the remains of the table he lay upon, but had died from the intense blunt trauma to the side of his head. Talos dipped his first two fingers in the congealing puddle of the mortal's blood, raising them to his speaker grille in order to inhale the coppery scent.

He hungered to taste it, to let the life matter flow through his gene-enhanced form and absorb it into his veins, so he might sense a ghostly echo of the man's dreams, his fears, his desires and terrors.

The wonders of Astartes physiology – to taste the life of those whose blood you have shed. Truly, a hunter's gift.

'You seem unimpressed by my assurance,' the Warmaster said.

'With respect, sir, all of your previous crusades have failed.'

'Is that so? Are you one of my inner circle, to judge whether my plans came to pass and my objectives were met?'

Talos flexed his hand, the gauntlet that would soon be replaced by sections from Faroven's armour. 'You do harm to the Imperium, but never truly advance our cause. Are you asking if the Night Lords will stand with you as you attack Cadia? I cannot speak for my Legion in its entirety. The Exalted will follow you, as he always does. I'm sure many more of our leaders will do the same.'

Abaddon nodded as if this confirmed his point, the veins under his cheeks darkening as he grinned.

'You speak of disunity. Your Legion lacks a figurehead.'

'Many claim to be the Night Haunter's heir. The Talonmaster has vanished, but his claim was no stronger than any other, even with his possession of one of our symbolic relics. Too many other leaders have similar items once carried by our father. Captain Acerbus leads the largest coalition of companies, but again, his insistence reeks of desperation and need. No true claimant has come forth, as you did with your Legion. Our father's throne sits empty.'

'Again, I hear the disquiet in your words.'

'I am not hiding it, Warmaster.'

'Admirable. So tell me: does your heart not cry out to take that throne yourself?'

Talos froze. He hadn't expected this. He'd suspected the Warmaster would seek to use his curse in some way, perhaps even drawing him into the ranks of the Black Legion as a pet advisor. But this...

This was new. And, he suspected, it was a bluff designed to throw his thoughts into disparity.

'No,' he replied.

'You hesitated.'

'You asked a difficult question.'

Abaddon walked closer to Talos, his boots crushing debris beneath each thundering tread. The helms and human skulls impaled upon the trophy racks rattled together, birthing a clacking melody like some barbarous musical instrument.

Threat, the rune flickered, and the Night Lord looked through his red vision at the Warmaster no more than ten metres distant. He couldn't help but compare him to the original bearer of the title. Horus, beloved son of the Emperor, Lord of the Eighteen Legions. Talos had only seen the First Warmaster once, but it was a moment of devastating potency in the storm of his memory.

'I saw the First Warmaster once,' he voiced aloud, without meaning to.

Abaddon chuckled, a series of throaty, predatory grunts. 'Where?'

'Darrowmar. We fought alongside the Luna Wolves in the capital city.'

'The Luna Wolves.' Abaddon openly sneered at the use of his Legion's first name, before they'd become the Sons of Horus in honour of their primarch, and long before they'd become the Black Legion to expunge the shame of their father's failure. 'Days of blindness and war based upon the darkest of lies.'

'True. But they were days of unity,' Talos said, recalling the majesty of Horus at the head of his Legion, his armour of grey-white polished to a finish of ivory and pearl. He was human, but... more. Astartes... but more. Contained within the First Primarch was all that was great and glorious within humanity, distilled to perfection by the fleshsmiths and geneweavers of the Emperor's hidden fortress-laboratories.

To stand within his sight was to bathe in light, to be flooded by inspiration more vital and real than the stinging chemicals pumping through Astartes blood. In his eye-aching brilliance, Horus drew everything to him – merely by taking the field, he ensured he was the fulcrum upon which everything spun. He became the heart of the battle, a maelstrom of slaughter, untouched by the mud and the blood of the battlefield even as he reaped the lives of the foe.

And Talos had barely seen him. He'd formed his opinion of the living god from the other side of a cityscape battleground, seeing little more than the juddering images allowed by his helm's zoomed vision as he sought to assess the Luna Wolves' front lines. It had been like glancing at a moving painting of an ancient hero.

He looked at Abaddon. *How times change.*

'What do you recall of Warmaster Horus?' Abaddon asked.

'My eyes hurt in his presence, even from a distance,' Talos said. 'I am Nostramo-born,' he added, knowing that would explain everything.

'You Night Lords. So literal.' The thought seemed to entertain him, which struck Talos as petty beyond belief. Clarity came upon him in that moment. Abaddon was an avatar for what the Traitor Legions had become. Talos watched him now, knowing neither of them were the equals of their primarch progenitors. None of the Legions could make that claim. They were all mere shadows of their fathers, and their fathers had failed.

The thought was a humbling one, and the weak claws of melancholy reached for his conscious mind again. These encroaching thoughts he dismissed with a scowl, refocusing his attention by acquiring target locks on the weakest points of Abaddon's armour plating. Precious few existed, but he felt his armour's machine-spirit responding, awakening again, teased back into anger. It helped him focus.

'You have still not stated your reasons for summoning me, Warmaster.'

'I will be blunt, then. After all, we have a crusade to forge in the coming days. Tell me, prophet, have you seen anything of the Crythe War in your recent visions?'

'No,' lied Talos immediately.

'No.' The Warmaster narrowed his eyes. 'Just... "No". How very declarative.'

'I have seen nothing that will help you plan, nothing that will bring you new information or aid in any way.'

'But you have seen something.'

'Nothing you have any right to know.'

The claws chimed quietly as they clanged together, Abaddon closing and opening his gauntlet just once. 'I am not famous for my patience,' he said slowly, his voice ripe with threat. 'But it is enough that my suspicions are confirmed. You are a seer, and you have seen what will come.'

'You seem to care a great deal about my visions. I thought you had sorcerers of your own.' A streak of amused pride coloured his words. Abaddon didn't seem to notice, or to care if he did.

'They are having difficulty piercing the warp's veil. You, evidently, have done what they cannot. You have witnessed the future. It should not surprise you that a commander would wish dearly for such information.'

Talos said nothing, knowing what this was building up to.

'Talos, my brother. I have an offer for you.'

'I refuse. I thank you for the honour of whatever this offer might have been, but my answer is no.'

'Why so blatant a refusal?' Abaddon scowled now, the first time he had, and the grimace revealed filthy, blackened teeth behind his bluish lips.

'If you are offering me the chance to lead the VIII Legion, I refuse because it is an impossible task, and not one within your power to grant. If you are asking me to leave my Legion, I refuse because I have no interest in doing so.'

'You reject my offer without hearing it.'

'Your offer will not be in my interests. There is little of any Legion in what remains to us, Warmaster. I no longer believe we will be the death of the Imperium. I no longer believe we are true to our fathers. Corruption has its claws deep within many of us.'

'Then why do you still fight?' Abaddon's glower remained, his teeth clenched and his eyes raw in their open glare.

'Because I have nothing else. I was born to fight, and forged in the fires of war. I am Astartes. I fight because it is right that we fight. The Emperor abandoned the Great Crusade, and demanded humanity pave the way for his ascension to godhood. I don't expect to topple him from the Golden Throne, but such hubris, such evil, must always be opposed.'

'And what of Curze?'

Talos stepped closer, his muscles bunched. 'You will not speak his name with such disrespect, Abaddon.'

'You think you intimidate me, worm?'

'I think I address your primarch by his title as the First Warmaster, despite his ultimate failure. You will do the same honour for the lord of my Legion, who was vindicated even in death.'

'Then tell me, what of the Night Haunter? Does his murder mean nothing to you?'

'The Emperor betrayed my gene-father. Even without the Great Heresy's ideals, the need for vengeance alone would be enough for me to live my life only to see the Imperium fall.'

At this, Abaddon nodded again. 'I respect the Night Lords as brothers, but you are right. You are a broken Legion.'

'And you are not?'

The Warmaster turned, his voice dropping to a threatening murmur. '*What* did you say?'

Threat, threat, threat, the rune flickered.

'Do you fight, Warmaster, because you believe you can still win? After centuries of defeat, after failed Black Crusades, after infighting and war has bled your Legion dry and draped you in ignominy among the other Legions? Is it not true your men are slaved to daemons to make up for the great losses you have sustained since the death of your primarch? You leech strength from other sources, because your own Legion's might is almost gone.'

Silence answered this proclamation. Talos broke it again.

'This meeting is a facet of that. You wonder about how my power will benefit your failing armies.'

Abaddon might have laughed. It would have been the act of a great leader to laugh, to humour a lesser warrior, to bring him around to his own way of thinking through persuasion and empathy – even were it all false. But Abaddon was not such a leader. He was shrewd enough, at least, to guess Talos would never be fooled.

The storm bolter barked once. Two shells roared from the muzzles, two bolts thrown by screaming daemon mouths shaped from dirty brass. Talos's chestplate – the defiled aquila of polished ivory resplendent upon it – cracked under the impact, but it wasn't the bolts themselves that brought him low. In a burst of inky mist, black gas streamed around him.

On his knees before he could even blink, his retinal display registered alarms and flashing runic warnings of life signs plummeting. His armour's machine-spirit was enraged, and he felt the rising desire through his connection junctures to slaughter anything living before him. The Astartes instinct. Defending oneself by killing all threats.

The machine-spirit of Talos's armour was a bastardised, hybrid sentience of anger, pride and caution, born from a meshing of the many suits of armour he had cannibalised for use over his years of war. It growled in his blood now, howling through the socket ports in his skull, his spine, his limbs, firing his own rage. He recognised its frustration instantly from the runic display on his visor. It was unable to reconcile depleted life warnings with the insane fact that, somehow, all of the ammunition counters still read at maximum.

He was wounded without returning fire. This was unnatural. It was not how wars were fought. It had never happened before.

'Preysight,' he demanded from his armour's soul. His vision blanketed in thermal vision, a facade of cold blues, but still somehow failed to pierce the choking gas.

And he *was* choking. That in itself was insane. Each breath drew in another wisp of the black gas, filtering in through his cracked chestplate, its scent like that of burning tar and its taste like the burned earth a week after a battle. He felt the muscles in his throat and chest spasm, tightening like cables of iron. Life runes flashed in alarm – runes he'd never seen before.

Poison. He was actually being poisoned.

'Abaddon!' he roared, immediately horrified at the breathy whisper of his voice. 'You die for this...'

It was when he heard the answering laugh that Talos drew *Aurum*. It took him an indeterminate number of heartbeats to realise the blade had fallen from his nerveless grasp to clatter on the wreckage covering the ground. All he tasted was blood and charred soil. All he felt was the cold, cold pain of his lungs going into spasming shock-lock.

'I have an offer for you, prophet,' the Warmaster's voice came from somewhere he couldn't see. He could barely raise his head. He hadn't even managed to look at the split aquila on his chest and assess the damage to his armour. The draining charts and numbers filtered across his vision told him all he needed to know about his condition.

Poisoned. How was that even possible? The gas... daemon-mist...

Kill him before you die.

The thought rose unbidden from the depths of his mind, and – for a moment – the unfamiliar sense of it left him cold. It was closer to a thought than a voice, an urge rather than an order, and in that doubt lay the answer. This close to death, the machine-spirit of his war-plate pushed easily into his fading mind. It was an invasion of unpleasant pressure, so much colder and more focused than the primal emotions and survival instincts usually massaged against his conscious thoughts. Those were easily ignored; tamed with a moment's concentration. This was a lance of ice to the brain, strong enough to twitch his limbs in a dying attempt at obeying the words.

'And,' the Warmaster continued, 'if you will not hear this offer from me, you *will* hear it from my allies.'

'THAT WAS A bolter.'

As soon as he'd said the words, Cyrion raised his own boltgun and levelled it at the bullish helm of Falkus. 'That,' he said again in a lower voice, 'was a bolter. Tell me I'm wrong.' He had the audio readout displays of his helm at the edge of his vision to assure him that he was absolutely correct, but he was caught off-guard and needed to buy time.

The Night Lords and Black Legion squared off in the central aisle, surrounded by a hundred and more kneeling prisoners.

'Abaddon,' they had been chanting. 'Abaddon... Abaddon... Abaddon...' with all the conviction and reverence of a religious rite. But they'd stopped the moment the Night Lords raised their weapons.

'Storm bolter,' corrected Uzas, and they all heard the smile in his voice. 'Not a bolter. Two barrels. Talos is dead. Life rune is unstable.'

It was true. A single bark of a bolt weapon in the distant mess hall, and the life rune had started flickering on the edge of their retinal displays.

As the standoff stretched out, the Black Legion Terminators remained impassive. *Easy for them,* Cyrion thought, *backed up by over a hundred fanatics.*

'Talos,' he voxed. Nothing. He switched channels with a blink at the right rune. 'Septimus.'

Again, nothing. He blinked at a third rune. '*Covenant*, this is First Claw.'

Silence.

'We're being jammed,' he voxed to the squad.

'Night Lords,' Falkus of the Black Legion murmured. 'There has been a regrettable incident with your Thunderhawk. Come. We will provide alternate transportation back to your ship.'

'Fight them,' Xarl voxed. 'Kill them all.'

'Blood and skulls and souls,' Uzas sounded like he was drooling again. 'We must fight.'

'Keep your damn heads, you fools.' This from Garadon, Hammer of the Exalted. 'Even we would be overwhelmed in this place.'

'Aye,' Cyrion nodded. 'We find answers first, then take whatever vengeance is deserved.'

'*Fight*,' stressed Xarl. The ignominy of being marched out of here was clearly too much for him. 'We can't leave Talos here.'

'The Legions stand on the precipice of battle with what happens in this moment,' Garadon's gruff voice cut into Xarl's threatened raving. 'And they outnumber us in orbit as well as on the surface. Bide your time, and strike when the prey is weakest.'

'You are a coward, Garadon,' Xarl snarled.

'And you will answer for that slur,' the Hammer of the Exalted replied. 'But lower your bolter. This is not a fight we can win.'

The Night Lords lowered their weapons and allowed themselves to be escorted from the hall. Jeers and laughter followed them as the prisoners rose to their feet. Several hurled bottles or fired stolen shotguns into the air, triggering alert runes across the Night Lords' visors.

'Every single one of these wretches will bleed for this,' Xarl promised. Affirmation blips came back from every member of the squad. A bottle struck Uzas on the side of the helm, and the others heard him laughing.

'What the hell is so funny?' Xarl snapped.

'They played us for fools,' Uzas was grinning. 'Killed Talos. Killed Thunderhawk crew. Captured our gunship. Clever moves. Is it wrong to be impressed that they outplayed us so easily?'

'Shut your mouth,' Xarl said. 'They didn't *kill* Talos. His life rune's still live.'

'Same difference. He's theirs now. Good riddance.'

Cyrion ignored their bickering. Surrounded as they were by kneeling mortals, his secret sense was afire with sensation. Every one of these humans was afraid beneath their masks of worship. Their fears bled into his consciousness in trickling spurts of conflicting voices.

...don't want to die...

...freedom, at last, will they let us go...

...a trick, they'll kill us...

Cyrion closed his eyes, feeling their mass fear threatening to overwhelm his own thoughts in a sickening blur of barely-understood emotion. As a child, he had fallen into the sump-lake in the depths of Joria Hive's underhive foundations. Unable to swim, in the endless seconds before his father had saved him, he'd been sinking slowly into the black, staring up at the fire-lit lightness rippling on the water's surface above. Being around too many humans always reminded him of that one moment, when he'd felt himself fading, swallowed whole and forgotten by some vast extraneous, remorseless force. He'd known he was dying, staring up at the dimming half-light above, feeling everything within his mind slipping from his grasp.

He knew the same now. The feeling was the same, coming with the familiar cold, dull realisation of inevitability. It was just taking much longer to happen.

Cyrion's vision focused as he concentrated on the voices in his vox instead of the whispers within his head. He switched to helm speakers again, letting some of his anger bleed into his tone.

'You. Son of Horus.'

One of the Black Legion Terminators turned, still lumbering forwards. 'Night Lord?'

'What, exactly, has occurred to our Thunderhawk?'

'An event of the most terrible misfortune,' he said, and Cyrion picked up the muted vox clicks as the Black Legionnaires laughed over their internal squad channel. 'As a courtesy, we will return you to orbit with one of our own transports,' Falkus said.

At the end of the hallway, the lift doors rumbled open again. An Astartes in black power armour walked towards them, a smile on his pale features and a glint in his dark eyes.

Cyrion voxed to the others as soon as the newcomer began walking towards them. 'You were right after all, Uzas.'

The Night Lords watched the approaching figure, each one recognising him, each one resisting the urge to aim their weapons and open fire.

Uzas nodded, still amused. 'I told you it was a trap.'

'My brothers, my brothers,' the newcomer said. The oily pools of his eyes drank them in one at a time. 'How it pleases me,' he spoke in fluent Nostraman, 'to see you all again.'

SEPTIMUS AND EURYDICE were still in the cockpit.

Septimus was both annoyed and worried, though he tried to let neither of these emotions show. In fairness, he wasn't doing a tremendous job of it. Eurydice could tell the words he occasionally muttered in Nostraman were curses. She was doing an equally poor job of seeming unafraid, but the Astartes had been gone for long enough to set Septimus's teeth on edge and she found herself infected by his worry.

The vox had died almost an hour before, as soon as the Astartes had descended into the prison spire. With a sudden, sharp crack of feedback, connection had been lost and static was all he'd heard from any of the Astartes since then. That in itself didn't worry him. He doubted there was anything here that could do the demigods any real harm. He was, however, worried about himself and Eurydice.

To no avail, Septimus had been trying the vox once every five minutes since it failed. He could reach neither First Claw in the complex below, nor the *Covenant of Blood* in orbit, and this was starting to smell suspiciously like a trap.

It was time to consider his options.

He'd briefly considered taking off and staying on-station by keeping the gunship in hover a few dozen metres above the platform. That, unfortunately, wasn't viable for two reasons. Firstly, his orders had been to stay where he was. Secondly, even had he broken his orders to take off, *Blackened* didn't have the fuel for sustained hovering on its atmospheric thrusters – at least, not if it wanted to break orbit and return to its waiting strike cruiser. The fuel readouts showed, at his best estimate, that he could burn the engines for perhaps fifteen minutes before he would need to return to the *Covenant*. If his master emerged and needed immediate extraction while he was away, or even while he was burning fuel in an unnecessary hover, they might not make it back into the void.

No. It wasn't even worth considering. So with the doors sealed, the gang ramp closed and the weapon turrets trained on the lift building, Septimus waited, eyes narrowed to slits, watching the ship's sensors and deluding himself into thinking he didn't look as worried as he was.

'Will you relax?' Eurydice asked, shattering his self-deception.

Her boots were up on the control console, and she leaned back into the oversized co-pilot's chair with creaking squeal of leather. Septimus, by comparison, was arched forward over the auspex display, watching the green pulse sweep over the screen every six seconds. It pulsed outwards from an icon of *Blackened* in the centre of the screen.

She made a noncommittal grunt, trying to get his attention.

'What?' he said without looking. Another pulse.

'You're worried.'

'Something like that.'

'When will they get back?' Another pulse, still nothing.

'Do I look like they involve me in their plans?' he laughed, though the sound was forced.

'Just asking. What are you worried about, anyway?'

'The prison below us. Specifically, the inmates.' He nodded to the data-slate resting on the arm of his chair. Its display screen listed a screed of information in tiny green letters. 'This is Internment Spire Delta-Two,' Septimus explained. 'The prisoners kept here are awaiting execution, though they are kept alive to serve a span of years in deep tunnel mining operations as slave labour. These aren't recidivists or minor criminals. They're murderers, rapists and heretics.'

'But the doors are sealed.' An edge of hesitancy crept into her voice now, just a thin suggestion of doubt.

'No door is invulnerable. The flank bulkheads would stop anything I can imagine, but the main gang ramp works through regular hydraulics. It's sealed and locked, but... Look, I'm not worried. Just being prepared.'

'Prepared for what, exactly? Why would anyone rush an Astartes gunship? Talk about a death wish.'

'I don't know. I expect most wouldn't come near us. If they did? Well, maybe some might want to try and flee the planet by stealing the ship. Or maybe, given their incarceration here, they're not all that sane to begin with. Or...' he trailed off.

'Or *what?* Don't just start a sentence like that and leave it hanging.'

He shrugged. 'Maybe if they had learned there was a woman on board...'

She nodded, but he could see she was struggling to maintain her bravado. 'This gunship has, well, guns, right?'

'It... does.'

'I don't like the way you said that.'

'Half of the weapons are inactive, including the main battle cannon. Ammunition is low, and the heavy bolters on the gunship's flanks are no longer slaved to servitors.'

'Why not?'

Another pulse. Another blank screen. 'Because the servitors are dead. They have been for years, and I was the one tasked with dragging the bodies from their ports.'

After several moments of silent staring, another console screen chimed. Septimus turned in his throne, leaning forward to examine the readout.

'Well, well, well...'

'More bad news?' she asked him, not sure she really wanted an answer.

'Not exactly. Another ship just took off – and not one of the bulk landers down there on the plains. This ship was a Thunderhawk-class vessel. Black Legion identification signals.'

'Meaning?'

'The auspex chimed because it registered First Claw on board the ship as it headed into orbit.'

'What? They left us here?'

Septimus was still watching the screen. 'Not all of them. No signal from Talos. He's still in the prison complex.'

He was not a man who enjoyed these kinds of mysteries. Septimus turned from the screen to hit a few console keys. *Doors: Secured,* a flashing icon on the console read. It was the third time he'd checked the doors in the past hour.

As Eurydice drew breath to ask another question, the auspex chimed again. There was nothing foreboding in the sound. It was almost melodic.

'Damn it,' said Septimus, rising from his throne.

Eurydice sat up. The auspex was singing now, tinny chime after tinny chime. 'Are we in trouble?' she asked.

Septimus was staring out of the forward window, at the open elevator doors, and what came spilling out of them.

'Oh, absolutely,' he said, drawing both of his pistols.

'Then give me one of those,' she said as she stood, following his gaze.

'Take them both,' he said, handing them to her before leaning over the control console. 'And don't think about shooting me.'

She gave him a withering look that he never saw. Septimus hit a long sequence of console keys, his fingers a blur.

'What are you doing?' she asked.

'This,' he said, and the gunship's functioning heavy bolter turrets lit up with fire as they unleashed their rage.

JERL MADDOX COULDN'T believe his luck. Freedom.

Freedom.

Freedom after eight years in this damn hellhole. Eight years of eating the cold, bitter grey paste that passed as food, morning, afternoon and night. Eight years of fourteen-hour shifts under the earth of this accursed rock, digging and digging and digging in the vain hope of striking a handful of ore. Eight years of backaches, blurred vision, gums burning from infection, and pissing blood after every beating from the guards.

Yeah, well, payback had come sure enough. He clutched the shotgun to his chest, racking the slide just to enjoy the feeling. Click-chunk. Oh, *hell yes.* This was something else. He'd taken the weapon from Laffian, but that was all good because Laffian had been one of the worst guards in R Sector.

R Sector – 'Omega Level Transgressions Only' – was home no longer for Maddox, and the fact he could still feel Laffian's blood on his face was just that little extra touch of victory.

That was payback, too. Payback for the time Laffian had smacked Jesper around so bad the poor fool's eye had popped out from his broken head. Maddox grinned, the stench of his teeth making his eyes water. Laffian hadn't looked so cocksure with his chest blown open and his leg hacked off at the knee.

He'd screamed about his kids, too. Yeah, like that would make a difference. Maddox's grin became a snigger.

'Shut your mouth, Blackjaw,' someone next to him said. Maddox swallowed, pressing his lips together. In the close confines of the lift car, which was an uncomfortable fit for almost fifty of them, several of the men curled their lips or swore at him in grunting monotone.

'Sorry,' he mumbled, but that just got them complaining again. It wasn't his fault. His gums were infected. His teeth were black and loose in his jaws – the few that remained, anyway. Wasn't like they had access to a doctor in R Sector, was it? And they smelled just as bad, anyway. Fifty of them all sweating and bloody in their white overalls...

'You stink, too,' he muttered. Bodies started to move, to turn in his direction. Maddox lowered his head a little, avoiding all eye contact as the man ahead turned around.

'What's that, Blackjaw?' It was Indriga, a solid two metres of tattooed muscle and knife scars. He'd been stuck on R Sector for killing and eating some poor habwife.

'Nothing. Nothing, Indriga.'

'Damn right, nothing. Now shut your mouth before we all throw up.'

He kept his head down, doing his best not to smile. He couldn't help it, though. He kept seeing Laffian howling and thrashing around with no leg... And the trembling smile became a blurted cough of a snigger. A droplet of warm, thick saliva plopped onto the stock of his stolen shotgun. Laffian's gun. He laughed again.

The men around him turned away, swearing. He likely would have died then and there had the lift not ground to a halt and the doors opened. The thin, ash-tasting air floated in to meet them as the prisoners looked out onto the landing platform.

'There it is,' Indriga said, already walking out.

It was a ship – a small vessel by troopship standards, and that was about the only frame of reference Maddox had; he'd been Imperial Guard before his arrest for... whatever they'd said he'd done. He hadn't done anything, and he knew it. No way. Not him. He was Guard, through and through. Damned if he could even remember what they'd insisted he'd done wrong, now...

Someone shoving him forward jolted his senses back to the present.

'Let's take it,' one of them said.

It was vaguely hawkish, with downswept wings, and it was dark blue, like the colour of the deepest oceans. The thought of that made Maddox's stomach quiver and bunch. He hated the sea. He couldn't put his head below the surface without imagining *something* deep down there, looking back at him.

He was one of the stragglers, while most of his fellow prisoners ran forwards with their stolen clubs and guns held high. Their saviours – the god-warriors in black – had chosen some of the strongest and fittest inmates in R Sector to come up here and perform this sacred duty. There were people in this ship, and they had to die. The gods had spoken.

And, *hell yes,* one of them was supposed to be a woman.

It was good to be free. It was good to be the chosen champion of the gods that had bestowed upon him the freedom he so richly deserved. Even the awful air tasted better than usual.

These were the thoughts swirling around Jerl 'Blackjaw' Maddox's mind as he died. When he went down, he was still too lost in his thoughts of freedom to really comprehend what was happening to him, and he died with his body in pieces, still smiling, and still smelling terrible as he laughed without any sound leaving his lips.

The turret cannons on the gunship blazed away, bolt rounds streaming out to thump home into yielding flesh only to detonate a moment after impact. Inmates were reduced to shattered husks of meat and bone, thrown across the landing platform in ugly smears. From the vox speakers mounted on the Thunderhawk's exterior, a voice spoke calmly in heavily-accented Gothic.

'Welcome, all of you,' Septimus said. 'Please enjoy the last mistake you'll ever make.'

Cyrion checked his bolter again, then clamped it once more to his thigh armour.

'Stop that,' voxed Malek. 'You look irritated.'

'I can't think why,' Cyrion sneered.

First Claw and their Atramentar escorts sat in the restraint thrones of a Black Legion gunship, their surroundings vibrating as the Thunderhawk juddered through the atmosphere.

'Will they take *Blackened*?' Cyrion asked. 'It would be a foolish error if they tried.'

'They just wanted Talos,' Xarl said. He clicked the blinking rune that confirmed a private channel with Cyrion. 'And the Atramentar knew it would happen. They were here to ensure we did not step out of line, and backed down at the first need to shed blood. The Exalted planned this.'

Cyrion's voice was tired. The weight of the prisoners' fears, although faded now, still rested heavily on his mind. 'I grow weary of this, Xarl.'

'Of what?'

'The treachery. The death of trust. Of my mind aching from the silent weeping terror of mortals.'

Xarl said nothing at first. Sympathy was not in his blood. 'You are tainted, Cyrion,' he said at last.

'Something like that,' Cyrion replied. He took a breath. 'The Exalted has always resented Talos's position in the Legion, as a favoured son of our father, but this was a step too far. To attempt to kill him? Is Vandred insane?'

Xarl's response came after a bitter laugh. 'What makes you so sure he wanted Talos dead? Out of the way, certainly. Perhaps among the ranks of the Black Legion. A gain for both Abaddon and the Exalted.'

'Like Ruven,' Cyrion said.

'Yes, brother,' Xarl said, his voice lower now. 'Like Ruven.'

EURYDICE SWORE WITH feeling as the Thunderhawk shook again.

'Throne, I don't want to die here.'

Septimus didn't turn to look at her. His focus was entirely on the ammunition readouts, which were dropping with heart-wrenching speed. He clicked the vox live.

'This is the VIII Legion Thunderhawk *Blackened*.'

'It's not working,' Eurydice swallowed her panic at his desperate attempts. 'The *Covenant* can't hear you. Talos can't hear you.'

'Shut up,' he replied. 'This is the VIII Legion Thunderhawk *Blackened*, hailing the battle-barge *Hunter's Premonition*. Do you read?'

'The... the what?'

'Another one of our ships is in orbit,' he said. 'One of the Night Lords' flagships.'

'Why aren't you shooting?'

He didn't even need to glance at the ammo displays. 'Because every gun that can track a target this close to the hull is out of shells.'

The cockpit shook again, this time hard enough to throw Eurydice back onto her chair.

'Throne!' she shouted. Septimus winced.

'That wasn't good. They're inside.'

'*What?*'

He didn't answer her. 'This is the VIII Legion Thunderhawk *Blackened,* hailing the battle-barge *Hunter's Premonition*. Please respond.'

Voices could be heard yelling in the deck below. The prisoners that had survived the annihilation offered by the heavy bolters were definitely inside now.

'Damn it.' Septimus abandoned the console and pulled the curved hacking blade that was strapped to his calf. 'Worth a try.'

Eurydice tossed him one of the pistols.

'Looks like I won't be guiding your heretic masters through the Sea of Souls after all.' She smiled a nasty little grin, somewhere between bitterness, terror and triumph.

Septimus raised his pistol at the closed cockpit door. 'We'll see.'

IX

FOUR GODS

'Our brothers run to the edges of the Imperium to cower in the shadows of the Dark Gods that protect them. Only we, the Night Lords, the sons of Konrad Curze, are strong enough to stand alone. We will bring our wrath upon the empire that betrayed us, and though the ages may see us divided and broken by the endless war ahead, we will stand untainted until the stars themselves die.'

– The war-sage Malcharion
Epilogue of his work, *The Tenebrous Path*

TALOS OPENED HIS eyes to nothingness.

To one who saw through pitch darkness as naturally as a mortal man saw in daylight, this was both unwelcome and unfamiliar. He turned, still seeing nothing, unsure if this was because there was nothing to see in the blackness or if he had lost his sight. It occurred to him with no small amusement that he'd inflicted this very fate on so many mortals over the years, forcing them to awaken in the darkness of the *Covenant's* interior. A cautious smile spread across his lips as he enjoyed the irony.

The air was cold on his flesh.

Flesh? At the first hints of the sensation, he could see himself now – his hands before his face, bone-white and blue-veined, and his tunic of dark weave. He was out of his battle plate. How could this be? Had his wound been so terrible that First Claw had cut him from his armour and...

Wait. His wound.

His pale hands pulled open the front of his robe, baring his chest to the darkness. His torso, a pale, sculpted echo of ancient Romanii marble statues of their warlike gods, was unbroken by any wound. Across his sternum were the junction plugs and connection sockets required to link into the powered systems of his armour, and he could make out the hard shell of the black carapace implanted beneath his skin, forming the sub-dermal armour that sheathed his form in additional protection and allowed him to interface with his battle plate's senses.

But no wound.

'Talos,' a voice spoke from the blackness. He turned to meet it, hands reaching for weapons that didn't exist here, wherever here was.

The speaker was a Night Lord. Talos recognised the armour instantly, for it was his own.

In the nothingness, he faced himself, staring at his armoured image with something approaching fury.

'What madness is this?'

'A test,' his reflection said, removing its helm. The face beneath the helmet was, and was not, his own visage. Eyes of silver stared back at him, and the centre of his forehead was branded with a stylised rune of sickening devotion. The burn mark was still fresh, still trickling blood down his reflection's face.

'You are not me,' Talos said. 'I would never wear the slave mark of the Ruinous Powers.'

'I am what you might be,' his image smiled, revealing teeth as silver as his eyes. 'If you were bold enough to unlock your potential.'

And if you will not hear this offer from me, you will hear it from my allies. The Warmaster's words came back to him now, trickling into his consciousness as the blood trickled into his reflection's alien eyes.

'You are not one of the Ruinous Powers,' he said to the image before him. 'You are not a god.'

'Am I not?' it replied, smiling indulgently.

'No god would be so brazen, so unsubtle. You would turn your eyes upon one soul? Never.'

'I turn my eyes to a trillion souls with each passing moment. It is the nature of a god to exist in such a way.'

An ugly thought clawed its way up from Talos's doubts to reach his lips. 'Am I dead?'

'No,' the god smiled again, 'though you are wounded in the world of flesh.'

'Then this is the warp? You have taken my spirit from my body.'

'Be silent. The others come.'

He was right. Other figures manifested about him – one behind, one to the left, one to the right, taking the cardinal points around where he stood in the darkness. He couldn't focus upon them. Each time he turned, he saw nothing except the others existing at the edges of his vision.

'This,' said the first figure, 'is what I offer you.' He reached out a gauntleted hand to Talos. 'You are keen of mind and great of vision. You know your armies of god-sons will fail without true gods to lead them. Your flesh gods have fallen. Your fathers are slain. You are godless, and in godlessness lies defeat.'

'Touch me and die,' the Astartes warned. 'Mark my words, false god. If you touch me, you will die.'

'I am Slaa Neth. I am the One Who Thirsts. I am a god, more than your gene-father ever was. And this,' the figure repeated, 'is what I offer you.'

Talos...

...opened his eyes to a battlefield.

A battlefield he claimed, heart and soul. The enemy, the Imperial army, was reduced to a graveyard of wrecked tanks and corpses that reached from horizon to horizon.

He stood above his warriors as they kneeled before him, feeling the pleasant sting of some vicious new battle chemical stimulant flooding his veins. He was wounded, for there were cracks in his swollen armour where reddish ichor flowed down his war-plate. These wounds, great rents and rips in his flesh open to the chill air of the battlefield, ached with a pleasure so intense he cried his thanks to the stars above.

Was this what it was to be a primarch? To laugh at wounds that would destroy even an Astartes? To feel war as an amusing diversion, while crushing a million enemies under the might of invincible armies?

Perhaps this was what the Night Haunter had felt. This exaltation. Blood-slick claws tore fresh rents in his cheek as he scratched himself, laughing at the delicious pain. Pain itself became a joke to those who could never die.

'Prince Talos,' his troops were shouting up at him. 'Prince Talos.'

No, not shouting. Worshipping. They bowed and cried and prayed for his attention.

This...

'...IS WRONG,' TALOS growled. 'The Night Haunter was never exalted above us as a perfect, immortal being. He was moribund and cursed, stronger for all the trials and agonies he endured.

'This,' he finished, turning from Slaa Neth, 'is not how he lived. It is not how I will live, either.'

'Cyrion,' the figure smiled. Talos hadn't ever smiled like that in his life.

'What of him?' the Astartes narrowed his black eyes, instinctively reaching for weapons that weren't there.

'His soul has felt my caress. Your brother hears the fears of every living thing. My gift to him.'

'He resists.'

'On the surface, he resists. The parts of his mind that shout silently relish the sounds of weeping souls. He feeds on fear. He enjoys what he senses.'

'You are lying,' Talos said, but his broken conviction was evident in the growl. 'Begone.'

The first figure faded with a laugh, unseen by Talos, who now stared at the second. He wasn't surprised to see another image of a Night Lord, his own armour facing him once more. Talos felt a smile creeping across his lips at the sight: it was his armour laid bare, the cannibalism and repairs left unpainted and visible to the naked eye. His chestplate was still the deep blue of the Ultramarines. The armour of his leg was the royal yellow of the Imperial Fists, and the thigh guard attached was the gunmetal grey of the crippled Steel Confessors Chapter. A harlequin's display of colours and allegiances made up the figure's war-plate, and Talos lost himself in the memories of where and when each piece was taken. Most, he'd not even thought about for years. Decades, even.

The shoulder guard ripped from the corpse of a Crimson Fists veteran was a particularly pleasant recollection. They'd fought hand to hand, an uncomplicated brawl of fury against fury, gauntlets pounding cracks in each other's armour until Talos had managed to crush the other warrior's windpipe. Once the loyalist Astartes was strangled into unconsciousness, Talos had broken his spine and smashed his skull open against the hull of First Claw's waiting Land Raider. With the Imperial Fist finally dead, the Night Lord let the body fall to the ground.

Strange, how the centuries were affecting his memory. He'd believed once that his recollection was almost eidetic. Now, he realised he'd forgotten the most ferocious three minutes of fighting in his entire life.

The second figure removed his helm, showing a face that mirrored his own but for the curving symbol tattooed on its pale cheek.

'You know me,' the second figure said, and it was right, Talos did know. He recognised the faintly patronising cadence in the man's speech, and the sickly sweet scent rising from his armour. The same smell emanated from the Exalted.

'You are the Shaper of Fate,' Talos said. 'Vandred is one of your slaves.'

The figure nodded, his black eyes a perfect image of Talos's own. 'He is one of mine. A champion of my cause, a beneficiary of my gifts. Not a slave. His will is his own.'

'I believe differently.'

'Believe what you will. He is of some value to me. You, however, could be so much more.'

'I have no interest in...'

...power.

That was the first sensation that drummed from his twin hearts, as though they pushed strength itself through his body with each dual beat. This was not the laughable power of blithe immortality and pleasure, but something altogether more familiar. He turned his head to regard the others on the command deck.

The Atramentar, all eight of them, knelt before him. Beyond them, the bridge crew worked their stations; each and every one a human with a servitor aide, all working diligently.

He gestured to the Terminators abasing themselves before him.

'Rise.'

They rose, taking their places flanking his throne.

As clear as the sound of his own breathing within his battle helm, as real as his own red-bathed sight, he felt the sudden surety that one of the Atramentar would speak. It would be about the Exalted's punishment.

'Lord,' growled Abraxis, the Atramentar warrior closest to the throne. 'The Exalted awaits your judgement.'

He knew then, before he even spoke, that the Exalted would break under thirty-eight night cycles of physical and psychic torture. The Atramentar could provide the former. Talos himself would provide the latter.

'Mark my words, brothers,' Talos said. 'He will not last forty nights under our care.'

The eight Terminators nodded, knowing he spoke the truth, knowing he had foreseen it in the winds of fate.

'We are one hour from our destination, lord,' said one of the mortal bridge officers. Talos closed his eyes, and smiled at the images he saw imprinted in his mind.

'When we re-enter realspace, seek the engine signatures of three freighters using the third moon as shield against auspex returns. Cripple them quickly, and ready First, Second and Third Claws for boarding actions.'

The whispers began. They thought he couldn't hear them – the whispers about his new power, about 10th Company's resurging strength. Let them praise him in whispers. He needed no obsequiousness to his face.

Talos relaxed into the command throne, letting his thoughts drift into the infinity of what was yet to come, feeling the skeins of fate like a thousand threads under his fingertips. Each strand led to a possible future that played out before his eyes, if he merely concentrated for a single moment. The future…

'…IS UNWRITTEN.' HE took a breath, feeling naked without his armour and swallowing the rising urge to slay these apparitions before him. 'I am a seer, and I know the path of the future is darkened by choices yet unmade.'

His reflection, in its salvaged armour, shook its head. 'I can offer you the secret sight any mortal must have in order to pierce the mists.'

'My second sight is pure.' Talos spat on the chestplate of the patchwork armour, where – much to his discomfort – the Imperial eagle still shone undefiled. 'Yours is the bane of sanity. Leave.'

He turned to the third, aware of a buzzing sound that felt almost tactile, crawling against his skin. Flies covered the armour of the third figure, fat and blood-red, though patches of occasional blue showed through the insect vermin as they swarmed over the armour's surface in a rippling, random tide.

The figure wore no helm. The face was his own, blighted by swollen sores and infected cuts. Through cracked lips which bled a thin orange fluid, the figure shook its head, and spoke with the voice of a grunting, drowning beast.

'I was summoned here,' it said, 'but you will never be one of my champions. I have no use for you, and you have no will to wield the power I offer.'

Talos fixed on the first point of cohesion in all this foolish madness. 'Who summoned you?'

'One of your kind wove his pleas into unspace for a flicker of my attention. A magus, begging into the warp.'

'An Astartes? A Night Lord? A human?'

The figure faded, taking its rank stench into oblivion as it went.

'Who *summoned* you?' Talos cried into the darkness.

When silence was the only reply, he turned to the fourth and final figure, the act of facing it bringing it into being.

The last figure showed the greatest deviation from Talos's own image, and that alone set the Night Lord's lip into a disrespectful sneer. This figure, unlike the others, was in motion as if unable to remain still. It swayed from foot to foot, hunched over akin to a beast ready to leap, breathing rasping from its helmet's vox speakers.

The armour itself was red, the red of a body's darkest blood, edged in bronze so filthy it looked as dull and worthless as copper. It was still his armour, but lacking his familiar trophies and sporting fresh battle damage, as well as the repainted surfaces and bronze modifications, made it an unnerving sight. Seeing his most treasured possession so twisted...

'Make this good,' he said, teeth clenched.

The figure reached up, removing its helm with shaking hands. The face it revealed was a mess of scars, burns and bionics, framing a malevolent grin.

'I am Kharnath,' it grunted through the toothy smile.

'I know that name.'

'Yes. Your brother Uzas cries it as he takes skulls for my throne.'

'He is one of your slaves?' Talos couldn't tear his eyes from seeing his own face so damaged. Half of the head was replaced by oil-smeared bionic plating that fused with raw, inflamed skin at the edges. The flesh that remained was blistered and uneven from burn scarring, or darkened by badly-sealed cuts from what must have been horrendous blows to offset the enhanced healing of Astartes physiology.

Most unnerving of all was the way he swayed, hunched over and ape-like, with the same dead-eyed grin Uzas wore when trying to maintain his attention on a difficult conversation.

'Blood,' it wheezed, 'and souls. Blood for the Blood God. Souls for the Soul Eater.'

'Is Uzas your slave? Answer me.'

'Not yet. Soon. Soon he will stand as a champion among my warriors. But not now. Not yet.'

'Whoever summoned you to win me to your allegiance has wasted their time. This is almost laughable.'

'Time is short,' the figure still grinned. 'And such sights I have to show you.'

Talos had more insults to offer, more rejections to voice, but found he couldn't speak. His lungs locked, feeling like slabs of quivering stone behind his fused ribs. It was a savage echo of the moment he'd been poisoned, and he felt the same sensation as the meat within his body shuddered, stealing his breath. This time, as he fell to his knees, his breathless wheezes weren't curses, but laughter.

The warrior of blood was fading. Talos knew in the world of flesh, his lungs were purging the taint that brought him here.

'Witness my gifts,' Kharnath said, desperate now, ferocious in his eagerness. 'See the strength I offer. Do not abandon this one chance!'

'Go back to hell,' the Night Lord grinned through bloody teeth, and vomited black mist into the nothingness.

TALOS OPENED HIS eyes again.

Immediately, he felt vulnerable. He was on his back. Prone.

Filtered through the red of his visor display, he recognised the scarred ceiling of the mess hall, and his targeting reticule marked three figures standing above him. He did not know who they were or what their presence indicated – all three were mortals in dark robes marked by blasphemous symbols, backing away as soon as his consciousness returned.

'Preysight,' he said, and their vague identities were further masked, reduced to the rich blur of thermal traces.

The first died as Talos rose to his feet and pounded his fist into the human's face. The Night Lord felt the man's head give with a wrenching snap of skull bone, and the corpse spun away without another sound. He was on the second robed figure before the first had hit the rubble-strewn ground, gauntlets clasped around the mortal's frail neck, eliciting several wet clicks as he squeezed and twisted. The mortal's eyes bulged as the sound of dry twigs snapping echoed into the air. Once the man's head was wrenched backwards, after several seconds of teasing enjoyment, Talos let that body fall in turn.

The third figure was trying to escape, running for a set of double doors that led deeper into the prison complex. Three sprinted strides brought the Night Lord within reach, and he clawed at the fleeing heat-blur. The thermal smear screamed in his hands.

He wasn't even hurting it, yet.

Talos lifted the smudged miasma of reds and yellows off the ground, and voided his preysight. A human face, male, middle-aged and weeping, met his natural vision.

'*Going somewhere?*' the Astartes growled through his vox speakers.

'Please,' the man wept, 'please don't kill me.' Through his helm's olfactory receptors, Talos scented the cloying incense on the mortal's robes, and the sour reek of his breath. He was infected with... something. Something within his body. A cancer, perhaps, eating at his lungs...

Taint. He reeked of taint.

Talos let the man stare into the impassive skulled face of his helm for several more beats of his panicked, mortal heart. *Let the fear build.* The words of his gene-father, the teachings of the VIII Legion: *Show the prey what the predator can do. Show that death is near. The prey will be in your thrall.*

'Do you wish to join your friends in death?' he snapped, knowing his helm's speakers turned the threat into a mechanical bark.

'No, please. Please. *Please.*'

Talos shivered involuntarily. Begging. He had always found begging particularly repulsive, even as a child in the street gangs of Atra Hive on Nostramo. To reveal that level of weakness to another being...

With a feral snarl, he pulled the man's weeping, pleading face against the cold front of his helm. Tears glistened on the ceramite. Talos felt his armour's machine-spirit roil at the new sensation, like a river serpent thrashing in deep silt. It woke again to feed on the mortal's sorrow and fear.

'Tell me,' the Night Lord growled, 'your master's name.'

'R-Ruv–'

Talos snapped the mortal's neck, and stalked from the room.

Ruven.

RUVEN RESISTED THE urge to shrink before the Warmaster's displeasure.

Abaddon's claw scraped less than lovingly over the sorcerer's shoulder guard, tearing the oath scroll that was bound there. Several strips of the hallowed parchment ghosted to the ground, floating patiently on the breath of an invisible wind.

'He has awakened early,' Abaddon repeated Ruven's last words back to him.

'Yes, my Warmaster. And,' – he hated to add this – 'he has slain my acolytes.'

Abaddon gurgled laughter through a fanged maw. 'You were of the Night Lords before you came to my Legion, yet their actions surprise you now.'

Ruven inclined his helm with its lightning bolts painted onto the black ceramite. He was both intrigued and confused by the Warmaster's rhetorical statement.

'Yes, my Warmaster.'

'That makes your carelessness doubly entertaining.'

Abaddon and Ruven stood on the ground floor of the prison complex, overseeing the ragged march of convicts towards the waiting slave ship that rested, slug-shaped and fattened for cargo capacity, on the dusty red plain beneath the prison mountain. Legion serfs, servitors and the hulking form of black-clad Astartes directed the column of convicts, occasionally serving out beatings or – in a few instances – executions, if a convict's jubilation at freedom brought him to attempt an escape.

Robed acolytes, dressed identically to the humans Talos had slaughtered only minutes before, walked alongside the column, proselytising about the glory of the Warmaster, the false rule of the Golden Throne, the abominations done in the Emperor's name by His armies, and the inevitability of the Imperium's demise in the name of justice. Several of these priests shrieked at the thousands of prisoners in gibbering tongues unknown to all but the Dark Gods' favoured servants, seeking any recognition within the convicts' eyes, hoping to stumble across a Chaos-tainted individual and raise such a blessed scion of the Ruinous Powers out of the ragtag cannon fodder regiments of slaves being formed from the prison world's population.

Solace would be stripped bare of life before the sun rose.

The sorcerer, Ruven, still said nothing.

'Your acolytes were worthless anyway,' Abaddon said. 'Listen to these preachers, howling about the unworthiness of the False Emperor. Such theatrics. And for what? Every soul upon this world was betrayed by the Imperium. Discarded, hated and forgotten – purely for the sin of living their lives as they chose. These men need no ideology beyond learning they will be given the chance to earn vengeance through bloodshed.'

'If my Warmaster does not approve of the methods of the acolytes I have trained–'

'Do I sound like I approve?'

'No, my Warmaster.'

'Cease scurrying, Ruven. Where is the Night Lord prophet now?'

Ruven closed his eyes, resting his gauntleted hand against the side of his helm as if trying to make out a sound in the distance.

'Making his way to the landing platform, my Warmaster.'

'Good.' The Astartes helms spiked by the Despoiler's trophy racks clattered together as Abaddon turned to the sorcerer. 'You were foolish to let your acolytes remain as long as they did.'

'I was, my Warmaster. Their chants were necessary to maintain the vision, but the prophet threw off the toxins quicker than I had anticipated.'

'Am I to assume he resisted your attempts at conversion?' Abaddon's voice betrayed just how little faith he'd had in the idea from the beginning.

'He refused the Dark Ones, my Warmaster. To their faces. This was not some minor conjuration – I summoned reflections of the Four Powers. A trickle of power from the winds of the warp, each to offer their gifts.'

The blasphemous symbols branded onto Abaddon's flesh burned and itched with maddening intensity. 'What did he see? What was so easy to refuse?'

'I know not, my Warmaster. But his vision was true. I felt the presence of the Four. A momentary glance of their attention, if you will.'

Abaddon chuckled. The sound lacked even a shadow of humour. 'Grotesque and unsubtle, but deeply amusing.'

'Yes, my Warmaster.'

'Return to orbit, Ruven. Your work here is done.'

The sorcerer hesitated, clutching his staff made from the fused bones of tyrannic-breed xenos. 'Do you not wish to me intercept the Night Lord and make another attempt?'

Abaddon watched the column ahead, where one of his Black Legion Astartes was dragging a screaming prisoner from the line. With a single swipe of a blade, the human's head left his shoulders.

'He has been made to feel vulnerable, and his Legion looks even weaker in his eyes. The cracks already in his resolve will soon split wide. This was never about converting the puritan bastard in one fleeting moment. It was merely the first move in a much longer game of regicide.'

'Shall I inform the Exalted of our failure?'

Abaddon grinned. '*Our* failure?'

'*My* failure, Warmaster.'

'Better. No, I will speak with the Exalted myself and inform him that his pet seer survived untainted. Vandred was a fool to think it would happen so quickly.'

'Then I shall do as you bid, my Warmaster.'

Abaddon didn't answer. Such an obvious statement needed no affirmation. Instead he turned, irritation touching his feral features for a moment.

'Did you at least kill the slaves?'

The Exalted had won the orbital battle for him in a fraction of the time Abaddon had planned for. The least he could do to repay the Night Lord commander was a little favour like that.

'Bleed the slaves on board the Thunderhawk,' the Exalted had asked. *'But allow nothing to be traced to either Legion.'*

'Whatever you wish, brother,' Abaddon had replied. *'What reason do you have for making this look like some nonsensical accident?'*

The Exalted had smiled to hear it described like that. *'A petty reason, but a necessary one. Eliminating the allies of a potential rival. My prophet gathers his resources. He will not take my place as commander.'*

Abaddon found that rather quaint. The Exalted's claws had to be clean of this murder. Amusing to see how subtle these Night Lords could be when they chose.

'I sent fifty prisoners, my lord,' said Ruven. 'Their Thunderhawk was overrun, and the other Night Lords returned to orbit in one of our ships.'

'Fifty.' How amusingly excessive. 'Against how many?'

'Two slaves.'

Abaddon nodded, looking back at the columns of freed convicts. Fifty against two, and the crime apparently blameless.

At least something had been done right.

* * *

Talos had been unable to reach any of First Claw on the vox, nor had he made contact with *Blackened* or the *Covenant of Blood*. He suspected jamming, though to what purpose, he couldn't begin to guess. Killing them all down here made no sense at all, for there would be no gain for the Black Legion. While Abaddon may have had a thousand faults, with overconfidence first among them, he was not a fool. His grasp of tactical insight had only grown stronger over the centuries.

Then again, nothing the Black Legion did was ever particularly predictable. Once, Talos thought, they were the best of us.

How the mighty are fallen.

As the lifter doors opened, he stared at the bodies spread across the landing platform. It took no time at all to see they had been sectioned by heavy bolter fire. Talos's attention immediately fixed upon the Thunderhawk, silent on its grey clawed landing gear, its forward gang ramp lowered. Black streaks of burned and twisted metal showed on the blue hull where explosives had been employed to wreck the ramp's hydraulics. The convicts had evidently been extremely well-equipped.

Talos was already walking forward, crushing meat and bone underfoot, his blade and bolter at the ready.

'Hnnngh,' one of the nearby corpses wheezed at him. Talos didn't break stride. He glanced at the black-toothed, bleeding ruin of a man, and destroyed its head with a single bolt shell. The gunshot's report echoed off the Thunderhawk's hull.

'Septimus,' he voxed.

The answer he received did not please him.

X
THE HUNTERS HUNTED

THEY HAD TAKEN her.

They had defiled *Blackened* with the foul mortal scent of panicked fear; they had torn Septimus to pieces, and they had taken Eurydice.

Talos sheathed his blade and locked his bolter to his thigh, kneeling by the command throne where Septimus lay unmoving. Dark smears of blood across the floor showed where the slave had dragged himself. He lounged in the pilot's throne, sprawled like a puppet with cut strings, a mess of bloody bruises, broken limbs and shattered bones.

He still breathed. Talos wasn't sure how.

The Night Lord kicked a convict's corpse aside, removing his helm and kneeling by his artificer. The rich scent of flowing blood and the reeking stink of recent death assailed his naked senses. Septimus coughed flecks of fresh blood to his sliced lips, turning to face the Astartes.

'They took her,' he said, his voice surprisingly clear. 'Master, I'm sorry, I can't see. They took her.'

Talos withdrew a syringe and a roll of self-adhesive synskin bandage weave from his thigh-mounted narthecium. The supplies he bore now were a hollow shadow of the old Apothecary tools he'd once carried, but those were lost an age ago, on a nameless world in the years after the Great Heresy split the galaxy.

The first thing he did was inject a cocktail of blood coagulant, painkillers and Astartes plasma into Septimus's thigh. The second was to bandage what remained of his slave's face.

'They took her,' Septimus said again as the weave was wrapped around his eyes.

'I know.' Talos rose to his feet again, after spraying disinfectant on the open wounds of the mortal's legs, torso and arms. He tied off the worst gashes with tourniquets, and left the bandages within Septimus's reach on the control console.

'You must use the rest yourself. The bandages are by the secondary thrust levers.'

'Yes, master.'

'They used explosives to breach the main ramp doorway.' It was not a question.

'Yes, master.'

'Understood. Rest, Septimus.'

'I can't see,' the slave repeated. His voice was still strong, but his head lolled with the onset of both shock and the effects of the syringe's contents hitting his organs. 'They took my eyes.'

'They took one of them. The other is damaged, but not lost.' Talos was searching the corpses, each one felled by las-rounds or vicious hacks of Septimus's feral world cleaver. The two serfs had fought like tigers before being overwhelmed – the evidence of their defiance was all around, mutilated and silent in death.

'If I can't see,' Septimus rested his head against the rest of his throne, 'I can't fly us back to the *Covenant*.'

'That is not important at the moment. Do you know what happened to First Claw?'

The slave swallowed, the sound thick and wet. 'Back in orbit. A Black Legion Thunderhawk.'

Talos breathed out through clenched teeth. An unsubtle trap that, nevertheless, they had all walked right into.

'Be silent,' he said to Septimus. 'Do not move.'

'Are you going for her?'

'I said to be silent.'

'Hunt well, master.'

'Always.'

Talos, Astartes of First Claw, 10th Company, VIII Legion, stalked towards the cockpit doors. He gripped his stolen power blade in one hand, and with the other he replaced his helmet, blanketing his sight in the murder-red of his targeting vision. Over his shoulder, the inhuman warrior spoke four words to his wounded slave, the promise emerging from the skull helm as a mechanical snarl.

'Back in a minute.'

IT HAD BEEN a long time since the hunter had moved with such purpose.

Too long, he realised. He had lost grip of his own purity, ignored the simple power brought about from being true to one's nature.

He found the instincts flared into life as soon as his twin hearts started beating faster. He ran, the boots of his ceramite second skin pounding on the metal decking. The sound was a welcome warning, a tribal war drum, the threatening heartbeat of an enraged god. The hunter would take no pains to mask his approach. Let the enemy know that death was coming for them.

He moved through the prison complex, corridor by corridor, not trusting the lift to deliver him, placing his faith in the strength of his own renewed vigour. It dawned on him as he sprinted that in the hour since his poisoning and the awakening from his magus-induced vision, a thick sluggishness had settled into his bones. This weakness faded now, purged in the flow of honest adrenaline.

Eurydice. Curse them for taking her, and curse the Black Legion for engineering this petty little trap. She was to be the *Covenant*'s Navigator. Talos would stand for nothing else, not after seeing so clearly in his vision how she would be discovered on the surface of Nostramo's remnants.

Lower and lower into the complex, he ran with unrestrained pleasure at the battle stimulants tingling through his blood. His war-plate's machine-spirit wanted this hunt. Its dim sentience was alive and sharing his joy. They both needed this.

In the corner of his visor, a rune burned its way into his sight. The Nostraman numeral 8. It pulsed with a heartbeat of its own, listing life signs and distance from his position in urgent red lettering. The surgery that blocked Eurydice's warp eye with a small iron plate was not the only modification the Legion's servitors had made to the Navigator. Implanted in her throat was a locator beacon, ticking its position to any Night Lords tuned to its frequency. A standard implantation for the slaves of the VIII Legion.

It took exactly six minutes and thirty-one seconds to reach the basement generatorium chambers. Almost seven minutes of running through stilled, lifeless corridors, past empty cells, and an equal number of hallways still dense with the sweating mortal flesh of convicts waiting to be loaded into slave ships. Some of them had reached out to him, mistaking him for one of their Black Legion saviours. The hunter answered their worship with swings of his blade as he ran, not allowing himself to slow down even to end their irritating blasphemies. Angry, scared cries followed in his wake each time the sword sang. These grunts and bestial shouts of animals herded for the slaughter, panicked by a larger predator, almost brought a grin to his lips. The hunter tried not smile, though their very existences amused him.

So weak. So scared.

Six minutes and thirty-one seconds after he had left the Thunderhawk on the landing platform, Talos reached the basement. Able to survive the drop, he'd fallen the final three floors by tearing open a sealed elevator chute door and leaping into the darkness. He landed with an echoing thud that rang out throughout the prelim chambers of the generatorium floors.

Wasting no time, Talos resumed his sprint, running headlong through the empty control room. Great windows took up one wall, facing out into a vast domed cavern, housing the grinding, clanking generators powering the sprawling prison complex above. Each of the twenty generators stood five storeys tall – edifices of hammering pistons, whirring cogs and thrumming power cell units wedged into their sides like the scales of some caged reptilian beast. Between this miniature city, walkways and gangways were illuminated by the flashing red of emergency lighting.

His vision wavered, rippling lines of distortion dancing across his lens displays. Runes warped and cancelled. Electrical distortion. A great deal of it. It was killing his helm's input receptors.

So much power. Talos scanned the control room, large enough for a staff of thirty or more, though devoid now of all life. *Void shields?* This much power couldn't be purely for lighting the multi-towered spire above. These generators must also power the prison's void shields, preventing orbital bombardment or meteor strike.

Defending a fortress full of criminals from death, though they were slated for execution anyway? *Ah, the wasteful ignorance of the Imperium of Man.*

Anathema boomed out a volley of bolt shells that hammered in a wide spread across the control consoles before him.

His vision cleared. Darkness fell. Silence, at last, followed.

It was not an immediate process. At first the darkness was broken by the crackling death rattles of the destroyed consoles, lighting the blackness like bolts of lightning. When the ruined control consoles spat their last, his vision stabilised just as darkness fell. True, absolute darkness, imaginable only by those who lived life without ever seeing the sun.

Next came the silence. The twenty generator towers took almost a minute to die. Great hulks, strangled of attention and starved of willpower without the guiding signal of the control consoles. Within the observation room, failsafe systems roared into life with flashing red sirens. Talos emptied the rest of his magazine into the failsafe station, turning his head from the resulting explosion.

Once more, there was darkness. The generator towers rattled and clanked and whined down into stillness over the course of another forty-six seconds, and then, blessedly, there was silence over the self-contained generatorium city.

Talos crashed through the control room windows, falling twenty metres, landing smoothly on the ground floor's decking with a tremendous bang of ceramite on iron. He looked into the darkness, listened to the silence, and breathed a single word.

'Preysight.'

* * *

Indriga wasn't spooked.

He was, however, losing his temper. The others were getting twitchy with the lights going out and the generator towers dying. The girl wasn't struggling anymore, but that was hardly any reassurance. She'd already bitten and clawed chunks out of Edsan and Mirrick, and Indriga had a feeling lurking at the back of his mind that the dangerous bitch was just waiting for the right moment to lash out again.

Between two powering-down towers, the four men froze in the darkness. The crash of destroyed glass had reached them even over the towers' death whines. Handheld lampsticks speared into life as Indriga and Edsan turned on the shotgun-mounted lights they'd taken from slain prison guards.

The girl moaned, coughing loud enough to make Indriga jump.

'Shut her up,' he whispered. 'And keep your damn light on the ground.'

Edsan obeyed, lowering his stolen gun so the beam was no longer lancing off into the avenues between the towers. 'You just messed your pants, Indri. I saw you jump like you were shot.' It wasn't mockery in Edsan's voice. It was something not far from panic.

'I ain't spooked,' Indriga whispered back. 'Just lower your Throne-damned voice.'

Edsan didn't reply at first. Indriga sure looked spooked, and that meant bad things. Indri was a hive ganger like most of them, but his skin was black with tats listing his kill counts and blasphemous beliefs. You didn't get that big without being vat-grown or significantly cut up and put back together by some augmetic-hungry doc, that's for sure.

When his nerves got the better of him, he said 'Indri. There's four of us, right? That's good, yeah?'

'Yeah.'

Edsan had the distinct feeling Indriga wasn't listening to him at all. That was nothing new – Indriga was big news in R Sector, he'd never had time for small-time players like Edsan – but this time, it wasn't like Indriga was brushing him off out of disrespect. This time, Indri just looked like he could smell fire around the corner and was thinking about making a run for it.

It was weird. Looking at him now, he was like one of the beefy attack dogs Edsan's boss used to use in pit fights. Gene-changed to be hulks of slab-like muscle and wide jaws, and before a dog fight they'd be tense and shivering, staring off at stuff only they could see. They were glanding stimms, sure, but it was still weird to see an animal so... focused. Indriga looked like that now. Shivering but rigid, staring at... Well, that was the problem. Like those ugly dog-things, he was staring at the Emperor only knew what.

'You see something?' Edsan whispered.

'No. Can hear it, though.'

And then, just like that, Edsan heard it, too. Maybe the girl did too, because she moaned again, earning a slap from Mirrick, who was still bleeding, still back there with her. A new noise blended with the fading howl of the generators. Something rhythmic, like the metal *thunk-thunk-thunk* of... of... of something. Edsan didn't even know what it sounded like. He'd never heard it before. His slippery mind fixed on the only comparison it could hold on to in his rising panic. *Like the footsteps of a giant.* When he would learn the truth of the matter less than a minute later, he'd be horrified to see how accurate he'd been.

Indriga raised his shotgun. 'Someone's coming.'

'For her?' Edsan swallowed. Indriga's slow caution was shredding his nerves. This was bad. Maybe they could leave the girl and get out of here. 'Indri... Are they coming for her?'

Eurydice spoke for the first time since she'd been taken. Through swollen lips, she sneered the words, 'No. He's coming for you.'

OF THE EMPEROR'S sons, one had always stood apart from his brothers.

Through a twist of fate that would herald the human race's eventual unmaking, the twenty progeny of the Emperor were stolen from their father. As vat-grown infants – who had been painstakingly flesh-forged as biological masterpieces in the labyrinthine gene-labs beneath the surface of Terra – they were engineered to be all that was idyllic and noble in the human form. Avatars, as it were, of mankind's perfection.

Their exaltations and degenerations are chronicled in numerous tomes of mythology and factual record, variously forgotten by most mortals of the Imperium in the ten thousand year span, sequestered by the Inquisition, or so distorted by the passage of time as to barely resemble the truth.

Though all twenty sons would one day be reunited with their sire as the Emperor reached out to conquer the stars in His Great Crusade, nineteen of these sons were raised, for better or worse, by surrogate mentors. Their incubation pods plunged from the skies of twenty worlds, and twenty planets played home and paid homage to godlike beings that would rise to shape the destiny of each world as they grew to adulthood.

On Chemos, a world of manufactories and pollution so thick it blanketed the sky in a drape of vile orange mist, the primarch Fulgrim rose through the ranks of drone workers and executives to become the lord of the fortress-factories, heralding in a new age of resource and prosperity for his people.

On Caliban, the austere primarch known as the Lion grew to lead a glorious crusade of knightly orders against the tainted beasts of his home world's forests. On Fenris, legends have the Primarch Leman Russ first raised by the vicious wolves of that icy world, then reaching his majority to lead the barbarous warrior clans as their greatest high king.

On a nameless world, its title long-lost to the mists of time, the Primarch Angron reached adulthood as a pit slave, shackled by the lords of his apparently civilised planet, forever twisted by the experiences of his bloodthirsty maturation.

For better or worse, fate had each Imperial son raised by others, shaped by instructors, guides, mentors, friends and enemies. Only one primarch grew up alone, hidden from the eyes of humanity, guided by no hand and taught by no elder.

He would come, in time, to be known by the name his father had chosen for him: Konrad Curze. To the people of Nostramo, the world forever wrapped in nightfall's embrace, he was – at least at first – altogether less human. Never did the primarch bear a human name there.

The child survived by living feral in the shadows of humanity's towers. He scavenged in the alleys and streets of Nostramo Quintus, the planetary capital, a sprawling metropolis that covered a sizeable portion of the northern hemisphere. Crime here, as it was across all Nostramo, was as rife as life itself. With no moral compass beyond the evidence of his own eyes, the young primarch began the work that would shape his existence.

The seed of his endeavour was humble enough at first, at least by the standards of Imperial justice. Street-level criminals; the murderers, the rapists, the thugs, gangers and muggers that populated the dark avenues of Nostramo Quintus soon began to whisper a name that flowed from their lips with fearful tremors.

The Night Haunter.

He would kill them. Barely into his teens, the boy would witness an act of violence or crime, and he would leap from the shadows, feral and enraged, butchering those who preyed upon their fellow humans. This was how the nascent core of his humanity sought to enforce order upon his surroundings.

Fear, primal and true, was something the young god understood all too well. He saw its uses and applications, and he saw how those in the thrall of terror were so much more pliant and obedient. In those black streets, he learned the lesson that would shape his Legion. Humanity did not need kindness, indulgence or trust in order to progress. People did not comply with law and live lives of order out of altruism or shared ideology.

They obeyed society's tenets because they were afraid. To break the law invited justice. Within justice was *punishment.*

He became that punishment. He became the threat of justice. Known criminals were left for all to see come the weak dawn: crucified and disembowelled, chained to the walls of public building and the ornate doors of the wealthiest gang leaders and syndicate bosses. Always, he would leave their faces untouched, twisted with the silent and fixed scream of an agonising death, for he knew the dead gazes of the slain triggered a deeper empathy and realisation within the hearts of those who met their glazed stares.

Years passed, and many more died. Soon enough, the Night Haunter was reaching his pale, grasping hands into the higher tiers of society, beating, strangling and slaughtering the ringleaders, the organisers, the officials at the core of the city's corruption. The fear that so thickly saturated the streets soon choked the halls of the wealthy and powerful.

The rule of law reigned. Victory and compliance through the threat of punishment. *Order through fear.*

It is said in the records of the VIII Legion that when the Emperor came to Nostramo, he spoke these words to his long-lost son:

'Konrad Curze, be at peace, for I have arrived and intend to take you home.'

The primarch's reply is also recorded. *'That is not my name, Father. I am Night Haunter.'*

Perhaps the sons of Konrad Curze, had their sire been raised upon another world and learned different lessons, would have been more typical Astartes, and the VIII Legion a far cry from the driven creatures they were at the edge of the forty-first millennium. But the sons of the Night Haunter learned every lesson their gene-father did, carrying the same truths with them down the centuries.

'Soul Hunter,' the primarch had once said to Talos.

'My lord?' he had answered, unable as ever to meet his father's direct gaze. He concentrated on the Night Haunter's midnight war-plate, decorated by lightning bolts painted by the finest tech-artisans of Mars, and bearing the skulls of so many fallen foes on chains like hanging fruit.

'Soon, Soul Hunter.'

The melancholic tone of his lord's voice was not new. The whispered reverence was. Surprise made Talos raise his eyes to his father's face, gaunt and nearly lipless, the pale, dull grey of sunrise on a dead world.

'Lord?'

'Soon. We run from the hounds my father set at our heels, and vindication must be bought with blood.'

'Vindication is always bought with blood, lord.'

'This time, the blood-price will be mine to pay. And willingly, my son. Death is nothing compared to vindication. Die with the truth on your lips, and your life's echo will never fade.'

His father spoke on, but Talos heard none of it. The words were like a blade of cold fire in his gut.

'You will die,' he breathed. 'I knew this would come, my lord.'

'Because you have seen it,' the primarch grinned. As always, the smile was without any mirth. The Night Haunter had never, to Talos's knowledge, displayed any human emotion approaching genuine humour. He was amused by nothing. He enjoyed nothing. Even the bloodiest moments of war set his features in a grim mask of concentration and infrequent disgust. Battle-lust seemed beyond him, or he had transcended its feverish joys.

This was the result of sacrificing one's humanity for the good of the Imperium's people. And he would be repaid for his great sacrifice – repaid by the Emperor's assassins seeking his lifeblood.

'Yes, lord,' Talos replied, his mouth drying, his deep voice like a child's compared to the throaty rumble of his father's. 'I have seen it. How did you know?'

'I hear your dreams,' the primarch replied. 'We share a curse, you and I. The curse of foreknowledge. You are like me, Soul Hunter.'

It didn't feel like an honour. Despite feeling no greater kinship with the primarch than in that moment, there was no honour, just a sense of vulnerability that threatened to eclipse even his awe at standing in the shadow of his godlike gene-sire. They would share words only once more before the Night Haunter greeted his death, and without it being spoken, Talos knew this, too.

What brought these thoughts flooding back to his mind now? The rush of instinct, the thrill of the hunt? Galvanised, Talos broke into a run. Eurydice's life rune pulsed on his retinas like the unstable ticking of a broken engine. She was wounded, that much was clear. Her implantation was crude and functional, revealing little of specifics. He heard Eurydice's muffled breathing, the heightened heartbeats of her captors, and exaggerated his footfalls so they would know he approached.

Then, when he judged the moment right, when he could hear them whispering their fears to one another, the hunter ghosted into the shadows, turning his tread soft, standing in wait.

One of the mortals walked past the Night Lord's hiding place between two man-sized capacitor cylinders, his skin reeking of grime and terror-sweat. Talos resisted the urge to lick his lips.

'Greetings,' he said in a low, smiling voice.

The shotgun bucked and blasted noise into the silence. The convict had fired his weapon in panic even before he turned. He had less than a heartbeat of looking into the blackness, seeing a pair of arched red eyes glaring, before Talos was on him.

His death was regrettably quick, and Talos mourned the chance to make it last. The corpse, its neck snapped, fell to the metal decking with a crumpling thud. The Night Lord was already gone.

'Edsan?' someone called. 'Edsan?'

'He's dead,' said a voice behind him. Mirrick managed a breathless, wordless grunt of surprise before his head left his shoulders. Talos ignored the tumbling body, but caught the head before it fell.

Gripping it by its lank, greasy hair, he moved on through the darkness. In his gauntleted fist, the head still twitched with facial tics for several moments.

The third to die was Sheevern.

Sheevern had remained with the woman, standing over her with a power maul in his hands. Like most of the prisoners, he'd acquired the weapon from an enforcer guard in the riot. Unlike most of the prisoners, he was innocent of the crimes he'd been incarcerated for.

Sheevern was no heretic. He was serving his sentence for ties to a deviant ruling cult from a world that had forsworn the Dictate Imperialis, and broken from Imperial rule. As a politician in the regime, he had been charged with heresy when the Imperium of Man came to take the world back from the grasp of the tainted rulers, despite the fact that he'd argued against secession from the Throne. He found it bitterly ironic to be serving a life sentence for heresy, when he'd spent a good twenty years in office, secretly indulging his true lusts and urges without any of his actions coming to the light. The blood of five women and two young men was on his hands. Sheevern regretted nothing. He didn't believe he had anything to regret.

'Indriga?' he called out. No answer. By his feet, the woman whisper-laughed again. He thudded a boot into her side, feeling something – a rib or two, maybe – snap under his kick. 'Shut the hell up.'

His ears itched. A buzzing, like a swarm of insects, was irritating his senses. 'What the hell is that sound?' he muttered, clutching the maul tighter in his thin-fingered hands.

It was the thrum of live mark IV Astartes war-plate. Talos emerged from the darkness ahead of him, illuminated only by the dim glow of Sheevern's personal lamp pack.

'Catch,' the Night Lord said. Despite the growl of his helm's vox speakers, he sounded almost amiable.

On instinct, Sheevern caught what was thrown. He cradled it one-handed for a moment before dropping it with a gasp. His hand and arm were warm with blood. Mirrick's head banged on the gantry floor.

'Wait,' Sheevern begged the resolving shape. 'I didn't touch her!' he lied. Eurydice's bare foot hit the back of his knee as she lashed out in a furious kick.

Sheevern stumbled, righting himself just in time to meet the Night Lord's bolter hitting his face. The muzzle of the oversized weapon hammered into his panting mouth, making shards of his teeth, the cold metal forcing its way to the back of his throat. He barely had time to squeal a muffled protest before the bolter bucked and sheared the chubby former politician's head clean off.

Talos backhanded the headless body aside and stared down at Eurydice. She was battered and bruised, her clothing torn, one eye swollen shut. She still looked a lot better than Septimus had, though. Nothing here wouldn't heal, at least in regards to the physical damage she'd sustained.

'We are leaving,' said Talos.

'There's one more,' she said faintly through slug-fat lips. 'The big one.'

'We are still leaving,' he said, reaching down for her.

With the Navigator over his shoulder and his bolter clutched in his free hand, Talos made his way back through the generatorium chamber.

'THIS IS INDRIGA,' the convict spoke into a hand vox. He crouched in the darkness under the foundation support girders of a silent generator tower, his words emerging as a sneering whisper. He wasn't made to hide. It took all of his willpower not to get out there and brain the armoured monster that was making its escape.

'Speak,' replied a sibilant male voice.

'Lord Ruven,' the prisoner said, 'he came for the witch.'

'This leads me to wonder, however, why you are still alive.'

The words were stuck in Indriga's throat for several seconds. 'I hid, lord.'

'Has he gone?'

'He's leaving now.' A pause. 'He took the witch.'

'What do you mean he *took* her? Why would he take a corpse?'

Indriga swallowed, and the sound travelled down the vox. Ruven growled a sigh.

'We brought her with us,' Indriga said. 'We wanted to–'

'Enough. Your mortal urges are meaningless to me. You failed to comply with the most basic orders, Indriga. And now, you will die for it.'

'Lord…'

'I would start running, if I were you.'

Indriga lowered the hand vox, his lip curling in disgust as he heard the armoured killer's footsteps drawing near again. Evidently, he was coming back to finish the job.

Must've heard me whispering…

Indriga needed to see. He clicked the shotgun's underslung lamp active, and leapt from his hiding place with the beam of light like a lance before him.

The towering armoured form swivelled in the half-dark, no doubt protecting the witch he was carrying. Indriga's shotgun barked once, twice, a third time and a fourth, each impact blasting a hail of shot that cracked and clattered against the ceramite war-plate.

Talos turned in the second Indriga's shotgun clicked dry. Eurydice, over his left shoulder, had been shielded from harm when he'd spun to avoid the gunfire. The massive bolter fired once, aimed low, and the bolt pounded into Indriga's stomach. It detonated a moment later, leaving the convict in pieces across the walkway. The largest piece, consisting of Indriga's chest, arms and howling face, remained alive for twelve agonising seconds. Talos ignored its shrieks, reaching for the hand vox the dying prisoner had dropped.

'Prophet,' said the voice on the other end of the channel.

'Ruven,' Talos said softly, 'my brother. It has been a while, brother. I should have recognised your unsubtle handiwork when your four "gods" babbled without sense for so long.'

'Ruven of the Black Legion now, and Eyes of the Warmaster. I assure you, Talos, you do not know of what you speak.'

'The Exalted says the same. I am weary of the protests of the corrupt and the ruined. The Warmaster has betrayed the other Legions before, but this is crude and brazen, even for him.'

'So you say, brother. You have no proof beyond a cracked breastplate that he was even involved. And who would care? The Exalted? He is Abaddon's creature, and always has been. One squad of the Night Lords walking into an obvious trap is no concern for the coming crusade.'

At Talos's feet, Indriga breathed his last. The silence was unwelcome, for the idiot's howls had been curiously pleasant.

'Your thuggish little cultist is dead,' Talos said as he moved away.

'I will hardly be weeping over that. Tell me, why was it so easy to refuse the Four Powers? Did they offer nothing that tempted you? Even for a moment?'

'The purpose of luring me to the planet's surface escapes me, brother,' Talos said, looking down at the human wreckage. 'You must have known I would never leave the Legion.'

'The VIII Legion is *weak*. The Exalted seeks to discard you; you have little love for your brothers; and above all – Abaddon himself takes an interest in you. Does that mean nothing to you? How can this be so?'

Talos was already moving, cradling Eurydice as he walked.

'I am going to kill you when next I see you, Ruven.'

The Night Lord had foreseen the Navigator's importance, and almost lost her only days later. This foolish venture had also almost cost him Septimus. Might yet still cost him Septimus, if he didn't survive the restorative surgeries.

Carelessness. Carelessness beyond reckoning.

'Mark my words, Ruven. Whether you are the Despoiler's pet or not, I will cut you down.'

'Why did you refuse the Powers? Answer me, Talos.'

'Because I am my father's son.' Talos cast the hand vox aside and kept walking.

'It was good to speak with you again, my brother. I missed your simple sincerity and literal nature. Talos? Talos?'

Talos felt Eurydice stir as he ascended the stairs to the next level.

'Thank you,' she said softly.

He had no answer to that. The words were too unfamiliar.

PART TWO

THE OLD WAR

'There will come a time when our Legion is shattered across the stars.
When the powers we spurn become allies to which many turn.

The paths of your future are closed to me,
And they are yours to walk alone.
But I know this.
The war that fires our blood now will still rage in ten thousand years.
Bleed the Imperium. Tear it down, tear it apart. Show no mercy.

But watch yourselves. There is no traitors' unity in the Old War.
Trust your Legion brothers.
And trust no one else.'

– The Primarch Konrad Curze.

XI

THREE WEEKS LATER

THE SLAVE LISTENED at the door.

From within, he heard sounds of movement, dully penetrating the metal. With a hand he was still not used to using, he pressed the entrance key, triggering a toneless chime within the room. Footsteps came closer, and the door opened on hissing gears, sliding to the left. In the doorway stood another slave.

'Septimus,' said the room's occupant with a smile.

'Octavia,' he replied. 'It's time.'

'I'm ready.'

The two Legion serfs walked down the darkened halls of the *Covenant of Blood*'s mortal decks, where the illumination strips along the ceilings were forever tuned to twilight. It was enough to see by, even for those unused to a sunless life, but it would hardly pass for twilight on most worlds.

Octavia still found herself glancing at him every few moments when they were together. The surgeries were still fresh, his skin still adapting, and where his augmetics met flesh, the telltale redness of fading inflammation was still in evidence. His left eye, the one he'd lost to the convicts that stormed the Thunderhawk, was now a violet lens set in a bronze mounting that reached out to cover his temple and cheekbone.

Octavia, in her life as the daughter of a Navigator House, had seen a great many augmetic enhancements in the courts of Terra, not least of all her own father's. By general standards, Septimus's bionic reconstruction was relatively subtle. It was certainly above the poorest-grade cybernetic 'slice and graft' surgeries available to even many wealthy Imperial citizens.

Still, she could tell none of that was any comfort to him. She watched him hit the door release with his gloved hand – the hand he had lost along with his eye. She had yet to see the augmetic hand and forearm he now bore, but she heard the rough mechanics of its servos buzzing and clicking as he moved. Upon his throat and chest, the outward bruises had mostly vanished, but the memory of the violence done to him was still clear in the way he moved. Although he was healing and the three weeks had shown huge improvement, he was still stiff and obviously sore – walking like an old man in the winter.

They walked together through the lower mortals' decks of the *Covenant*. Octavia doubted she would ever get used to the... the community down here. Unlike the upper decks, which housed valued serfs and officers, the non-essential mortal crew inhabited these darkened decks, occupying civilian quarters much as on any other military vessel, but they were twisted and shaped by their allegiance to the Night Lords. They reminded her of vermin, living down here in the darkness.

In the untraceable distance, down unknown numbers of winding corridors, someone screamed. Octavia flinched at the cry. Septimus did not.

As the two serfs moved down the wide steel corridor, a cloaked figure, hunched over almost onto all fours, scrambled across their path from one adjacent passage to another. Octavia didn't even want to know who or what it was. Cold water dripped in an irregular rhythm from a tear in the metal overhead. A punctured coolant feed somewhere, a hole in the vessel's veins, slowly leaking icy water through a rusty wound. It was hardly an uncommon sight. Maintenance servitors never made it to this part of the ship.

'Why did we have to go this way?' she asked quietly.

'Because I have business here.'

'Why are these people even tolerated? Do the Astartes hunt them for sport?'

'Sometimes,' he admitted.

'Is that a joke?' She knew it wasn't, and wasn't even sure why she voiced the words.

He smiled, and she almost froze in her tracks. It was the first smile she'd seen from him in almost a month. 'They have their uses, you know. Future artificers. Potential servitors. Failed officers that may be useful one night in a position of lesser responsibility.'

She nodded as they approached what looked like a market stall made of scrap metal, raggedly built into the side of the corridor.

'You need power cells?' the sore-ridden old man at the stall asked. 'Cells for lamp packs. Fresh-charged in a fire. Good for another month, at least.' Octavia looked at his withered, gaunt face, at the cataracts milking over his eyes.

'No. No, thank you.'

She assumed they didn't need money in the bowels of the *Covenant*, but she couldn't imagine how anyone acquired anything new for barter, either. She also had no idea why they'd stopped here. She gave Septimus a look. He ignored it, speaking to the elder in the worn serf tunic.

'Jeremiah,' he said in Gothic.

'Septimus?' The elder offered a shallow bow, respect evident in his bearing. 'I'd heard about your misfortune. May I?'

Septimus flinched at the question. 'Yes, if you wish.'

He leaned closer, and the old man's trembling hands rose to meet the serf's face, shivering fingertips lightly stroking across the healed skin, the bruises that remained, and the new augmetics.

'This feels expensive.' The man's smile was missing several teeth. 'Good to see the masters still bless you.' He withdrew his hands.

'Apparently they do. Jeremiah, this is Octavia,' Septimus gestured to her with his ungloved hand.

'My lady.' The elder offered the same bow.

Lacking anything else to say, she instinctively forced a smile and said, 'Hello.'

'May I?'

Octavia tensed just as Septimus had before. She could count on one hand the number of times another person had touched her face.

'You... probably shouldn't,' she said softly.

'I shouldn't? Hmm. You sound like a beauty. Is she, Septimus?'

Septimus didn't answer the question. 'She's a Navigator,' he cut in. Jeremiah's reaching hands snapped back, fingers delicately curled in indecision.

'Oh. Well, that was unexpected. What brings you here?' the old man asked Septimus. 'You don't need to scavenge like we do, so I'm guessing it's not a need for my fine wares, eh?'

'Not exactly. While I was wounded,' said Septimus, 'the void-born must have had her birthday.'

'That she did,' Jeremiah nodded, absently rearranging the fire-blackened power cells, stringed trinkets and handheld machine tools on his scrap metal stall. 'Ten years old now. Who'd have guessed, eh?'

Septimus gently scratched. His gloved fingertips stroked the irritated seam where his bronze augmetic plating met his temple.

'I have a gift for her,' he said. 'Would you give her this, from me?' The artificer reached into his belt pouch and withdrew a silver coin. Octavia couldn't make out the detail stamped upon its face – Septimus's gloved fingers obscured the majority of it – but it looked like a tower of some kind. The old man stood motionless for several moments, feeling the cold, smooth disc in his palm.

'Septimus...' he said, his voice lower than before. He was edging on whispers now. 'Are you sure?'

'I'm sure. Give her my best wishes, along with the seal.'

'I will.' The elder closed his fingers around the coin. Octavia could tell the gesture was reverent and possessive, but there was a sick desperation in there, as well. It reminded her of the way a dying spider's legs curled close to its body. 'I've never held one before,' he said. After a pause, he added 'Don't look at me like that; I won't keep it.'

'I know,' said Septimus.

'May you continue to be blessed, Septimus. And you, Octavia.'

They said their goodbyes to the trader and moved on. Once they were around a few corners and safely out of earshot, Octavia cleared her throat.

'Well?' she asked. Her own fate was forgotten in the wake of the enigmatic gift-giving she'd just witnessed.

'Well, what?'

'Are you going to tell me what that was about?'

'Time flows in an uneven river within the void. You're a Navigator – you know that more than most.'

Of course she knew. Her look told him to get on with it, and she noticed his false eye whirring and focusing as its socket mechanics tried to mimic the raised eyebrow on the undamaged side of his face.

'There is a soul on this ship, more important than most. We call her the void-born.'

'Is she human?'

'Yes. That's why she's important. The Great Heresy was thousands of years ago. But to the *Covenant,* it has been less than a century. Less than a century since this strike cruiser hung in the heavens of Terra, as part of the greatest fleet ever amassed – the horde of the First Warmaster, Horus the Chosen.'

Octavia felt her spine tingle at the words. She was still new to this, new to the *Covenant,* new to her own developing treason against the Golden Throne. She could barely even frame her own evolving place on this ship in words that confessed to her treachery. To hear of this very vessel that harboured her being part of the Horus Heresy's final moments, the assault on Terra, and only scant decades ago by the ship's internal chronometers... She shivered again. The blasphemy made her skin crawl, but there was a delicious edge to the sensation. She was living in the echo of mythology. She stood with the shadows of a greater age, and even being near the Astartes was invigorating. They felt more than any souls she had ever met – their rage burned hotter, their bitterness was colder, their hatred ran deeper...

It was the same within the metal threaded bones of the *Covenant.* Until Septimus had spoken the words, she'd never been able to form the feeling into something comprehensible. But she *felt* the ship. She felt its wounded pride in the rumble of its engines, like an eternal growl. Now she understood why. The Heresy was not mythology to the VIII Legion, not some sequestered insurrection that was more legend than history. It was a memory. A recent memory, seared into their thoughts, just as their ship bore weapon-fire burns that still scarred the skin of its hull. The vessel itself was marked from the war it lost, and its crew shared the grim recollection, their lives stained with the knowledge of failure.

A mere handful of decades ago, this vessel had rained its fury upon the surface of Terra. A mere handful of decades ago, the Astartes on board had walked the soil of Imperial Earth, screaming orders to each other as they slaughtered the loyal defenders of the Throne, their bolters barking in the shadows cast by the towers of the God-Emperor's vast palace.

Neither fable nor ancient parable to these Astartes. Recent memory, twisted by time's loose grip in the warp.

'You look light-headed,' said Septimus.

She had slowed down without realising, and met his unmatching eyes now with a weak smile.

He continued. 'It's easier to understand when you realise where the *Covenant* makes its haven.'

'The Eye of Terror,' she nodded slowly.

'Exactly. A wound in our reality. The warp reigns there.'

Even as a Navigator, even as one of the rare few with the genetic deviance allowing them to see into the Sea of Souls and know the warp more intimately than any other mortal, it was a struggle for Octavia to cling to this shift in her perceptions. Stories forever abounded of vessels lost in the warp for years or decades, and arriving weeks ahead or behind the intended translation date was an unbreakable, unchangeable part of flight through the immaterium. When ships sailed through the second reality, they surrendered themselves to the realm's unnatural laws.

Even so. This was a span of time she could barely comprehend. The differential made her mind ache.

'I understand,' she said. 'But what has this got to do with your gift?'

'The void-born is unique,' Septimus replied. 'In the decades the *Covenant* has been active since the Great Betrayal, she is the only soul to be born on board.' He saw the questioning look in her eyes, and cut her off. 'You have to understand,' he clarified, 'even at full crew complement, this was never a vessel that ran with decks full of conscripted slaves. The crew was always small and elite. It is an Astartes vessel. With the decline over the years... Well. She is the first. That's all that matters.'

'What was the gift?'

'A seal. You'll receive one yourself after your surgery tonight. Do not lose it. Do not give it away. It is the only thing that will keep you safe on these decks.'

She smiled at this habit of his. Every crew member of the *Covenant* said 'tonight', never 'today'.

'If it's so important, why did you give it to her?'

'I gave it to her *because* it's so important. Each seal is inscribed with the name of one of the Astartes on board. The rarest of them show no names, and ensure the bearer is protected by the entire Legion. In ancient nights, it was tradition for a personal serf to attend to each warrior. They carried a seal marked with their master's name, signifying their allegiance and dissuading other Astartes from entertaining themselves by harming such a valued slave. The coins mean little now the old traditions are remembered by so few. But they are still acknowledged by some. My master is among them.'

'You wish her to be protected?'

'Most of the Astartes do not even know she exists, and would not care if they did. Their attention is forever elsewhere. But she is a talisman to we "mere mortals" of the *Covenant*.' He smiled again. 'She's a lucky charm, if you will. With my seal, she is under the guardianship of Talos. Any who meet her will know this. Any who threaten her will die by his hands.'

She considered his generosity, not liking where her thoughts led. 'And what about you? Without that seal...'

'Priorities.'

'What?'

'Priorities, Octavia. Focus on your future, not mine.' He nodded to the doors ahead, dark and sealed at the end of the corridor. 'We're here.'

'Will you be waiting?' she asked him. 'When this is over?'

'No. I am retrieving First Claw from the surface within the hour.' He hesitated. 'I'm sorry. If I could...'

'Fair enough.' She touched the metal band implanted on her forehead. Strange, the things one could get used to. With a smile, she said, 'I'll see you soon.'

Septimus nodded and the Navigator entered the apothecarium. As the doors opened, the servitor surgeons powered up from their sterile silence. Septimus watched them until the doors closed again with a grinding clank. They were a familiar sight for him, having been in their care for weeks himself.

He checked his wrist chron once Octavia was out of sight, and made his patient way back through the ship. The war on the surface of Crythe once again demanded his presence.

OCTAVIA EMERGED TWO hours later. The band of restrictive metal was gone from her forehead. She wore a headband of black silk, given to her by Septimus for this purpose, to use when the time was right. It neatly covered her third eye.

In her pocket was a silver Legion medallion, handed to her by a nameless Astartes who presided over her surgery. He hadn't said a word the whole time.

She turned it over in her hands, seeing the same tower symbol minted into the metal. A hive spire. Somewhere on Nostramo, most likely. On the other side, the impression of a face, lost to time's wear, with the faint inscription *'Ave Dominus Nox'*.

This she could read, for it was High Gothic, not Nostraman. *Hail the Lord of the Night.* The ruined face, smoothed by age, must be their father – the Night Haunter. She looked at the featureless visage for a long moment, then pocketed the coin.

Staring into the darkness, she suppressed a shiver of fear. This was the first time she'd been out of her quarters without an escort. The seal in her jacket pocket was cold comfort in the bowels of the *Covenant*. What guarantee did she have that anyone down here would care if she carried the coin?

Her hand vox crackled, and she knew who it would be. Only two people ever voxed her, and Septimus was planetside.

'Hello, Etrigius,' she said.

'Are you coming for another lesson tonight?'

She reached up to touch the silk bandana, and a wicked little smile creased her lips.

'Yes, Navigator,' she said.

'I will send servitors at once,' he replied.

She thumbed the coin in her pocket, and stared into the darkened corridor ahead.

'No need,' she said, and started moving, her heart beating in time to her hurried footsteps. Eyes – unseen by Octavia but not unnoticed by her – watched as she walked the blackened halls of the tainted ship.

LONG BEFORE HE had earned the honour of wearing the war-plate of the VIII Astartes Legion, Talos had ghosted through the streets of his birth hive on his home world. It was a life lived in the darkness, a life of avoiding stronger predators and carefully choosing weaker prey.

He knew he'd come late to the Legion, and the fact pained him. Nostramo was already forgetting the lessons learned under the claws of the Night Haunter. Scant years after the great Konrad Curze had ascended into the heavens to wage war with his Imperial father, the world he left behind began its inexorable backslide into familiar degeneracy.

Street gangs carved out territories in the habitation and industrial sectors; little princelings marking their claimed turn by runes painted on walls and – in echo of the Haunter himself – the remains of enemies prominently displayed where their kin and brethren would take heed.

Talos had known Xarl even then. They had grown up together, sons of mothers widowed in the underworld wars that broke out once the shadow of the Haunter was a fear of the past. Before their tenth birthdays, both boys were accomplished thieves, inducted into the same gang claiming their hab sector as its domain.

By the time the boys were thirteen, both were killers. Xarl had killed two kids from a rival gang, peppering their bodies from an ambush with his heavy-calibre autopistol. He'd needed both hands to hold that gun, and the sound it made when it fired... A deafening boom that split the silence.

Talos had been there when Xarl made his first kills, but had shed no blood himself that night. His own first murder had been the year before, when a storekeeper had sought to beat them for stealing food. Talos had reacted before his conscious mind even gripped the situation – a brutal, primal flash of instinct that saw the storekeeper coughing and gasping on the floor, Talos's knife buried to the hilt in his heart.

Even now, even over a hundred years later for Talos, while the galaxy had turned ten thousand years since that old man had last drawn breath, he still remembered the strange friction of the blade slamming home.

It stayed with him, that sensation: the scratching twist as the first thrust buckled, defeated by the weak armour of the man's rib bones. Then the way the blade had sped up as it slid between the ribs, sticking fast with a sickening, meaty whisper of a sound.

Blood immediately came from the man's lips. A spluttering spray. Talos felt the flecks of spit-thinned blood on his cheeks, his lips and in his eyes.

They'd run in a panic, Xarl half-laughing and half-crying, Talos in stunned silence. As always, they took to the streets, hiding there, making the dark city into the haven their homes would never be. Places to get lost, ways to stalk prey, a million ways to move unseen.

These were the lessons he took with him to the stars, when his own ascension came. These were the instincts he relied on when he stalked the night-time cities of a hundred and more worlds.

Uzas's voice, voxed from some distance away, was agitated.

'I've found a Black Legion Rhino. It's a wreck. This must be what happened to Ulth Squad.'

'Survivors?' Talos asked.

'Not even any bodies.' They all heard the regret in his voice. Bodies meant armour, and armour meant salvage.

'Mass laser fire damage.'

'Skitarii,' put in Cyrion. The Mechanicus footsoldier elite. It stood to reason – no one else would have laser fire capable of totalling an Astartes transport.

'You hear that?' Uzas said. 'I hear something.'

'How truly specific,' Cyrion chuckled.

'I'm getting it, too,' Xarl cut in. 'Broken vox, scattered chatter from other frequencies. Other squads.'

'The Black Legion?' asked Talos.

'No,' Xarl replied. 'I think it's us.'

Talos moved through the ruined manufactory as he listened to his squadmates. His red-tinted sight took in the stilled machinery, the idle conveyor belts, the tall roof with its shattered stained glass skylights where once the scene of the Emperor-as-Machine-God, coming to ancient Mars, had filtered the brilliance of the night sky.

Stars shone down now, illuminating the gargoyle-decorated building with silver silence. Whatever they had made here would never be made here again. The place was a tomb.

'The vox is unreliable,' Cyrion said. 'What a revelation. Everybody, hold positions, I'm going to contact the Warmaster and let him know.'

'Shut up, fool,' Xarl snapped. 'Talos?'

'Here.'

'Frequency Scarlet sixteen-one-five. You hear that?'

It took a few moments for his helm's vox-link to shift and scan nearby signals. He continued to walk through the silent manufactory, bolter and blade at the ready. Soon enough, voices prickled at the edge of his hearing.

'I hear it,' he voxed back to the others.

'What should we do?' Cyrion asked, dead serious now. He'd heard it, too. 'That's Seventh Claw.' There was a pause as he called up data, most likely on his auspex's data screen. 'The armament manufactorum, to the west.'

Talos idly checked his bolter, whispering praise to the machine-spirit within. The vox on the surface of Crythe was a savage, fickle thing, never reliable, always punctured and scrambled by the Mechanicus's arcane technology. Since the Legions had made planetfall, squads had grown used to the violated vox and being cut off from one another.

The fleet orbiting Crythe was blessedly free of the worst of the forge world's twisted vox-screeching, but the squads on the surface were forced to listen to an unending howl of code mangling their signals. Even vox fed through the ships' systems were still often subject to bizarre ghosting, added voices, and delays of several hours. Many times now, squads had responded to positioning information and orders that were half a day out of date.

'They're trying other frequencies to summon reinforcements,' Talos said.

'That's my guess,' Cyrion agreed.

'The Exalted will not be pleased if we abandon our recall orders.' Uzas sounded pleased, his voice low and scratchy. Talos forced the image of himself so battered and bloody, speaking with the same voice, from his mind. *Blood for the Blood God,* he'd said in the vision... *Souls for the Soul Eater...Skulls for the Skull Throne...*

'To hell with the Exalted,' said Xarl.

'We're going to Seventh Claw,' Talos said, already blink-clicking a Nostraman rune to open another channel. 'Septimus.'

'Here, master.' The signal was choppy, swamping the serf pilot's voice in jagged crackles. 'Scheduled retrieval in fourteen minutes. En route to your position.'

'Change of plans.'

'I don't dare ask why, lord. Just tell me what you need. This isn't *Blackened*, there's only so much I can do in a transporter.'

'It's fine. Full burn to my position, combat retrieval protocol, then full burn to coordinates Cyrion is transmitting now.'

'Lord... Combat retrieval? Is the sector not clear?'

'It's clear. But you will be taking First Claw and our Land Raider to an engagement zone west of here.'

'By your command, lord.' Talos heard Septimus take a breath. The mortal knew the Exalted had demanded First Claw's recall. 'Actually, I've changed my mind. I do want to know. May I ask what exactly is going on?'

'Seventh Claw is pinned down. We are going to break them out.'

'Forgive me for asking again, lord. What is pinning them down, that requires First Claw *and* its Land Raider?'

'A Titan,' Talos said. 'Now hurry.'

XII
SEVENTH CLAW

THE STREET SHIVERED under its tread.

Dozens of windows facing the avenue shattered in their frames and dust rained from the walls of broken buildings. The thunder of its splay-clawed feet wasn't even the loudest aspect of its presence. Louder still were the roaring whines of its great joints, great mechanical shrieks that split the air as it walked. And louder yet, the cacophonous bellow of its weaponised arms, burning the air when they sucked in power to fire and illuminating the world around it with the light of blinding dawn as they released their fury.

Adhemar of Seventh Claw crawled through the rubble of what had, moments before, been a habitation block. His vision flickered and hissed, all sense lost with the damage taken to his helm. Even his life readouts were scrambled, displaying nothing of use, nothing he could make out. With a curse, he tore the helm from his head, freeing his natural senses. The air was ash-thick and vibrating with the resonant booms of the Titan's stride. It was still some way down the avenue, bringing its guns to bear once more. Seventeen metres tall, almost as many wide, it hunched in the road, taking up so much of the street that its brutish shoulders made squealing tears in the buildings as it raked them with its bulk.

The Astartes knew those armoured shoulders shielded several crew members at work around the inner reactor, chanting their irritating prayers to the Emperor in His guise as the Machine-God. The fact he could not slay them, the fact he had nothing which he could even deal damage with, galled him almost beyond apoplexy. He glared at the canine head of the Titan, picturing the three pilots inside, leashed to their control thrones by hardwiring and restraint harnesses.

How they must be laughing right now...

Adhemar's throat and lungs tightened, filtering out the dust in the air as though it were a poison. Ignoring this biological reaction, the Night Lord dragged himself to his feet and ran behind the still-standing wall of a nearby building. The street, which had once been the main thoroughfare of a habitation sector, was a tumbledown wasteland in the wake of the Titan's anger. One of its weapons, like a gnarled right fist, was a multi-barrelled monstrosity that hurled hundreds of bolt shells a second at its targets below. Every impacting shell chewed a metre-wide hole in the Warhound's steel and stone surroundings. With thousands of shells fired every minute, Adhemar wasn't surprised at the level of destruction. He was merely surprised he still drew breath.

Most of his squad didn't share that fortune.

An ugly chime rang out, reminiscent of a cracked bell calling the Imperial faithful to morning prayer. Adhemar's muscles locked solid as he remained where he was. It was the echolocation pulse of the Titan's auspex. If he moved, it would know where he was. Hell, if it even sensed the minimal heat of his power armour, it would know... but he was counting on the Titan's systems being aligned to hunt larger prey.

Fifty metres down the road, shadowed from the moonlight by two towers that had escaped its opening wrath, it stood on its backwards-jointed legs, wolfish cockpit-head grinding left and right on servos that whined at agonising volume.

He heard the next attack before he saw it – the grunted cough of a missile launched nearby. From the second level of a ruined building, a streak of howling smoke slashed across the street. Adhemar moved to watch the missile's course, narrowing his eyes as his Astartes cognition instinctively took in the details of the warhead's angle and the certainty of its impact point.

Denied his vox, he whispered to himself.

'Mercutian, what are you doing...'

The missile exploded in a fragmentary starburst against the Titan's faintly-shimmering void shields, and the Warhound was already responding. The great left fist came up on roaring gears with punishing speed.

Inferno gun.

Adhemar was back in cover within a single heartbeat, not because he was in the line of fire, but because to look at the weapon firing would be to invite hours of blindness. Even with his eyes closed and head turned away, the son of Nostramo felt the brightness assault his retinas with jabs of migraine-coloured pain. The massive gun fired with the challenging roar of a feral world predator, blasting searing air in all directions from its heat exchange vanes.

Adhemar exhaled a lungful of the burning air, feeling it scrape his throat. He knew without looking that the chemical wash of vicious liquid fire had flooded the building, dissolving everything within. The expected crash came moments later, as the building's structure withered under the superheated force of the assault.

Was it his imagination, or had he heard a moment's cry from the vox of his helm in his hands? Had he heard one of his brother's death screams?

Mercutian was undeniably dead. Brave, without a doubt, to think to harm the Titan with one of his last rockets, but the gesture was futile even before he took aim. Picking the god-machine apart once its layered shields were down was one thing. Getting those shields down in the first place was quite another.

Adhemar hooked his sundered helm onto the magnetic coupling of his belt, and reached for his auxiliary vox within a thigh pouch. The earpiece felt alien; he was so used to the enclosing sensory magnification of his helm.

He doubted there was anyone still with him, but it was worth the attempt.

'Seventh Claw, status report.'

'Adhemar?'

'*Mercutian?*'

'Aye, brother-sergeant.'

'How in the infinite hells are you still alive?' It was an effort not to raise his voice with incredulity.

'You saw me take that missile shot?'

'And I thought I heard you die.'

'Not yet, sir. I made a tactical withdrawal. At speed.'

Adhemar resisted the urge to laugh. 'So you ran.'

'Ran *and* threw myself from the third storey of that building's south-facing side. My armour's a mess and I lost my launcher. Adhemar, we've got to get to the Rhino. The plasma gun is–'

'Not going to take down a Warhound Titan.'

'You have any better ideas?'

A grinding chorus of immense gears started up down the avenue again. Adhemar risked another glance around the edge of the wall.

'Bad news. Do you have visual?'

'I'm in the adjacent street, sir. I can't see the beast.'

'It's found the Rhino.'

The Titan had indeed. It hunched, every inch the feral predator, glaring down at Seventh Claw's troop transport nestled in a narrow alleyway. The collapse of the last building had revealed its dark armoured hull. Rubble from the fallen hab block was scattered across its roof, leaving bursts of gunmetal grey where the blue paint was scraped away.

'I have an idea,' Adhemar voxed.

'Adhemar, sir, with respect... we need to get out of here. There's no honour in this death.'

'Be silent. If we can get its shields down...'

'That's an impossible "if". If we could fly or piss plasma, we'd have the job done, too. None of those things will happen.'

'Wait. It's moving.'

The howl of great gears intensified. Adhemar watched, whispering a prayer to the machine-spirit of his Rhino, the faithful vehicle that had carried him across countless battlefields. He knew its interior as well as he knew his own armour. He could read the tank's temperament in the grunts of its idling engine, and feel its arrogance in the clank and ding of every gunshot that sparked harmlessly from its hull.

The Rhino's name in High Gothic was *Carpe Noctum*. 'Seize the Night'.

The tank that had carried Seventh Claw since the Legion's founding on pre-Imperial Terra died an ignoble death, expiring with a twisted, protracted groan of tortured metal. The Warhound Titan stood for half a minute, its splayed right foot-claw grinding the tank into the street. The greatest injustice was that the tank had met its end in such an undignified manner purely to spare the Titan's ammunition reserves.

You'll pay for that, Adhemar swore. *You will bleed and scream and die for that.*

The Titan finally raised its foot clear of the wreckage, scraps of bent metal falling from its talon-toes. In its wake, still in the behemoth's shadow, the crushed hull of *Carpe Noctum* looked especially pathetic. It was impossible to reconcile the image of miserable ruin with the great-hearted, indomitable tank that had raced him into battle a thousand times and more.

Seventh Claw was dead. Heart and soul. Even if he and Mercutian somehow survived the next few minutes, they were destined to join one of the other Claws in the ragtag remnants of 10th Company.

Adhemar watched the lumbering Titan stalk down the avenue, hunkering left and right, coming closer with each pounding tread.

'Mercutian...'

'Aye, brother-sergeant.'

Not brother-sergeant after this. Not a chance. 'We need to find Ruhn and Hazjarn. They had melta bombs.'

The Warhound thundered past.

Adhemar froze, back pinned against the wall. A great shadow fell across him as the Titan blocked out the moon. It stood only thirty metres away, pistons hissing and venting air pressure – a beast breathing, sighing after a long hunt. Its back was to him now, as it stared down the avenue, seeking targets. Another dull clang rang out as its echolocation auspex sought returning signals of movement or heat. The wolf was sniffing for prey.

'Repeat, sir.'

'Ruhn and Hazjarn. They had our melta bombs.'

'They're useless with the Titan's shields up. You know that.'

'They're our only chance. We could mine the road ahead of it. Have you got anything better to be doing, or did you come here in midnight clad just to die with the others?'

'I've got Ruhn on my locator, sir. But not Hazjarn. Can you see him?'

'I can't see anyone's signals; my helm is damaged. I saw him fall when the hab block came down on us. I know where to dig, but we'll need to be fast.'

'I've got no life signs from anyone except you and I,' Mercutian said.

Not at all surprising, Adhemar thought, watching the Titan panning left and right on its torso axis. The sound was like thunder in a valley.

'It's facing away. There's a sixteen second break between its auspex signals. The scanner wave will pass over us within the first second or two. Move only three seconds after the damn thing clangs. Freeze the moment you hear it pulse.'

'Yes, sir.'

They waited for several heartbeats, until the dull ring chimed once more. More windows facing the street shattered under the reverberation.

One. Two. Three.

'Move.'

THE TRANSPORTER HANDLED with weighty sluggishness compared to *Blackened*. Although the Thunderhawk variant was marked by a more skeletal mid-frame, it cradled the bulky shape of the squad's Land Raider in its underside hull claws. The weight counted. Septimus felt it in every bank and turn.

Septimus brought the flyer lower, streaking over the tips of hab blocks, stabiliser thrusters burning hot. Go too low, and he risked entering the Titan's weapon range before they knew for sure where it was. Stay too high, and their auspex wouldn't give an accurate return on where the enemy machine was.

'I'm getting significant thermal flare at the end of a major avenue just north of here.'

The voice of his master came over the vox. First Claw waited within their battle tank. 'Pull in low, release clamps at the other end of the avenue. If you get killed while causing the distraction, I'll lose my temper, Septimus.'

He grinned. 'Duly noted, lord.'

The transporter's stability engines burned hotter and angrier as they took the vessel's weight in full, all forward thrust lost as it coasted lower to the ground, between the stunted remains of Titan-killed hab blocks. Engine wash blackened the street below.

Six hundred metres or more down the avenue, the Titan saw them. The Warhound reared around, back-jointed legs easing it into an awkward reverse turn. Its arms rose in lethal salute.

'Imperial machine is acquiring target lock,' Septimus voxed. 'Twenty... Fifteen... Ten metres above ground.'

'*Ave Dominus Nox*,' Cyrion said over the channel.

'Hunt well, Septimus,' Talos added.

'Claws detached!'

Freed of its burden, the Thunderhawk transporter bucked skyward, overcompensating engines roaring.

Warning runes flashed across his console screens. *Target lock.* The serf wrenched the guidance sticks to pull the flyer into a vicious roll. From the avenue below, streams of massive-calibre bolt shells sliced through his engine wake. He punched out at two levers either side of his control throne, and the protesting boosters cried out with fresh fury. The amount of thrust he was demanding from the transport was usually reserved for breaking back into orbit after a landing. To use it in atmospheric flight, to use in a cityscape...

Septimus knew *Blackened.* He knew the Thunderhawk could've taken this and more. He wasn't so sure about the transport. It juddered and creaked and whined all around him, complaining down to the rivets in its hull.

Spires flashed by in a dizzying blur. Septimus climbed and brought the flyer into a sharp turn. As he lined up the nose with his target below, acquisition runes glimmered across his main data screen.

The transport's missile launchers came alive, pods opening like unfurling flowers.

'I hope this works...'

THE TREADS OF First Claw's Land Raider had been in motion before it even hit the ground. They whirred and spun, chewing air, hungry to grind over the street's surface.

'First Claw!' came a voice over the tank's interior vox.

Talos blink-clicked a tuning rune. 'Adhemar?'

'Talos, by the claws of our father... What are you doing here?'

The Land Raider lurched as it crashed to the street, its cycling treads already tearing up the concrete at full speed. Cyrion, at the tank's driving throne, turned the huge vehicle to the right, moving through a wide alley into a parallel side street. Within the tank's gloomy, red-lit insides, the rest of the squad checked their weapons.

'Take a guess,' Talos replied, and pounded his gauntlet against the door release. Night swept in, temperature gauges on retinal displays falling as the chill wind hit their armour. Talos, Uzas and Xarl leapt from the moving tank, scattering into the ruined hab towers.

'It's not the scenery, is it?' Mercutian's voice crackled. 'We'd have warned you away.'

'We appreciate the effort, brothers,' Adhemar voxed, 'but even a Land Raider is scrap metal against a Warhound. We're honoured you would join Seventh Claw in death.'

'Silence,' Talos barked. 'Where are you in relation to the Titan?'

'I could spit and hit it,' Mercutian replied. 'We're in its shadow, with melta bombs to mine the road.'

'Save them,' the prophet ordered. 'First Claw, move up through adjacent streets to link with Seventh Claw. Cyrion, bring *Storm's Eye* in fast, just as agreed.' There was no sense trying to hide the Land Raider. The Titan's auspex would scent its heat and power source from a kilometre away.

'You plan to take it down with your Land Raider?' Mercutian whistled low. 'A good death.'

'Enough of your negativity,' Adhemar snapped. 'Brother, tell me you've landed with a plan.'

'I landed with a plan,' Talos said. He ran through the rubble-strewn street, sighting the Warhound as it unleashed withering rivers of fire into the sky. 'The Titan is about to become the victim of an unpleasant distraction. When we strike from the sky, follow my orders exactly.'

'Compliance, Soul Hunter,' Adhemar said.

THE THUNDERHAWK TRANSPORT was lightly armed compared to its troop-carrying gunship counterpart, but not entirely lacking in offensive capability. Wing-mounted heavy bolters made up the anti-troop complement of its weapons array, backed up by the capacity for six under-wing hellstrike missiles.

Septimus had been flying the Thunderhawk *Blackened* for years, and had performed strafing runs on enemy positions many times in the past. This attack run was marked by several uncomfortable differences to his usual participation in a battle. First among these was that the transporter lacked the main cannon armament of the more familiar Thunderhawk. Secondly, it could withstand significantly less damage on its hull mid-sections. Thirdly, as Septimus ran the flight path adjustments through his conscious thoughts, he reached an ugly conclusion: *This bastard turns like it's underwater.*

The tank-carrier dived, and dived hard, like a spear from the night sky cast at the cruellest angle.

The Titan fired up at him. He could imagine its crew in their restraint thrones, unwilling to allow such a prize as an Astartes lander to escape its clutches, commanding their god-machine to send its anger skyward in a relentless hail of bolt shells, thousands at once.

The transporter jerked away from its dive, rolling so hard the pressure slammed Septimus painfully against his throne. The inertia of his attack run would, if he kept this up for much longer, either kill him, tear the ship apart, or both. But the lance of lethal shells slashed past.

Altitude meters chimed in alarm. Velocity readouts did the same. The vessel itself was screaming at him.

Septimus dragged at the control sticks, ramming the thrust levers a moment later. The transport powered closer, its angle less insane. Septimus had held out as long as he could, not wanting to broadcast his intent, but the Titan crew had to know now. They would recognise this manoeuvre. Not a strafing run with the cannons. A bombing run.

TALOS CROUCHED WITH Adhemar in the ruined ground floor of the hab block. With the walls almost completely levelled, they had an unopposed view of the street. Both warriors gripped plate-sized melta bombs in their hands, watching the Titan in the middle of the avenue as it fired into the sky.

Adhemar, older than Talos and showing it with his head bare, grinned toothily at the prophet. 'If this works...'

'It'll work.' Talos was almost smiling behind his own helm, glad that Adhemar had survived the Titan's initial assault.

Above, the transporter began its howling descent, racing closer by the second. The Titan locked its legs for support, and opened fire with a fresh volley from its Vulcan bolter cannon.

SEPTIMUS CAME IN between the towers of hab blocks. Low now. Even lower.

Low and close enough to graze the Titan's shoulders with heat wash when he passed overhead. When only two hundred metres separated the knifing flyer and the firing Titan, as he heard dangerous clashes on the hull from shredding bolter fire, Septimus pulled back and climbed again.

The Titan tracked its flight, but the ancient, time-honoured joints couldn't keep pace with the speeding flyer as it nosed up into the final stage of its attack run.

Septimus was holding to the thrust and altitude levers too tightly to risk letting go. The flyer was wounded, venting black smoke from several critical points, and he didn't dare take his hands from the controls for a moment. Leaning sideways in his throne, he cursed the fact this ship was made to be piloted by oversized gene-forged Astartes instead of mortals. With a Nostraman invective, he kicked out at the clamp release console the very second his targeting rune flashed green, green, green.

Septimus's boot heel smacked the lever up from *Secure* to *Armed*.

Aimed downward like six separate blades, the missiles spat from their pods and fell, howling, from the sky.

AT THIS RANGE, near-suicidal as it was for the Thunderhawk, the Titan had no chance to intercept the missiles.

The impact was a sight to behold. It burned into Talos's memory as fiercely as it burned into his eyes.

The missiles struck with savage force, hammering into the Titan's void shields with the force of a falling building. They exploded as one, and the flare momentarily blinded the one Night Lord that couldn't resist watching it all play out.

Talos stared, seeing nothing until his eye lenses frantically cycled through filters to compensate for his blindness. Sight returned, blurred by smears of retinal pain, just in time for the Astartes to see the Warhound stagger back a step, its right leg moving back to support its tilting weight, clawed foot grinding into the ground.

Its shields seemed fluid and malleable, swirling like oil on water, dissipating and sparking back to life as the internal generators strained to maintain the power feed to the void shield projector. Talos could almost see the tech-adepts working around the central column of the Titan's juddering fusion reactor, like a spine running through its torso and beneath its dense shoulder armour.

The Titan's shield crackled and flared with a sudden burst of dissipating energy. Deep within its armoured body, a low and rising thrum built up, muted but still audible to the Astartes in hiding. The Warhound's internal systems were bracing, feeding additional power to prevent a complete shield shutdown. Its voids were on the very edge of failure.

'Night Lords,' Talos voxed, smiling his crooked smile. 'Move in for the kill.'

THE MACHINE-SPIRIT HOUSED within the immense bulk of the VIII Legion Land Raider *Storm's Eye* had been honoured time and again for its aggression. Scrolls and pennants marking dozens of glorious victories moved in the wind as they hung from its hull. On treads that had churned the earth of countless worlds, it powered from the side street, acting as much on its own bloodlust and instinct as it was obeying the suggestions from the flesh-master at the controls.

Its prey... Its prey was immense. *Storm's Eye* sensed the boiling heat of the Titan's plasma reactor; felt the fierce pressure of the giant's glare as it drew a target lock. Yet *Storm's Eye,* the soul of the machine, knew nothing of fear, nothing of retreat, nothing of cowing to intimidation. It tore into the avenue, treads crushing and grinding the rockcrete beneath its weight, flanking the towering foe.

Storm's Eye clawed and spat at the larger predator – its spitting venom was a withering hail of high-calibre bolt shells from its hull-mounted turret, its talons raking the enemy's flesh were Kz9.76 Godhammer-pattern lascannons, each side turret unleashing eye-aching beams of merciless laser energy from two barrels slung side by side.

It clawed and clawed and clawed, ripping at the prey's fragile shimmer-skin, tearing at the half-seen protective shield.

Something burst. The shimmer-skin. *Storm's Eye's* talons had peeled the final layer of shimmer-skin away, leaving the foe cold and exposed. The enemy staggered with violent kinetic feedback as something broke within its body.

Storm's Eye heard the flesh-masters shouting to one another. It sensed their blood-excitement and shared their hunt-hunger. The joining of battle-hate pushed the tank's soul even harder. Its claws ached with death-heat. The cooling touch of maintenance would be a blessed relief after this hunt.

The prey was still strong, and it was still fast. The flesh-master guided *Storm's Eye* at hunt-kill speed across the avenue, reversing from the larger foe without ceasing fire. It was a battle to keep the tank's hull-body away from the murder-claws of the colossal predator. Like a shark seeking prey, *Storm's Eye* moved left and right in a weaving motion, engine-heart burning hotter and hotter, claws tensing and hissing with the killing heat.

The foe finally turned fast enough. No longer prey... No longer threatened...

It roared its own reply at *Storm's Eye*, machine-soul to machine-soul, and with the wrath of a predator-god, it clawed back.

TALOS VAULTED ANOTHER broken wall, sprinting across the avenue into the shadow of the firing Titan. With its Vulcan bolter cannon chattering a thunderstorm of shells at the Land Raider's retreating form, the enemy war machine had a greater threat to worry about than the Astartes at its feet. Still, it knew they were there. A clanging auspex return from the Titan sent warning runes flashing across Night Lord retinal displays, but even as the towering foe turned and sought to crush its weakling prey, the weakling prey was already acting.

Talos was the first. *Aurum* crackled with energy in his fist before a single slash carved a malicious streak through the armour and engineering of the Titan's ankle. Even one-handed, the blow would have felled a tree or carved a mortal in half. Talos's own gene-enhanced strength, amplified tenfold by the artificial muscle fibre of his war-plate, was the pinnacle of mankind's genetic manipulation coupled with some of the Machine Cult's closest-guarded secrets rediscovered from the Dark Age of Technology.

The golden blade sliced and sank into the armour plating, biting deep into the mechanics beneath. This alone was nothing, a pinprick of a wound caused in a heartbeat's span. Talos snarled with effort, his muscles unused to being so tested as he wrenched the blade deeper, impaling and sawing through the cables and rods and pistons that served the Titan as tendons.

Machine-blood spat from the carved metal, sheeting Talos with discoloured lubricant and oil. Its next auspex pulse sounded like a wail. With a replying cry of exultant anger, Talos slammed his other hand against the jagged wound he'd carved. There was a hollow clunk as the melta bomb adhered fast.

Adhemar and Xarl were next, clamping their own explosives to the wound's edges. Talos was already sprinting to safety as Mercutian slammed his incendiary home. He sighted Uzas.

Uzas, who was not laying his explosives with the rest. Uzas, who stood under the towering, stamping Titan and fired his bolter up at the war machine's chin. Did he think small-arms fire was ever going to puncture a hole in the armour of a Titan? Did he think the crew within that head-cockpit felt his gunfire as anything more than a whispered irritant against the hull-skin of their walking sanctum?

Xarl's voice barked over the vox, caught between anger and disbelief. 'What's that damn fool *doing*?'

Talos didn't answer. He was already running back.

Cyrion's influence made it all the more difficult. Sight-stealing brightness flashed in colourful blurs across Talos's eyes as the Land Raider down the avenue maintained heavy fire with its Godhammers. Talos closed his useless eyes, running blind between the Titan's crushing legs, relying on his other senses to guide him.

Beneath the pounding stamp of the enraged Titan's tread...

Beneath the mocking, deafening waspish buzz of constant lascannon fire...

There. The thrum of power armour. The heavy chatter of a bolter like an impish giggle in the wake of the superheavy weapons at play. Most identifiable of all was Uzas's gleeful voice risen in the howling of names Talos had no wish to know. Names which cast him back – just for a moment – to his vision of Abaddon's 'allies'.

He threw himself at the sounds, shoulder-charging Uzas ten metres across the street with the dull crash of ceramite armour plates clashing hard. Still blind, he ran to his brother's rising body, and powered his fist into Uzas's helmed face.

Once, twice, a third time and a fourth.

With a weak growl, Uzas staggered on shaking legs. Talos headbutted him, the Nostraman rune on his forehead shattering one of Uzas's red eye lenses. Feeling his brother go limp, the prophet hooked his fingers in Uzas's armoured collar, and dragged the fool into the relative cover of a half-fallen hab block.

He looked up to see his death. The Titan's arm, the one not releasing a torrent of murder down the avenue at Cyrion and *Storm's Eye*, aimed directly down at him. The arm itself was longer than a battle tank, sucking in light and heat through side-vanes as it amassed the power to fire.

An inferno gun. It would liquidate him, Uzas, the stone of the building, the concrete of the street, in a wash of sun-fire.

One thought burned through his mind as Talos stared up at the trembling cannon.

This is not how I will die.

The explosives bolted to the Titan's ankle detonated, as if the prophet's silent words shaped fate itself.

PRINCEPS ARJURAN HOLLISON grunted a weak murmur, because it was the only sound he could make. Something was crushing his chest, blocking all attempts to breathe, and pressing him back against his throne. The pressure that forced him hard against his throne made the hardwiring needles and probes socketed to his spine and skull push far deeper than they should, effectively impaling him. He could feel the dim, pulsing throb of internal bleeding in his head and chest as his vision swam, and...

No. It was the Titan's pain. Still linked to the enraged, crippled form of *Hunter in the Grey,* the princeps was drowning in the god-machine's overwhelming pain.

And its overwhelming indignity.

It had fallen. Not in glorious battle. Not in war against a stronger foe. The Titan, Warhound-class, assembled in the hallowed and sacred forge-factories of Alaris II – noble and knighted Mechanicus world – had *fallen*. Stumbled. Crashed to the ground, now prone to the ant-like bites of lesser prey.

The cooling reactor core of the humbled giant bled helpless rage into Arjuran's mind. Just as the Titan lay prone, so too was he defenceless against its maddening anger. He couldn't move his head to unplug himself. Rage flooded him, terrifying in its intensity and inhumanity, rendered worse by the very fact it could not be escaped. The twisted metal crushing him (the pilot throne of his faithful morderati primus, Ganelon...) was unmovable. His hands beat weakly, worthlessly, against the restraining weight.

He became aware that not only was he crushed, but that he was at an angle. His right arm and leg, as well as the right side of his head, were numb with dull pain from being forced against the metal wall of the cockpit. *Hunter in the Grey* had twisted as it fell, coming down on its side.

Arjuran had a fragmentary burst of short-term memory. The pain in his left fist as the inferno gun streamed killing fire into the sky, a useless release as the Titan toppled.

Then the thunderous crash.

Then blackness.

Then pain.

Now the rage.

ARJURAN WAS SHIVERING and drooling, half-senseless from the fury of his fallen Titan, when the roof of the wolf-headed cockpit was torn away. Not that he was aware of it, but his body was spasming every few seconds with violent jerks, banging his cracked skull and broken leg against the wall. The Titan's mortis-cry, an ululating wave of channelled hatred, was slowly killing the one crew member still alive. But then, *Hunter in the Grey* had always been a wilful and vindictive engine.

Arjuran gasped and wept as a dark figure dragged him from the throne. He gasped in relief, wept in thanks, as the plugs and cables snaked from his skull and spine.

Even now, deprived of the invulnerable shell of his *Hunter*, he could not care that he had traded one death for another. Blessed succour from the dying Titan's poisonous emotion. That was all that mattered.

Held limply in the gauntlets of the enemy, Princeps Arjuran Hollison, born of the dynast-clans ruling the Legio Maledictis of Crythe Primus, once the commander of one of his home world's precious god-machines, stared into the emotionless red eyes of his captor.

'My name is Talos,' the dark warrior growled. 'And you are coming with me.'

XIII
SEEDS OF INSURRECTION

'It is possible to win and lose at once.
Think of the war that rages for so long that a world is left worthless in its wake.
Think of the swordsman that slays his foe at the cost of his own life.
Think, finally, of the Siege of Terra.
Let those fateful nights burn into your memory.
Never forget the lesson learned when Horus duelled the false god.
Triumph bought with too much blood is no triumph at all.'

– The war-sage Malcharion
Excerpted from his work, *The Tenebrous Path*

TEN THOUSAND YEARS ago, before humanity was riven by the betrayal of Horus the Chosen, 10th Company returned home to Nostramo.

10th Company, 12th, and 16th – three battle companies returning from the Great Crusade to be honoured by their home world.

The Night Lords were never like their brother Legions. They came from a world without warrior traditions stretching back through the centuries. The fortitude that girded them for the rigours of the Emperor's Great Crusade was born of a world that knew fear, knew blood, and knew murder – more than any other globe in the Emperor's grip. The people of Nostramo knew these aspects as a natural part of life. The acceptance of such darkness bred a Legion colder than any other; a Legion willing to discard its humanity in service to the Throne.

And this is exactly what it did.

This was an age when the Night Lords were the emergent Imperium's most powerful threat. A world resisting the Imperial Truth could be conquered by the drudging half-mechanical Iron Hands or the massed precision of the ever-loyal Ultramarines. It could be brought to compliance by the howling hordes of the Luna Wolves – who would one day become the Black Legion – or the avenging wrath of the Blood Angels.

Or it could suffer the crippling evisceration of society offered by the untender talons of the Night Haunter's chosen sons.

Fear was their weapon. As the end of the Great Crusade neared, even as the Night Haunter's brother primarchs looked askance at their moribund, wayward kinsman, the Night Lords were the Emperor's most potent weapon. Entire worlds would surrender their arms as their scanners revealed that the Astartes vessels that had translated into orbit bore the runic symbols of the VIII Legion. In these waning years, the Night Lords encountered less and less resistance, as deviant societies abandoned their defiance rather than die under the claws of the most feared Imperial Legion.

Their reputation was hard-won through hundreds of campaigns, unleashing their specific brand of terror upon those they conquered. It was never enough to take a world in the Emperor's name. To cement the

Master of Mankind's rule, populations must be utterly quelled into obedience. Obedience through fear. A Night Lords strike force would ravage the heart of a world's leadership, crucifying the bodies of its rulers on public address pict-screens, burning the monument-houses to the planet's false gods, and systematically peeling back a society's skin to expose the weaknesses beneath. In their wake, shattered populations lived the lives of loyal, silent Imperial citizens, never even whispering a word of rebellion.

And as the years passed, resistance faded.

The gene-forged warriors of the Night Lords grew discontent with this. Not only discontent, but bored. When the order came from Terra – the insane demand that the Night Lords and their primarch father return to suffer the chastisement of the Emperor – discontent and boredom faded to be replaced by the birth of a new emotion. The Night Lords grew bitter.

They, who had whored their humanity away in the fires of the Emperor's wars.

They, who had allowed themselves to be moulded into the Imperium's truest weapon of terror.

They were to *pay* for these deeds, like sinners kneeling before an angry god?

Indignity. Madness. Blasphemy.

The last Night Lords to set foot upon the surface of Nostramo were the warriors of 10th, 12th and 16th Companies. A homecoming of special rarity, for few Astartes ever saw their home worlds again, and Nostramo was hardly renowned for doing honour to its sons fighting away in the Emperor's wars.

The parade was modest, but sincere. A gesture from the captain leading the three companies, as the expeditionary battlefleet refuelled and made repairs in the docks above Nostramo. Fifty Astartes from each company would make planetfall and march down the main avenue of Nostramo Quintus, leading from the spaceport.

Talos remembered thinking even at the time it was a strangely emotional gesture. Yet he'd descended to the surface in *Blackened*, along with the other nine Astartes of the full-strength First Claw.

'I do not understand,' he'd said to Brother-Sergeant Vandred, who was still decades away from becoming the Exalted, and still months away from becoming 10th Captain.

'What is there to understand, Brother-Apothecary?'

'This descent. The reception on the surface. I do not understand why the 10th Captain has ordered it.'

'Because he is a sentimental fool,' Vandred replied. Grunts of agreement sounded from the others, including Xarl. Talos said no more, but remained sure there was more to it than something so simple and senseless.

There was, of course. He wouldn't find out what for many months.

During the parade itself – which was almost alarmingly populous – Talos clutched his bolter to his chest and marched bare-headed with his brothers. The experience was dazzling, though almost without sound at first. Little cheering took place, but the clapping soon became thunderous. The ambivalent people of Nostramo, in the actual presence of the Night Haunter's sons, cast aside their apathy and welcomed their champions home.

It was not humbling. Talos was more confused than anything else.

Were these people so ardent in their love for the Imperium that they welcomed the Emperor's chosen born from their own world? He had spent his youth on this world, hiding and running and stealing and killing in the black backstreets of its cities. The Imperium had always been a distant, ignorable thing at best.

Had so much really changed in a mere two decades? Surely not.

So why were they all here? Perhaps curiosity had dragged them from their habs, and the uniqueness of the moment was breeding the excitement now.

Perhaps, he realised with a bolt of guilty unease through his spine, the people thought they had returned permanently. Returned to reinstitute the cleansing laws laid down by the now-distant Night Haunter.

Throne... That was it. That was why they were glad to see them. In the absence of their lost primarch ruler, the populace hoped for the Haunter's sons to return and take up his duties. The primarch's lessons were being unlearned, the imprint of his silent crusade on society was a thing of the past. Talos had lived here himself, barely believing the world had once been a bastion of control and order under a gene-god's rule.

Now it became humbling. To feel the weight of terrible expectation willed from the crowd. To know they were destined for crushing disappointment.

It became worse when the crowd started shouting names. Not insults, *real names.* It wasn't en masse, but individuals in the groups lining the avenue shouted names at the Astartes, for reasons Talos couldn't quite guess. Were they yelling their own names, to receive some kind of blessing? Were they screaming the names of sons taken by the Astartes, hoping those very same warriors now walked this wide street?

Few moments in life had been as difficult for Talos as this. To feel himself so separated from the life he once led, that he couldn't even guess what other humans were thinking.

The thin line of enforcers keeping the crowds back broke in several places. Small-arms fire banged out, putting down the few members of the mobbing crowd that sought to walk with the Astartes. Only a handful made it to the ranks of marching warriors. They weaved this way and that, looking lost, looking drunk, staring up like frightened, fevered animals into the faces of the walking warriors.

A middle-aged man scrabbled at Talos's chestplate with dirty fingernails.

'Sorion?' he asked. Before Talos could answer, the man fled, repeating the same whispered question to one of the Astartes two rows behind.

At no point did the Legion stop marching. Pistol-fire broke out as the enforcers, in expensive business suits, took out one of the mortals in the avenue that strayed far enough from the Astartes to guarantee a kill-shot without hitting one of the armoured giants. None of the enforcers wished to risk his own death by missing and hitting the revered armour of the Night Haunter's sons.

An elderly woman harassed Xarl. She was barely over half of his height.

'Where is he?' she shrieked, wasted hands scratching at the marching warrior's armour. 'Xarl! Where is he? Answer me!'

Talos could read the discomfort in his brother's face as Xarl marched on. The old woman, beneath her mop of wild white hair, saw him paying attention. Talos immediately faced forward again, feeling the old woman clawing at his unmoving arm with her weak grip.

'Look at me!' she pleaded. *'Look at me!'*

Talos didn't. He marched on. Weeping, wailing after him, the old woman fell behind. 'Look at me! *It's you! Talos! Look at me!'*

An enforcer's gunshot ended her demands. Talos hated himself for feeling relief.

FIVE HOURS LATER, back aboard *Blackened*, Xarl had sat next to him on the restraint couches.

Never before – and never again – would Talos see his brother's face marked by such hesitancy.

'That wasn't easy for any of us. But you did well, brother.'

'What did I do so differently?'

Xarl swallowed. Something seemed to dawn behind his eyes. 'That woman. The one from the crowd. You... didn't recognise her?'

Talos tilted his head, watching Xarl carefully. 'I barely saw her.'

'She said your name,' Xarl pressed. 'You truly didn't recognise her?'

'They were reading our names off our armour scrolls,' Talos narrowed his eyes. 'She said your name as well.'

Xarl rose to his feet, making to move away. Talos rose with him, gauntlet clamped on his brother's shoulder guard.

'Speak, Xarl.'

'She wasn't reading our names. She knew us, brother. She recognised us, even after twenty years and the changes wrought by the gene-seed. Throne, Talos... You must have recognised her.'

'I didn't. I swear. I saw only an old woman.'

Xarl shrugged off Talos's grip. He didn't turn around. His words echoed with the same finality as the gunshot that had silenced the old woman's pleas.

'The old woman,' Xarl said slowly. 'She was your mother.'

* * *

THESE THOUGHTS ECHOED in Talos's mind now, on the return to orbit from the war-torn surface of Crythe. The memories, which so safely hid within his unconscious at all times, broke through the surface now.

The mood aboard the transport was grim, despite the victory First and Seventh Claws had just achieved. The death of a Titan, even a Warhound-class Titan, a lesser cousin of the city-crushing Warlords and Imperators... This deed would be etched onto their war-plate, and machined onto the armour plating of *Storm's Eye*. Nostraman runes would tell the tale of their triumph until the night when their bodies lay cold and Legion brothers came to scavenge the relic armour.

But the mood remained dark. Victory at such a savage cost was barely a victory at all. Talos recalled similar words written by the war-sage Malcharion, in the years after the Haunter's assassination.

And with that thought, with that connection made, Talos's roiling mind – already lost in the coldest, deepest and most furious pits of memory – turned blacker still.

Assassination. Murder. *Blasphemy.*

The last time he had wept was on that night, that night of wrenching agony, standing with thousands of his brothers and watching the traitorous whore leave the fortress-monastery, her gloved hands clutching their father's head by its lank, black hair.

Hours before, Talos had shared his last words with his gene-sire.

'My life,' the primarch had said, head bowed before a gathering of his captains and chosen, 'has meant nothing.'

The bowed god weathered the shouted denials of his favoured sons, who all fell silent as he spoke again.

'Nothing. Yet, I will amend that with my death.'

'How, lord? What glory will your sacrifice bring to us?' These words from the Talonmaster. *Zso Sahaal.* First Captain.

The same questions were uttered from a dozen lips.

'We cannot prosecute the crusade against the Imperium without you,' declared Vandred, not yet the Exalted, not yet Captain of the 10th, but already considered so gifted by the Haunter in matters of void war.

The Night Haunter smiled, somehow without animating his face beyond warping the blue veins beneath his cheeks.

'Our crusade of vengeance against the Imperium, against my father's false ascension to godhood, spins upon a fulcrum. Every life we take, every soul that screams in our wake – the rightness of what we do hangs upon a single aspect of balance. Name that aspect. Name it, any of you, you who are my chosen.'

'I will,' said a voice from the loose crowd.

The Haunter nodded. 'Speak, Captain of the 10th.' At those words, Talos glanced at his own captain. So did Vandred.

Brother-Captain Malcharion stepped forward, leaving the ranks of the company leaders, to stand one step closer to his primarch.

'The rightness of our crusade is justified because the Imperium is founded upon a lie. The Emperor is wrong in all he does, and the Imperial Truth his preachers propagate is flawed and blinding. He will never bring order and law to mankind. He will damn it through ignorance.

'And,' Malcharion nodded his head, mimicking the primarch's earlier bow, 'his hypocrisy must be answered with revenge. We are right because he wronged us. We bleed his flawed empire because we see the truth, the decay beneath the skin. Our vengeance is righteous. It is justice for his scorn of the VIII Legion.'

Malcharion was taller than many Astartes, his bare head showing seven implanted silver rivets around his right eyebrow, each one a mark of honour meaning nothing to any outside the Legion. A ferocious fighter, an inspiring leader, and already composing works of great tactical and meditative value. It was all too easy to see why the Night Haunter favoured him with captaincy of the 10th Company.

'All true,' the father said to his sons. 'But what is the Emperor learning by our defiance? What do the High Lords of Terra learn as we slaughter the citizens of their void-kingdom?'

'Nothing,' said a voice. Talos swallowed as he realised it was his own. Every unhelmed face turned to look at him, including the primarch's.

'Nothing,' the Night Haunter said, closing his black eyes. 'Nothing at all. Righteousness is useless, if we alone know we're right.'

He had told them before. Told them his intent. Yet this cold, ironclad confession still undermined the inner preparations each one had made to deal with the death of their gene-sire. All the questions previously quelled broke loose, and the grim acceptances paved over doubts were shattered.

Here was the chance to argue. To defy. To challenge fate. Voices rose in protest.

'It is written,' the Night Haunter murmured. His whispered words were always enough to bring his sons to silence. 'I feel your defiance, my Night Lords. But it is written. And more than that, even were this a destiny to be battled and resisted, it is *right* that I die.'

Talos watched the sire of the VIII Legion, his own black eyes narrowed.

'Soul Hunter,' the Night Haunter said suddenly, gesturing with a hand that resembled a marble claw. 'I see understanding dawn in your eyes.'

'No, lord,' he said. Talos felt several of the captains and chosen eyeing him, hostile as ever at the way their primarch singled him out for the honour of such a deed name.

'Speak, Soul Hunter. The others understand, but I hear your thoughts. You have framed it in words better than any other. Even our honourable and verbose Malcharion.'

Malcharion nodded in respect to Talos, and the gesture gave him impetus to speak.

'This is not entirely about the Legion.'

'Continue.' Again, the marble claw invited more.

'This is a lesson from a son to his father. Just as you instruct us in the principles to continue this crusade, you will show your own father, who watches all from the Golden Throne, that you will die for your beliefs. Your sacrifice will echo in your father's heart forever. You believe your martyrdom will set a fiercer example than your life.'

'Because...?' The Night Haunter smiled again, a fanged smirk that had nothing to do with delight.

Talos drew a breath to speak the words he'd seen in his dreams. The words his gene-sire would speak before the assassin's blade fell.

'Because death is nothing compared to vindication.'

'SIXTY SECONDS TO dock,' Septimus said in muted tones.

Talos would not be jarred from his reverie. Deeper. Deeper. Away from the sight and scent of damaged power armour and bleeding skin, away from the pitted and cracked hull of both the transport and *Storm's Eye* gripped within the carrying claws. Away from the two squads of men with their annihilated numbers, their tainted souls, and their bitter victory.

Deeper.

'Nostramo was blighted,' the primarch said.

It would be the final time Talos spoke to his father. Konrad Curze held his son's helm, turning it over in his hands, white fingertips tracing the Nostraman rune upon its ceramite forehead.

'Soul Hunter,' he whispered the name. 'Soon, in the nights to come, you will earn the name I have already given you.'

Talos did not know what to say, so he said nothing at all. Around them, the black stone chamber of the Haunter's throne room remained silent but for the sounds of their armour reflecting off the walls.

'Our home world,' the primarch said, 'was more than blighted. It was ruined. You know why I killed our world, Talos. You sense the honourless, murderous nature of the Legion now.'

'Many sense it, lord.' Talos drew in the ice-cold air. His breath steamed out. 'But we are a weapon against the Imperium. And we are righteous in our vengeance.'

'Nostramo had to die.' The primarch continued as if Talos had said nothing. 'I tried to tell my brothers. I told them of Nostramo's backslide into lawlessness and cruelty. The recruitment had to halt. My Legion was poisoning itself from within. The planet *had to die*. It had forgotten the lessons I taught with blood and pain and fear.'

The Night Haunter stared past Talos, at the black wall of his chamber. A thin trickle of saliva made its way down his chin from the corner of his mouth. The sight made Talos's main heart beat faster. It was not fear. That would be impossible, for he was Astartes. It was... unease. Unease at seeing his primarch so unstable.

'Assassins come. One will reach this palace. Her name is...'

'M'Shen,' Talos whispered. He had dreamed the name himself.

'Yes.' The primarch's tongue flicked out to lick at the trailing drool. 'Yes. And she, too, does the work of justice.'

The Night Haunter handed the helm back to Talos, closing his eyes as he lowered his slender, armoured form onto the throne. 'I am no better than the millions I burned on Nostramo. I am the murderous, corrupt villain that the Imperial declarations name me. I will greet this death gladly. I punished those who wronged. Now my own wrongs will be punished in kind. A delicious and balanced justice.

'And in this murder, the Emperor will once again prove me right. I was right to do as I did, just as he is right to do as he does.'

Talos stepped closer to the throne. The question that left his lips was not the one he'd intended to voice.

'Why,' he said, eyes burning with something akin to anger, 'do you call me Soul Hunter?'

The Night Haunter's black eyes gleamed, and the enthroned god smiled again.

'AND WE'RE DOWN,' Septimus said. 'Docked and locked, powering down now.'

Talos rose to his feet, leaving the restraint couch.

'Septimus, see to the Navigator. Ensure her surgery occurred without complications.'

'Yes, lord.'

'First Claw, Seventh Claw,' Talos said. 'With me. We are going to speak with the Exalted.'

* * *

'The war on the surface is costing us dearly.'

'The losses are acceptable.'

Talos eyed the Exalted's visage, twisted and leering in a parody of pale Nostraman flesh.

'Acceptable?' the prophet asked. 'By what standards? We have lost nine Astartes since we made planetfall. The Warmaster is throwing us against the hardest targets on Crythe.'

'And we break them.'

Imbedded within every pure Astartes was the capacity to generate acidic spit. In loyalist Chapters descended from flawed gene-seed, this ability was occasionally hindered, stunted or absent altogether. The Night Lords were not impure. At the Exalted's obdurate display, Talos felt his saliva glands tingling, responding to his annoyance. With a whispered curse, he swallowed the burning venom, where it would dissipate harmlessly in his stomach acids. It stung on the way down his throat.

'Yes, we break them. And we break ourselves upon them. We are fighting the *Mechanicus.* The Warmaster is bleeding us against targets ill-suited to our Legion's warfare. Titans and servitors and tech-guard? We are wasted against an enemy too inhuman to feel fear.'

'It is not the role of a warrior to whine when he is deployed outside his ideal battlefield, Talos.'

'Then by all means,' Adhemar interjected, spreading his arms wide, 'come down to the surface, Excellency. Bloody your claws with the rest of us. Allow your precious Atramentar to fire some bolts in anger. See for yourself!'

The older Astartes grinned, wolf-like and keen, as the Atramentar either side of the Exalted's throne growled through their tusked helms. 'We just crippled a Titan,' Adhemar's dark eyes shone with amusement, 'so don't think you raising those weapons is any deterrent to us telling the truth.'

The Exalted burbled a wet chuckle. 'You are in fine spirits for a sergeant that so recently led his men to their deaths.'

The smile was wiped from Adhemar's face. Talos looked between the two Atramentar – Garadon and Vraal – in their bullish Terminator plate. Tense. Ready.

But they would not act. He was sure of it.

'Enough of this madness,' Talos said. 'We are hurled like fodder against insane resistance, and ordered to scout ahead of the mortal armies. *Scout ahead? Astartes?* This is no way to wage war. Fear is our greatest weapon, and that blade is blunted in this conflict.'

'You will fight because it is the will of the Warmaster,' the Exalted sneered. 'And it is *my* will.'

'Seventh Claw is destroyed.' Talos's fingers ached to draw *Aurum*. He knew, with icy certainty, he could ascend the dais and ram the golden blade home in Vandred's chest before the Atramentar cut him down.

Sorely, sorely tempting.

'Did you harvest their gene-seed? You were my Apothecary once. It would grieve me to think you had forgotten your former duties completely.'

'I cut them from the bodies of the slain myself,' Talos replied. And he had. With his combat knife, he'd cut the progenoid glands from the chest and neck of each killed warrior. Adhemar, with tears in his eyes, had packed the discoloured organs in freezing gel, storing them in a sealed stasis crate aboard *Storm's Eye.*

Six souls lost. Lost to the warp. He imagined his men, brave warriors all, their shades howling as they drifted through the Sea of Souls.

'Adhemar and Mercutian are First Claw now.' Talos was adamant. 'That is not a request.'

The Exalted shrugged, moving weighty armour and bone spikes. Matters of unit size and assignment were beneath him.

'And let us be clear, Brother-Captain Vandred. This war will see us dead. The Warmaster will bleed the 10th to the bone, because we are expendable to him. The survivors will, by virtue of no other choices remaining to them, join the Black Legion.'

'The Warmaster, a thousand praises upon his name, has granted his forgiveness for your... outburst... on the surface of the prison world.' The Exalted's ruined teeth glistened unpleasantly. 'Do not abuse his generous nature, Talos.'

Talos looked to the Atramentar. Garadon had been there. Had he not explained the truth of the matter?

'The Warmaster sought to create divisions between the landing party. He wanted me because my second sight is not blinded, as his own seers suffer. I cannot believe you still refuse to the see the light of truth. Garadon was with us. Surely he–'

'The Hammer of the Exalted relayed all that occurred. The only flaw the Black Legion was guilty of was allowing our Thunderhawk to be overrun by prisoners.'

'Are you *insane*?' Talos took a step closer. Both of the Atramentar brought their weapons to bear: Garadon hefting his hammer, and Vraal's lightning claws sparking into hostile life. 'They blew the main ramp door open with explosives.'

The Exalted did not answer, but the smile revealed all. It knew. The Exalted knew, had always known, and did not care. The loss of Talos, no matter how precious a commodity his prophetic gift was, would be an acceptable sacrifice in the name of the Warmaster's continued goodwill.

Talos's next words came out as a whispered threat. 'If you think I will allow you to lead the 10th into the grave because you hunger so feverishly for Abaddon's good graces, you are sorely mistaken.'

'You seek to usurp me, Soul Hunter?' The Exalted still smiled.

'No. I seek leadership for the surface conflict. I want to win this war and still have a company to come back to.'

'Promoting yourself? How droll.'

'Not I, Vandred.'

Finally, the Exalted reacted. It rose from its throne on squealing armour hinges, its slanted, birdlike eyes narrowed.

'Do not speak his name. He slumbers too deeply. He will not awaken. *I* am the Exalted. *I* am Captain of the 10th. You will obey *me*.'

'Enough, Vandred. You will not lead us on Crythe, and we are dying to your desire in order to please the Warmaster. We are fighting an enemy that lacks any human emotion. They do not feel fear, and they will not panic. It is costing us life and resources to destroy such a foe in grinding, traditional warfare. If their morale can yet be broken, it will not be done with bolters and blades. So we will use our own machines. The machines they once made for us.

'I am going to the Hall of Remembrance,' finished Talos. 'First Claw, with me.'

With those words spoken, he stalked from the bridge, guarded by the sacred weapons of the newly-forged First Claw.

OUTSIDE, CYRION STOPPED.

With the doors closed behind them, he leaned against the wall, head down, as if stunned. A tremor overtook his right arm, and he held onto his bolter only because his fist tightened in an uncontrolled clenching of tendons.

In a broken voice that reached only Talos, he said, 'Brother. We... must speak. The Exalted's terrors are flooding him. He is finally drowning in them.'

'I do not care.'

'You should care. When you spoke of the Hall of Remembrance, what remains of Vandred within that tainted shell was weeping in fear.'

THE EXALTED AND its guardians watched the squad leave. As the doors slammed closed in the Astartes' wake, Garadon lowered his ornate hammer, resting its haft on his shoulder once more. The black lion's face of his shoulder armour roared silently in the direction of the sealed doors.

'I will never understand why the primarch honoured Talos so highly,' the Atramentar said.

Vraal, on the other side of the Exalted's command throne, voxed his own thoughts. 'He is fortunate. Luck favours him. He dreamed of the Navigator. Now he takes a Titan princeps prisoner. The Warmaster himself will praise that capture.'

'You sound disgusted, brother.' Garadon's own voice was as cool and toneless as ever. 'Does his fortune offend you?'

Vraal had still not retracted his lightning claws. They hissed and sparked in the gloom of the bridge, sending harsh illumination flashing along the contours of his bulky Terminator armour like sheet lightning.

'It does. He offends me with each breath he draws.'

'Vraal,' the Exalted slurred, its voice thick with bitter mucus.

'Yes, my prince?'

'Follow them. I do not care how it is done, but the ritual of reawakening must be desecrated.'

'Yes, my prince.' Vraal nodded his tusked helm. The servos in his ancient war-plate growled at the movement.

The Exalted licked its fanged teeth, uncaring of the blood it drew.

'Talos must not be allowed to awaken Malcharion.'

XIV
CAPTAIN OF THE 10TH

'I do not want this.
I have served with loyalty and honour…
Throw… my ashes into the void.
Do… not… entomb me…'

– Final words of the war-sage Malcharion

THE SLEEPER DREAMED.

He dreamed of battle and bloodshed, dreams that warped the boundary between memory and nightmare within his sluggish mind.

A world. A battlefield. *The* battlefield. Armies of millions laying waste to each other in a relentless grind. Bolter fire, bolter fire, bolter fire. So loud it bleeds into other senses. So loud it becomes blinding, so loud it tastes of ash. The sound of bolters firing is more familiar to him than the sound of his own voice, so deeply is it ingrained within him.

The spires of a palace that spans a continent. The towers of a fortress like no other – a bastion of gold and stone to rival the imaginations of even the greediest gods.

He would die here. This he knew, for it was memory.

He would die here, but would not be granted peace.

And still, the bolters fired.

THE ORNATE PLATINUM surface of the sarcophagus stared back in silence, still draped in thin, gentle tendrils of wisping steam as the stasis field powered down.

It was ornate and beautiful in the way *Storm's Eye* would never be. The Land Raider, enhanced by vicious spikes and ornate armour restructuring, was artistry of a sort: revelling in the Legion's reputation, fitted with chain racks to display crucified enemies even as the battle tank cut down hundreds more.

Storm's Eye was limitless aggression and the infliction of woe upon the enemy. The machine-spirit within, reflected by the ceramite without.

But this was artistry of a different, nobler breed.

The sarcophagus was rendered in platinum and bronze, depicting one of the greatest days of battle ever to take place in the history of 10th Company. A warrior in ancient war-plate stood, head raised back to the sky, clutching two Astartes helms. His right boot rested upon a third, driving it into the ground.

The image had never been defiled with exaggeration. No mound of skulls, no cheering crowds. Just a warrior alone with his victory.

The helm in his right hand sported a jagged lightning bolt etched onto its forehead, with a barbaric rune upon its cheek. The helm of Xorumai Khan, swordmaster-captain of the White Scars 9th Company.

The helm in his left hand was crested and proud, even when torn from the body of its wearer. It was marked only with a clenched fist upon the faceplate, and the High Gothic rune for *Paladin*. Here was the helm of Lethandrus the Templar, a renowned champion of the Imperial Fists Legion.

Lastly, beneath the warrior's boot, the helm of a third Astartes. This helm was winged, marked by a tear-shaped drop of blood – displayed here as a ruby – on the helm's forehead. Raguel the Sufferer, captain of the Blood Angels 7th Company.

The warrior had slain these three souls in the span of a single day. A single day of hive warfare outside the walls of the Imperial Palace, and the warrior had cut down three champions of the loyalist Astartes Legions.

Clanking cranes lifted the huge sarcophagus from its stasis pit in the marble floor of the Hall of Remembrance. Servitors operated the lifting equipment, their mono-tasked mechanical precision a necessary part of the ritual of reawakening. Talos watched the hulking coffin of platinum, bronze and black ceramite – the size of two Astartes in full Terminator plate – as it was lifted clear of the pit's restraints. Tubes, feeds and cables, each with a sacred use, trailed down from the sarcophagus as it hung aloft. These fibrous snakes dripped coolant, beads of moisture collecting in the funereal air after such a long immersion in the stasis field.

First Claw watched in silent reverence as the sarcophagus was carried across the chamber and lowered with programmed care. Several more servitors waited below the lowering coffin, clustered around the towering form of an armoured carapace three times the height of an Astartes. Their hands, replaced with industrial claws and technical tools, busied over the machine body, making the final preparations for the sarcophagus's mounting upon its front.

Dreadnought.

The word itself sent a pulse of ice through his blood, but it was nothing compared to the reality before his eyes. A Dreadnought: the ultimate blend of man and machine. The form of an Astartes hero, encased within an ornate sarcophagus and forever suspended in amniotic fluids on the very edge of death, controlling the nigh-invulnerable ceramite body of a walking war machine.

The ritual so far had taken almost two hours, and Talos knew several still lay ahead. He watched the servitors at work, machining clamps into place, locking struts, testing interface ports…

'My lord,' said Tech-Priest Deltrian. 'All is ready for the Third Juncture of the Ritual of Reawakening.'

The man, robed in black, had augmented himself to the height of an Astartes with none of the inhuman muscle-bulk. To Talos, he resembled the skeletal harvester of life from pre-Imperial Terran mythology. It was an image shared across the stars by so many colonised worlds, even those that had evolved independently of far, far distant Earth. *A reaper of souls.*

Deltrian's face, visible from under the black cowl, seemed to play to this conceit for reasons Talos had never fathomed. A silver skull grinned at the Astartes. The face was formed from chrome and plasteel shaped to the man's facial bones – perhaps even replacing skin and bone itself.

A voxsponder unit, like a coal-black beetle on his still-human throat, emitted Deltrian's mechanical voice.

The unblinking eyes were glittering emerald lenses, dewy with a faint sheen from the moisture spray that hissed subtly from Deltrian's tear ducts once every fifteen seconds. Talos had no idea why the tech-priest's eye lenses must be kept moist, they were hardly human eyes in need of lids and juices to prevent them drying out.

As with all of Deltrian's inhumanities, it was something Talos respected as personal, despite his curiosity.

'You have the Legion's thanks, honoured tech-priest,' the Astartes said, continuing the traditional phrases expected of him. He glanced around the marble-floored chamber, its walls thick with arcane machinery, pits sloping into the floor holding even more wondrous technology. He looked back to the tech-priest, and added on a whim: 'Our thanks, as always, Deltrian. You are a dutiful and trusted ally to us.'

Deltrian froze, machine-still. The servitors banged and clanged and fused and attached and drilled. The tech-priest's emerald lenses clicked and whirred, as if seeking to adopt some form of facial expression. The skull of his face never stopped grinning.

'You have violated the traditional exchange of vocalised linguistics.'

'I merely meant to show gratitude for the duties you perform. Duties that too often remain thankless.' Talos's black eyes didn't break the sincere stare. 'I apologise if I caused you offence.'

'It was not an error to amend the vocalised linguistical exchange?'

'No. It was intentional.'

'Analysing. Processed. In reply, I would state: thank you for your recognition, Astartes One-Two-Ten.'

Astartes One-Two-Ten? Talos smiled as understanding dawned. First Claw, Second Astartes, 10th Company. His original squad designation.

'Talos,' the Night Lord said. 'My name is Talos.'

'Talos. Acknowledged. Recorded.' Deltrian turned his death's head grin on the lowering sarcophagus. 'Through the invocation of the Machine-God, through the blessed sacrament of unity between the enlightened Mechanicum and the Legions of Horus, I shall endeavour to revivify the warrior before us if the cause aligns with the First Oath. Make your vow known to me.'

Slipping back into the formal exchange, Talos replied, 'In the name of my primarch, who loved and served Horus as the brother he was, I give you my vow. The VIII Legion makes war upon the Golden Throne and the Cult of Mars. Return to us our fallen brother, and Imperial blood shall run. Renew his strength with your secrets, and together we will bleed the false Mechanicum of its lore.'

Here Deltrian paused again. Talos wondered if he had spoken the oath incorrectly. He'd studied the texts, but this was the first time he had undertaken the ritual himself.

'Your avowal aligns with the First Oath. My secrets will be employed in our mutual favour.'

'Wake him, Deltrian.' Talos met the tech-priest's gaze, his voice lowered. 'A storm is coming. A reckoning. We need him to stand with us.'

This, too, was a break in the prescribed ritual. Deltrian paused to process it.

'You are cognitive of the probability of failure? This warrior-unit has resisted reawakening on all four previous attempts.'

'I know.' Talos watched the sarcophagus, golden with great deeds, being fastened in place on its war machine body. 'He has never awoken. He did not wish to be entombed.'

Deltrian said nothing. To refuse the honour of becoming so close to the Machine-God made no sense to the Mechanicum priest. With no comprehension of the emotions at play, he simply remained silent until Talos spoke again.

'May I ask a question?'

'Permission is granted, with the acceptance that no lore of the blessed Mechanicum shall leave the minds of its holy servants.'

'I respect that. But I will be leaving an... honour guard here. To watch over the ritual. Is that an unacceptable breach of tradition?'

'It was once considered tradition to maintain an honour guard in the Hall of Remembrance at all times,' Deltrian said. In a moment of almost eerie humanity, the machine man tilted his head to the side while the smile remained on his unchanging face. 'How times change.'

Talos nodded to that, smiling himself.

'Thank you for your patience, Deltrian. Cyrion, Mercutian and Xarl will remain here. They will not interfere with your work and worship, I assure you.'

'Your orders are recorded.'

'I wish you well, honoured tech-priest. Please summon me for the final stage of the rite. I wish to be present.'

'Compliance,' the augmented man said. After several seconds, Deltrian added almost awkwardly, 'Talos?'

The Astartes turned with a growling whirr of armour joints. 'Yes?'

Deltrian gestured with a long-fingered skeletal hand to a wall-mounted life support pod. Within its glass walls, suspended in amniotic fluids and connected to external systems by a tangled weave of cables and wires, the naked form of Princeps Arjuran Hollison floated in chemical-induced slumber.

The tech-priest emitted a blurt of machine code from his throat-vox; the sound equation of a pleased smile. 'This one will have many uses. Much to be learned from him. My thanks for the gift of this most valuable weapon.'

'Return the favour,' said Talos, 'and we'll consider the matter even.'

'We need to discuss matters of rank.'

Bare-headed, sporting a short black beard salted with flecks of grey, Adhemar walked alongside Talos through the darkened halls of the *Covenant*. They were descending deeper through the ship, heading from the artificer and machinery deck, making their striding way to the mortal crew quarters.

'What is there to discuss?' Talos asked. A rare vitality was flowing through him. *Hope*. Something he'd not felt in a long time. He'd not lied to the tech-priest; a storm was coming. He could feel it in his blood. It threatened to break with every beat of his heart. 10th Company would be changed forevermore.

The two Astartes' bootsteps echoed from the black steel around them.

'I outrank you.' Adhemar's voice came as if he were grinding rocks with his teeth.

'You do,' Talos agreed. 'Why does that seem to make you uncomfortable?'

'Because rank means nothing with the 10th ruined. Beneath the Exalted is the Atramentar. Above the Exalted is no one but his hateful gods. All else is unworthy of his notice. Ninth Claw has been leaderless for three months now.'

Talos exhaled, shaking his head. Truly, the Legion had fallen apart.

'I had no idea.'

'I am First Claw now,' Adhemar affirmed. 'But who leads First Claw? The former brother-sergeant of Seventh? Or the former Apothecary of First?'

'Do I look like I care?' Talos rested his hand on the pommel of sheathed *Aurum*. 'I'd be satisfied with the company holding together for the duration of this war. You lead. You earned your rank.'

'Has it never occurred to you that perhaps you've earned a higher rank than the Exalted grants you?'

'Never,' Talos lied. 'Not for a moment.'

'I see the lie in your eyes, brother. You are not gifted with deception. You know full well you should lead First Claw. You merely offer me the position from respect.'

'Maybe. But the lie is sincere. You have the rank. Lead and I would follow.'

'Enough games. I have no wish to lead your – our – squad. But hear me well. Your actions for the betterment of the Legion may be altruistic and made without thoughts of personal glory. But they do not look that way to the Exalted.'

They waited at the sealed doors to an elevator, staring at one another in the pitch blackness, seeing each other's features perfectly. Talos breathed slowly before answering. Even the mention of the Exalted was fuel for his suppressed fury.

'These are not your words, Adhemar. This talk of suspicion and deception... It is not your way to learn of such things. Who is this warning from? Upon whose behalf are you speaking?'

From the hallway behind them, a voice said: 'Mine.'

Talos turned slowly, cursing himself for being too lost in his inner conflicts to have heard another close by. Even though the newcomer was unarmoured and wearing only the traditional Legion tunic, the prophet should have heard his approach.

'My behalf. Adhemar speaks on my behalf.'

Adhemar nodded his head in respect, as did Talos, to Champion Malek of the Atramentar.

* * *

Xarl and Cyrion had never been close. Conversation, such as it was, always remained stilted between them when it occurred at all. Idle chatter was not an Astartes trait, and that tendency was only magnified when the two Astartes in question despised one another.

Bolters held to chests, they walked in opposite directions around the marble-tiled chamber of the Hall of Remembrance, passing each other twice on each circuit. Mercutian, his armour sigils yet displaying his allegiance to Seventh Claw, stood guard at the great double doors, his helm turned to face the form of the Dreadnought.

Deltrian puppeteered his servitors with occasional blaring snarls of machine code. According to his directions, the cyborged minions went about the painstaking process of readying the Dreadnought for a full reawakening. Upon its front, the mounted sarcophagus stared across the room, brazen with its glory in a way Malcharion never was in life.

On the sixth time Cyrion passed Xarl, he opened a vox-channel to his brother.

'Xarl.'

'Make this good.'

'What are the chances of this working?'

'Of the war-sage waking?'

'Yes.'

'I am... sceptical.'

'As am I.' A pause stretched out, and the channel fell dead after several minutes. Cyrion blink-clicked it open again.

'The Exalted will not allow it to happen.'

'That is not news to me, brother.' Xarl sighed over the link. 'Why do you think we are here? Of course the Exalted will attempt to stop this ritual. What still eludes me is why. I can scarcely believe things are falling apart so completely.'

'The Exalted fears this. He fears Talos, but he fears the awakening of Malcharion even more. You haven't sensed what I have.'

'I have no desire to. Let us not dwell on talk of your corruption.'

'I *sense* fear. I do not feel it. It's a... perception. Like people whispering on a detuned vox, where only scraps of meaning break through.'

'You are touched by the Ruinous Powers. Enough.'

Cyrion pressed on. 'Xarl. Listen. Just this once. Whatever war is taking place within the Exalted, it is one Vandred lost long ago. He barely exists as the man we followed into battle after the Siege of Terra.'

They passed one another again, neither warrior giving sign of acknowledging the other, despite their argument over the vox. Mercutian still stood in orderly silence.

'*Enough,*' Xarl snapped. 'Do you think I will react favourably to learn you understand the mind and soul of that twisted wretch? Of course you know his secrets. You are as warped as he is. His corruption is on the outside, bared to the eyes and displayed in the ravaging of his flesh. Your decay is within. Hidden, and all the darker for that fact.'

'Xarl,' Cyrion said, his voice softer. 'My brother. In the name of the father we share, listen to me now if never again.'

Xarl didn't reply. Cyrion watched his silent brother approaching as they came around to meeting on another half-circuit of the chamber. As they passed, Xarl gripped the rim of Cyrion's shoulder guard. It was a strange and awkward moment. Even though the red lenses of both their helms, Cyrion felt his brother making eye contact for the first time in several years.

'Speak,' Xarl said. 'Justify yourself, if you can.'

'Imagine,' Cyrion began, 'a secret voice within everyone. A voice that speaks of their fear. When I am with you, with Talos, with Uzas... all is silent. We are Astartes. "Where fear fills the mortal shell, we are hollow and cold".'

Xarl smirked as Cyrion quoted Malcharion's writings. Apt, very apt.

Mercutian's voice crackled over the vox. 'Keeping secrets from your new squadmate?'

'No, brother,' replied Cyrion. 'Forgive us this momentary disagreement.'

'Of course.' Mercutian's link went dead again.

'Continue,' Xarl said.

'It's... different around mortals. I hear their fears, like a chorus of shameful whispers. You kill a mortal and see the light die in his eyes. I hear him silently weeping, hear him whispering of a home world he will never see again, of a wife he was so afraid he would never lay eyes upon one last time. I... rip these thoughts from every mind I am near.'

The taint of the psyker, Xarl thought. In the years of the primarch's glory, such wretches would be purged from the Legion, or shaped according to rigid codes of behaviour and use. A wild psychic talent was an open door to possession and corruption by the soulless beings of the warp.

'Continue,' he said again. The word was much harder to speak this time.

'You cannot imagine what the Exalted sounds like to me, brother.' Cyrion's own voice was broken and hesitant, struggling to give the concepts a form in words. 'He shrieks... lost in the darkness of his own mind. He shouts our names, the names of Legion brothers dead and alive, imploring us to find him, to save him, to kill him.'

He took a breath before continuing. 'That is what I hear when I stand near him. His torment. His terror at the loss of control he suffers throughout his existence. He is no longer Astartes. His possession has allowed him to feel fear, and it has rendered him truly hollow. Terror bores through him like the tunnels of a hundred worms.'

Xarl realised he was still holding Cyrion's shoulder guard. He released it immediately, fighting down the snarl in his voice. 'I could easily have lived without that knowledge, brother.'

'As could I. But my revelations were not spoken to make you uncomfortable. The Exalted is two souls – Vandred, shrieking his slow way into oblivion, and something else... something formed from his hatred and meshed with the mind of another. When Talos threatened to awaken Malcharion, it was the first time I have heard both souls howl. Vandred's remnants and the daemon that claims him; both feared this moment.'

'We are here,' Xarl insisted. 'We stand watch over the rites of resurrection. If the Exalted truly fears this event and sends... dissuasion, it will not matter. Threats and oaths. Who of the Atramentar is truly ignoble enough to make war upon his brothers? Malek? Never. Garadon? He is the Exalted's creature, but he is no match for three of us. Any of the Atramentar would fall, and the Exalted is precious with the lives of his chosen elite.'

'You assume their lives are equally valued. No, brother,' Cyrion said. 'He will send Vraal.'

Both warriors turned as the great doors rumbled open again. Cyrion was already voxing to Talos.

'My brother, it's beginning.'

The reply was terse. 'First Claw. At any sign of aggression, you will engage and slay the target. *Ave Dominus Nox.*'

'Cyrion,' Xarl racked his bolter as one of the Atramentar entered the Hall of Remembrance, 'I hate it when you are right.'

MALEK SHARED THE lift to the lower levels with Talos and Adhemar.

'You cannot afford to be this naïve,' he said, his face as grim and set as white granite.

'I am not being naïve,' Talos said. Despite his respect for Malek, the Atramentar's tone fired his blood. He couldn't keep the edge of defiance from his voice. 'I am acting in 10th Company's best interests.'

'You are acting like a blind child.' Malek's voice was iron-stern now, and his black eyes glared. 'You talk of 10th Company's best interests? That is exactly my point. 10th Company is *dead*, Talos. Sometimes preservation of the past is a step backwards. I do not advocate change for change's sake. We are talking about the reality of our war.'

'The Night Haunter would never–'

'Do not dare speak of our father as if you know him better than I.' Malek's eyes narrowed, and his voice became an animalistic growl. 'Do not dare assume you were the only one he held private counsel with in his final nights. Many of us ranked among his chosen. Not you alone.'

'I know this. I am speaking of the legacy he wished for us.'

'He wished us to survive, and to defy the Imperium. That is all. Do you think he cared about the ranks we marched in and the titles we wore while we did our duty? We are barely over thirty Astartes. Squad unity is destroyed. Leadership is weak. Resources are stretched to the limit. We are not 10th Company of the VIII Legion. We haven't been for almost a century of our own time... and ten millennia of the galaxy's span.

'Do you truly remain blind to what you are doing?' Malek finished. He shook his head, as if the mere thought was impossible to fathom.

'I am willing to concede–'

'The question was rhetorical,' Malek grunted. 'Anyone can see it. You chance upon a hundred servitors just as our resources are almost bled dry. You walk the surface of our shattered home world, and anyone with their eyes open saw that as an omen. Then you steal a *Navigator,* of all the things to discover! Now a Titan princeps. You rail against the Exalted and speak of awakening the war-sage...'

Adhemar cut in. 'Talos, my brother. You are rebuilding the company to your vision. The Navigator was the boldest step. If the *Covenant* somehow lost Etrigius, the entire company would depend upon you, upon the Navigator you control. We couldn't even break into the warp without your... permission.'

'Etrigius is in fine health,' Talos said. But they were words he couldn't back up. Navigators may enjoy inhuman longevity because of their mutations, but Etrigius – who forever kept himself shrouded in his personal observation chambers close to the ship's prow – had barely been seen by anyone except the Exalted in decades. Octavia had access to his section of the ship, but her meagre reports through Septimus had mentioned nothing of Etrigius's mental or physical state. He seemed unchanged.

'I am of the Atramentar,' Malek said, the tones heavy with import. Talos understood immediately. Malek would never break an oath to reveal the secrets of his liege lord, even if he despised the Exalted. But he was free to let Talos know he had obviously accompanied the Exalted into Etrigius's presence.

Perhaps the discovery of Octavia on Nostramo's surface was a more direct threat to the Exalted than Talos had realised.

She would need to be guarded. Guarded vehemently. And Malcharion's reawakening…

'Mercutian, Cyrion and Xarl stand watch in the Hall of Remembrance,' he said to Malek. The robed warrior nodded, his statuesque face resigned.

'That is probably wise. How long has the ritual been taking place?'

'Four hours. The Dreadnought's chassis was being powered up and consecrated when I left. They had not yet begun to wake the sleeper.'

'The odds are not in our favour,' Adhemar said. 'He has never awoken, even once.'

'And he did not go into that sarcophagus willingly,' Malek added.

Talos's vox crackled live, interrupting further discussion.

'My brother,' said Cyrion. 'It is beginning.'

Vraal strode into the Hall of Remembrance.

The roaring lion's head of his right shoulder guard, marking him as one of the Atramentar, sported a pattern of random gashes and cuts, the marks of infrequent repairs after countless battles. The rest of his Terminator war-plate followed suit. Scars marred the midnight surface, the lips of these carved chasms gunmetal grey where repainting was in order.

Old blood still flaked his gauntlets. Although any matter on his lightning claws was burned away each time he activated them, gore would streak his gauntlets for weeks after he bloodied himself in battle.

The others misunderstood this as irreverence. As *disrespect.* It was almost laughable.

What greater honour to the machine-spirit of his armour was there than to display the wounds it had won in battle? What nobler reverence could be paid than revealing with pride all the scars that had failed to see him slain?

Thrusting from his armour's hunched back were trophy racks made from bronze spikes, each with Astartes helms and their oversized skulls clattering together with every step he took.

Vraal licked his teeth as his red-tinted displays locked onto every living being in the chamber. There, the servitors tending the silent Dreadnought, like mindless worshippers. There, the tech-adept Deltrian working over a console of arcane lights and switches and levers. There, the new blood of First Claw, dour Mercutian, standing in the shadows of the great doors to Vraal's left. There, Cyrion and Xarl, bolters held to chests.

The Atramentar noticed a warning rune flicker briefly. He was being scanned by an auspex. Deltrian, surely. Vraal gave the watching tech-priest an acknowledging nod as he stalked further into the room. The spindly machine-creature bowed back in respect. Hateful thing. A curse on the Mechanicum, that such filth was necessary to the Legion's operation.

Vraal was under no illusions about his presence here. The Exalted was playing its game with care, for to oppose Talos openly might incite full-blooded rebellion. What remained of the 10th would be broken, some following the Exalted, others joining the prophet. For Vraal, the choice was no choice at all. The past or the future. Talos represented the former. What was there in the past but failure and shame?

It would be a relief when the prophet was finally killed. Well did Vraal remember his disappointment when the Exalted's plan to whore Talos off to the

Ruinous Powers failed so completely. The Despoiler had allowed the prophet to escape with no resistance – Abaddon had even failed to kill the two slaves Talos evidently treasured – and 10th Company was burdened with the prophet's irritating anachronistic meddling once again.

Maddening. Like an unscratchable itch.

No, Vraal was under no illusions at all. Open conflict was out of the question. It would galvanise Talos's emergent faction. One of the favoured Atramentar could never be used. It would be undeniable proof the Exalted was acting against the prophet. But not wild, unpredictable Vraal. Oh, no. Vraal would be mourned for his 'vicious temper' and 'choleric humours', while the Exalted waxed lyrical about how he deeply regretted Vraal's terrible disruption of the resurrection ritual.

His bitterness left him uncontrollable, the Exalted would say. *Vraal's actions bring shame upon us all. Such disunity...*

Yes, Vraal could almost hear his eulogy spoken now. The Exalted had sent him here to die, spending his life for the good of the warband. So be it.

Of course, this new plan to awaken Malcharion had to be put down with tact.

With nuance.

With *subtlety.*

Vraal's claws slid from the sheaths on his gauntlets. They sparked and crackled, wreathed in killing lightning.

'Brothers!' he called joyously into the vox. 'Everyone in this room is going to die!'

A moment later, he was wading into bolter fire, laughing through the speakers on his tusked helm.

Chunks broke away from his trophy racks, the shattered pieces thrown behind. A tusk from his own helm splintered. His chestplate cracked. His knee guard split, spraying ceramite debris to the ground. A storm of bolter fire hacked and chipped at his Terminator war-plate.

This was almost fun.

The three weaklings from First Claw were falling back, presenting unified fire that was doing nothing to suppress the Atramentar's advance. Vraal heard Deltrian's mechanical voice bleating over his vox.

'Why would you do this! This is blasphemy! This chamber is consecrated to the Machine-God!'

Ugh. Would that Vraal's armour had any ranged weapons… He could silence the wailing tech-priest once and for all. As it was, his lightning claws flared as if in response to his anger.

The three Astartes opposing him were backing away, edging towards the still form of Malcharion and unrelenting in their fire. This was irritatingly tactical. Vraal knew killing them was only a secondary concern, no matter how pleasurable it would be. He needed to end Malcharion's resurrection, once and for all. They stood in the most obvious way of that: simply tearing the Dreadnought's form apart with his claws.

Ah, well.

Vraal broke into what approximated a run for an Astartes encumbered by the near-invulnerable shell of Terminator armour. Not making for the defiant Astartes. No, that would be suicide without doing his duty.

'Tech-priest!' Vraal staggered as the withering hail of bolter fire shattered his lower leg plating and interrupted the workings of the servos. 'Come! We must talk, you and I!'

His stumbling, limping run had a sickening speed all its own. The reaper-like tech-priest did not leave his control console, even as Vraal slammed his right claw through the sacred machinery. Disappointingly, nothing exploded.

A particularly well-aimed bolt threw his head to the side for a moment. Most likely from Xarl. That bastard was known for being a wicked shot.

But the Astartes held back now. Vraal stood among the control consoles, thudding closer step by step to Deltrian. They wouldn't risk exploding bolts damaging the machinery. He raked both claws out to the sides, lacerating more blessed Mechanicum technology.

How curious. The defilement made the tech-priest weep. He was weeping what looked like oil, running down his skullish silver cheeks in dark tracks. Vraal took in this intriguing fact in the span of half a second. He used the rest of the second to ram the four curved knuckle-blades – each a metre in length – straight through Deltrian's torso.

'Hnnkhsssssshhhh–' the tech-priest wheezed, cutting off in a blurted babble of static.

'Very wise,' Vraal chuckled, pulling the blades back. The resistance within the adept's body had felt unpleasant and inhuman. There was little joy in rending apart false machine-life. Deltrian fell back, his black robe clutched closed even as he fell to the marble floor.

A proximity warning rune flickered a moment too late. One of First Claw was on him.

Spinning, claws up to guard, Vraal faced the other Astartes.

Xarl's bolter kicked at close range, snapping one of Vraal's claws off in a shower of bolt shell debris. His chainsword howled down a heartbeat later.

'Just... *die...*' Xarl breathed over the vox. His grinding chainsword blade skidded across the Atramentar's hulking armour, biting into surface metal without penetrating deeper.

Vraal disengaged with a shrug of his shoulders. His Terminator war-plate boosted his already inhuman strength far beyond standard Astartes armour. And as to the odds of a chainsword piercing it... Well, at least Xarl was keen. It made things all the more amusing.

Vraal raised his right gauntlet – now missing a talon – and caught the chainsword between crackling sword-claws on its second descent. The revving blade immediately started eating its way through the softer joint armour and servo fibres of Vraal's gauntlets. With a grunt of effort, the Atramentar twisted his arm. The claws sparked with a flare of power as they met the trapped chainblade, and severed it with a wrenching snap.

Disarmed, Xarl leapt back, casting his ruined sword hilt aside as it coughed into death, and bringing his bolter to bear again.

He didn't fire. A warning rune told Vraal why, and he spun to meet the threat of Cyrion and Mercutian behind.

They came at him together, leaping with gladius blades drawn and reversed like plunging daggers in the hands of assassins. Cyrion's stab clattered aside from the dense war-plate, and Vraal smashed the Astartes aside with a slash of his claw that tore through Cyrion's armour.

Mercutian's thrust bit, and bit deep. It was a moment of shocking, sickening intimacy – a wrath-inspiring violation – when the two Astartes met one another's gaze through their crimson eye lenses. The gladius was a cold, hateful heaviness in Vraal's stomach, and even as his enhanced physiology coped with the wound by sealing the haemorrhage, he felt it being torn open again with Mercutian yanking the blade upwards.

He'd breached a soft joint in the armour. *And this... this was pain...*

Vraal hadn't quite remembered how much it hurt, it had been so long since he'd felt it.

Impacts struck him from behind in a staccato burst. The rhythm was utterly familiar. A bolter on full auto. *Xarl was... firing... and he needed to...*

Free himself... from the blade...

Vraal lifted his claw. The suit answered slowly, sluggish with the damage it was sustaining. Mercutian kept pulling the blade up, carving through Vraal's innards even though the blade was blocked from moving too far by the Atramentar's dense chestplate.

He spat blood into his helm and backhanded Mercutian away. The other Astartes snapped back like a puppet with its strings tugged too hard, and smashed into the ruined control console.

Mercutian was down. Cyrion was... *Ha!* His blow to Cyrion had severed the wretch's arm at the elbow. He was still picking himself up, shouting his hate through the vox as he looked for his bolter.

Xarl. He had to deal with Xarl. Xarl was always the dangerous one.

Blinking blood and sweat from his eyes, Vraal turned to do exactly that. He launched forward, claws powering towards Xarl like seven short lances.

Xarl cursed even as he moved, throwing himself to the side, muscles aflame, faster than he had ever moved in his gene-extended life.

The tips of Vraal's right claws caught him. Xarl clenched his teeth as the three blades sliced and penetrated his armour. A moment of agony pulsed through his left thigh, and he crashed to the ground on dead legs.

Vraal's estimation of the situation changed. Deltrian, that spindly machine-freak, was crawling away towards another wall-mounted console. He looked injured. Was that right? Did machine-men suffer injury? Damage, perhaps.

Cyrion was advancing again, one-armed and gripping his gladius, the pain of his wound doubtlessly swallowed whole by his armour's injection of stimulants and nerve-killers directly into the bloodstream and brain. Mercutian was back up as well, unarmed. His blade had broken in the fall, and he must have expended all of his bolter ammunition. Xarl, ever defiant, had drawn his bolt pistol and was aiming it from where he lay on the ground, unable to stand with his leg half-severed.

That was the moment Vraal realised he was probably going to win.

'Brothers, brothers,' he laughed. 'Who dies first?'

'Do your worst,' Xarl barked, opening fire again. Flashing runes blinked across Vraal's display as the bolts hammered into his head and chestplate. *Aiming for the neck joint,* Vraal knew. He was still laughing, still advancing, when Xarl's pistol clicked empty.

But... that sound...

...wwrrrrRRRRRRRRRR

Vraal's bloody face contorted as he scowled at the rising noise. *What the hell?*

It was the sound of a Reaper-pattern double-barrelled autocannon powering up. It was followed by the throaty mechanical *clunk-clunk-clunk* of autoloaders cycling into life.

Vraal turned in time to see it open fire. When it did, the Hall of Remembrance shook with the sheer volume of the weapon's discharge. Storms ferocious enough to bring down hive towers had done their destructive work with less volume and rage. Servitors too mind-wiped to cover their ears suffered ruptured eardrums.

The helms of First Claw filtered the sounds to tolerable levels, but every one of them had teeth clenched against the noise.

Vraal heard it all, with damning clarity, because it was happening to him.

Six mass-reactive explosive shells – each one capable of killing a Rhino transport on its own – smashed into the Atramentar in the space of three seconds. The first destroyed his chestplate and would have seen him dead in moments through the horrendous blood loss from his mangled insides. He was spared this death as the second shell killed him instantly, exploding against his tusked helm and annihilating his head and right shoulder.

The other four shells impacted and tore the remains to pieces. In three seconds, nothing remained of Vraal of the Atramentar beyond shards of broken armour and the wounds carried by First Claw.

The storm passed.

The thunder faded.

On ancient servos, the massive form of a bronze-edged, blue-armoured Dreadnought stepped forward. It was heavy enough to shake the room. The cannonfire had been nothing compared to its howling servo joints and cacophonous tread.

'L-lord?' Mercutian whispered.

'You're awake…' Cyrion breathed. 'How…'

In a guttural, vox-altered boom, the Dreadnought spoke from speakers wrought into its ornate chassis.

'I heard bolter fire.'

XV
REBORN

THE EXALTED RECLINED on its throne, forcing its face into a smile.

'It is a blessing to see you, brother.'

The hulking shape of Malcharion dominated the *Covenant's* bridge. Light from the console screens flickered across his body's dark ceramite hull.

With the ship idle in orbit, the crew, those human enough to care, were free to cast sidelong glances at the incredible sight in their midst. Malcharion stood alone before the commander's raised central dais. The Dreadnought was tall enough that its sarcophagus was level with the seated figure.

Alongside the walls, every Astartes not engaged in planetary operations had gathered to witness the resurrection – and the first meeting with the Exalted. Talos and Adhemar stood in rapt awe. So did most of the others.

Around the Exalted's throne stood the Atramentar. All of them, except for Vraal. Seven warriors, the Terminator elite, in an orderly half-ring behind the throne. Malek and Garadon stood closest to the Exalted, as always.

For the longest time, the war machine said nothing. The Exalted watched with its slanted black eyes, raptor-like in his attention to detail. It fancied it could almost hear, under the ever-present hum of the Dreadnought's back-mounted power generator, the occasional bubbling swish of the amniotic fluid within the sarcophagus as whatever remained of Malcharion's mortal body twitched.

'You have changed,' the Dreadnought boomed.

The Exalted's smirk did not fade, indeed it became suddenly more genuine. 'As have you, brother.'

The machine made a noise akin to a grunt of acknowledgement. It sounded like a tank shifting gears.

'You are uglier than I remember.' Another gear-change grunt, this one closer to a chuckle. **'I would not have believed it possible.'**

'I see your decades of inactivity while the rest of us waged our father's war have not dimmed your... humour.'

'Do not bore me back into slumber with your dour nature, Vandred.'

'I am the Exalted now. You would do well to heed that, Malcharion. Time has changed many things.'

'Not everything. Hear me, Vandred. I have awoken. Torn from a century of nightmares, each one a memory of our greatest failure. The Soul Hunter tells me that war calls once more. You will tell me of this war. Now.'

The Exalted's lips curled. *The Soul Hunter.* Sickening.

'As you wish.'

THE BATTLEFIELD HAD several names. None of them quite carried the weight of true import. This was to be the decisive conflict, the moment of truth.

Located in the highest reaches of the northern hemisphere's mountain range, it was the bastion of Mechanicus strength above the equator.

To the invaders, grudgingly impressed by the curving rock formations and the fortress-factories built into them, it was the Omnissiah's Claw. A theatrical name, but apt: the mountains resembled steel fingers reaching for the heavens, as if the fortresses could tear the invader vessels from orbit.

To the cold cogitators and tactical logic engines of the Mechanicus defenders, it was simply Site 017-017.

Seventeen-Seventeen, the main foundry of the Legio Maledictis, heart and soul of Crythe Prime's Adeptus Titanicus forces.

And void-shielded so densely that orbital bombardment was utterly beyond hope. Ironically, such a defence was pointless. Abaddon had made it clear to his captains and commanders that Seventeen-Seventeen was to be captured, not destroyed. Such a base would be able to repair, outfit and construct Titans to serve in his coming crusade. At the very least, huge quantities of materiel and resources could be plundered from the fortress-factories here.

Time, however, was growing short. Astropaths across the fleet told of whispers within the warp. The Imperium's response to the invasion would arrive within weeks.

The Blood Angels. The Marines Errant. Countless regiments of the Imperial Guard. Abaddon had ventured far from his haven within the warp anomaly known as the Eye of Terror, where the Imperium could never follow. While he had chosen a fine target in Crythe and hit the world with the decisive power of this hastily-assembled fleet, victory must now come quickly or be abandoned altogether. Already the month of war had been drawn out too long, and ground taken at too high a cost. The Mechanicus and their accursed champions in the Legio Maledictis were defiant, indefatigable foes.

If astropathic premonitions were accurate, the Imperium's battlefleets en route would present unbreakable might. Here, the forces of the Throne sensed their chance to bring the Despoiler to justice. Navigators and other psychically-sensitive souls among the Chaos fleet told of a great wave of pressure rolling from the warp, like the thunderheads of a coming storm. Every warrior within the Warmaster's armies knew this for what it was. A convergence of warp routes, the way a fleet of ships would drive waves of water before their prows. Invisible currents within the Sea of Souls lashed at the Crythe Cluster as countless Imperial vessels burned their engines hot to defend the forge world and avenge the worlds already fallen.

It all came down to Seventeen-Seventeen.

Crythe Prime had to be taken.

The endgame had begun.

THE NIGHT LORDS of 10th Company's remnants were tasked with making up part of the spearhead in the initial assaults. Alongside them would be their kin from the *Hunter's Premonition*.

With masses of traitorous Imperial Guard now siding with the Warmaster, along with the penal legions harvested from Solace, the Night Lords of *Hunter's Premonition* and the *Covenant of Blood* had a handful of foundries and fortress-factories marked as objectives.

The Black Legion, far outnumbering the Night Lords contingent, was assigned to larger numbers of similar factorum objectives. Talos no longer detected any obvious signs of the Warmaster seeking to bleed the VIII Legion ahead of his own troops.

Necessity stole any such favouritism.

* * *

First Claw's arming chamber was a hive of activity.

Serfs and servitors attached armour into place, machining it closed and sealed. Septimus was one of them, checking the joint seals of Talos's armour, ignored by the Astartes as they spoke.

Cyrion held his arm out as a servitor attached his vambrace and gauntlet. Everyone in the room caught a glimpse of the new augmetic limb, its metal surface a dull, oceanic grey, still uncovered by synth-flesh. Soon enough, the naked steel and titanium arm was armoured in the midnight blue of his battle plate.

Weapons were blessed and honoured. Oaths were sworn. Spinal sockets were penetrated by the invasive connection needles of power armour locking into place. Vision was tinted murder-red by helms descending over faces.

'I have not seen Octavia since long before her surgery yesterday,' Cyrion ventured. 'How does our Navigator fare, artificer?'

Septimus did not look over from where he was fastening an oath scroll to Talos's shoulder. The parchment was the white of fresh cream, detailing in Talos's flowing Nostraman handwriting all of the mission objectives, and his blood-sworn promises to succeed in each one. Oaths of Moment like these were no longer common within the Legion. Xarl also wore one, but Mercutian, Uzas, Cyrion and Adhemar abstained from the tradition.

'She is well, Lord Cyrion,' said Septimus. 'I expect she is with Navigator Etrigius again. They spend much time in discussion. They... often argue, apparently.'

'I see. My thanks for the work you did on my bolter.' As he spoke, he held the weapon up, looking over it as he cradled the weapon in his gauntlets. The name '*Banshee*' was written upon its side in swirling Nostraman script.

'A pleasure to serve, Lord Cyrion.'

'How is the void-born? Is she well?'

Septimus froze as he checked the rivets of Talos's shoulder guards. 'The... the what, Lord Cyrion?'

'The void-born. How is she?'

'What's this now?' Uzas asked, suddenly interested.

'She is a mortal, brother. Beneath your concern,' said Cyrion.

'She is... well, thank you, Lord Cyrion.'

'Good to hear. Don't look so surprised, we're not all blind to the goings on of the ship. Take her my regards, will you?'

'Yes, Lord Cyrion.'

'Did she like her gift?' asked Talos.

Septimus forced himself not to freeze again. 'Yes, lord.'

'What gift?' Uzas sounded irritated to be excluded.

'A Legion medallion,' said Talos. 'This mortal is treasured by some of the crew. Apparently, treasured enough to warrant my protection.' Talos turned to Septimus again, and the slave's blood froze. 'Without my permission.'

'Forgive me, master.'

'I heard holes were drilled into the coin, and she wears it as a necklace,' Talos continued. 'Is that desecration, Cyrion? Defiling Legion relics?'

'I think not, brother. But I shall take the matter up with the Exalted. We must be certain of such things.'

Septimus's smile was forced, and he swallowed again. He tried to speak. He failed.

'Forgive us a moment's levity at your expense, Septimus,' Talos said. He flexed his fists, rotating his wrists, testing the ease of motion. His right gauntlet was definitely stiff. A replacement must be found soon.

Faroven. Faroven, the brother that Talos saw die in a dream. From his body, would the new gauntlet come.

His end cannot be far away now.

Cyrion clamped his bolter to his thigh on its magnetic coupling. 'Aye, it's been a long time since we were mortal. Strange how you forget how to joke.'

Septimus nodded again, unsure if even now Cyrion was making fun of him, and still far from comfortable with such 'humour'.

'By the way,' Cyrion added. 'Take this.'

Septimus caught the coin easily, one hand taking it out of the air on its downward arc. It was a twin to Talos's own coin, silver and marked the same, but for Cyrion's name in the written runes.

'If you're going to give mine away and doom me to watching over a ten-year-old girl,' Talos said, 'I need to keep you alive somehow.'

Septimus bowed in deep thanks to both of them, and finished his duties in humbled and confused silence.

IT HAD TAKEN Octavia barely five minutes to decide that she didn't like Etrigius at all.

According to the *Covenant's* Navigator, he had known upon first seeing her that he disliked her. This was the kind of fact he found necessary to share.

Etrigius wasn't even remotely human anymore. That was little concern to Octavia, and nowhere near as shocking to her as many of the more mundane aspects of life aboard the *Covenant.*

She was a Navigator, a scion of the Navis Nobilite, and even if her House name wasn't worth an iota of respect in the great and wide galaxy, she was still a daughter of humanity's most precious bloodlines.

She knew what the Navigator gene did to all of her kind in time. In that regard, sitting with the no-longer-human form of Etrigius was disconcerting, but never truly unnerving.

Much worse was his penchant for glorifying his own existence.

These nightly lessons were now her duty – he'd made that clear the first time he'd demanded her presence weeks before – but they were far from pleasant.

Etrigius's domain was the antithesis of the gloom that pervaded the *Covenant's* innards the way blood ran through a body's veins. He claimed a modest chamber close to the ship's massively-armoured prow, and bathed the room in oppressive white light from glow-globes mounted on the walls. Octavia found the brightness hard to bear after the ship's dark halls. Her warp eye remained covered, but her human eyes wept stinging tears each time she came to visit the other Navigator in his den. The illumination of false sunlight after a month of night.

'Can you dim these lights?' she asked the first time she'd been granted admittance by Etrigius's robed slaves.

'No,' he said, seeming to muse. 'I dislike the dark.'

'It might be said that you're on the wrong ship.'

Camaraderie had threatened to bloom between them at that moment. They had one thing in common that no other soul shared. Yet instead of a unity forming, they'd quickly descended into bickering and vague tolerance.

Etrigius's attendants – not one of them unaugmented and younger than sixty – admitted her to 'the master's gallery'. The title was appropriate. An entire wall was taken up with pict screens reflecting dozens of views from different points of the ship's outer hull. As it was, the screens showed the rest of the Warmaster's battle-fleet, and the world the *Covenant* orbited.

In the warp... the screens would come into their own. Octavia had to admire the wish to see every angle of the ship as one guided it through the sea of souls.

The rest of the chamber was much less admirable. And much less tidy. Clothes were piled here and there, strewn across the floor, as well as jewellery. When she'd first entered, her boot had crunched a golden earring into the ground. Etrigius, thankfully, hadn't noticed.

Octavia suspected Etrigius had been handsome at one point. If not handsome, then at least well-presented. Before his service in the Great Crusade and the century of chronological time since. She formed this opinion from his voice and bearing, both of which remained cultured and polite despite his many other changes from the near-human he'd been at birth.

His skin was grey. Not the wan tone of a sunless existence, nor even the pale grey of the dead or the dying. It was grey the way a deepwater shark's belly was grey: fish-like but unscaled, thick, completely inhuman.

His fingers were almost armoured in gold and ruby, such was the number of rings he wore. Octavia was no expert, but what confused her was that the rings varied in quality from the exquisitely valuable to the almost worthless. What seemed to be the only common factor was that each ring was a shade of red set in a mounting of gold.

The Navigator's many-ringed thumbs and fingers each possessed an extra joint. Octavia would lose track of what she was saying if she got lost in their eerie, hypnotic, curling movements. Fingernails more akin to a feline's claws sickle-curved from the tips of Etrigius's grey fingers. These he used to stroke the tattered leather of his observation couch, forever seeming to engineer new splits in the material.

The rest of Etrigius's body was masked by a robe of the same deep blue favoured by the Legion's warriors. His domed head was smooth enough for Octavia to be sure no hair ever grew there, and his 'human' eyes were always masked in pressurised goggles with thick clear lenses, featuring some strange violet fluid swirling within. She'd asked what the liquid in his lenses was, asked how he even saw through the murk, but he'd deigned not to answer. Etrigius did that a great deal. Evidently, he only answered topics he found worthy of discussion.

'They have freed your warp eye,' he murmured, with something resembling awe.

She touched the bandana tied around her forehead. 'I think they must be coming to trust me. I mean, after I took the name... After Talos saved me...'

'I was not informed of this. Why was I not told you were to be unblinded?'

'Is it any of your business?'

'I am the Navigator for the *Covenant of Blood*. Any issue pertaining to the warp is within my purview.'

'I've been sitting here an hour listening to you. You only just noticed the metal was gone from my forehead?'

'This was the first time I have bothered to face in your direction,' he said, and it was true enough. Etrigius was not enamoured of eye contact.

'I am tired of feeling helpless on this ship,' she said, more to herself than to him.

Etrigius smiled, for once, with apparent sincerity. 'Do not expect that to fade, girl.'

She watched him in silence for several moments, hoping he would continue.

'We are at once slaves and slavemasters,' he said. 'Enslaved, yet valuable beyond measure.' Etrigius gestured to the screens, displaying the Chaos fleet orbiting Crythe. 'Without us, these traitors are crippled. Their endless crusade could never be fought.'

Octavia's gaze never left the grey man's.

'Did you choose this life?'

'No. And neither will you. But we will both live it, all the same.'

'Why would I wish to seal myself away in here?' she countered.

'What Navigator can be satisfied without a vessel to guide?' The words left his lips with a sickeningly condescending sense of kindness.

Octavia shook her head without realising she was even doing so. An unconvincing denial, truly no more than an instinctive need to say no.

Etrigius smiled that same smile. 'You hunger to sail the stars, as we all do. It's in the blood. You can no more hide that desire than you can hide the need to breathe. When the time comes, when the Astartes ask you to guide them... you will say yes.'

Octavia once more felt the potential for a connection between them. She could have used that moment to ask for revelations about navigating the warp without using the guiding light of the Emperor's Astronomican. She could have said any one of a hundred things to bridge the gap between herself and her fellow Navigator.

Instead, she rose to her feet and left.

A cold-blooded sense of inevitability had stolen her tongue.

WHEN SEPTIMUS FOUND her, she was in Blackmarket.

In the *Covenant's* mortal decks, a communal chamber linked many of the individual halls and quarters, and as the Great Crusade played out across the galaxy, the Legion's loyal servants and slaves came to use the chamber as a trading post and a place to gather. The black market, as it was back then, derived its name from the perpetual darkness of the chamber, only marginally dispelled by lamp packs and glow-globes. Even with a full crew in better days, the mortal decks had endured the same scarce illumination as they did now.

Fifty or so people crowded the chamber. His status ensured he received respectful nods or greetings from most of them, even from the clusters of rival gang emissaries here to trade for ammunition and power packs. Here, in all its shadowed glory, was a microcosm of fallen Nostramo, born afresh in the blackness.

One old woman pressed her grimy hands to the bronze surface of his augmented temple and eyebrow.

'It's not so bad,' she smiled, exposing rotten teeth in her otherwise kindly, lined face.

'I'm getting used to it.'

'The surgery took you from us for too long. Weeks! We worried!'

'I thank you for your concern, Shaya.'

'Nale's gang was killed close to the enginarium decks.' She dropped her voice. 'None of the others are claiming responsibility. There's talk it's another beast, come from the deepest dark.'

Septimus felt a grim mood settling firmly on his shoulders. He had been part of the hunting party to slay the last warp-creature that spawned in the bowels of the ship.

'I will speak with the masters. I promise.'

'Bless you, Septimus,' she said. 'Bless you.'

'I... heard Octavia was here?'

'Ah, yes. The new girl.' The old woman smiled again, gesturing to a market stall with a small group of people stood around. 'She is with the void-born.'

With the...? Why?

'My thanks,' he said, and moved on.

Octavia was indeed with the void-born. The little girl, her pupils eternally huge in the gloom into which she was born, was showing Octavia a selection of articulated string puppets. Octavia stood at the stall, run by the void-born's ageing mother and father. She smiled and nodded down at the girl's presentation.

Septimus came alongside the Navigator and bowed to the void-born's parents. They greeted him and remarked on how his wounds were healing.

'I had to get away from Etrigius,' Octavia said in Gothic. 'I have the medallion now,' she added almost defensively. 'So I went for a walk.'

'The ship is still dangerous, medallion or not.'

'I know,' she replied, not looking at him.

'Do you understand anything she's said?' Septimus nodded to the little girl.

'Not a word. Her parents have been translating some. I just wanted to meet her. The respect she receives is incredible. People keep coming over, just to speak with her. Someone paid for a tiny lock of her hair.'

'She is revered,' Septimus said. He looked down at the void-born, who was staring up through her ratty and snarled mop of long black hair.

'Athasavis te corunai tol shathen sha'shian?' he asked.

'Kosh, kosh'eth tay,' she smiled back. A beaming smile on her face, she held up the silver Legion medallion, holed through and strung on a leather thong cord. She wore it like a medal of honour. 'Ama sho'shalnath mirsa tota. Ithis jasha. Ithis jasha nereoss.'

Septimus offered her a little bow, smiling despite his black mood.

'What did she say?' Octavia asked, trying to hide her disappointment at the Nostraman conversation.

'She thanked me for the gift, and said she thinks my new eye is a very nice colour.'

'Oh.'

The void-born started babbling, pointing up at Octavia. Septimus smiled again.

'She says you are very pretty, and asks if you are ever going to learn Nostraman, so you can talk to her properly.'

Octavia nodded. 'Jasca,' she said, then in a quieter voice to Septimus, 'That's "yes", isn't it?'

'Jasca,' he replied. 'It is. Come, we need to talk. I'm sorry I've been away since your surgery. It has been an interesting day since we last spoke.'

He should never have been awakened.

Had he not served with heart and courage and loyalty? Had he not slain the primarch's enemies? Had he not obeyed the orders of the First Warmaster? What more did life demand of him?

Now he walked once more, striding through the waking world. *And for what?* To witness the degeneration of everything the Legion had once been. To stand defiant against Vandred while 10th Company crumbled in the final moments of its decay.

This was not life. This was an extension of an existence he had rightfully left behind.

He was two bodies. A mind divided between two physical forms. On one level, through his most immediate perceptions, he felt what was now: the vehicular strength of his tank-like body. The massive arms jointed by grinding servos. The claw capable of mangling adamantium and ceramite. The cannon capable of annihilating entire platoons of men.

An unbreathing, tireless avatar of the Mechanicum's unity between flesh and machine.

All of that could be dissolved within a single moment's lapse in concentration. These immediate sensations were an effort to maintain. In the moments when the ancient warrior let his focus waver, he would feel himself, his mortal husk, encased within the sarcophagus and suspended in cold, cold, cold amniotic fluid.

These truer sensations were sickening to dwell upon, but Malcharion's attention tore back to them time and again. His legless, one-armed husk of a body, gently cradled in icy, gritty fluid. The back of his head and spine was a vertical splash of jagged, awkward pain as machine tendrils and MIU brain spikes needled his ravaged body, forcing his thoughts into junction with the Dreadnought body.

Sometimes, when he tried to move his left arm – the claw-like power fist – he felt his true limb, the wasted fleshly limb, thumping weakly against the side of the amniotic coffin that housed his corpse. The first time he had tried to speak to Vandred, instead of the piercing tendrils within his mind carrying his thoughts into vox-voice, he had felt his true mouth open. Only then had he realised he *breathed* the freezing fluid now. It was how he stayed alive. Oil-thick and numbingly cold, the amniotics circulated through his respiratory system. The ooze caked his lungs, a dead weight within a helpless, strengthless body.

A long time ago, he had battled alongside his brothers of the Iron Hands Legion. After those wars had ended, he battled against those same brothers. Malcharion knew their beliefs well. It was unconscionable to him that such stoic, resilient warriors found this eternal entombment to be some kind of glorious afterlife.

'I will lead the next surface assault,' he'd boomed at the gathered Night Lords. The warriors of his Legion bowed their heads or thumped fists to breastplates in respect. In pride! Incredible. They saw only what was on the outside. They had no conception of the withered corpse within as its starved face pressed against the front of its coffin.

'We are the Lords of the Night. We are the sons of the VIII Legion. And we will take Seventeen-Seventeen, so that for a thousand years the Imperium will lament the hour of our coming to Crythe.'

The cheers had been loud and long.

'Prepare a drop-pod,' the Dreadnought demanded. **'I stand in midnight clad once more, and my claws thirst for Imperial blood.'**

The cheers roared louder.

An eyeless, tongueless, one-armed corpse floated within the god-like machine, knowing it would soon taste war for the first time in ten thousand years.

XVI
SEVENTEEN-SEVENTEEN

'I HAVE NOTICED *an anomaly.*

Many Imperial records have come to deal very kindly with the Crythe Cluster Insurrection, but praise is most often levelled at the saviour fleet led by the arriving Astartes of the Blood Angels Chapter, rather than the initial defence of any individual world. Critical eyes were most often cast at the 'dubious resistance' put up by the Adeptus Mechanicus in the defence of its principal bastion in the northern hemisphere, Site 017-017.

Indeed, that site's survival is often entirely attributed to the instability of the Archenemy's forces upon Crythe Prime and the well-noted tendency of the Traitor Legions to fall upon one another at the slightest provocation.

Entire mountains were hollowed out to make room for the blessed Titan foundries of the Legio Maledictis. Had the Despoiler's war been successful, these would have been a resource of overwhelming value: used, plundered and stripped of their worth before the arriving Imperial fleet bestowed its infinite vengeance upon the accursed forces of the Warmaster.

Those rugged mountainsides were thick with elite Mechanicus skitarii, like lice in a beggar's hair.

Arranging thousands of individual landings across the entire mountain range would have taken a great deal of time that remained unavailable to the Despoiler.

At this stage, the Warmaster believed only weeks remained before the first Blood Angel battle-barge would soar into the system to bring the God-Emperor's justice. Abaddon, a thousand curses upon his name, knew this from his own astropathic sources. Prisoners captured after the war confirmed this to us.

Such foreknowledge is the only conceivable explanation for a massed surface landing on the plains before Site 017-017's foothills. In essence, Abaddon cast his hordes planetside and hurled them 'at the front gates', as it were.

I have heard it said that our greatest weapon against the Archenemy is the foe's own nature. That may indeed be so. Fate was most certainly on the side of righteousness the day the Night Lords and Black Legion within the Crythe offensive turned against one another.

No Imperial record I have been able to trace details exactly why Abaddon's command over portions of his army broke so completely, nor does it explain what – if anything! – the forces of the Archenemy sought to gain from their untimely division.

If such internal conflict is down to anything more than the maddened behaviour of tainted, once-human beasts, it is unlikely to ever come to light.'

– Interrogator Reshlan Darrow
Annotation in his pivotal work:
Faces of the Despoiler

FIRST CLAW SHUDDERED as one.

'Breaching atmosphere,' Adhemar said to the others within the confines of the drop-pod. 'One minute.'

'Why the rough deployment?' Cyrion asked.

'Anti-air fire,' Mercutian grumbled.

'This high? Not a chance.'

'It's just a rough ride down,' said Adhemar. 'Weather patterns, rising heat, high pressure. Stay focused, brothers.'

'Blood,' Uzas was mumbling. 'Blood and skulls and souls for the Red King.'

'Shut up,' Adhemar growled. 'Shut up or I'll tear your head off, stuff it with frag grenades, and use it as the ugliest explosive ever made.'

'He can't hear you,' said Cyrion. 'Ignore him. He always does this.'

'Blood for the Blood God,' Uzas's voice was thick and wet. He was salivating again, venomous drool coating his chin. 'Skulls for the–'

Talos slammed the palm of his hand on Uzas's helm, crashing the side of the helmet against the headrest of his brother's restraint throne.

'Shut *up*,' he snapped. '*Every* mission. *Every* battle. *Enough*.'

Uzas didn't react at all.

'See?' Cyrion said to Adhemar.

Adhemar just nodded, his thoughts his own. 'Thirty seconds.'

'This is not going to be easy,' Mercutian said. 'Are we going in with the Violators and the Scourges of Quintus?'

'They're to the east,' Talos answered, 'between us and the Black Legion. Just remember your targets. We break in, we kill the unit commanders as ordered, and we break out to our own lines.'

'Twenty seconds,' Adhemar noted.

'This is not about attrition,' Talos said, repeating Malcharion's words at the briefing, 'and we're dead if anyone tries to turn it into a fair fight.

'Ten seconds.'

'Kill, and break away. Let Abaddon's mortal followers bleed for him.' Talos couldn't resist the grin that coloured his words. 'That's not our job.'

IT WAS A decent plan on the surface, but with obvious risks.

The squads that volunteered for this, across all of the Traitor Legions and renegade Chapters, were given poor odds of survival.

In front of the Exalted and Malcharion, Talos had demanded First Claw be part of the assault.

Like all troops, the Mechanicus's skitarii, despite their training and augmentations, had proved time and again they suffered when severed from their battlefield leadership. The Warmaster's forces, seeking to capitalise on that potential weakness, hurled elite squads of Astartes into the warzones below – each unit tasked with the assassination of several tech-adept commanders.

First Claw's pod crashed to the earth, throwing soil skyward from its landing crater. With timed bursts, the walls slammed down to form ramps, and First Claw charged from their restraint thrones, bolters up and blazing as they ran out onto the plainsland – a vast plateau before the foothills of Seventeen-Seventeen's crag fortresses.

Their pod had come down onto a battlefield, in the middle of an enemy regiment.

An ocean of foes writhed beyond the clearing dust of their downed pod. The distant figures of Titans, a host of classes and patterns, duelled in the distance.

The closest of the god-machines was at least two thousand metres away – a towering, enraged Reaver spraying the ground with immense firepower – and still it was huge beyond reckoning compared to the surrounding enemy. Instinctively, it drew the eyes.

As the Astartes disembarked, weapons opening up, their vox calls to each other immediately took on a tone of amused desperation.

'Try not to die here, brothers,' Mercutian muttered. 'I'm in no spirits to look for another squad.'

Cyrion laid waste to three heavily-augmented tech-guard, bolts detonating in the flesh-parts of their bodies and blowing them apart.

'This looked much easier on the holo-maps!' A brute with four mechanical extra arms rumbled towards him, waving a bizarre array of mining tools formed into weapons of war. Cyrion dodged a drill the size of his leg as it powered past his head, and rammed his gladius into the skitarii's bawling mouth. The blade bit, sank in, and impaled the skitarii's altered brain.

'I've got zero confirmation of the first target,' he said, holding back several more tech-guard with full-auto bolter fire. His aim was off. Shaky and loose. Hard to align his bolter with his targeting reticule.

The new arm. A hasty surgery and a simple augmetic. It would need a great deal more reconstructive work before he was satisfied with its performance. Still, with these odds, it was impossible to miss.

The ground was treacherous underfoot, rendered uneven by the bodies layering the plain. Their drop-pod had killed a fair few of the enhanced Mechanicus soldiers when it hammered down into the heart of the regiment's formation. Those around the impact zone were still scattered and fighting to form a decent resistance to the enemy in their midst.

'Landing is never an exact science, eh?' Adhemar ended a brief duel with a skitarii possessing treads instead of legs. He wrenched his combat blade from the creature's eye socket, launching at the next closest. 'Zero sighting of the main target.'

Talos's attention kept flicking to his retinal display, keeping track of the squad's increasing spatial division.

'Xarl?' he voxed. No answer. He spun as he lashed out with *Aurum*. The distance was bad. The blade's tip snicked through the throat of a looming tech-guard behind him, instead of taking the head clean off.

'Xarl, answer me.' Talos kicked the staggering skitarii with the severed jugular away. Cycling through sight modes, he tried to get a clear view of his brothers through the mass melee.

'North,' came Xarl's voice. 'Closer to the front line. I can't confirm. The fighting is densest there.'

'I'm too far away for confirmation,' Adhemar voxed back.

'As am I,' Talos cursed. 'Cyrion? Mercutian?'

'Little... busy...' Mercutian replied.

'Too far,' breathed Cyrion. 'Can't see. Fighting.'

'Souls for the Soul Eater!' Uzas screamed. 'Skulls for the Skull Throne!'

'No one asked you.'

Through a sea of stabbing drills, slashing blades, punching fists and cutting las-fire, Talos carved and gunned his way forward.

Something impacted on the side of his helm. *Anathema* barked in that direction, ending whatever threat had been there. *Aurum* twisted to deflect a skitarii's two lashing machine arms. Talos thudded his ceramite boot into the chest of a tech-guard to the right, caving in the warrior's armour and puncturing his lungs with broken ribs. *Aurum* flashed again in a vicious arc, cleaving through another tech-guard's torso as *Anathema* roared three shells into the heads of three other skitarii.

The downed tech-guard, carved in two, flailed at Talos's legs with its remaining functional arm. The Night Lord stamped on the howling saw blade to smash it into uselessness and crushed the soldier's head a moment later.

'I'm having a wonderful time,' Cyrion voxed to him, breathless and sarcastic.

'You and I both,' Talos said, his teeth clenched. He spared a half-second's glance in the direction of the monstrous Reaver. It was closer now, but only barely, siren horns wailing above the battlefield – a challenge or a warning to those underfoot. It dwarfed the defeated Warhound by no small degree.

'Traitors!' one of the attacking skitarii yelled. 'Kill the Chaos Marines!'

Talos gunned him down with a bolt in the face, and waded on.

UZAS MADE THE kill.

The tech-adept was called Rollumos, a name he'd chosen himself, and any name he'd been born with was forgotten long, long ago. He was, by the calculations of his own internal chronometers, one hundred and sixteen years of age. At least, the few remaining flesh parts were. Close, so very close, was his ascension to perfection. Only seventeen per cent of his flawed mortal form remained. A glorious and worshipful eighty-three per cent was iron, steel, bronze and titanium, all consecrated and ritually thrice-blessed daily in the name of the Machine-God.

He hesitated to call himself a Master of Skitarii, not out of modesty but out of private shame. His role was a vital one, certainly, and not without its honour. Yet a grim, too-human ache remained within his cranial cogitators. A master of what? Slave soldiers?

He deserved better. He deserved more.

Solace lay in deception, and shame could be quelled by the same deceit. Outwardly he embraced his role, endlessly modifying his physical form so that he might wage war alongside his augmented warriors. He lied to his peers and fellow adepts. How they believed him! How they processed and chattered confirmation for his apparent scholarly focus within the physicality of front-line tactical/battle immersion.

Like the avatars of the Machine-God that they were, the great engines of Legio Maledictis strode across the plains, towering above Rollumos's own pedestrian, humble, insignificant accomplishments. Oftentimes he would ascend the gantries when only menials were present, and run a mechadendrite across the armour of an inactive Titan, his inner processors generating picts of himself working on a god-machine, striving to bring forth the soul of the engine from its silent bulk.

Tormented by his own position in the Legio's hierarchy, at least he hid his displeasure from the unblinking eyes of his more respected brethren. That was cold comfort, but enough to keep his shame hidden.

It was no matter that this hierarchical deceit placed him within harm's way. His body was significantly enhanced to deal with the kind of threats faced by tech-guard infantry, and he had no worries of sustaining personal harm.

And yet, this deceit was one he came to regret in the final minutes of his life.

They were dropping Astartes into his regiments.

Astartes. Entire squads of them. A night-dark drop-pod lashed groundward, pounding into the plain some five hundred and eleven metres from where he stood, deep within a phalanx of his favoured skitarii.

Rollumos cogitated their allegiance. The winged skull symbol. The forks of lightning inscribed upon their armour. The… immediate and total viciousness of their assault, bolters discharging and blades hewing into precious augmented skitarii flesh.

Night Lords. This was not optimal.

As Rollumos directed a greater number of his soldiers in the direction of this closest pod and its troublesome burden, the first regrets were just beginning to sink in. These regrets reached their peak – and ended abruptly – exactly seven minutes and nine seconds later.

'Kill,' Uzas voxed to First Claw. He wasn't even out of breath. 'Target slain.'

Uzas raised Rollumos's metal head in one hand, like a primitive tribesman bearing the skull of a murdered foe. The tech-guard around him shrank back as he howled.

'Who's next?' Cyrion asked. The others heard the pounding of weapons against his armour transmitted over the vox. 'I'm already bored of this.'

'Skitarii Captain Tigrith,' Talos answered. 'Look for banners. Further north.'

FIRST CLAW RETURNED to the *Covenant of Blood* nine hours later.

Septimus and Octavia were waiting for them in the hangar bay, both mortals dressed in their Legion serf uniforms. The Thunderhawk bringing them back was *Nightfall*, one of the only other gunships still functional within 10th Company. Two other squads disembarked first. First Claw came last, and Octavia swore softly under her breath.

Almost ten hours of solid fighting at the front line had taken a clear toll. Cyrion's arm was limp and unmoving, the hastily-attached augmetic limb having given out hours before under the relentless demands of battle. Xarl's collection of skulls hanging from his armour was reduced to no more than scarce fragments of bone dangling on a few remaining chains. Uzas and Mercutian both bore horrendous damage to their battle armour: las-burns had carved blackened furrows through the ceramite or burned it black on deflected impact; huge axes and chainblades had chopped the images of their edges into the dark plate elsewhere.

Adhemar was bareheaded, his face decorated with bloody cuts, already scabbed and sealing with his enhanced physiology.

Talos was the last to leave the Thunderhawk. The defiled Imperial eagle upon his chestpiece sported some intriguing new desecrations. One wing was now severed by a blade's impact, unjoined to the rest of the image, and the eagle's ivory-white body was black – charred by a flame weapon was Septimus's guess. Talos's right hand was locked into a curled claw, rigid and unmoving. Evidently, the gauntlet had finally failed, and would need a great deal of care in its repair.

Septimus noticed two things immediately, the first of which was how much effort it was going to take to repair Talos's armour. The second made his blood run cold.

'Where's his gun?' Octavia asked. She'd noticed it, too.

'I lost it,' Talos said as First Claw strode past.

'Lord, where are you going?' Septimus said.

'To see the tech-priest, and the 10th Captain.'

* * *

DELTRIAN ATTENDED TO Malcharion personally.

The damage he'd sustained in the desecration of the Hall of Remembrance was almost fully repaired, though several joint-motors within his upper body were still functioning at half-capacity, their systems untested at full power.

Although it wounded him with secret shame to adopt such a human reaction to his injuries, he cursed Vraal each time his diminished physical aptitude caused an adjustment in his motion and movement.

The tech-adept and several of his servitors worked on the Dreadnought's hull, resealing, repairing, amending and reshaping. The Hall of Remembrance echoed with the sounds of maintenance.

Talos had greeted Deltrian formally upon entering, but quickly lapsed into vox conversation with the ancient warrior.

'Forgive me for the rudeness, tech-priest,' the Astartes said, replacing his helm back over his head. 'It is necessary if we are to speak over the noise.' Deltrian had bowed in response. The sounds of holy maintenance were loud by necessity. Through such song was praise offered to the Machine-God.

'Captain...' Talos voxed.

'Captain no longer. Speak, Soul Hunter.'

'The plains are ours.'

'A fine landing site, they shall make. The siege begins with the dawn.'

'It will be close. Even if we take the city within the week...' Talos trailed off. Malcharion knew as well as he did. Time was not their ally. The Blood Angels were less than three weeks away.

'Abaddon's seers are still sure, are they not?'

Talos snorted. 'I heard from his own lips that they are failing him all too often these nights.'

'Then why does he trust them?'

Irritation – and doubt, Talos realised with a jolt of unease – had crept into Malcharion's vox-tone. He was a warrior from an age when almost no psychic tolerance pervaded the Legions. Such abominations were either barred from loyal service or strictly trained and regulated, not relied upon as part of a war's planning.

'He works with what he has. In this case, astropaths across the fleet confirm it.'

'Does Krastian agree?'

'Krastian is dead, sir. Slain sixty years ago. We have not had an astropath on board since.'

'For the best, perhaps. Psykers. They are deviants and not to be trusted.'

'The astropaths aboard *Hunter's Premonition* align their predictions with the Warmaster's own. The relief fleet is still weeks away.'

'Hnnh.'

'How was your first battle, sir?'

Malcharion had already answered this question several times. Upon his own return to the *Covenant*, visitors from several squads came to pay their respects and speak about the surface conflict.

'Glorious, brother. The splash of blood against my armour... The exaltation of ending a legion of lives with cannon and fist... It will be a great triumph when we take this world in our father's name.'

Talos smiled. Barely.

'Now tell me the truth.'

The servitors attending Malcharion paused momentarily as the Dreadnought made a gear-shifting grind of a sound.

'Joyless. Passionless. Lifeless.'

'Are you are angry at me for waking you?'

'Were I angry, brother, you would already be dead. I would erase you from my sight the way I annihilated that Atramentar bastard Vraal. I never liked him.'

'No one did.'

'I do not understand what is needed of me. That is all.'

Talos considered this for a moment. 'Do you realise how you sound to me, sir? To all of us? How your voice hangs in the air like the echo of thunder, and stampedes across the vox?'

'I am not obtuse, boy. I am not blind to this form's inspirational qualities. But I am dead, Talos. That is the truth, and it will tell in the end.'

'Tonight was a fine victory. Not a life lost. We make planetfall again in three hours. Dawn will see the mountain fortress-foundry breached.'

'And I will pretend to care, brother. Have no fear.'

'I heard how you rallied Ninth and Tenth Claws on the field of battle.'

'All I did was kill for hours and bellow at the enemy.' Another grinding sound clunked from the depths of the Dreadnought.

'What was that?'

'My auto-loader cycling,' Malcharion lied. It had been how his behemoth body translated a chuckle. **'Now dispense with the formalities, Soul Hunter.'**

'I could live without you calling me that, sir.'

'And you think I am inclined to agree with your desires? I am Malcharion the Reborn, and you are an Apothecary with delusions of command.'

'Point made,' Talos smiled.

'Enough foolishness. Why are you here? What troubles you?'

'I lost my bolter.'

'Hnnh. Have mine.'

'*"Have mine"?*' Talos laughed. 'With such great reverence you treat Legion relics.'

'I certainly don't need it any more.' The war machine raised and lowered its twin-barrelled autocannon. Two servitors working on the barrels emitted error sounds from throat-voxes as their work was interrupted.

'Sorry...' the Dreadnought boomed in its true voice.

Deltrian bowed, reaper-like and sinuous. 'All is well, lord.'

'Fine,' Malcharion spoke into the vox again. **'Get on with it, Talos.'**

'I had a vision, sir.'

'This is hardly remarkable to me.'

'This one was different. It is... wrong. Some of it, at least. It's not coming true. Right from the first moment I woke from it, everything within the images felt unlikely. It felt like a lie uncoiling inside my mind. Uzas of First Claw, killing Cyrion. And now, as the planet stands on the very precipice of being conquered, I wonder at the rest of the vision. Faroven has not died, as I dreamed he would.'

'Are you so certain these events must take place on Crythe?'

'I was,' Talos admitted. 'Now I am unsure they will take place at all. I look at so many of our brothers – even Cyrion and Uzas. I fear their taint has spread to me. Could my second sight be corrupted by exposure to the Ruinous Powers?'

'How many visions have you suffered? Are they as frequent as they were before my entombment?'

'More than before. They grow more frequent.'

'Hnnh. Maybe he will die on Crythe. Maybe he will die later. Maybe he will not die in the manner you

have foreseen, and you worry over nothing. I don't recall you whining this much in the past.'

'Whining? Sir...'

'Even the primarch's visions were nebulous at times. Vague, he would say. Clouded. What right do you have to claim infallibility when even our gene-father's second sight was imperfect?'

'Wait. Wait.' Talos stared up the giant machine, his vision coloured killing-red. The image of Malcharion in life, clutching those three helms, stared back at him.

'Our father's dreams,' Talos whispered, 'were sometimes *wrong?*'

'The virtue of such dreams is sometimes in the symbolism.'

'This... cannot be true.'

'No? This is why you always bred enemies within our ranks, brother. A Legion is a hive of one million secrets. You, Soul Hunter, have always assumed you knew everything. I always liked that about you. Liked your confidence. Not everyone felt the same.'

'Did the gene-sire ever speak of me?'

'Only to tell me why you were named as you were. I laughed. I thought our father joked at my expense. It seemed so unlikely that anyone would disobey his final order.' Malcharion made the strange gear-changing growl again.

'Least of all you.'

XVII
SOUL HUNTER

'Because the name suits you.
One soul, my son. One hunt, in the name of revenge.
You will hunt one shining soul when all others turn their backs on vengeance.'

– The Primarch Konrad Curze
Addressing Apothecary Talos of First Claw, 10th Company

TALOS HAD CALLED to her from the darkness. He'd called the assassin's name, spoken in a whisper that emerged as a crackle of vox.

'M'Shen,' he hissed.

The assassin broke into a run. Talos followed.

The others would follow later. When the shock broke, when their tawdry and infantile ambitions overcame their grief. When they would look at the body of their slain father and weep not for his death, but for the fact his relics were taken from their greedy grasp.

Talos cared for none of this. The Imperial bitch had murdered his father, and she was going to die for it.

This was the age before *Aurum*. In his gauntlet he gripped a chainsword, gearing it into howling life as he pursued her. Although bareheaded, his vox-bead was in place. The shouts of his brothers transmitted with punishing clarity.

'Does he hunt her?'

'Brother, do not do this!'

'You defy the father's last wishes!'

Talos let them rant and rage. The hunter had no concern for anything beyond his prey. Bolts streaked past her as he fired and she dodged in blurs of dark lightning. Each bang was a storm's echo within the black halls of the Night Haunter's palace on Tsagualsa.

The assassin dared a laugh. And well she might. What was a lone Astartes to a trained agent of the Imperial Callidus Temple? Nothing. Less than nothing. She ducked and weaved and flipped over the bolts.

Outpaced with ease, Talos cursed as he slowed to a halt, and melted back into the shadows.

The hunt was not over.

M'SHEN LICKED HER lips to moisten them. The air of Tsagualsa was bitter and dry, an effect only magnified by the stilted air within this palace of the damned. Her fingers curled in the hair of her slain prey, the head of the Traitor Primarch clutched hard in her grip.

Drip. Drip. Drip.

She was painting the onyx floor with trickles of blood from the severed neck. The blood's scent was cloying and too rich, like powerful spices. This was the holy blood of the Emperor, soured into rancidity by corruption and evil. M'Shen resisted the urge to cast the grisly trophy away. Evidence. She needed evidence the deed was done.

It was strange. The primarch's genetic inhumanity was revealed once more even in death – the severed head had taken several minutes to start bleeding. Clotting agents within the blood were finally breaking down, releasing this dark trickle.

She could have simply taken the artifacts he wore, such as his simple crown circlet, the silver blade sheathed on his back, or the cloak of black feathers draped across his shoulders. But these relics, while valuable, could be stolen from the living as well as the dead. She needed overwhelming evidence to cast before her superiors. In the form of the dead god's head, the assassin had all she would require on that score.

The artifacts she'd taken were for her personal honour, not just the honour of her temple. *And oh, how they would praise her for this.*

M'Shen's pict-link back to her ship's data recorders, while scarcely reliable over such a distance, was gone now. She'd felt it die as she leapt at the Night Haunter and that, too, reeked of the most poetic corruption. The timing of such severance... Something about this place...

It made no sense. Her memory was as close to eidetic as the human mind allowed – yet still, she was lost. These black and bone-lined corridors, how they shifted and weaved. Sound carried strangely here. Sometimes it carried not at all.

The wall next to her head exploded in a shower of debris. She was already moving, already leaping to the side and falling back into her sprint with infinite grace. She was Callidus. She was the most murderous art rendered into human form.

On and on she ran. Constantly she passed Astartes in their outdated mark III and newer mark IV warplate. At the sight of her, these warriors would freeze. Some trembled with the suppressed urge to draw weapons and meet her in combat. She felt their bloodthirst as an overwhelming presence in the air. A few, a rare few, shouted curses at her as she fled past. But not many. These were the stoic sons of a most moribund father.

And their gene-sire had died willingly. Still this most astonishing of developments assailed her thoughts. Fully half of the Callidus Temple, beloved instrument of the God-Emperor, hunted across the galaxy's Eastern Fringe for the lifeblood of Konrad Curze, Eighth Primarch, father of the Night Lords Legion.

Here, on barren Tsagualsa, within this palatial fortress of onyx and obsidian, of ivory and bone and banners of flayed flesh she had found him.

Willingly, he surrendered his life.

She, M'Shen, was the death of a primarch. *Godslayer,* her mistresses would name her...

Tremendous weight smashed her to the ground. The primarch's head rolled from her clutch, her own face smashed against the tiled floor. Stimulants flooded her blood and she hurled the burden away. Within a heartbeat's span, the assassin was on her feet once more, looking back at the Astartes she'd thrown back against the wall.

Him. Again.

TALOS'S OWN BLOOD burned. His armour squirted fast spurts of searing chemicals into his body, through sockets in his spine, his neck, his chest and wrists. His chainblade shrieked in a series of enraged whines as it cut nothing but air. The assassin weaved aside from each blow, seeming barely to move, her body slipping into the minimal amount of movement necessary to dodge each swing.

The assassin's blue eyes, the blue of seas long boiled away on Terra, regarded him with fading amusement. She had nothing to say to him, and no reason to fear him, Astartes or otherwise. She was an Imperial assassin. She was the limit of human perf–

Talos's blade edge nicked her black weave armour, slashing a cut in the synskin over her bicep.

Eyes wide in alarm, she made a diving roll to the side, grabbed the trailing black hair of the primarch's head, and sprinted away faster than any Astartes could hope to follow.

Talos watched her go. The voices of his brothers were heated in his ear. Even his brothers within First Claw railed at him for this most disrespectful of disobediences.

'The Haunter *chose* this fate!' Vandred screamed.

'Talos, this was his final wish!' Cyrion implored him. 'She must escape back to Terra!'

Talos moved back into the shadows, a crooked smile on his face.

His vox-link screamed in a hundred tinny voices, others now joining the raging arguments.

The sons of Night Haunter had recovered their desperate ambitions quickly enough. Acerbus, Halasker, Sahaal and the others – the other captains, the other Chosen. Talos heard them whining and raging in his ears, and he found himself smiling at their furious and helpless disbelief.

'She has taken his signet ring,' one stormed.

'His crown!' another wailed like a lost child.

'Our father had not foreseen this,' one of them said. And then the ultimate hypocrisy – they demanded the entire Legion do now for greed what they had been cursing Talos for attempting in the name of vengeance.

'She must be slain for this!' they cried.

'She has transgressed against us all!'

The names of Legion relics stolen from their rightful inheritors was a litany Talos had no desire to listen to. He tuned out their voices, so suddenly full of righteous indignation.

How soon his brethren turned from faith and love in their gene-sire to grave doubts – the very same moment they realised the assassin had stolen weapons and relics they believed were theirs to inherit.

Such greed. Such pathetic, disgusting greed.

Talos despised them all in that moment. Never before had the sickening ambition of his corruptible brothers been shown so clearly.

And so was born the hatred that would never heal.

THE ASSASSIN ESCAPED the palace, and did so with apparent ease.

The Night Lords took their ships, ragtag gatherings of claws and companies, racing to their Thunderhawks to return to their vessels in orbit. The entire Night Lord fleet ringed the world of Tsagualsa, and they gave chase in unprecedented force.

Four vessels pulled ahead of the others. These were *Hunter's Premonition* of 3rd and 11th Companies; *Umbrea Insidior* of 1st Company; *The Silent Prince* of 4th and 7th Companies, and *Covenant of Blood*, of 10th.

The assassin's ship, no matter how sleek, fast and exquisitely-wrought it was, stood no chance at all. As it powered away from the dark orb of Tsagualsa, the pursuing cruisers lanced in its wake, weapons roaring at their quarry's essential systems.

She fell from the warp, powerless and crippled, dead in space. Boarding pods spat from all four Astartes vessels, crashing home and locking fast in the metal flesh of the Imperial ship.

The hunters bit into their prey, each one desperate to be the first to taste blood, and with it, victory.

ON BOARD THE assassin's ship, Talos ran with the other hunters in his pack. Menials, mortals, servitors – all fell before the howling Night Lords as they flooded the decks from a hundred hull breaches.

It was to be a day forever imprinted in the annals of Legion history, as well as one held in the hearts of every Astartes present in that moment of denied vindication.

As the hunters found her – squads from 1st Company claiming that honour – a fresh anger broke out across the vox-network.

Talos stood in the charnel pit of the crew habitation quarters, surrounded by brothers from the 10th and the ruined meat of so many mortal crew members. Blood painted the walls, the floor and the dark fronts of their armour plating. Not a soul would survive the culling of the murderer's ship.

At first, the reports had difficulty filtering through to the Astartes engaged in the hunt on board. Their blood was up, and the alerts were lost within the chaos of howling voices taking hold of the vox-channels.

Talos was one of the first to hear. He powered down his chainsword, tilting his head as he listened carefully.

How can this be?

'We are under attack,' he voxed to the others in proximity, his voice cold, calm, but edged with the taint of disbelief.

'We are under attack, *by the eldar.*'

In the centuries to come, the warriors of the VIII Legion would argue over the exact nature of the xenos ambush. Riding from their unknowable pathways through the void, wraith-like eldar ships ghosted around the embattled Night Lords vessels, alien weapons bringing light to the blackness, cutting into yielding shields without mercy.

Some claimed the assault was to claim the relics of the primarch, just as the assassin had. Others argued that an alien race would have no need of such treasures, and it was either indecipherable xenos reasoning – or merely a night of ill-fortune conspired by fate – that brought the fleets into contact at such a moment.

Umbrea Insidior would be lost, and with it, the betrayer Sahaal. *The Silent Prince* would suffer devastating damage, but ultimately the xenos fleet would be annihilated.

Yet few of the Legion claimed any satisfaction in the hollow triumph won that night.

During the evacuation, eldar warriors materialised in the hallways of the assassin's ship, manifesting before the packs of enraged Night Lords to be cut down even before they were free of the shimmering smears that marked the aftermath of alien teleportation technology.

First Claw, along with the other squads on board, fought their way back to their boarding pods.

'Whatever they've come for,' Cyrion voxed as he cut the head from an eldar female even as she appeared, 'they want it badly.'

'Back to the ship!' Captain Malcharion was shouting over the disorderly fighting retreat. 'Back to the *Covenant*!'

The vox was no clearer now. Jubilant cries clashed with the calls for withdrawal and hateful curses levelled at the aliens. Somewhere in the verbal melee, Talos could hear the victorious shrieks of Captain Sahaal, and the fevered raging of 1st Company.

Something was wrong. He could hear it in their voices.

He slowed in his stride, falling behind the rest of his claw, his attention pouring into the myriad cries and conflicting reports coming over the vox. A pattern emerged soon enough.

Captain Sahaal had reclaimed one of the Night Haunter's relics... and immediately fled. He was taking *Umbrea Insidior* away from the fleet, breaking formation and trying to run from the eldar.

He has abandoned 1st Company. Talos swallowed. Had he heard that right? Had one of the Legion's most respected commanders left his own warriors to die at the hands of the eldar?

Talos stopped dead in his tracks, the corridor silent now that the rest of his squad had raced so far ahead.

Sahaal had fled with his treasure, running into the void. 1st Company were battling their way to their boarding pods, and would be stranded, forced to die fighting or rely on the charity of the other vessels to save them.

Talos cared little for most of this. The struggles of 1st Company were 1st Company's own trouble. The Legion was in retreat from this grotesque ambush, and 10th Company would be fighting to save itself.

But M'Shen's death had still not been confirmed over the vox-network.

In his greed, Sahaal was fleeing with his trinket, all thoughts of vengeance forgotten... *and the assassin was still alive.*

Talos turned from his path of escape, and moved deeper into the ship.

THE POWER WAS out, leaving her in darkness, but she was safe at last.

As quickly as they'd come, the Astartes had fled.

Her ship still shuddered, but it seemed to her that the alien attackers, the filthy xenos creatures that named themselves eldar, had withdrawn with the Night Lords' retreat.

One of them had taken her hand with a swing of his blade. She could not fight off five of them at once, and the blow had severed her wrist in a clean slice. Her training made any pain from the wound utterly ignorable, but M'Shen bound her wrist with a tourniquet and a temporary seal of synthetic flesh nevertheless. The bleeding had been a danger, even if shock and pain had not.

She stood on the bloody ruin of her bridge, listening to the laboured breathing and shivers of the few crew members that yet drew breath.

None of them could see. The auxiliary power should have come online by now, resurrecting the lights. The continuing darkness was a bold enough statement that her ship was almost certainly damaged beyond easy repair.

M'Shen spun on her toes, her blade in her remaining hand. She could see nothing in the pure blackness, but she didn't need to. The thrum of live power armour filled her senses. The low growls of its servo-joints and false muscle fibres flexing told her all she needed to know. The Astartes's location, his posture, everything.

The assassin edged to the right, allowing herself a smile. Despite her exhaustion and blood loss, a lone Astartes would prove no threat. She–

Talos closed his hand around her throat.

He could sense she was duller, slower, and the beat of her heart was quicker than it had been in the palace. The assassin was weakened from her escape and the recent battle.

But she would kill him before his hearts had time to beat twice if he tried to hold her. Everything about this creature was engineered to end life, and with infinitely more skill and grace than the blunt efficiency of the Astartes. He was a warrior, but she was a murderer. He was trained for battle and war. She was bred only to kill.

The same second his hand gripped her throat, he was already acting.

Not to squeeze. Her armour of precious synskin would resist such trauma. He jerked her close, risking a headbutt to daze her. That was a mistake. The assassin leaned her head back like a recoiling serpent. Curse her, she was *fast*.

Talos felt her fisted hand coming up to unleash the lethality within her rings – each one a digital weapon of some unknown configuration. He wasted no time.

The Night Lord spat into her face, and hurled her away.

SHE HAD NOT screamed in many years.

It wasn't that pain was new to her, nor even a surprise, but this was no neat severance of limb from the body – this was the dissolving of her eyes in her skull, and never before had pain eclipsed her senses so completely. Even through the agony, she imagined the wretched Night Lord stumbling away in his cumbersome armour, amused at her momentary helplessness.

And she was right. In the darkness, Talos relished the sound of her scream. Even sweeter was the subtle, mellifluous hiss of acidic venom eating into the soft tissue of her beautiful blue eyes.

Panting now, seeing nothing but milky white sunfire, the assassin swallowed the pain, remembered her teachings, and used the agony as a focus. Over the vicious *tsssssshhhhh* of her melting eyes, she heard the humming rumbles of his armour.

He had to die. He had to die *now*.

She launched at him to make the need become reality.

* * *

TALOS FIRED AT the floor, bolt shells masking his movements as their rapid explosions overwhelmed the bridge chamber with noise. He cast a black-eyed glance at the assassin blindly fighting the air, her lashing kicks and blade sweeps utterly lethal – aimed at audible joints and weak points of his armour – but utterly useless. Talos was already across the bridge away from her, bolter still barking.

Deafened and disoriented, the assassin slowed her movements. Desperately poised, muscles taut, she seemed to be trying to filter the noise of his armour through the banging detonations.

He risked another shot to distract her, aiming squarely in her direction. She weaved a minimal amount, just as she had in the palace, and the bolt went wide.

Talos breathed out a curse as however she sought to sense him succeeded perfectly. The assassin turned to face him, and started running.

With his free hand, he slammed on his helm.

THE NIGHT LORD was a fool.

Every explosion ringing from the floor betrayed the shell's point of origin. It was complex, a matter of rigid concentration and training, and M'Shen was slowed by the pain she struggled to overcome. That was why triangulating his location took almost four entire seconds – an age to her preternatural senses.

Bolts started tearing directly at her, which confirmed her belief that the Astartes was a fool. Even rendered sightless, these she dodged with ease.

A new sound overrode the slicing whoosh of missing bolts. A sound she had only heard once before. His voice, speaking a single word.

'Preysight.'

* * *

HAD HER BLOWS landed, he would have died. He knew this with cold certainty.

Assassins, those from the Imperial-sanctioned temples, were already legends in the young Imperium. Her remaining hand would have thrust, blade-like and steel-hard, into the joints of his armour, crushing nerves and perhaps even breaking the enhanced bone of an Astartes warrior's skeleton. From there, his death would have taken mere moments. The pain he'd inflicted would be repaid tenfold.

None of her blows landed, because she made no attempt to strike him. As the blur of dull thermal movement came charging towards him, as every bolt he fired was dodged with ease, Talos filled his three lungs with the blood-rich air of her wrecked bridge.

As deep and echoing as the first thunderclap of a breaking storm, he roared his hatred at her.

WITHIN A CALLIDUS assassin, training and instinct met in honed, focused fusion. That fusion split within M'Shen as she lost the second of her senses. The depriving assault hit as hard and fast as the first. A moment of ear-splitting pain lanced through to the core of her mind, shaking her hearing, and all was suddenly silent.

She had no idea if the Night Lord was still screaming or had fallen quiet after detecting his triumph. Her senses were killed. She felt only the air shaking around her as her enemy moved again, and as bolts slashed past.

Blinded, deafened, clutching a shimmering blade that had taken the head of a fallen god, she twisted in her sprint and leapt at where she was certain the Astartes must be.

Her estimation was, as always, perfect.

* * *

Talos held her with the gentleness of a lover.

'My father told me of this night,' he whispered to her. 'And I never believed him. I never believed I would disobey him, until you came into our home and took him from us.'

M'Shen never heard his words. She would never hear anything again in her life, which was now measured in seconds. The assassin dropped her blade. As her gloved fingers uncurled almost against her will, she felt the heavy weapon thump against her foot.

Strengthless arms wouldn't move. Trembling fingers couldn't crook to fire digital weapons within the ornate rings. Painkillers choked her veins with no effect beyond an irritating tickle of sensation. Her stomach was aflame. It hurt even more than the hissing holes where her eyes had been. Some violation, some iron-hard presence pressed her in place, transfixing her torso.

She guessed correctly what it was. The Night Lord's chainsword. He had impaled her on his blade.

A dim, fading part of her mind tried to assess this damage, but the brutal and human edge to her consciousness overrode a life of combat narcotics and relentless training. She was dying. She would be dead within moments.

'Godslayer,' she said to him, never hearing her own words. 'That... is how I will... be remembered...'

Talos blinked stinging tears from his eyes. His thumb edged closer to the chainsword's activation rune.

Threat, threat, threat the warning runes flickered. Talos blink-clicked them away, clearing his red visor display of all but the assassin's masked face and her hollow, bleeding eye sockets.

'*Ave Dominus Nox,*' he whispered, and gunned the impaling chainsword into life.

* * *

He drifted for sixteen hours, alone in one of the boarding pods left by the ravaged survivors of 1st Company. In the absolute silence, he had only his grief and satisfaction to pass the time.

They did so admirably.

When his brothers found him, when the pod was brought aboard the *Covenant of Blood* as it returned to seek survivors and salvage, Talos was still sitting in one of the pod's thrones, his armour spotted with dried blood.

The pod's doors opened into ramps, and Talos looked out into the *Covenant's* starboard launch bay.

First Claw stood watching him, their weapons raised.

'She's dead,' he told them, and rose to his feet, movements sluggish and weary.

His chainsword's teeth were clogged with dark, chewed meat and shards of bone. Before leaving her vessel, he had sawn her into nothing more than gobbets of biological matter, venting his final frustrations on her remains. In the darkness of the bridge, the surviving mortal crew members heard everything, with only their fearful imaginations to provide the imagery.

'Talos...' Captain Malcharion, the war-sage, approached slowly. 'Brother...'

Talos raised his head with equal slowness.

'She killed our father,' he said in a crackle of vox.

'I know, brother. We all know. Come, we must... deal with the aftermath.'

'The Haunter said I would do this,' Talos looked at the gore-caked blade. 'I did not believe him. Not until I felt the rage of her presence in our palace.'

'It is over,' said Malcharion. 'Come, Talos.'

'It will never be over.' Talos dropped the blade to the ground with a crash. 'But at least now I know why he named me as he did. *"One soul,"* he said. *"You will hunt one shining soul while all others turn their backs on vengeance".'*

'Brother, come...'

'If you touch me, Malcharion, I will kill you next. Leave me. I am going to my chambers. I need to... to think.' Talos left his weapons where they lay. Primus would gather them.

'As you wish,' the war-sage said, 'Soul Hunter.'

'Soul Hunter,' Talos chuckled in response, the sound laced with bitterness. 'I believe I could get used to that.'

THE INTERLOCKING CAVERN network beneath the Omnissiah's Claw mountain range was home to miracles of immense scale and ingenuity. Here lay the living core of the Legio Maledictis, and the sacred heart of the Adeptus Mechanicus's operations on Cryhe Prime.

A million humans, one million souls in varying states of augmentation, worked in these hallowed underground tunnels. The air was fever-hot with smoke, shimmering with heat blur, and rancid with the metallic reek of incense and industry.

Entire cave systems were given over to railroaded conveyor carriages, huge trains transporting resources, ammunition, servitors and machine parts from one colossal chamber to the other. The myriad chambers themselves reached hundreds of metres in height, each capable of housing a battle-ready Warlord-class Titan. The stone skin of this great lair was masked in machinework attached to the walls: consoles, sensor relays, gantries, elevators, storage loaders, promethium fuel tanks, and grand icons of the Mechanicus of Mars. Little remained of the original red stone that had once reached as far as – and indeed farther than – the mortal eye could see.

A city of factories and forges hidden beneath the armoured skin of the world's crust. A city founded to provide the Imperium of Man with invaluable god-machines to stride across distant battlefields in the crusades of a dying empire. A city that had prospered for almost two thousand years.

The plains before the mountain range had fallen to the Warmaster after the previous day's fighting. The Mechanicus's last-breath attempt to deter the siege of Seventeen-Seventeen's front gates had failed, and the evidence of that failure stretched from horizon to horizon. Troop bulk landers and Astartes Thunderhawks carried soldiers and warriors down from the void and from elsewhere on Crythe, massing on the plains in one unified horde. The bodies of slain skitarii and mortal fodder smothered the rest of the plain, punctuated by the occasional corpse of a downed Titan. The mortal dead bloated in the morning sun. The skitarii's flesh-parts were already starting to stink and discolour. The fallen Titans crawled with ants – the Warmaster's own tech-adepts recovering the slain god-machines for use on other worlds.

Crythe Prime was well-chosen by the Warmaster not only for its resources, but because the majority of its Titan Legion was engaged in battle elsewhere in the segmentum. Not only could resources be harvested from Seventeen-Seventeen if it fell, but the Imperium would be denied yet another bastion of strength in the future.

The great gates would not hold for long. Seventeen-Seventeen had grown too far beyond its original plans. The Avenue of Triumph leading into the main undercity now stood outside the protection of Site 017-017's invincible void shields. The main gate was naught but adamantium and Mechanicus ingenuity; despite its strength, it would fall to massed fire within hours. Wide enough to allow three Titans marching out abreast, it was also wide enough to allow the Warmaster's army within.

Under siege, threatened with destruction, the hidden city called upon its chosen sons. The few that remained answered this call. They marched through their home caverns, immense shoulders bristling with city-crushing weaponry, beneath banners of a hundred past glories. At their heels, a million adepts, servitors and skitarii warriors braced to repel the invaders.

The last sons of the Legio Maledictis had awoken, and Seventeen-Seventeen shook with their tread.

BLACKENED STOOD READY on the deck. It was a howling, dark-armoured vulture, with its engines whining as they gushed heat-shimmer into the air. It breathed readiness, and the Astartes felt inspired just seeing it.

First Claw marched in loose formation towards the lowered gang ramp, their armour as repaired as the handful of hours back on board the *Covenant* had allowed. Each suit of war-plate still bore a wealth of scars. Mercutian and Uzas, with no access to trained artificers, looked as though they had no right to walk away from the last battlefield. Pits, cracks, chips and cuts spoiled the surfaces of their ceramite plating.

Mercutian had complained of his armour's machine-spirit responding sluggishly. Small wonder, with the damage its skin had taken.

As he marched, he cycled through sight modes, swearing softly over the vox.

'My preysight is down.' The words came out hesitantly, and for good reason.

'Bad omen,' Uzas chuckled. 'Bad, bad omen.'

'I do not hold any faith in omens,' Adhemar said.

'Strange then,' Uzas replied, 'that you serve in a squad led by a prophet.'

'Uzas,' Talos said, turning to face him.

'What?'

Talos said nothing. He didn't move.

'What?' Uzas repeated. 'No lecture?'

Talos still said nothing, standing unmoving.

'His life signs are... insane,' Cyrion was watching his retinal displays. 'Oh, hell. Xarl!'

Talos half-turned, staggered, and fell on nerveless legs. Xarl caught him with a clash of battle armour.

'What ails him?' Mercutian asked.

'Seven eyes open without warning,' said Talos over the vox, 'and the sons of the Angel fly with vengeance in their hearts.'

'Isn't it obvious?' Cyrion said to Mercutian. 'Septimus! You are needed here.'

'The Angel's sons seek the blade of gold, and justice for their brothers with blackened souls...'

'Now, Septimus!' Cyrion yelled.

THE EXALTED TURNED its horned head to a mortal whose name he had never even tried to learn.

'Launch status,' he drawled.

The officer straightened his outdated uniform as he checked his console displays. 'Lord Malcharion's pod reads as already down, master. All squads already engaged or en route to the surface... except First Claw.'

The Exalted craned itself forward. Bone creaked and armour growled. 'What?'

'Confirming, master.' The officer affixed his vox-mic to his collar. 'This is the command deck. Report launch status, First Claw.'

The Exalted, ever a student of fear in the human form, watched in perverse fascination as the officer's face paled. The soft drumming of the mortal's heart thumped a touch harder and faster. Bad news, then. News the mortal feared to share.

'First Claw reports, master, that Lord Talos is incapacitated. He has suffered another... malady.'

'Order them to leave him and proceed to the surface at once.'

The officer relayed the order. As he listened, he managed to swallow on the third attempt.

'Master...'

'Speak.'

'First Claw has refused the order.'

'I see.' The Exalted's claws gripped the handrests of his exquisite throne. 'And on what grounds do they refuse to prosecute the enemy in this holy war?'

'Lord Cyrion said, master, that if you are so worried about the surface battle, you are free to borrow their Thunderhawk and take a look down there yourself.'

The fact the officer relayed all of this without more than a minor tremor in his voice impressed the Exalted considerably. He valued competence above all.

'Fine work... mortal. Inform First Claw their treachery has been noted.'

The officer saluted and did exactly that. The response, from the Astartes known as Lord Xarl, was immediate and obscene. The mortal decided not to relay that part back to the Exalted.

More voices buzzed in his ear. The Astartes of First Claw again.

'Lord?'

The Exalted turned, intrigued by the rising unease in the man's voice.

'Speak.'

'Lord Cyrion wishes a direct link to you. It's a most grave and urgent matter.'

'Open it.'

'Vandred,' Cyrion's voice echoed across the bridge. 'Recall the claws from the surface immediately.'

'And why would I do that, Brother Cyrion?'

'Because we do not have three weeks before the Blood Angels arrive.'

The Exalted tongued its lipless maw, feeling the veins under its cheeks ache in sharp pulses. 'Your belligerence grows tiresome, First Claw. I will listen to this and this alone. Link me to Talos's vox.'

'...breaching the hull. I kill him. He recognises my sword as he dies...'

The Exalted listened in silence for over a minute. When his next words came, they did so with savage reluctance.

'Open a channel to the *Vengeful Spirit*. I must speak with the Warmaster.'

MALCHARION TRUDGED THROUGH the cavernous chamber of the under-mountain citadel. The siege had been grinding on for over an hour, and although Malcharion's forces from 10th Company were charged with entering as part of the second wave, the reforming resistance in the early caverns was punishing the Chaos advance.

Flanking his hulking form, yet giving him respectful – and prudent – distance with which to fire his weapons, two Night Lord claws advanced, their bolters spitting into the disorganised ranks of the enemy.

The resurrected warrior knew them by name, knew their individual suits of armour even through the scars earned in the many battles each of them had survived and suffered without him.

Yet with the passion of battle-lust rendered cold in this immortal shell, he felt little connection to the brothers he once commanded as captain of the 10th.

They fought because they still hated with a ferocity he no longer shared. They shrieked curses with a bitterness he no longer tasted.

Dark thoughts, these. Dark thoughts that threatened his focus.

The Dreadnought's armoured feet, splay-clawed and ponderous, crushed bodies beneath his weight. The double-barrelled cannon that served as his right arm boomed over and over, ripping vicious gaps in the skitarii's lines. On they came, drawn by the blasphemy of his existence, desiring nothing more than to end the unlife he suffered because of warped Mechanicum lore.

Perhaps a part of him was tempted to let them succeed. A small part. A part that remained silent and dead while battle raged. This was not joy – war had never been joyous for the war-sage – but the immersion allowed him to focus elsewhere, to concentrate upon the external. Such focus diminished his awareness of his true form, husk-like and cold within the sarcophagus.

A skitarii with four shrieking saw-blade limbs battered itself against the Dreadnought's front. Malcharion clutched it from the ground, squeezing it with the unbreakable strength of his power fist. Lightning flared into life as the dying tech-guard's blood spurted onto the electrified metal claw that crushed him. Malcharion fired his arm-mounted flamer unit, bathing the man in liquid flame, roasting the skitarii's flesh-parts even as the soldier was crunched into death. This organic wreckage he threw into the soldiers before him, lamenting their lobotomised indifference to such magnificent slaughter. Blood of the Ruinous Ones, what a foul waste of the Legion's talents this war was.

'Malcharion,' said a vox-voice.

It was significant effort to tune into speaking within the vox-network instead of transmitting his voice to the speakers mounted within his armour. The battle raging in the caverns hardly helped.

'It is I.'

'It's Cyrion.'

His autocannon hammered shells into a towering skitarii – a champion or a captain, surely. The cyborged warrior fell into the teeming horde in pieces. The shouts of thousands of soldiers locked together rang around the arching cavern.

'You are supposed to be here, are you not? You woke me to kill everything for you?'

'Sir, you have to pull back from Seventeen-Seventeen. Lead the claws back to the Thunderhawks.'

Ghost-pain travelled through him in an acidic rush. Malcharion – his true form – screamed within the coffin of sustaining fluids. He felt the silken play of ooze across his ravaged face. Psychostigmata bruised his corpse's pale flesh.

The skitarii drilling into the Dreadnought's knee joint was pulped into a wet smear a moment later. Malcharion spun on his waist axis, power claw outstretched. Several other skitarii about to besiege his towering body flew back into their fellows, bones smashed to shards.

'We are within the cave city,' Malcharion boomed, his pain flooding his vox-voice. **'We cannot retreat. The day will be ours.'**

'Talos is being wracked by another vision. He says the Imperial relief fleet isn't weeks away. It's barely even hours away. The Blood Angels are coming.'

'What of Vandred?'

'He has apprised the Warmaster, but will not recall our forces. Likewise, the *Hunter's Premonition* has been ordered to keep its troops on the surface.'

Malcharion panned his power claw in an arc before him, unleashing streams of fire from the mounted flamer. Next to him, in orderly formation with bolters and blades striking, two squads of 10th Company's Night Lords advanced in his shadow.

The Dreadnought halted. Slowly, he turned. Watching.

Noise erupted around him. Noises previously unheard over the snarling of his own joints and the rage of his weapons. Solid shells clanked and clinked from his armour. *Bizarre. Almost like rainfall.*

'The Black Legion and their mortal slaves are engaged alongside us. Are we to abandon them? The Soul Hunter's second sight is not without flaw.'

'Malcharion, my captain, what do you believe?'

The Dreadnought's power plant thrummed louder as Malcharion re-engaged the enemy, fist crushing, cannons firing. The speakers on his hull blared loud as he shouted in Nostraman.

'Night Lords! Fall back! Back to the ships!'

ABOARD THE COVENANT, the Exalted watched blurry pict feeds of the surface battle. The creature cycled through views – the helm picters of each squad leader and image-finders mounted on the hulls of 10th Company's tanks. Orbital imagery was worthless with the battle now taking place in the opening chambers of the Omnissiah's Claw. It was left to this series of juddering, frenetic scenes out of necessity. It offended the Exalted's tactician sensibilities.

On its left stood Malek, on his right, Garadon.

'Do you see this?' The Exalted focused on the crimson view displayed by one Astartes's vision lenses.

'Yes, lord,' both Atramentar warriors said.

'Intriguing, is it not? Why would all of our squads be moving back through the Warmaster's forces? One has to wonder.'

'I can guess, lord,' Garadon said. His fist clutched the haft of his double-handed hammer tighter.

'Oh?' The Exalted allowed a rare smile to split its face. 'Indulge me, brother. Share your suspicions.'

Garadon growled before speaking, as if dredging up enough bitterness to put into the words. 'The prophet is making his move to usurp your leadership of the warband.'

Malek shook his bullish helm. 'Talos is incapacitated by his second sight. You are seeing conspiracies in guiltless corners, Garadon.'

'None of us are blind to your support of him,' Garadon replied. 'Your ardent defence of his every failure.'

'Brothers, brothers,' the Exalted no longer smiled. 'Peace. Watch. Listen. I suspect any moment now–'

'Incoming message, my prince,' the vox-officer called from his station.

'Delicious timing,' the Exalted breathed. 'Put it through.'

'This is Captain Halasker of the 3rd,' crackled the bridge speakers. All present knew the name. Halasker, Brother-Captain of 3rd Company, commander of the *Hunter's Premonition*.

'I am the Exalted, lord of the 10th.'

'Hail, Vandred.'

'What do you wish, Halasker?'

'Why are your squads falling back to the landing site? Blood of the Father, the war-sage is ordering a retreat of all VIII Legion forces. What the hell kind of game are you playing?'

'I did not order the withdrawal. Malcharion is acting according to his own maddened will. The Warmaster has demanded we continue the war's prosecution.'

'You cannot control your own forces?'

The Exalted breathed through its closed fangs. 'Not when the war-sage is on the surface, acting as if he ruled the 10th.'

'And why are *you* not on the surface, Vandred?'

The edge of derision in Halasker's voice rankled more than anything the Exalted had endured in a long, long time... until the other captain's next words.

'Vandred, where is the prophet? Malcharion and your claws are voxing news of a new prophecy. I must speak with the Soul Hunter.'

'He is *incapacitated*,' the Exalted managed. Its teeth were clenched so forcefully that one cracked like porcelain. 'Our father's ailment has befallen him once more.'

'So it's true?'

'I did not sa–'

'Fall back!' Halasker cried to his squads over the vox. 'Fall back with the war-sage!'

The Exalted roared at the ceiling of the command deck, loud enough to send the mortal crew cowering.

HE OPENED HIS eyes. The sight of bright, proud armour faded from before him, replaced by the dark red of his visor display. Flickering, tiny runes streamed across his vision. His hearts slowed. He swallowed the coppery tang of blood in his mouth.

Targeting reticules locked on familiar aspects of his own chamber. A quick glance at the digital chron reader in his lens display told him exactly how long he'd been lost to sense.

It could have been worse.

'Cyrion,' he voxed, and the door to his chambers opened the moment he spoke.

'Brother,' Cyrion said. He was still in full war-plate.

'Cy, the Throne's forces are coming. The Marines Errant, the Flesh Tearers. The Blood Angels, first of all. They are almost here.'

'You've been out three hours, Talos.'

'I know.'

'The Exalted has called a war council.' Cyrion moved away from the door, gesturing for him to follow. 'The Blood Angels are already here.'

XIX
FOR THE LEGION

THE WAR ROOM was being used for its intended purpose for the first time in decades.

Banks of monitors and consoles stood active, attended by servitors – many of whom were reprogrammed by Tech-Priest Deltrian following their capture on the asteroid chunk of Nostramo. A huge occulus screen showed the open link to a similar chamber on the *Hunter's Premonition*, though that room was far grander and larger than even this, the largest room on the *Covenant of Blood*. The battle-barge was built to carry three entire companies, whereas the strike cruiser housed only one.

A huge central table projected a distorted green hololithic display of Crythe and the dozens of ships surrounding it. In angry red blurs, a second fleet a short distance from the planet was depicted. They wavered in jagged, flickering detail.

The pict link to *Hunter's Premonition* showed Captain Halasker in his Terminator plate, unhelmed as he stood at the head of his own holoprojection table.

'They are holding off, then.'

The Exalted dragged its spiked bulk closer to the projected display, and gestured with a swollen, pale claw. 'Two battle-barges, three strike cruisers. This represents overwhelming force. Perhaps two-thirds of the entire Chapter.'

'We are aware of numbers. What we are not aware of is why they arrived so soon.' Malcharion stood opposite the Exalted, dwarfing the daemon-twisted former captain. The division in the room was obvious for all to see.

'The Warmaster lied to us,' Halasker insisted. 'He must have known.'

'Why would he lie and endanger his own forces on the surface?' the Exalted countered.

'Maybe so. But can that many seers truly be wrong?'

'Did not your own astropaths agree with the Warmaster's declaration?' the Exalted asked. 'The wake of that many ships casts great waves through the sea of souls. Your astropaths confirmed the judgements of the Warmaster's own. The tide should not have broken upon us for another month.'

'The seers are mortal.' Halasker wouldn't concede the point. 'I placed no overt trust in them at all.'

Talos spoke from his place close to Malcharion. 'A larger fleet is still incoming. We are dealing with nuances in the immaterium – a dimension none of us understand. Can you, Captain Halasker, look into the warp and see which waves are natural tides in an unnatural realm? Can you, Captain Vandred, see whether the war-wake of one fleet is masked by the tidal wave caused by another? Everything we do is guesswork compounded by inexperienced estimation.'

The Exalted met Halasker's black eyes over the screen link. 'If the Blood Angels will remain at bay, they can be ignored while Crythe falls. We can recommit our forces and avoid the Warmaster's further displeasure.'

'You are free to commit the 10th wherever you wish,' the other captain replied. 'I am done with this fool's errand. A fine concept in the simulation displays. A fine concept that has bled us dry when it came to the moments of bolter and blade.'

'The Warmaster has carelessly spent our blood,' Xarl snarled low. 'We owe him nothing.'

'I agree,' Talos said. 'We should disengage from the fleet as soon as all of our forces have been recovered from the surface.'

'Agreed,' said Halasker.

'Agreed.'

'I am enjoying this display of supreme naivety.' The Exalted's tongue bled as it licked its fangs. Eyes as black as dead stars turned upon Talos and Malcharion. 'But the Despoiler will not allow this. He has the strength to prevent us breaking away, and he will never forgive such a betrayal.'

'Enough, Vandred.' Halasker shook his head. 'Your loyalty to the Old War is commendable, but Abaddon is a fool. Yet again, he has committed too much, too hard, too far from support. He holds tenuous lordship over Legions that are greatly-enamoured of endless infighting. This is just one of many betrayals he will forgive because he will need allies again in the future.'

'Hear, hear,' the Dreadnought rumbled.

'The last of my forces will be on board the *Premonition* within the hour.'

'And how are we supposed to placate the Warmaster? I promise you, Halasker, he will fire upon us if we run.'

'Cripple his ships.'

All eyes turned to Talos.

'What did you say?' the Exalted asked, softer than he'd spoken in years.

'When we break from the fleet, we cripple the *Vengeful Spirit*, or any other vessel that challenges us.' Talos met the Exalted's stare.

'And leave them at the mercy of the Angels?'

'Do I look as though I will shed any tears over that?'

'Nor will I,' Halasker added. 'Abaddon is hardly short on ships. Even without us, he outnumbers the Blood Angels eleven to five.'

Chatter began to pick up around the room as the gathered Astartes discussed the imminent treachery.

'No,' the Exalted growled. 'This cannot, and will not be.'

'And why not?' Halasker narrowed his eyes.

'Almost all of the Warmaster's forces are engaged upon Crythe. If the Blood Angels strike – if they *board* the Black Legion's cruisers – the Warmaster will struggle to escape with any of his fleet intact. There might be as many as *six hundred* Blood Angels waiting on their ships on the other side of this world! They will sweep through any resistance on board the Black Legion's vessels.'

'Then he should have begun the recall of his men hours ago, as the prophet's vision suggested. Warnings were sent. You sent them yourself. Abaddon chose to leave them unheeded.'

'Malcharion,' Halasker addressed the Dreadnought now. 'Are the 10th's full forces back on board the *Covenant?*'

'Yes, brother.'

'Then make preparations to leave. I still have fifteen squads on the surface, with armour support. They were deep in the caverns, and their fighting withdrawal is taking lamentably long. Vandred?'

'Yes, "brother"?'

'Even after all this time, you are still a worm,' Halasker finished. Then the screen went dead.

The Exalted looked at its shattered company, with no more than thirty Astartes remaining. They watched him from where they stood around the table. Their armour was pitted and cracked. Their bearing remained strong and tall despite this pointless war. How had it come to this? Betrayal after betrayal. The erosion of trust. The death of brotherhood.

'Incoming transmission,' a servitor intoned from a wall console.

The screen came alive again. This time, the face wasn't Halasker's, it was a dark helm with slanted eye lenses. The Astartes there inclined his head in greeting. Armour of black and gold shone in the flickering light of his own bridge.

'*Covenant of Blood*. The Warmaster demands to know why you have still not recommitted your troops.'

'Tell the Warmaster he will be losing this war without us, if he still aims to fight it. The Blood Angels have arrived, and more Imperial forces will be here soon.'

'Silence, Dead One. Exalted, hear me. You know who I was, and who I am now. As the Eyes of the Warmaster, I speak with the Despoiler's voice. Lord Abaddon cares nothing for the presence of the Sons of Sanguinius and their quaint fleet. He demands that the *Covenant* pull alongside the *Vengeful Spirit* in defensive formation.'

'No.'

'No? *No?* You will risk allowing them to board us?'

The Exalted shook its horned head. 'Ruven, you were once of the 10th yourself. So you know we will not comply. We are not enslaved to the Warmaster's will. You know this as well as any other. Malcharion speaks the truth. Pull your own forces off Crythe before it's too late.'

'It is not that simple. We have committed much to the battle for Seventeen-Seventeen.'

'Leave the mortals. Let them die. Who cares if they do not live to be slaughtered on another world in a later war? Recover your Astartes and be ready to engage the Blood Angels. Perhaps if we move quickly, we can decimate them before other Chapters fall out of the warp in support.'

'We have *Titans* on that world. Thousands of Astartes. Hundreds of tanks. We are the Black Legion, not some shattered, impoverished horde weeping over its misfortunes and the memory of a martyred primarch.'

The Exalted tongued its broken teeth again, feeling his veins ache with the need to see this bastard's blood. Who was this wretch, this traitor, to speak of the Night Lords Legion in such a way...

'If you will not comply,' Ruven said, 'you will be fired upon for trying to flee.'

'The Throne's vengeance is here,' the Exalted spoke low. 'My prophet insists more will arrive within hours. We will not be selling our lives to preserve yours. We will not be repeating our warnings again.'

'Your prophet is unreliable. You have indicated as much yourself.'

The Exalted grunted a breathy sigh. 'That may be so. But he is my brother, and you are nothing more than a betrayer who fled to wear the black of Abaddon's many failures. I trust his words, as I trusted my father's.'

With a too-long claw, the Exalted dragged a finger across its throat in the demand for silence. The servitor at the vox console killed the link.

'Battle stations,' the Exalted said. 'Be ready to disengage from the fleet.'

THE MINUTES PASSED with agonising slowness. More signifier runes appeared on the hololithic display as the minutes became hours. Vessels belonging to the

Marines Errant, and the cousin Chapters of the Blood Angels – the Flesh Tearers and the Angels Vermillion – pulled alongside their fellows.

The Exalted's expert eyes roamed over the formation, seeing the possibilities playing out within his mind. Loose. Their formation was loose, as if the captains had no experience with one another, or any desire to work together. This may indeed have been true, for all the Exalted knew. Either way, it was an opening.

They will come at us soon.

He knew that because, had he commanded the gathering fleet, it would have been what he'd do. Strike hard, ramming the point of the lance through the heart of the Warmaster's fleet. Such a gambit held grave risks and definite casualties. The Despoiler's ships bristled with immense firepower, and still outnumbered the loyalist vessels.

Strange, in truth. Not only had this approach been so masterfully masked, but the sense of opposition emerging between the two fleets was almost poetically startling. *The advantage we hold is in the external force we can bring to bear against them. The advantage they hold is in the internal threat they bring.* In a straight clash of vessels, the Throne's Astartes would be annihilated. But no void war was ever so clearly defined. When boarding actions came into consideration, the Warmaster's fleet would be lost.

Distances within void conflict are matters of thousands and thousands of kilometres. As the runes depicting the enemy fleet began to blink and move, the Exalted rose to its full height and addressed Malcharion – the only other Astartes still in the room.

'Alert the *Premonition*. We have forty minutes before they reach us.'

* * *

Orbital pict imagery was useful again with the ground forces in retreat. Talos watched on the bridge's occulus as the blurry forms of Astartes and rolling tank armour sheared back from their attack on the city beneath the mountains. Individuals were impossible to make out and the images were rendered even hazier by the shroud of pollution across the world's skies, but the stuttering, distorted picts still told their tale.

Talos saw the Black Legion falling back to their troopships spread across the conquered plain. Behind them in a routed wave came a teeming mass of humanity. Titans and tanks seemed like pockets of calm in the swarm.

'Will they be able to get more than a few hundred Astartes back into orbit before the Angels reach us?' he asked.

The Exalted watched the same picts. 'No. They will rely on the renegades that still have sizable forces on board their ships. The Purge, the Scourges of Quintus, the Violators... Here, look.' The Exalted gestured to other vessels in the fleet, their hololithic images flickering and sending streams of smaller craft between them.

'Thunderhawks,' Talos said.

'Exactly, my prophet. The Black Legion is begging its lesser allies for aid. Warriors from renegade Chapters are to be pressed into service, defending Abaddon's own ships.'

The Exalted shook its head as it sighed. 'Once more, our Warmaster has grievously overcommitted his forces onto a battlefield. At least he was wise enough to leave many of his allies in orbit in the event of disaster.'

Talos nodded to the creature on the throne. As much as it galled him to admit it, the Exalted was sinking into his element now. The myriad plays and ploys of void war lit up his eyes from within.

'If this is the spearhead of the Throne's force,' Talos said, 'I would hate to see the relief fleet arrive in full.'

'The odds still favour us.' The Exalted's gaze only left the pict screen to glance at a miniature hololithic tactical display generated from the armrest of his throne. 'Two battle-barges and six strike cruisers, with frigate support... We would survive, at crippling cost, should they be unable to board us.'

The Exalted summoned a naval rating to the side of his command throne. 'You. What's the status of the *Premonition's* withdrawal?'

'The last report still has fifty Astartes and their transports on the surface, lord.'

'Get me a link to Captain Halasker.'

'Yes, my lord.'

'Halasker,' the Exalted said. 'What is taking your men so long?'

Pictureless, the vox-link crackled back. 'I have five squads fighting through to the landing site now. This is madness, Vandred. The Black Legion is shooting down our Thunderhawks.'

'I demand confirmation.'

'This is not the time to argue over picts! I have the sworn oaths of fifty men on the surface that they are embattled with the Black Legion, and that they have seen Abaddon's own forces tearing our gunships from the sky. They are led by some kind of warp-sorcerer... My men cannot kill him.'

'Ease your choler, brother. Be aware that no more than twenty minutes remain before we'll need to engage the Angels or break into the warp.'

'No. I will not leave half a company to die in the dust of a world Abaddon failed to take.'

'You are the commander of one of our Legion's last remaining battle-barges,' the Exalted's voice lowered to a dangerous snarl. 'If you are going to sell your lifeblood, do it in tearing down the Imperium, not a vainglorious last stand. I will recover your Astartes. I have Thunderhawks and transporters standing ready. We will rendezvous in the Great Eye as soon as we are able, where the dogs of the Throne will not follow.'

'Brave, Vandred. Very courageous. You think your little *Covenant* will survive where the *Premonition* would not?'

'Yes. It will.'

'Because it's a less tempting target, eh?'

'No. Not because of that.'

'I sense you have an idea, brother.'

'Halasker,' the Exalted's monstrous face lowered slightly, and its black eyes closed. 'Enough of this. Just run while you still can. Abaddon's mistake must not be allowed to kill us all. The *Premonition*, at the very least, must survive. Be ready to move the moment I give the word.'

'*Ave Dominus Nox*, Vandred. Glory to the 10th. Die well, all of you.'

The Exalted took a rattling, sticky breath. 'We shall see.'

After the link was silent, it spoke again. 'Transmit the following message to the Warmaster's flagship: *"The Covenant of Blood is reengaging."* Then bring us alongside the *Vengeful Spirit*, as the Warmaster ordered.'

The vox-officer nodded, and did as he was told. The helmsman did the same. The vessel shuddered as its drive engines awoke.

'Vandred–' Talos began.

'All is not as it seems, my prophet.' He fixed Talos with a haunted, fierce look. The web-like veins splitting his cheeks curled as he smiled. 'Trust me.'

* * *

In the infinitely slow ballet of void movement, the *Covenant of Blood* drifted through the scattered fleet, coming alongside the Warmaster's flagship. A blue-black and bronze blade of a ship, it reached barely half the size of the *Vengeful Spirit*.

'Launch Thunderhawks,' the Exalted said, reclining once more in its command throne.

'Thunderhawks launching,' an officer called back.

'Report the moment they're clear of the fleet.'

It took less than a minute. 'Thunderhawks clear. All five are in the upper atmosphere.'

'Drift to the following heading.' The Exalted's claws hit keys embedded in his throne's console. 'Engines cold. That is imperative. *Drift*. Use attitude thrusters, and no greater duration than two seconds from each. Keep all thrust emissions untraceable by casual auspex sweeps.'

The *Covenant* obeyed. The Exalted watched the images displayed by the external picters, seeing the skin of the flagship edging closer to the hull of his own vessel. He was reminded briefly, as he always was in these dark and silent moments, of two sharks passing one another in the open ocean.

'Open a one-way channel to the *Premonition*. Do not allow a reply.'

'Done, lord.'

'Halasker, this is the Exalted. Run.'

Engines burned into angry life, propelling the *Hunter's Premonition* from its position in the invasion fleet. The Exalted watched the hololithic display and the sensor readings of his focused auspex scans, but spared no attention for the disengaging Night Lords battle-barge. His focus was on the rest of the fleet.

Several cruisers showed their weapons going live.

'Incoming message, lord.'

'From the *Vengeful Spirit*, I imagine,' the Exalted said.

'Yes, lord. They request we move, immediately, to a station at their starboard.'

'Oh, woe,' the Exalted grinned. 'Are we accidentally within their firing solution? My, however will they open fire on the *Premonition* before it breaks into the warp?'

Several of the bridge crew shared self-satisfied smiles.

'They've repeated the demand for immediate compliance,' the officer said.

'Inform the flagship we require confirmation of that order. Only a short while ago, we were ordered to this position. Now we are required to move? With the Blood Angels inbound?' The Exalted's smirk was as ugly and inhuman as the creature itself.

While the vox-officer sent the message, the Exalted watched the hololith again. Three other cruisers were powering up their lances to rip the *Premonition* apart for its betrayal. These, he disregarded. They would either be too slow to inflict more than minimal damage, or too late to do anything except watch the battle-barge escape.

Pride uncurled within his stomach, hot and welcome. Perhaps some nobility could be salvaged from this night after all.

'Orders confirmed,' the vox-officer called.

'Do as the flagship orders,' the creature nodded to the helm. 'They won't even be able to come about in time.'

As the *Covenant* shuddered in obedience, the Exalted opened a vox-link to every speaker on the ship.

'This is the Exalted. We are remaining within the fleet until the recovery of our brothers on the surface. We must buy our Thunderhawks time, during which we will endure assault from our former brethren, the

Blood Angels. Seal all bulkheads. Atramentar, to the bridge. Claws, to your posts. All hands, to battle stations. Stand by to repel boarders.'

XX
THE ANGEL'S SONS

THE FLEETS MET only briefly.

'These battles are won and lost in the opening manoeuvres,' the Exalted said as it stared at the Astartes fleet bearing down upon them. 'If one side is in a strong enough position, the other – commanded by intelligent souls – would do better to retreat rather than be annihilated in a hopeless engagement.'

Garadon regarded the three-dimensional hololithic performance as a dull mystery. 'They will not back down, my prince.'

'No. They will not. Another opportunity lost. Helm, be ready to break orbit on my mark.'

'Break orbit?' Malek grunted. 'But lord–'

'We are not going away from Crythe, Malek. Quite the opposite.'

The Exalted closed its eyes, breathing deep and slow. It remained in this state for several moments. Finally, it spoke, without opening its jet eyes. 'The first lances will be firing… now.'

The Atramentar, all seven of them in their Terminator plate, watched as the hololithic display began to add weapons fire to its projection.

'The lead battle-barges, bearing the Blood Angels' insignia, will be hit by lance fire from the first of our perimeter ships... now.'

The Exalted opened its eyes, seeing its predictions confirmed. Officers and servitors at consoles started working frantically. 'We have a Blood Angels strike cruiser inbound, do we not?' the Exalted asked.

'Yes, lord!' called a rating.

'How predictable. Sometimes, we do not even need Talos to see the future for us. Our foes' grasp of tactical potential is so *coarse.*'

Garadon grunted acknowledgement, but said nothing.

'Fire lances,' the Exalted ordered, even as the weapons officer was drawing breath to announce the Blood Angels cruiser had just entered lance range.

'Firing lances, lord.'

The Exalted went back to its hololithic staring even as the ship started shuddering with the first impacts.

Shields holding. Six per cent drain.

'Shields holding!' an officer called. 'Seven per cent drain.'

Close enough.

'Weapon batteries, ready for my signal.'

'Weapon batteries, aye.'

Come on. Closer. Closer.

The bridge shivered again. The rune depicting the Blood Angels strike cruiser *Malevolence* bore down like a spear. That was the one. It would release boarders onto both the *Spirit* and the *Covenant*. They were well within scanning distance now. They would know how vulnerable the Warmaster's capital ships were. How empty the internal corridors stood without the Astartes to defend them.

The bridge lights dimmed, then failed for a handful of seconds. The fleets, as they crossed each other, exchanged a ferocious volley of fire. The smaller capital ships like the *Covenant* had void shields far below the punishment capacity of battleships like the *Vengeful Spirit*.

'Shields are down,' a rating called out on cue. The tremors shaking the ship intensified tenfold.

'My prince,' one of the weapons officers said. 'They're in weapon battery range.'

Wait. Wait...

'Lord, enemy cruiser *Malevolence* has fired boarding pods.'

The Exalted burbled a sound that might have once been a chuckle.

'All batteries fire.'

Two of the eight pod-runes flickered out of existence from the hololithic display. The others streamed home into their target ships. Four impacted into the *Covenant*.

The Exalted calmly demanded a vox-channel to the entire ship. A rating at the console nodded back.

'All claws, this is the Exalted. Between twenty and forty Blood Angels have breached us with assault pods. Hull impact locations are routed to squad leaders. Find the loyalists, my brothers. Kill them.'

The Exalted rose from its throne, dragging its armoured bulk to the dais railing. It stared into the occulus, at the greyish orb of Crythe below.

'Damage report.'

'Minor structural damage, primarily the starboard side.'

'Order the enginarium to vent plasma from the reactors. Bleed power directly into the void.'

'Sir?' his human bridge attendant stammered.

'Do as I command, mortal.'

'As you wish, lord.'

'Vox-officer.'

'Yes, my prince.'

'Transmit emergency crash landing signals to the *Vengeful Spirit.* Inform them we've taken glancing damage that has managed to wound our reactor. Tell them we are losing our orbit due to the pull of the planet's gravity, and our engines are locked at full power.'

As the confused vox-officer obeyed, the Exalted turned to face the row of helmsmen.

'Are we bleeding plasma? Self-scan the *Covenant.* Do we appear to be haemorrhaging from a reactor leakage?'

The helm officers bent over their consoles. 'Yes, lord,' one replied.

'Then dive,' the Exalted grinned.

'What?' Malek stepped forward. 'Lord, are you insane?'

'Dive!'

Like a sword falling from the sky, the *Covenant of Blood* tilted downward and fired its engines. Flame wreathed the shieldless strike cruiser as it tore through the pollution-clogged atmosphere.

Septimus burned Blackened's engines, coming in tight and low over the plain. Behind him came another two Thunderhawks and two transporters, forming a loose 'V' formation.

'Be ready to break at the first sign of attack,' he warned over the vox.

'Compliance,' replied three servitors.

'Understood,' came a deeper voice. An Astartes. Septimus had no idea which one.

A trickle of sweat made its uncomfortable way down his back, seeming to pause at the bump of at each vertebra. It was one thing to know you'd eventually die in service to the VIII Legion. It was another thing to realise you were going to meet that fate imminently. Even if the Black Legion had stopped shooting down Night Lords gunships, what hope was there to get back into orbit and survive a docking operation in the middle of a void war?

Septimus swore under his breath and activated a general vox-channel.

'All VIII Legion units, this is the 10th Company Thunderhawk *Blackened.* Report your locations.'

The voices that came back to him were strained, angry, embattled. He throttled up, letting the engines shout harder, approaching the storm of disorder that engulfed the landing site of the Warmaster's forces.

'Look to the skies, Night Lords,' he said in fluent Nostraman. 'We are inbound.'

'Be swift,' one voice said. 'Most of us are down to killing them with our bare hands.'

The chorus of replies detailed exactly what needed to be recovered from the surface. A Land Raider, four Rhinos, a Vindicator and forty-one warriors.

Mere minutes later, Septimus kicked *Blackened* into hover, his altitude thrusters burning to keep the gunship aloft over the landing site. The landing platform erected by the 11th Company of the *Hunter's Premonition* was a bare bones setup – and Septimus was being generous calling it even that. The surviving tanks and men clustered around an engine-scorched patch of land, their weapons turned outwards into the ranks of the Black Legion's mortal slaves. The humans had seen the incoming gunships and sought to escape, charging the encircled Night Lords vehicles.

As the Astartes had said, several of the VIII Legion warriors were reduced to beating the mortals to death with their fists. Ammunition had not been landed and supplied to the front line in several hours. Even the guns of the tanks spat their deadly payloads only intermittently into the seething horde laying siege to their position.

'They've not got room to get the tanks into a loading position. Should we open fire on the crowd?' Septimus asked. 'My ammunition counters are practically voided.'

The gunship hovering fifty metres to his port bow immediately opened up with a vicious hail of heavy bolter fire, punching holes in the panicked mortal horde.

Foolish question to ask a Night Lord, really.

Septimus added his fire to the chaos below.

BROTHER-SERGEANT MELCHIAH MOVED with purpose.

In units of five, his men moved through the enemy ship.

The darkness was nothing to him. This, he pierced with the vision modes of his helm. The winding corridors offered no mystery to his senses. These, he navigated by memory, for one Astartes strike cruiser was the same as almost any other. Such was the wisdom contained with the Standard Template Construct patterns of all noble machines birthed by the Adeptus Mechanicus.

On he stalked, chainsword purring with rev-breaths, his plasma pistol raised before him. The blackness of the Traitors' vessel yielded before him, his vision stained emerald green by his helm's lenses, picking out details of walls, side corridors, and the heat smear of recent footsteps.

'Auspex,' he voxed to Hyralus.

'No movement,' Hyralus replied. 'Vague heat traces all around. A nexus of them in the chamber ahead.'

'Forward, in the name of the Emperor,' Melchiah said, moving on. He removed his helm, trusting to his own senses even in the pitch dark. He was Astartes. It was the way of things. Immediately, he felt more in tune with his surroundings, his senses no longer caged by the helm. Even with its enhancements, it was not always the perfect replacement for true perception.

Corruption was rife here. Even the air of the ship tasted foul. Too long in the warp, too long with the same recycled air. Warm and stale, it tingled against the steel studs implanted above Melchiah's eyebrow. Three of them, in recognition of his long service.

Upon the shoulders of each warrior, a ruby-red drop of blood the size of a mortal's fist was winged by marble angel pinions. It was a symbol that had endured for thousands of years, and one the Night Lords were sure to recognise. The Traitors' own symbol was the corrupt opposite – a fanged skull instead of a primarch's holy blood, and arching bat wings instead of the pure aileron of the murdered Angel, Sanguinius.

With the ancient hatreds hot in his heart, Melchiah entered the chamber, plasma pistol raised. The shuddering of the ship was growing savage. Curious, that it wasn't the jagged shaking of battle, but something much more regular. An atmospheric entry burn? Perhaps. But with little indication of why the Traitor Legion ship would be reacting this way, Melchiah put it out of his mind. He had a duty. He was oathed to this moment.

The chamber was large. Almost impressive. On board the *Malevolent*, this room was a chapel to the Emperor of Mankind. On the *Covenant*, it looked to be some kind of communal haven for slaves. Detritus decorated the floor. Tables stood abandoned and bare. Bedrolls lined one wall.

'Auspex?' he said. 'I see nothing.'

'And that's why you're dead,' Talos hissed as he dropped from the ceiling.

LIKE SPIDERS, THEY had lain in wait, clinging to the ceiling. With the Blood Angels in their midst, First Claw dropped the ten metres to the ground, their weapons spitting death at the loyalists below.

Talos hit first, *Aurum* deflecting a bolt from the Angels and lashing out to ram home in the chest of the helmless squad leader.

'*Aurum!*' the sergeant snarled. 'The blade!'

Talos's reply was a headbutt that crashed against his foe's reinforced skull, hammering the long-service studs through the bone and into the soft tissue of the brain beneath.

The two squads tore into each other, equal in all ways but for the fact First Claw had the advantage of surprise.

Talos powered the sword to the side, ripping through Melchiah's spinal column, lungs, one heart and his ceramite armour as if none of it existed. The blade's arc was as smooth as if Talos chopped air. As the Blood Angel staggered back, the Night Lord pounded a bolt into his neck, just a single shot. Melchiah had a single moment to claw at the wound before it exploded, removing his head in a shower of organic mess.

'For the Emperor!' one of the Angels cried. The darkness broke in the face of bolter flashes and clashing power weapons.

Talos leapt at the shouter, his golden sword cleaving through the warrior's bolter on the downswing. The Astartes met the blade's backslash with his own combat gladius.

'For the Emperor,' the Blood Angel said again, this time in a snarl.

'Your Emperor is dead,' Talos growled back. The moment came; the moment when the Angel's gaze flickered to the blade in the Night Lord's dark hands. Talos couldn't see his enemy's eyes, but he felt the minute movement of the Angel's muscles as his attention wavered. In that critical moment, Talos hurled the Blood Angel back against the wall. Three bolts to the head downed him for good, and Talos nodded his thanks to Cyrion.

Uzas, Mercutian, Xarl, Adhemar, Cyrion and Talos stood in the darkness, listening to the hiss of cooling bolter muzzles, watching the last Blood Angel in the doorway. He turned and ran, boots pounding down the corridor.

'I... wasn't expecting that,' Talos almost laughed. 'Uzas, do the honours.'

Uzas sprinted into the darkness, chainsword howling.

THE BLOOD ANGEL wasn't fleeing. Uzas knew that.

He hated to indulge the thought, even to himself, that the Angels were an admirable force – back in the Great Crusade, at least. These thinbloods left much to be desired. So far removed from the gene-seed of their primarch as to be almost mortal. But even so, the Angel wasn't fleeing. The only time an Astartes backed down from a battle was when he had an idea for how to fight it better elsewhere. The trick, Uzas had learned, was to kill the enemy before they got that chance.

He was on the Angel in under a minute, but the loyalist wasn't giving up easily. Without the element of surprise – and really, that was an inspired idea he grudgingly gave Talos credit for – the two of them were close-matched.

The Blood Angel pulled his gladius free from its ornate scabbard and lunged. Uzas parried the first thrust and dodged the second, third and fourth. *Kharnath's boiling blood,* the Angel was fast.

'I'm better than you,' the Angel mocked, backhanding the Night Lord with a fist that crashed hard against Uzas's helm. 'Will you call for your brothers, Traitor?'

Uzas gave ground, deflecting the gladius with his chainsword each time it sought his heart or throat. Teeth sprayed from his chainblade as the Angel hacked them away.

'I will eat your gene-seed,' Uzas grunted, 'after I claw it out of your throat with my bare hands.'

'You will die.' The Angel lashed out with a boot, thudding the Night Lord into the wall behind. 'And be forgotten.'

The Blood Angel's helm distorted with a tremendous *clang,* then exploded in a shower of red-painted shards.

Uzas breathed out slowly. The dead Blood Angel crashed to the ground in a metallic chorus of plate. Talos lowered his bolter and shook his head at his brother.

'You were taking too long,' he said, and moved back down the corridor.

THE COVENANT OF BLOOD was constructed in the shipyards of Mars in the age before Mankind's sundering. Since its birth in those fleet-raising forge-foundries, it had landed a total of zero times, and performed an equal number of atmospheric flights. As it burned through the atmosphere of Crythe and violently tore through the cloud cover, the Exalted's eyes remained closed, not seeing anything on the strategium command deck.

Its ship, the ship it knew better than the creature knew his own twisted body, was shaking itself apart. The painful shudders wracking the *Covenant* transmitted through to the Exalted's own spine in sympathetic torment.

But it vowed it would die before it failed in the promise to that preening glory-hound Halasker.

The bridge crew gripped their consoles or remained strapped into their own control thrones. The Atramentar Terminators were forced to their knees, even their enhanced muscle fibres unable to resist the gravity forces taking hold. They resembled worshippers before the Exalted's throne, which brought a sick little smile to the creature's face, even if only for a moment.

'Position,' it demanded of the helm. At the reply, the Exalted turned to the vox-officer. 'Hail our Thunderhawks. Inform them they have two minutes to be skyborne or they will have no mothership to return to.'

'We will be above Seventeen-Seventeen in ninety seconds, lord!'

'Slow my ship down, mortals. I care not how it's done, but make it happen. Give the Thunderhawks time to dock.'

THE SHAKING THREATENED the hunt.

Talos cursed as gravity reasserted its grip on them at another inconvenient moment, and his bolt went wide. Across the chamber, a second squad of Blood Angels stood their ground beside an unopened boarding pod. They crouched behind what little cover existed in the Blackmarket hall, returning fire at First Claw. Talos and his brothers used the corners of linking corridors as cover.

Neither side was getting anywhere.

'Brother, I have grim news,' Adhemar voxed. He crouched next to the prophet, twinning his fire with Talos's. 'That pod they're guarding?'

Talos unleashed another three bolts to no effect. 'I see it.' The hull was mangled and blackened where the red-metal pod had pierced the ship's skin. 'Hard to miss, Adhemar.'

'It's a Dreadnought pod.'

'What? How can you tell?'

'The size of the damn wound in our hull!'

Talos's retinal display outlined the measurements as he glanced around the corner. He resisted the powerful urge to sigh.

'You are right.'

'I'm always right.'

The ship juddered again, violently enough to throw two of the Blood Angels from their feet and onto the black decking. Uzas and Xarl similarly lost their footing, accompanied by Nostraman curses.

Like a steel bloom greeting the new season, the pod's cone-shaped front opened to the bay. The hulking form within began to grind forward, a tower of reddened metal and vox-roared challenges.

'I will end you, Traitors. I will end you *all*.'

The air between the squads roiled with barely-seen heat blurs, and the temperature readings on Talos's retinal displays shot up with sickening speed. The Dreadnought's massive multi-melta, capable of blistering tanks into sludge, was only just warming up.

'It's got a vaporiser cannon!' Mercutian voxed. 'We're dead.'

'Fine by me, I've had enough of your doom and gloom,' Cyrion answered.

Talos hunched behind his scarce cover, firing his bolter blindly around the corner and speaking into the vox.

'This is Talos of First Claw, requesting urgent reinforcements in the aft mortals' decks.'

The voice that answered was balm to his soul.

'Understood, my brother.'

XXI
FINAL UNITY

'Many will claim to lead our Legion in the years after I am gone.
Many will claim that they – and they alone – are my appointed successor.
I hate this Legion, Talos.
I destroyed its world to stem the flow of poison.
I will be vindicated soon, and the truest lesson of the Night Lords will be taught.
Do you truly believe I care what happens to any of you after my death?'

– The Primarch Konrad Curze
Addressing Apothecary Talos of First Claw,
10th Company

SEPTIMUS WRENCHED THE control sticks hard, begging for altitude. Crowded around him were Astartes from 11th Company, each one a stranger to him, each one now discovering the unwelcome fact that a blessed Legion relic was being piloted by a mortal serf. He expected at any moment one of them would demand the controls from him.

This didn't happen. He doubted it was because they were too exhausted – in his experience, Astartes didn't tire as humans did – but they were certainly worse for wear. Their dark, skulled plate was as shattered and bloody as First Claw's had been.

Turbulence buffeted *Blackened* with an angry fist, and a sickening lurch in his gut betrayed the loss of altitude even before his console instruments did. The serf threw levers and wrenched the sticks again. *Blackened* climbed.

Behind them, a transporter exploded in mid-air. Its shell, and the hulks of two Rhinos it was carrying, crashed to the ground in flames. Dozens of mortal soldiers died beneath it.

'The Black Legion,' one of the Astartes said in a low, dangerous voice. 'They will bleed and scream for this. Each and every one of them.' The promise met with general assent. Septimus swallowed; he couldn't have cared less about vengeance in that moment. He just wanted the damn gunship to climb, climb, *climb*.

He had to break into orbit. He had to reach the *Covenant*.

And that's when he saw it.

'Throne of the God-Emperor,' he whispered for the first time since his capture.

The *Covenant of Blood* was on fire. It streaked across the sky like a burning meteorite, trailing flame and smoke in a thin plume. The heavens rang with thunder as it pounded through the sound barrier – not speeding up but slowing down.

'This is the Exalted,' the vox crackled live. 'Brothers of 7th Company. We have come for you.'

THE VOX WAS alive with reports from the other claws. The Blood Angels, even with their numbers fewer than thirty, were spread throughout the ship and putting up ferocious resistance to the hunt that sought their lives.

Talos coughed blood. The bolts that had struck his chestplate and helm left his armour a broken ruin. Although his nerves were deadened to the worst of the pain by combat narcotics pulsing through his veins, he knew spitting blood onto the decking was a bad sign. His gene-enhanced healing was failing to heal whatever the hell was wrong with him.

He'd seen Adhemar die.

It was over in a moment.

A blur of motion as the former sergeant rushed the Dreadnought with his blade held high. The war machine had turned with unbelievable speed, whirring around on its waist axis, breathing invisible but searing heat from its multi-melta. Adhemar's armour baked and split within a heartbeat, the joints melted, the empty war-plate clattering to melt into sludge on the decking. Nothing biological remained.

Over in a moment.

All to save Mercutian and Uzas, who were wounded on the other side of the chamber. Talos had added his bolter fire to cover them, and taken hits from the Blood Angels for his trouble.

Were the Blood Angels suicidal? To fire a melta-weapon within a ship? It was a miracle the hull wasn't liquefied yet and every one of them torn out into the rushing air.

Talos gripped *Aurum*, feeling his strength waxing again. Good. Not lethal, perhaps. Something was wrong, but it could be dealt with later. The Blood Angels had to be slaughtered, skinned and crucified for their accursed presence on the *Covenant*.

At first he'd thought the deck shaking was merely more of the atmospheric turbulence. Shells still exploded around his fragile cover, and only when Malcharion strode past, his armoured bulk barely fitting within the linking corridors, did Talos realise what was happening. The Dreadnought stalked into the chamber, ignoring the small-arms fire from the Blood Angels.

Revitalised by the war-sage's presence, First Claw's survivors doubled their fire. Astartes armoured in red died. Mercutian and Cyrion went down as well, struck by bolts.

Talos felt his newly-recovered strength desert him. Back to the wall, he slid down to the decking, clutching his shattered breastplate. The Dreadnoughts regarded each other in a moment of almost hilarious calm.

'Kill it!' Talos screamed. *'Kill it now!'*

'I already have once,' Malcharion boomed.

The Blood Angels Dreadnought made the same gear-shifting grind of a sound Talos had heard from Malcharion. The Night Lord's eyes fell upon the sarcophagus mounted within the war-sage's new body. There stood the image of Malcharion in life, clutching the three helms. One of those belonged to...

The Blood Angel champion... Raguel the Sufferer.

'Even in death,' the Blood Angel growled, **'I will avenge myself,'**

'You deserve the chance, Raguel.'

With power fists crackling, the two war machines did what they were resurrected to do.

The fight played out in two worlds, and until his dying night Talos was never sure which battle he truly witnessed. In the immediate, painful, shaking world of the shallowest senses, the two armoured behemoths tore at each other with rotating claws and bludgeoning fists. Ceramite ripped in those mauling hands, and shards of armour flew from the combatants like hail on some blizzard-touched deathworld.

Neither of the suspended corpses saw this, and neither felt it.

The walls were gold where these warriors duelled. Both men wore the proud armour of their Legion, and both men fought for Terra – one to defend it and die for the Imperium, one to conquer it and kill for the same reason.

Their blades spun and struck until both were broken. Then it came down to gauntleted fists and the strength to strangle.

Talos watched the Dreadnoughts tearing each other to scrap, and saw exactly what the dead men saw.

Blackened roared through the air, engines screaming as the racing Thunderhawk drew alongside the *Covenant*.

The others had already docked, bringing their precious cargo on board the strike cruiser as it tore across the sky. *Blackened* was the last.

Warning runes flashed across console displays as Septimus pushed the engines past all safe limits. The control sticks juddered in his fists, shaking almost in sync with the wailing sirens that screamed at him to cease what he was doing. The dark dart of the Thunderhawk banked closer to the racing shape of the *Covenant*, the turbulence intensified with *Blackened* on the edge of entering its mothership's slipstream.

It was starting to climb.

He could see it himself, even without the Astartes in the cockpit – warriors he didn't know – pointing it out in curses and complaints.

These, he did his best to ignore along with the warning runes blinking migraine-red everywhere.

But the *Covenant* was definitely climbing now, and even slowly, it made a near-impossible landing almost inconceivable. Its prow came up, cutting the polluted sky, in the beginning incline for orbital re-entry.

'Just a little more,' he mouthed the plea, wrenching the three thrust levers into the blank sockets past the red zones marked on the helm consoles. *Blackened* kicked, howling louder, and burst forward in pursuit of its carrier.

The thought occurred, as he climbed alongside the strike cruiser, banking ever closer to the open hangar bay, that there was a very good chance one – or all – of the Thunderhawk's engines would explode under this punishment.

Septimus pulled back, climbing parallel to the larger ship, boosting ahead of the open bay doors, ready to fall back and weave inside. The gunship veered gently, shaking hard, within thirty metres of the hangar bay.

They were going too fast to deploy the landing gear. The claws would be torn off the moment they cleared the hull. Septimus would need to lower them late, as soon as *Blackened* came into the bay, and pray they were down enough to take the ship's weight.

'Now or never,' he whispered, and banked hard right at more than full thrust. The Thunderhawk wrenched to the side, rolling directly at the hangar bay.

The next ten seconds lasted an age to Septimus – an eternity of insane shaking and the loudest noises he had ever heard.

The port booster exploded as the Thunderhawk veered home, amplifying the turbulence tenfold. Septimus had been ready for one or more of the engines to go, and compensated immediately. *Blackened* would have fallen short of its target, either smashing headlong into side of the *Covenant*, or glancing from the larger ship and then falling from the sky after sustaining severe damage in the impact. Septimus compensated by overloading the remaining boosters, destroying them all in one momentary burst of thrust that threw the gunship at the open bay.

He risked it, so close to the target, and deployed the landing gear. The hideous sound of wrenching metal told the fate of the front landing leg. The others held.

Darkness blanketed over the view windows as they hurtled at the *Covenant*. Septimus had a split second to realise they were on course, but not *perfectly*, before they were in the bay itself with a blur of motion. Another almighty crash shook the Thunderhawk as the gunship's tail cleaved into the edge of the bay doors. *Blackened* bucked and lurched, twisted off its already chaotic course, and slammed into the floor with savage force.

The rear landing claws carved into the decking as the gunship's nose hammered down and ploughed a squealing, sparking furrow through the deck floor. After several dozen metres of skidding, the rear landing gear gave way, torn from their sockets and thudding the gunship's winged rear end to the decking with a thunderous crash.

With its engines dead and thrusters burned out, the only thing that brought the howling gunship to a final halt was its collision with the side wall of the hangar bay.

Septimus was jolted forward with this last indignity, but his restraint belts remained strong, keeping him in his throne.

Motionless at last, his heart pounding, Septimus let out the deepest breath he'd ever held.

'We're... we're down,' he said, unsurprised at the tremor in his voice.

The Astartes squad unbuckled from their own thrones and left the cockpit without a word.

Even as the ruined engines continued the short process of terminally cycling down in an orchestra of mechanical whines, the Astartes on board were disembarking, summoned by the Exalted in defence of the *Covenant*. Throne-loyal Astartes were apparently on board.

Septimus was almost too tired to care as he stood slowly, trying to keep his balance on unsteady legs.

His neck ached. His back ached. His hands ached.

Everything ached. A pilot all his life, he'd not even believed such a docking was survivable. The Astartes left without a word of acknowledgement. He was also too tired to care.

Well. Almost.

Stumbling down the gang ramp, he blinked blurry stress-exhaustion from his eyes. *Blackened* creaked and hissed behind him as its strained hull settled into inactivity once more.

The gunship's tail was gone, torn off in the crash with the hull. The landing gear was a mangled memory. All across the Thunderhawk's proud, hunter's form, damage showed in stark, black burns and dark, twisted metal.

'I am never doing that again,' he said. Servitors approached, their simple programming taking several moments to calculate how to deal with the wreckage of what lay before them. Several looked at him curiously, wondering if he'd spoken a command.

'Get back to work,' Septimus said. He reached up to activate his vox-bead. 'Octavia?'

Her voice was weak. Wet with tears.

'You have to help me,' she said softly.

'Where are you?'

She told him, and Septimus broke into a pained run.

* * *

On the strategium, the Exalted watched the mountain ranges below falling away. Its ship climbed, tearing into the sky like a spear. The bridge crew cheered. The sound shook the Exalted, having never heard it before.

Within seconds, the blue palette of the occulus was replaced by black.

The black of the void. Blessedly, the *Covenant* ended its tormented shaking. Artificial gravity resumed, and limbs became less heavy.

'Punch a hole through between these two ships,' the Exalted ordered. It was already sat back in its throne, studying the reactivated hololithic display. Keen senses raced to unravel the mysteries, the flight paths, the destructions and deaths since he had last seen this image.

The shaking began again, and this time, damage reports flooded in.

'I do not care what damage is sustained.' The ship jolted hard under another volley of lance strikes. 'Just get us into the warp.'

Arrow-straight and lethally fast, the *Covenant* ripped from Crythe Prime's orbit, racing through the battling fleets.

'Navigator Etrigius,' the Exalted said. 'Answer me.'

'He's... he's dead,' said a female voice.

First Claw came to the downed machines.

The healthiest of the Astartes were limping. Uzas and Mercutian dragged themselves by their hands.

The Blood Angel Dreadnought still twitched as it lay on its back. Its claw opened and closed, grinding nothing but air. Talos nodded to the sarcophagus, too pained to point.

'Cut that open.'

Xarl and Cyrion went to work with their chainswords, carving through the coffin's surface, the tearing teeth offering no respect for the funerary declarations and acid-etched glories depicted in Baalian glyphs. With grunts of effort, the two warriors hauled the sarcophagus's lid away, revealing the pilot within.

Their blades had ruptured the inner coffin. Clear amniotic fluid, blood-pinked in patches, seeped from the pierced box in sloshing trickles.

Talos stepped on the downed Dreadnought's hull, looking down at the limbless, augmented wreck of a human being.

'I am Talos of the Night Lords. Nod if you understand me.'

The slain hero nodded, skin tightening in doubtlessly painful spasms as his life support interfeeds failed. Talos smiled at the sight.

'Know this, Blood Angel. Your final mission was a failure. Your brothers are dead. We will wear their armour in battle against your False Emperor. And know this also, champion of the IX Legion. Twice now, the sons of the Night Haunter have seen you slain. Greet the afterlife within the warp knowing you were too weak to triumph over us, even once.'

Talos locked eyes with the spasming remnant in its fluid-filled coffin. In a sure grip despite the weakness of his arm, Talos raised *Aurum*, the blade of another fallen Angel.

'Your bones will be made into trophies for our armour. We will feast upon your gene-seed. And whatever remains of this glorious walking tomb will be salvaged by our tech-priest to house a champion of our own Legion.'

He plunged the blade down. Its golden length stabbed through the casket, impaling the mutilated Imperial hero's open mouth.

'Die,' Talos finished, 'with the taste of your Chapter's eternal failure on your tongue.'

OCTAVIA WIPED THE blood from Etrigius's face.

The Navigator's eerie features seemed somehow childish in death, peaceful and innocent. She could almost believe he hadn't seen a lifetime of sights and secrets few mortals should be cursed to witness.

One of his rings had slipped from a too-long finger. She replaced it on his hand, not even sure why she bothered. It just felt right. Throne, she'd not even liked him. He was an insufferable and condescending ass.

Still. He'd not deserved this. No one did.

Octavia rested her hand over the bleeding puncture where his warp eye had been. A sniper... some kind of lightly-armoured Astartes youth... He'd stolen into the chamber and dropped Etrigius with a single shot. The Navigator died in the middle of complaining about the turbulence. Octavia had been too shocked to move, too stunned to reach for her autopistol, even when the Navigator's robed servitors deployed their claws and tore the Blood Angel youth limb from limb.

'He's dead,' she'd told the daemon-thing on the bridge when its voice blared over the vox. 'They killed him.'

The daemon-thing, the Exalted, had screamed. The ship shuddered as if in the grip of some huge, angry god.

Septimus's voice came to her again. Not over the vox this time. She looked up and saw him standing at the doorway.

'Octavia.'

'They killed him,' she said again, her teeth clenched. Throne, why was she crying? Why wouldn't the ship stop shaking... just for a moment...

'Octavia,' Septimus came to her, helping her to her feet. 'The *Covenant* is being destroyed. We are all dead, unless...'

'Unless... I guide us into the warp.'

'Yes.' He wiped flecks of blood from her face, his augmetic eye whirring as it focused. She heard it click once, very quietly.

'Did you just take my pict?'

'I may have,' he said. His smile answered for him, slow and mournful.

Octavia glanced at the bloodstained meditation couch, and did not look back at him. 'You should go. This is never pleasant to watch.'

He hesitated, reluctant to let her go even as the ship was being annihilated by Imperial guns. She pushed him away, not unkindly.

'You know,' she said, walking to the couch, 'I'll see you after. Maybe.'

'Maybe.'

She finally looked back, seeing him standing by the door. 'I have no idea what I'm doing. I can find the Astronomican, guide by the Emperor's light. But I have a feeling that would invite pursuit.'

'It would. Just... do your best.'

'I could kill you all, if I wanted to.' She grinned. 'You're heretics, you know.'

'I know.'

'You should go.'

He didn't know what else to say, so he left without saying anything at all. The door to Etrigius's – no, Octavia's chambers – sealed closed and locked tight.

'Navigator,' came a growl from the vox speakers around the room.

'Here,' she answered.

'I am the Exalted.'

'I know who you are.'

'Do you know the region of space, close to the galactic core, that houses a warp wound known as the Great Eye?'

Eurydice Mervallion, now called Octavia of the *Covenant*, took a deep breath.

'Link me to the helm,' she said, strength returning to her voice. 'I will commune with your pilots.'

IT WASN'T SO difficult, really.

The ship hated her. Oh, how it loathed her presence. She felt its soul recoil from her probing meditation, like a viper protecting its young.

I hate you, the *Covenant* hissed. Its presence thrashed in her mind, shrieking and hateful.

I hate you, it warned again, far from the docile and sedate soul of Kartan Syne's *Maiden of the Stars*.

You are not my Navigator, it spat.

'Yes,' she spoke to the chamber, empty except the corpse of her predecessor. 'I am.'

Octavia closed her human eyes, opened the third, and dragged the *Covenant of Blood* into the space between worlds.

'YOU FEEL THAT?' Xarl asked as the ship seemed to slip forward in a strangely smooth lurch that had no similarity to weapons fire.

Talos nodded. He'd felt the translation into the warp as well.

'We made it,' Cyrion grunted. 'Most of us.'

Malcharion was no longer moving at all. First Claw clustered around the ruined warrior, and Xarl's chain-blade revved again.

'Should we?' he asked Talos. 'Deltrian might be able to save him, if he still lives within.'

'No. Let him sleep, as he wished. We already have an image of him that should stay with us down the ages.' The prophet's eyes didn't leave the triumphant engraving on the front of the sarcophagus for some time.

'It was grand to see him fight,' Uzas conceded, 'one last time.'

The others snorted or stared to hear such a thing from him.

'I swear, I saw the fight at the Palace of Terra again,' Cyrion said. 'Not these... war machines clubbing each other.'

Talos didn't reply.

'Deltrian,' he voxed to the Hall of Remembrance.

'Yes, One-Two-Ten. I am present, Talos.'

'Malcharion the War-Sage has fallen in battle.'

'Your voice indicates you grieve at this development. If condolences from others will ease your torment, I will offer them.'

'The sentiment is appreciated, but that is not all.'

'Your voice patterns now show a trace of amusement.'

'Send two teams of lifter servitors to the aft mortals' decks, to the area known as Blackmarket.'

'Processing. One team is enough to recover the holy relic of the entombed Malcharion. I require reasoning for your request of two lifter teams.'

'Because, honoured tech-priest,' Talos turned his gaze to the wreckage of Raguel the Sufferer in his priceless war machine shell, 'First Claw has a gift for you.'

With the link cut, Talos narrowed his eyes at the corpse of one dead Blood Angel. The warrior's breastplate remained intact despite grievous damage to his thigh, leg and shoulder armour. An Imperial eagle spread its wings proudly across the chestpiece, forged from platinum, gleaming gold in the dim light.

The prophet nodded weakly at the dead Blood Angel's beautiful armour.

'That is mine,' he said, and slid back down to the decking, too exhausted to move.

EPILOGUE
PORTENTS

In the bowels of the *Covenant of Blood*, a mother and father wept.

The human crew had not come through the battle unscathed. Some fell victim to the Blood Angel boarding teams, cut down as they fled from the righteous indignation of the Emperor's finest warriors. Others perished in the explosions that wracked the ship as it sustained severe damage from other Imperial cruisers. Still more died as gangs of mortals used the chaos of the orbital war as a cover to launch attacks on the rival gangs that shared the blackness with them.

One man clutched the body of his daughter, holding her light, lifeless form to his own scrawny chest. Blood still marked the girl's lips and face from where she had choked out her last wet breath, less than an hour before. Her eyes, dark from the eternal gloom, stared sightlessly at the crowd that came to gather.

She had no legs. These were lost to a Blood Angel chainblade as one of the Imperium's heroes had sought to exterminate his way through the heretic crew of the *Covenant*. His grinding blade had claimed the lives of many before he was finally slain by Astartes from one of the *Covenant's* claws.

Her father cradled what remained of her, and cried out his sorrow.

The witnesses began to whisper, speaking in quiet tones of curses, of omens, of the blackest portents. On the girl's chest, a Legion medallion glinted in the dim light.

Her father held what remained of the ten-year-old girl, and yelled at the walls of the silent ship all around.

'This vessel is *cursed*! It is *damned*! *She has been taken from us!*'

More humans gathered in the darkness, their eyes wide and wet with tears, each of them sharing the same thoughts and fears as the mourning father.

TAISHA WAS NOT at peace, despite the harmony of the garden.

Beneath a dome that revealed the glory of the silent void, beneath the twinkling light of a million distant suns, Taisha came to the garden in search of answers. Her bare feet whispered over the cool soil, the grass soft on her toes. A robe of shimmering jade silk clung to her lithe figure, hanging off one shoulder to leave it bare. Hair the deep red of human blood, long enough to reach the small of her back, was tied up in a sharp topknot.

Her slanted eyes regarded a figure kneeling upon the grass. His own robes were the black of the unending space between the worlds. He spoke without looking up at her.

'Greetings, daughter of Khaine and Morai-Heg.'

Taisha inclined her head to the appropriate angle, politely acknowledging his superior rank and the honour he did her by speaking first. She did not kneel beside him. Such would be a breach of decorum. Instead she stayed several metres away, her fingers lightly stroking the wraithbone sword hilt at her waist. The curved blade's tip almost reached the ground, such was its length. The belt it hung from was all that kept her green robe closed.

'Greetings, noble farseer. Are you well?'

'I am well,' he said, still not looking up.

'Have I disturbed your meditations?'

'No, Taisha.' The kneeling male regarded the ground before him, where a spread of coin-sized rune stones lay among the dewy blades of grass. 'You have come for answers, yes?'

'I have, noble farseer.' She was not surprised he knew of her unease, or that she would be coming to him. 'My slumber is troubled.'

'You are not alone, Taisha.'

'So I have heard, noble Farseer. Several of my sisters are likewise uneasy in their hours of rest.'

'Oh, but the turmoil reaches so much further.' Now he looked up at her, his ice-blue eyes like frozen crystals. 'War threatens the craftworld once more. A war that will see you shedding the blood of the mon-keigh, daughter of the Fate goddess.'

'We are Ulthwe.' She inclined her head again in respect. 'We know little else but war. But who comes, noble farseer? Which of the mon-keigh?'

The farseer scooped his runes from the grass of the garden, feeling them hot and portentous in his palm.

'The Hunter of Souls, Taisha. The one who will cross blades with the Void Stalker.'

ABOUT THE AUTHOR

Aaron Dembski-Bowden is a British author with his beginnings in the videogame and RPG industries. He was the Senior Writer on the million-selling MMO *Age of Conan: Hyborian Adventures*. He's been a deeply entrenched fan of Warhammer 40,000 ever since he first ruined his copy of Space Crusade by painting the models with all the skill expected of an overexcited nine-year-old.

He lives and works in Northern Ireland. His hobbies generally revolve around reading anything within reach, and helping people spell his surname. His first novel for the Black Library was *Cadian Blood*.